The First Day in Paradise

The First Day in Paradise

Stuart Walton

ROUNDFIRE BOOKS

Winchester, UK
Washington, USA

First published by Roundfire Books, 2016
Roundfire Books is an imprint of John Hunt Publishing Ltd., Laurel House, Station Approach, Alresford, Hants, SO24 9JH, UK
office1@jhpbooks.net
www.johnhuntpublishing.com
www.roundfire-books.com

For distributor details and how to order please visit the 'Ordering' section on our website.

ISBN: 978 1 78535 235 5
Library of Congress Control Number: 2015952234

A CIP catalogue record for this book is available from the British Library.

Design: Stuart Davies

Printed in the USA by Edwards Brothers Malloy

For Lucas Hunt

And if I had in speaking as much wealth
As in imagining, I should not dare
To attempt the smallest part of its delight.

Dante Alighieri, *Paradiso* XXXI

Chapter 1

Mount Purgatory

The road to Hell, we are occasionally reminded, is paved with good intentions. But they all are. All roads are built from honest resolve, even those that lead nowhere and those that converge on the gates of Heaven.

We start out in apprehension, stilling our fears by meaning to do well. Failing either makes us revise the intention or disintegrate. Success can be chalked up to our determination, which didn't come up short when the going was rocky and the sun beat down. That at least is the myth. We don't believe it ourselves, but hope that somebody, distracted by his own despair, might believe it for us. Fortune, whom only the fortunate love, commands the wheel, no matter how we try to wrench it, and refuses her favours at least as much from petulance at the lack of love as from having her hands full.

The crucial day may begin like most days, with an awakening to soft light through cream curtains, a good night's sleep inside you and the untroubling hours ahead. There are voices and music, hot water spraying your skin, runnels of it creeping through your hair, something to eat, something to drink, and then a perfectly tolerable entry to the great world, where a pleasant faint haze is melting into the pleasanter warmth of lemony sunlight. Duty calls, but duty isn't onerous. You earn your survival by mildness and modesty, are not dishonourably rewarded, and accept what there is of peace and satisfaction when the working day is done.

Isn't this what we say we want? But the landscape of an undemanding life, in which we seek and find sustenance, can turn arid with habit until the soul calls out of its shelter to the unexpected. Innocent multitudes toil and are heavy-laden, tried in the fire, over-acquainted with grief and then tried again. A ring at the door is what's needed, something thrown at us from the blue, containing the thrill of a decision to be made. It's the decision that matters.

We may wonder whether we want it all to change. There is a snugness to a life without surprise, though nobody feels much inclined to admit it. Surprises can go either way. There is no telling. Who could have warned Agamemnon, tranquil in perfumed bathwater amid the rippling silence of his palace, that stealing among the columns with a roll of netting and a double-headed axe, was his wife? Who save Cassandra, and nobody believed her.

What is so exasperating about chance is that it is distributed according to its own principle. There is neither regularity nor inevitability in it. There may be one chance or two, there may be a hundred. There may be thickets of them all at once, choking one another like weeds, or they may only spot the monotonous earth here and there in little tufts, scarcely noticeable as we continue on the way. Or there may be none at all. Should we not grasp the one in case it is only one? One chance to be saved. One chance to be ruined. To become rich beyond the dreams of depravity, or be broken on Fortune's wheel.

Helped out of the water by his friends, their comradely jeers having died in their throats when he dived after all, a boy of thirteen knew that he was growing into his goose-pimpling skin. His mother came forward along the poolside with a big white towel, his father was suddenly behind him. He shivered into the towel's embrace, laughing with their laughter, letting his teeth chatter, his knees braced, abdomen quivering, hair dripping. He was light-headed with achievement. They clapped his back and held him.

'So proud of you, my love,' said his mother.

'You've shown what you can do,' his father said. 'You've

shown everyone.'

He shook his soaked head. He knew that they knew he nearly hadn't left the board. It had taken many months for him to overcome his twin fears, of the height and the sudden immersion. There had been a moment when, as the last boy, he knew that he could just edge back and not follow the others. He wouldn't be interrupting the sequence, only curtailing it. But they were all looking up at him. He knew he had to. So he hadn't earned the praise, not properly, but his parents wouldn't be denied the pleasure of bestowing it.

'Oh yes,' his mother said. 'You can do anything. This is only the start.'

'You'll make us proud,' said his father. 'And we'll be behind you. Every step of the way.'

'Yes we will,' his mother said.

And they would. He knew they would.

* * *

The approach over pristine tiles laid in sweeping scallops, now finished, was good. The access from the first entrance created a sense of entering a forbidden domain, the soaring gilded columns offset with spandrels in turquoise and flame. Daring to follow the eye's ascent, the beholder was met with recessed tiers that seemed to reach into the celestial, the distant atrium roof opalescent with autumn dawn. Could there be clouds somehow, the creator wondered, made to pass in puffs across the face of the firmament, entirely benign, knowing nothing of rain? He filed the thought for later. All around were the illuminating fascias of storefronts, where the displays were still being assembled, or where assembly had scarcely begun. It was gathering. It was happening. The finished vision danced in his head as surely as sugar-plums.

And yet there was a lack. At the centre of it, like a missing tooth, was an absence that gaped and chafed.

Like everything in the civilised world, though, it would be well. All manner of things would be well.

'When will those houses fall down?' said Luke.

Adam came to the end of a sentence in his book, held the spot in the text with his fingertip and looked up. Luke was kneeling on the seat, his forehead pressed against the window. The train was slowing again with a suppressed long squeal of its brakes, and Luke's attention, sorely famished over the past two-and-a-half hours, was hungering for something to fasten on. The latest halt they were coming to was in a dilapidated neighbourhood on the outskirts of somewhere, where a row of Victorian terraced houses, preternaturally red in the wintry sun, offered a view of broken windows and desertion.

'I expect they'll be pulled down before too long, by the looks of it,' Adam replied.

Luke continue to stare out, evidently trying to imagine the final devastation.

'If they didn't fall down soon, we could live there, couldn't we?'

'Would you like to live there?' his sister, Joanne, asked him.

'*I* would,' he said.

It had been a slow tormenting journey with frequent changes of train, some scheduled, others not, and Luke had held out remarkably well. Joanne was too polite to be tiresome, having reached an age, fourteen, at which it was possible to behave like an adult and be taken seriously, instead of provoking smiles of indulgent amusement. She had discovered somehow that a measure of civility was one of the signs of approaching adulthood, a style of keeping your cards close to your developing chest and not loudly stating your preferences, or asking perversely unanswerable questions. For Luke, at six, that last was still a privilege and a birthright, and he was just growing into it as she was bidding it a none-too-fond farewell.

It was announced over the speakers that the latest delay was regretted, and that, as a token of the rail company's goodwill, a steward would now come through the train with free bottles of water. The trolley, pushed by a woman who came from a little hill-town in the Carpathians, duly trundled into earshot, its approach heralded by advancing mumbles of complaint, as passengers discovered that the bottles of water were not chilled and all fizzy. By the time it reached Adam, he took one of the bottles from her, more from pity than desire, but Luke was happy to try it. Adam encouraged him to think of it as lemonade, only without the taste, as he put the bottle to his lips.

The first cautious gulp produced no reaction whatever, but when he tried to polish off half the bottle at a swig, the bubbles attacked his throat and, with something between a belch and a retch, he brought a quantity of the fizzy water back up again. The man in an Arsenal shirt who was sitting at the fourth place at their table moved, with lightning reflexes, to pull his newspaper out of the path of the gush, but the tabloid supplement got drenched. Adam and he exchanged glances, the man offering a painted-on smile of forbearance.

'Yurk!' Luke shouted.

'Anybody could have seen that coming,' said Joanne.

At the outset of the journey, which now felt like days ago, they had been seen off by ailing Auntie Mary, bidding a final farewell to Adam and the children. Their four years living under her roof had not been easy. She was still mourning the loss of Uncle George, and the sudden billeting of a family on her, even amid grievous circumstances, couldn't have been, and wasn't, the antidote to her own bereavement. George and Mary's house was large enough to accommodate the four of them, and yet the shrieking of children's voices upstairs, the sudden fights, the prolonged sulks, even the habitual daily energies of them all, had all crowded in too close. Luke had been too young to remember Uncle George, and Adam had never got on with him, but Joanne at least was able to talk to her aunt about him. What she remembered of him, though, lacked the fondness the recently bereft need to hear, so that instead of recalling touching incidents of George's generosity, she brought to mind memories that were hurtfully absurd, as when they had all got into the lift in a department-store and George had pressed the alarm-button by mistake, resulting in a hue-and-cry and a stern dressing-down by the security officer.

For the past few months, Mary had been receiving treatment for some respiratory ailment, and the presence of Adam and the children had become a burden. The doctor advised her that stress was an exceptional risk in her condition, and that some other solution for the family must be found. There was only really one, which took the joint form of her sister Mirabelle and brother-in-law Jimmy, and it was to their flat above the shop in Gutford that the three of them had now been packed off.

Joanne had handled the departure from Auntie Mary with sanguine calm, but Luke had been unexpectedly traumatised. On the platform, he had clung fiercely to Mary, his arms around her hips in a gesture of revolt. Once on the train, staring balefully out at his rattled aunt, he had begun to howl, great gobs of wailing wordless misery escaping from him between gasps for woeful breath. Joanne looked on impassively while Adam tried soothing the separation for him, invoking the gorgeous promise of Gutford. When that failed, he resorted to trying to make Luke feel embarrassed at his own behaviour, but if he had been insensible of the lures of Gutford, he nonetheless now sensed the modulation in Adam's tone from sympathy to something harsher, and only howled all the louder. The man at their table, fixing his expression into one of tenderness, asked Joanne gently how long the family was going away for. Her flat reply – 'Forever' – succeeded in raising Luke's despair to tragic hysteria, so that there was no other sound in the carriage, or the world, than his anguished screaming.

'I'll bet he'll have forgotten all about it in five minutes,' offered a woman across the aisle from them.

'I wish,' Adam replied doubtfully, but indeed, five minutes after Auntie Mary had dwindled to an insignificant white smear, Luke's tears dripped dry, and he turned his attention to his crayons.

Now, though, they had reached that point where the elastic of everybody's nerves was being tested. People were beginning to inhale noisily through their nostrils, letting their eyes wander more desolately to the scene beyond the windows, glancing at their watches. The man at their table put both hands over his face as though bathing it in bracing cold water, but left them there, to obliterate the unchanging surroundings. A sudden buzzing in the speakers indicated that another announcement was about to be made. Heads tilted attentively.

'Apologies once again for this continued delay to your service, ladies and gentlemen. This is being caused by a signal failure up ahead. We hope to be on the move again as soon as we can. As soon as we have more information, we'll communicate it to you. Thank you for your cooperation.'

A sharp tut from the man at their table added the full stop.

Every now and then, almost surreptitiously, the train crept forward for what felt like about eighteen inches, before just as furtively stopping again. It was reminiscent, to Adam, of family holidays in the car when, after hours of driving, the coastal town in which they were to spend the next week lay just before them, like the shining city of Oz, with only an immobile mass of traffic, a mighty river not rushing but static, barring their entry to it. All there was for it was to wait in exasperated silence, a silence made the more profound by the clicking of Mum's knitting-needles, while Dad's bare forearms rested heavily on the steering-wheel. It was as though, in these dead times, the promise of happiness, distantly embodied in the architecture of fairgrounds and the dotting of the sparkling grey sea with the vivid colours of bathing-costumes, began to desiccate. The prize bloom was there for the plucking but, rather than withering when touched, it withered for lack of being grasped. Sometimes a stray horn would sound, more in impotent complaint than hope, and the air around them rippled in a sickly miasma of exhaust-fumes and heat. Everything lay in a state of tremendous suspension. Nothing happened, in the ponderous way nothing does when it happens.

Adam would once more take up the Summer Special bumper edition of his weekly comic. It had pages to colour in, puzzles and quizzes, and a big centrefold picture, in which all the regular characters appeared in a single holiday scene, released from their separate worlds into one great union, like a strip-cartoon version of Heaven. Pranksters lay in ambush to trip up pompous waiters carrying trays of ice-cream sundaes. They squirted water-pistols at the well-behaved, and drew comical faces on the exposed bald heads of their dads as they snored in deckchairs. It was a pranksters' world, in which only two facial expressions could be discerned – a manic guffaw of triumph and the red-faced indignation of the victims. Adam didn't want to play these pranks himself, he just wanted to be part of a world in which they went on.

There was a general stirring around them on the train, as people got up and began, with much weary huffing, retrieving bags from overhead racks and from between the seats.

'What's happening?' Adam asked Joanne.

'We're being thrown off at the next station. Do keep up.'

It was true. There followed a mass struggle of disembarkation and, the station being only a small village stop, the platform was soon densely packed with hundreds of passengers. Collisions of luggage threatened to trap small children, and those who had scooped up their belongings in a hurry now battled to make sense of the miscellaneous bundles. The train that had disgorged them sat obstinately by the platform for some time, emitting sharp exhalations of wounded dignity. An announcement told them that it had developed a defect, and that alternative arrangements would be put in place as soon as possible.

Luke looked up into Adam's face for reassurance.

'We'll get there eventually,' Adam told him.

'Yes, one day we'll get there,' Joanne sighed.

Luke's gaze clouded as it passed from Joanne to a woman standing next to her and, on observing the same haunted hopelessness there, began to crumple altogether.

'Now, come on, fella,' Adam coaxed him, scruffling Luke's head. 'We have to be brave soldiers, don't we?' But he was beyond bravery. His face set solidly into a screwed-up picture of pain, which it likely wouldn't relinquish in hours, not even when the wind changed back again.

Adam sat down on the biggest rucksack. Their departure from Auntie Mary felt like another era. It was already late afternoon and getting cold, and the time ahead of them only seemed to stretch ominously away out of sight. He took his phone out of his trouser pocket and called Uncle Jimmy to tell him they were going to be late. Jimmy was sorry to hear of their delay, but warned Adam that he hoped they weren't going to be *too* late, as he and Mirabelle liked to be in bed by ten.

The feeble cold sun threw a salmon-pink ray over Adam's shoes. An indistinct murmur of people sympathising with each other went on all around. Joanne studied the timetable on the wall. Luke's pained face cast about in search of the dimmest glimmer of hope. Despite their great numbers, the stranded passengers took on an air of eerie calm, as though only the most patient resignation would get them through the coming hours. Adam's thoughts drifted to the sleepless night a thousand years ago, when his father came into his bedroom and tried to distract him from insomnia's ache by making shadow-shapes on the wall in the sodium street-light.

After what seemed an age, another train arrived to rescue them. It was a smaller train than the previous one, and those who lost out in the race for seats had to stand shoulder to shoulder in the aisles. Luke sat on the floor among the feet, holding his colouring-book to his chest like a talisman against the disintegration going on all around him. A ticket-inspector tried to squeeze among them, eager to punch something, but so few people could find their tickets in the confusion that he gave up. There were isolated outbreaks of shouting, but they could only be answered with shrugs. It wasn't his fault, the inspector had to remind people.

Once the train picked up speed, it went at a satisfying lick. Through acreages of farmland, with desolate scrubby hills in the distance, it tore along, suddenly possessed of the sense of purpose that its passengers had lost. Sometimes, when it negotiated a long graceful curve in the track, those standing had to grip the handles on the seat-backs to prevent themselves toppling into the laps of the seated.

The train had been cold when they first got on, but the enforced huddling of bodies meant that it was soon uncomfortably warm. They stood and swayed, while some of the seated ones slept. Joanne stood and read. Adam tried to read but couldn't concentrate. Did the police detective know that the psychiatrist knew that he was now the chief suspect? Or had he only feared as much? Adam turned again for help to the back cover. 'If there is a better crime novel published this year than Denzil Croft's, I'll gratinate my granny and destroy the evidence.' 'A compelling work. Hideously addictive and insidious. It will gather you in tentacles of suspense and squeeze you mercilessly till you scream.'

'Swap?' asked Adam, holding the novel out to Joanne, who was reading *The Making of the English Working Class*.

'Not in this life.'

On the train rattled and ran, the greenish dusky blur beyond the windows gradually suffused by the cheerless dark of countryside after nightfall. Gutford lay a little nearer within their reach with each passing minute. They would soon be arriving in the overlit home of Auntie Mirabelle and Uncle Jimmy, sitting down to pasties, beans and chips, with the telly yapping reassuringly in the corner. There would be an awkward few weeks while they tried to find somewhere of their own, made contact with social services, got the kids settled into their new schools, and Adam went in search of a job. And then what? A blank white blind, flimsy but opaque, was drawn down over the years beyond, the better to enhance their joy, he told himself, when it was suddenly rolled up.

The queue for taxis at the station extended in a right-angle around the side of the building. Intermittent rain-drips leaked from the station roof as they stood and waited. Instead of the hoped-for flotilla of willing vehicles, there was a shortage of taxis, just the odd one creeping in at intervals of minutes. Adam called again, and this time Mirabelle answered, saying that Uncle Jimmy had got tired of waiting for them and had gone to bed. She said the spirit had been willing but the flesh was weak, although it didn't sound to Adam as though either medium had been especially robust.

As they trudged forward in the queue, their spirits began to rise a little. Joanne pointed out to Luke, who was almost asleep on his feet, that there were now only fifteen people ahead of them. A boy in front rootled in his rucksack and pulled out a half-finished sandwich wrapped in foil, abandoned during the journey, and to which he now returned with some gusto. The sight of him cramming his face reminded them how long it had been since they had eaten.

Finally, they found themselves bundling their belongings into a taxi the size of a minibus. The driver hadn't heard of Flint Street, and had to radio his control-room to ask for directions.

There was the sound over the radio of somebody leafing through a street-map. It was almost as though they had arrived on a clandestine mission in a country whose language they didn't properly speak. The driver said that it wasn't a part of town he was at all familiar with. Adam heard himself apologise, and Joanne asked him why he was apologising.

As they drove through the rain-soaked streets, a deep sense of forlornness came over Adam. This was truly what it meant to be orphans – the undergoing of arduous long journeys, ending in the deserted night-time streets of an inhospitable town, streets alive with the neon signs of takeaways and taxi-firms but bereft of human society, as they were borne towards a greeting of halting formalities and the uneasy settling in strange comfortless beds. Luke was already half-oblivious, but Joanne's taut expression told its own story. The driver drummed his fingertips on the steering-wheel as they waited before a red light at a trafficless junction. Apart from Luke, they all stared at the signal, willing it to change. Adam's gaze dropped to where it reflected, emergency-room red, in the puddles beneath. It felt already like the dead of winter, calling back from years ago.

Winters came fast and hard in those northern years. You were hardly back at school in brand-new woollens before woollens weren't enough, and a heavy topcoat, cap and scarf were essential. To trudge through slush on streets glistening with peril in the grudging grey of 8.45 was a penance Adam couldn't wear lightly. None of them could, snot-streaked kids with poor eyesight and skin, many of them less scrubbed of a morning than Adam was, some not scrubbed at all. You stood in squishy shoes in the high-ceilinged hall singing a dirge of praise to the Lord from raggy red hymnbooks that felt crumbly and soft in the hands, as though they had conceivably seen service to the glorious war dead. The odd book was crisper and redder to the touch, like crinkling crêpe paper at Christmas, but most had this papier-mâché feel, with well-thumbed pages on which the print had blurred over the years so that, in the blear reluctant light of a November morning, you couldn't make out whether you were praising the Almighty, his arch-rival, or Isambard Kingdom Brunel. The words, nonetheless, were all viscerally familiar. 'O God, our help in ages past.' 'Hills of the north rejoice.' 'Mine eyes have seen the glory of the coming of the Lord.' What was it he had trampled? Something better left whole, very likely. Under the wan lights in the school hall, to sing as one of trampling seemed a triumphalism delicately obscene in tiny infants. But there. It set the tone for the day.

Adam bent to his schoolwork, doing tolerably well, but everything scared him. Teachers in a temper. The headmaster who looked kindly enough, but was not above carrying a cane into the classroom to intimidate the unruly. A thunderstorm that one day rattled the high windows throughout their panes and frames. The lightning was pretty, sizzling through the violet sky like the crackle at the top of dodgem poles at the fairground, but the thunder that battered the building was a menace beyond appeasing. It threatened to split and consume the world, pulverise it prior to ingesting it whole, until some other kid told him it was exactly the other way round. It was the flashes that did the damage, whereas the crash was just the drumroll that presaged the circus feat. So then. Things were not as they seemed. Who saw that coming?

Some of the other lads frightened him too. Nor were they the obvious hard cases, the ones who didn't flinch or bruise or snivel at the impact of fist or foot. They were, by contrast, the ones who already, at the ages of five and six and seven, seemed to have reached an easy accommodation with the world. They were the ones who gave inspired answers to the teachers' questions, who didn't evoke gasps of shouty laughter from the throats of those who knew no better themselves. On the physical side, they were fit, but so was Adam. They weren't as skinny as Adam, though, which made a difference. And while Adam could jump and spell, as well as run like stink, these turned out not to be the most-respected capabilities. Anything that involved a ball lay claim to that status. The bigger the ball, the less interesting it was. In that, they were like voices, or personal fortunes.

'Hell-*oh*?' Joanne was saying. 'Earth to Adam.'

They were here, Auntie Mirabelle coming along the path to greet them. While Adam paid the driver, she pitched in with Joanne, who had begun to haul all their bags out of the taxi. She crushed a cigarette out on the pavement and, standing on her toes, gave Adam a kiss on the neck.

'You must all be famished,' she said. 'Look at the little 'un. Hardly awake, aren't you?'

Luke gazed up at her with an open-mouthed look of puzzlement. He'd no idea who she was.

'What time did you set off?'

Adam reflected. 'Er, about midday?'

'Ten-thirty, in fact,' Joanne stated.

'And look at it now,' Mirabelle tutted. 'Gone ten.'

'It's been a long day, for sure,' said Adam.

They stood looking at each other blankly, until Joanne suggested that standing about in the rain wasn't the best idea, and Mirabelle shepherded them towards the front door.

The hallway had the same smell that Adam remembered from childhood visits, a mixture of old brown carpet and cigarettes, with a fugitive note of cooking oil in the background. There were piles of shoes, both hers and Jimmy's, stacked four and five pairs high against the walls, which their bulky luggage toppled over as they struggled in. Mirabelle cheerily invited them to disregard 'the usual chaos', but as they tried to hoist the bags over them, the shoes seemed to be everywhere. In the confined space, Luke stumbled and hurt his hand on a stiletto heel, which brought forth a peal of sympathetic laughter from Mirabelle.

'Oh my Lord,' she chuckled and, seizing the offended hand, gave it a vigorous rub. 'You'll have to get used to it, my love. We live in a permanent state of chaos here.'

'Should we leave our shoes here too?' Joanne asked.

'If you wouldn't mind, Jo,' Mirabelle answered. 'Otherwise, it plays havoc with the carpets, and it's cost us an arm and a leg to have the upstairs done.'

Amid the confusion of bags, they took off their shoes and left them amid the existing pile, before following Mirabelle upstairs.

'Is that them?' a voice called gruffly from the landing.

'Oop, Old Faithful's woken up.' Mirabelle laughed as they trooped into the living-room, where a dressing-gowned Uncle Jimmy, eyes straining against the light, had blundered in.

'Adam.' He nodded, and scowled at the younger ones, whose names had evidently escaped him.

Jimmy looked nothing like the Uncle Jimmy of memory. His face, once set in a continuous cheery beam, now looked extravagantly weathered, even frazzled. Deep black lines criss-crossed it from side to side, there was a pronounced droop to his lower lip, and his ears seemed twice their original length. Most startlingly of all, the colourless dark hair he had once worn oiled and parted at the side was now replaced by a feathery thatch, brushed forward on his forehead and coloured a shrill daffodil-yellow.

'Give the younguns something to eat, Mish. Their bellies'll think their throats have been cut.' He winked at Luke, who stared back unwaveringly. 'Well,' he sighed, as though the night had been half worn away with badinage and cheer, 'I must get to my bed. I've not the stamina you youngsters have. You can't teach an old dog new tricks.' And he disappeared back into the bedroom.

After turning on the oven, Mirabelle showed them where they would be sleeping. An extra single bed had been jammed into one of the back bedrooms, so that Adam and Luke could share, while Joanne had the other all to herself. In her room was an old dressing-table with an inset mirror, a comb, hairbrush and hand-mirror laid out in fan formation on the surface. There were no such amenities in the boys' bedroom, although one wall was decorated with a poster of a Gutford Athletic team of many years past, while one of the beds sported what looked like a brand-new Spiderman duvet-cover. The window offered a view over the back garden to the back of the house behind, where a security-light shone brightly.

By the time they all sat down to eat, they were so tired, they had almost lost what remained of their appetites. The enormous array of Chinese and Indian ready-meals Mirabelle had warmed up looked far too extravagant anyway, but they did their polite best, Luke sticking mainly to the egg fried rice.

Just as they were coming to a satiated halt, Mirabelle said that she'd meant to offer them some wine, but had clean forgotten it. Did they want some now? Joanne replied that she didn't drink, but Adam gratefully accepted the offer and Mirabelle made a show of being gracious enough to join him.

'I'll get Luke ready for bed then,' Joanne said. Normally, this would have been a cue for a prolonged whine of protest, but for once he hadn't the energy.

Mirabelle went into the kitchen, clattered about in the cupboards, and brought back a bottle of red wine and two glasses. She pushed the bottle at Adam, while she went round the room looking for cigarettes.

'I can't tell you what a relief it is to be here,' he said, as convincingly as he could, while he filled their glasses.

'Don't mention it, duck,' said Mirabelle, finding the cigarettes under a cushion and lighting one up. 'It's what we're here for.' She took a gulp of the wine and pulled a comedy sour face. 'Takes me back though. It was only yesterday you were tearing round that garden in your little fire-truck. Now look at you.'

She went on to give Adam a full account of her and Jimmy's medical trials. There had been endoscopies and blood-tests, anal probes and barium meals, all to establish nothing in particular. They didn't get about much, it was true, but then evidently

Gutford had become a rather unpleasant place. Not that she wanted to scare them, but there wasn't the same community character any more. You could see it in people who came into the shop. Where once they would have stopped and chatted, now they simply put what they wanted on the counter, paid and left, often without so much as the odd word. Then again, you wouldn't want to get too friendly with some of the types that came in. True, you had to live and let live, but if only other people felt the same. With this, though, she caught herself coming over all philosophical, which could only end in tears before bedtime, and she suggested that Adam might top their glasses up PDQ before she got on to the meaning of life.

Taking another couple of sips of Shiraz brought Mirabelle to the other delicate matter she had to touch on.

'I would love it,' she said, with a grimace of regret, 'if I could offer you something to help us out, but I can't. These are not good times on the financial front, and there's no way we can squeeze the takings any further than they're already going, and still keep me and Jimbo in the style to which we're accustomed.'

Adam replied, truthfully, that he hadn't in any way taken it for granted that they would pay him to work in the shop, and that his intention had always been to find work elsewhere, rather than be an extra burden on them. It was quite enough that they had offered to accommodate the three of them for the time being. But he was sorry to hear that things were a struggle.

'It's the way everything's going now,' sighed Mirabelle. 'People go into the town centre to shop, mainly. They've all got cars now. In this street alone, we used to have a clothes-mender's, Farrelly's the butcher, a betting-shop, somewhere that did your nails, and a chippy. And us, of course. Oh, and the little sub-post office. Now it's just us. We've branched out as much as we can, but basically, we're still just the tatty old corner-shop that people only use if they realise they've forgotten something from the big stores. And what things are going to be like when this place opens,' she said, waving a hand in a vague north-easterly direction, 'Lord only knows. I think that's when we'll admit defeat.'

'What place?' Adam wondered.

'The new shopping centre. Except it's going to be so much more, as they keep telling us. Looks it too. It's the size of a sodding airport, at least. What the council were doing when they gave permission to plonk it down round here, I do not know.' And with each of the final three words, Mirabelle gave an emphatic jerk of her head that made her earrings dance about in indignant sympathy.

'Who's that talking?' Luke asked, interrupting the story Joanne was reading to him.

They held their breaths while they focused on the muffled voices next door.

'It'll be Adam and Auntie Mirabelle,' she told him.

'Why are they talking like that?'

'Well, they've got a lot of news to tell each other, I expect. Do you want to know what the wizard turned the bad pixie into?'

'A little dog,' replied Luke, sliding under the Spider-Man duvet.

'Oh, you've heard this before, have you? You should have said.' But he was in no fit state to concentrate anyway, with sleep advancing on him like an express train. Within the next minute, he had surrendered to noisy sleep-breathing, and Joanne slipped out of the room.

She paused at the door to the living-room and heard Mirabelle instructing Adam to fetch another bottle of wine from downstairs. As his footsteps came to the door, she quickly dodged into what she thought was her own room, only to realise from the prolonged sputtering fart that came from the bed that she had stumbled in on the slumberous Uncle Jimmy.

Into the darkness of the shop, the strong beam of the street-lamp penetrated, lighting up the shelves with a vivid amber glow. Adam made his way around, past tins of dog-food and packets of instant noodles, rechargeable batteries and stacked egg-boxes, to where the bottles stood, five shelves high. Unfamiliar brands of whisky lorded it at the top over the ranks of wines below. He recognised the Shiraz they had just been drinking, and turned the bottle into the lamplight. On the label was a picture of a mountaintop swathed in mist.

As he walked back into the living-room, Adam found Mirabelle in the act of lighting a fresh cigarette off the butt-end of the previous one.

'Oops, caught red-handed,' she chuckled.

They continued to talk for a while about the state of things, the economy, the uselessness of politicians, but the onslaught of the powerful red wine and the asphyxiating impact of the smoke in a closed room had begun to make Adam feel headachey. It had been a long day. He said that he might, if the rain stopped, go for a bit of a walk around the block before turning in. Mirabelle said she was ready for bed herself. She told him to leave the side-door on the catch when he went out, and to put the chain-lock back on when he got in again. Not that they had anything worth stealing, but there was no harm in being careful. And with that she got up, trod carelessly back into her slippers, and slouched off towards the bathroom, holding the wine-bottle.

Adam threw back the half-glass he had left, and crept back down the stairs. He undid the chain-lock and stepped into the drizzle.

Even though it wasn't yet late, there were surprisingly few lights on in the houses opposite, as though everybody was either out partying, or had already gone to bed. He looked up and down the street. There were one or two former shop premises that were boarded up, as Mirabelle had said, but most appeared to have been converted into homes. He recalled Mirabelle's contemptuously waved hand. In which direction had she gestured? He decided it was up the street and probably to the right, and started off that way.

Nothing about the area, which he had not seen for many years, seemed familiar. The streets seemed narrower, the houses smaller. Even the street-lamps seemed less bright, as though the whole area were gradually winding down to a final demise, expending less and less energy as it did so. The first side-street on the right was a short cul-de-sac. He walked on. It was cold, and the drizzle appeared to be strengthening towards another downpour. A girl passed him, her face muffled in a fluffy hood, her urgent pace in the rain only making his own T-shirted state of exposure seem the more ridiculous. Peering up ahead, he saw the next side-street in the near distance and decided to walk as far as that.

An illuminated shop on the corner turned out to be an off-licence, in which a couple of people were idly scanning the shelves, watched from behind a plate-glass screen by a man at the till. Adam paused and looked in the window. A feeling of gentle desolation was beginning to settle over him, composed partly of alcohol but largely of a sense of being far from home, wherever that was. It was a feeling only curable by sleep. He was just turning to head back when it occurred to him to look along the side-street.

On the right, a row of terraced houses stretched back a quarter of a mile or so. Facing them was the remains of a row of exactly similar houses, but these terminated abruptly about halfway along, beyond which the rest of the terrace had evidently been pulled down. Protruding just into the gap left by the demolished houses, somewhere distantly behind them, was a very strange sight. Apparently part of some larger construction, there was a vast cylindrical tower of shining silver, soaring seemingly hundreds of feet into the air, and ending in a domed top sprinkled with white lights. It looked like one end of a nuclear power station. Adam started up the street so that he could get a fuller view of the building, which extended itself bit by bit from behind and above the old row of houses. When he crossed over the street at the point where the terrace ended, he found his heart was thumping with some unfathomable sense of cheer.

The whole view, across the wasteland left by partly torn-down housing, through the now-heavy splashes of rain the wind kept driving into his wine-dark eyes, was astonishing. A colossal irregular structure of glinting silver had risen up, looking both immense and immensely fragile in the wet night. It looked like the building inside it had been swathed in silver paper, uncrumpled and spread over its curving contours, with flashes of iridescence where it caught the beam of the blazing floodlights that surrounded it. Had he not guessed it at once to be the hated 'place' Mirabelle had mentioned, he might have thought it was a new sports stadium. Its architectural promiscuity extended from the one towered end he had first glimpsed to a pair of what looked like steeples at the other, their asymmetrical points rising high into the black sky, one topped with a flagpole, the other tapering into a graceful pinnacle, wound about with what looked like a length of pink chiffon, apparently fluttering in some celestial breeze. The lower part of the façade was partially obscured by a chain-link fence hung with many large warning notices, but he could just make out what must be the top of the main entrance, where a kind of pediment of white stone was set above tall panels of dark glass. Above this was mounted an as-yet-unilluminated sign, a row of about seven or eight letters in fairground shapes, forming a word that he couldn't quite make out. Panache? Pastiche? Just in front of the building, absurdly dwarfed by its magnificence, was a yellow crane. It was turning this way and that on the spot, operated by a hard-hatted man sitting in its cab, whose image was the last and smallest detail of the tableau that Adam's rain-battered eyesight could discern. It was as though, standing alone in the night-time street, he had seen a miraculous vision, which nobody tomorrow would believe.

The next moment, he was running back to the flat in pelting rain.

Inside, all was quiet. Treading gently, Adam slipped into the bedroom where Luke was sleeping, and began rummaging through his rucksack to find his washbag, which had efficiently buried itself among the layers of folded clothes. He pulled things out on the floor, and heard Luke turn over and evidently half-wake up.

'Wha?' he began mumbling, and gave a faint burble of the lips.

'It's OK, it's just me,' Adam whispered, but his brother was already unconscious again.

Eventually the washbag came to light, and more rummaging unearthed his toothbrush. He tiptoed creakily along the landing and found the bathroom. In the dark, reaching for the right-hand tap, he found unexpectedly that it was the hot water, and the boiler juddered to life somewhere with a violent hammering and groaning. Surely that had woken everybody up? He listened but there was no sound.

Standing over the toilet, aiming more in hope than expectation, he found the vision of the almost-finished new shopping centre swimming back into his head, accompanied by a gentle rushing in his ears from the drinking.

No sound at all, not even breathing, came from Luke's bed as Adam settled himself under his own quilt. He hoped the dank feeling of melancholy that had overtaken him as they arrived at the station would have lifted by morning. He screwed his eyelids shut. Sleep was a skill he had only ever imperfectly learned and, unlike riding a bike, once learned could always be forgotten again. The whole of Gutford was asleep, but not him.

A bomb going off in the middle of the crowded railway station made everybody drop into a crouch of panic. The intake of breath and sudden convulsion of his upper body brought him back to a room in which the door had just banged shut. Luke was evidently up and about already. He looked at the alarm-clock. It was nearly eleven.

'Ah, the prince has awoken,' Jimmy said, looking up over the tops of his glasses from the local paper.

'No, it's just Adam,' Joanne interjected. 'Tea?' She was stirring a large pot.

Failing to stifle an enormous yawn, Adam settled for a nod in reply. He stood in his shorts at the door, a mess of indecision, before going in search of a shower.

'Does he always get up this late?' Jimmy asked.

'Not usually, but it probably took him about three hours to get to sleep in the first place. Shall I pour one for Auntie Mirabelle?'

'Oh yes, better had, love. She never misses a trick.'

The bathroom lock was broken and, no sooner had Adam turned on the shower and taken his shorts off, than the door flew open and Luke let out a martial scream and pointed something at him. A thin jet of icy water hit him in the groin. A shriek of victorious laughter followed.

'Oh great, someone gave you a water pistol,' Adam said.

'It's an atom gun,' Luke corrected him, before adding, with an emphatic air of triumph, 'an Adam gun!'

'Close the door, will you? I'll deal with you in a minute.'

'Sounds like someone's having fun,' Jimmy said, as the living-room door burst open.

'I hit Adam!' Luke screamed, charging behind Jimmy's chair on a lap of honour around the room.

'Calm down, Luke,' said Joanne, but there was no quelling his excitement. He knew he was living somewhere new, he had already guessed this was going to be a less censorious regime than Auntie Mary's, and – best of all – he had a water pistol.

The first few days were a good-humoured confusion of jumbled clothing, continuous TV and squirting water. Jimmy didn't venture out much, appearing to do the lion's share of serving in the shop, but Mirabelle accompanied the family on trips to the park, liberally buying ice-lollies and fizzy drinks as occasion and Luke demanded. Adam found himself regularly apologising for their intrusion, but she assured him that she positively welcomed the change to their normal routine. It wasn't only that Jimmy had become so set in his ways. It would turn out, she was sure, to be a great benefit to be surrounded by children, to keep in touch with younger minds. They had never had any of their own, which made it all the easier, she said as she and Adam watched Joanne trying to teach the rudiments of see-sawing to Luke, to be indulgent of nephews and nieces. She said it was obvious that Luke was going to be very bright when he grew up – as bright, she quickly added, as his older brother. The only thing was, and she hated having to be mercenary about things, they would be glad of any extra income now the household had more than doubled in size.

On the Monday after their arrival, Adam began hunting for a job. He looked in the columns of the local paper, only to be advised by Jimmy that that was pointless. 'Someone's always beaten you to it.' He arranged an appointment at the job centre, and was asked to bring with him some document he had never been given. At his meeting, he was advised not to narrow his vision too much, and was sent for an interview in the office of a demolition contractor. The office manager there asked him where he saw himself in five years' time, and when he said he had no idea, replied that they would be in touch.

Back at the job centre, he was asked whether he was interested in football. There was an office-admin job at Gutford Athletic. Pay wasn't great, but the working environment would be stimulating, and benefits included use of the gym facilities at restricted times and family tickets for three home matches per season. At the interview, Adam was asked whether he was passionate about

Gutford Athletic. When he said that he was from out of town, the interviewer replied that Gutford's fan base wasn't confined to the town. Did he know the name of the official supporters' club? He didn't. It was the Guttersnipes. Adam left with the advice that he needed to 'do a little homework'.

An interview in a restaurant kitchen foundered on Adam's inability to hear anything the chef was asking him amid the din. Another at the swimming-baths ran aground on his woolly description of cardio-pulmonary resuscitation. Offices of all designs, but of a strangely homogeneous torpor, embraced him briefly, before gently letting him go, their managers always wearing an air of mild suspicion at the outset, melting to warm-hearted courtesy as the door was held open to release him. Would he ever consider enrolling as a police cadet, he was asked at the job centre. The challenges were highly rewarding, the starting salary was competitive, and there was a generous occupational pension. Adam didn't think it was him, and was once more told he mustn't keep narrowing his vision. Things weren't getting any easier out there.

Dawdling back to the shop one afternoon, he bought a can of beer and sat on a bench on a traffic island. He gave a pound to a man who asked him if he had any change, and drank half the can in one long gulp. This couldn't go on. He didn't want to find himself doing something he didn't want to do, but what did he want to do? He had nobody's expectations to measure up to, other than immediate financial ones. A moment of obligation had come, but nothing suggested itself. How had he come to this time of nothing, a broad sterile plain that stretched away in every direction?

At the time Adam came to light, you could hardly get a knife-edge between the realms of bliss and the vale of tears, so close did they press against each other. When you waded in the one, you could hear the jingle-bells of the other on the scented air. It helped to have a big wide mind of course. A wide mind, capacious lungs and eyesight that could go uncorrected. Who he was would take a lot of explaining in the years to come, but at the instant of his parturition, it didn't much matter. He was here and he was healthy, despite a short burst of intra-uterine hysterics, and the folk whose joy his arrival appeared to guarantee weren't complaining. No sir.

His dad rode monumental red fire-engines to tiny blazes caused by deep-frying mostly, rattling and trumpeting through the streets with two-tone sirens intoning sedate cadences. They sounded like the opening motif of the closing movement of some nineteenth-century symphony, as full of non-negotiable life-or-death urgency. Nothing was life-or-death though, not really. The fire station was a broad-fronted municipal glory, like a museum case behind which five red engines the colour of life's blood snuggled until the days when two of them at least – no emergency was treated to the indignity of one – would come raring out of the traps, Adam's dad in the high cab of one of them. He never got burned, though he did smell burning flesh once or twice, but one day, descending the brass pole with just too keen a sense of duty, he landed badly, broke his foot and skewed his ankle forever. It left him with a distinctive walk, his feet splayed outwards, a stance that Adam himself, a lifelong stranger to brass poles, found himself taking on as he grew. How did that happen? How did anything happen?

What remained right now, to light the last of dejected consciousness, was the image of a big silver building in the distance, making its presence felt in outline only, evanescently, like something already dreamed.

When he woke again, there was twilight all around and most of the traffic had vanished. He pulled himself upright and rubbed his eyes.

As he made to cross back to the pavement, a cranberry-red Alfa Romeo came around the corner. He stood back to let it go but, as he crossed behind it, the car abruptly slowed and pulled towards the kerb a few yards further up. The passenger window glided down. He could see a figure inside the car leaning across from the driver's seat to the open window, in anticipation of speaking to somebody. There was nobody else about.

Adam hesitated, then strolled over to the stopped car.

A young man with tanned skin and short-chopped yellow-blond hair sat at the wheel, his hands now resting demurely in his lap, as though driving the car had been nothing to do with him.

'Hello,' he said.

'Can I help you?' Adam asked, bending to the window, unsure who had approached whom.

'I was looking for...' He thought. 'Latimer Road?'

'Can't help,' Adam replied. 'I'm a stranger here too.'

The driver laughed. 'Not for long, I hope.'

'Pardon?'

He turned, picked up something from the back seat and handed it to Adam. It was a publicity flyer. Against a night sky alight with fireworks was printed, in shivering pink letters, the word 'PARADISE', and underneath, 'You don't have to be good to get there.'

The car was already pulling away.

Chapter 2

The Sphere of Fire

In something shimmering and red, a torso stepped up on a small ladder and, with the gentlest breeze, blew tinkling music into the hanging icicles of quartz above his head. He wasn't supposed to move, but Vincent Beresford's eyes turned up and saw the photographer's assistant blowing on the dangling shards of chandelier glass through a plastic straw. It had the effect of making them look misty with condensation, to emphasise the staging of the whole tableau amid bleak midwinter. His own body was arranged semi-recumbent against a drift of powdery snow, the impression to cruder eyes perhaps suggestive of a skier who had taken a tumble on the slopes, but intended to evoke a holiday spirit of abandonment of toil. For the purposes of the shoot, it was imminent Yuletide. In a world where no snows fell at such a season, the first snows had indubitably fallen. Christmas was coming, things were getting fat, and there was no time to lose in preparing for the great feast. The dully conventional figure of Santa had been usurped in favour of a more pagan tradition, at least partly since Vincent, it was felt, hadn't the 'physical definition' to be Santa. Instead, he was Jack Frost, a mercurial spirit winging and flitting across the frozen fields, spreading spangles of white, turning trees to bare bone, settling a spellbinding quietness upon the land, before coming to rest on a snowbank of his own making. Here he lolled to watch the farmer huffing past behind his meagre herd, following the line of dismally clanking cowbells back to the byre. They might curse him for a hard heart, but didn't the world look pretty?

The assistant done with her blowing, Vincent's head of admin, Javine, appeared in her place, dropping to one knee by the set. Balanced on one of her hands was a large hexagonal box filled with dozens of chocolates wrapped in purple foil. Their eyes met, as though Vincent were guiltily soliciting her connivance in a forbidden act, before he reached out and took one. Javine withdrew somewhere to the right as Vincent unwrapped it. Shaped like a priest's biretta, it was made of blackest Caribbean chocolate. When crushed in the mouth, it exuded a mauve-coloured fondant flavoured vividly with lavender and vanilla, the bitterness of the shell contrasting with the sweetly perfumed filling. One was enough to linger on the palate for many minutes. To consume two in anything less than half-an-hour was reckless avarice, Vincent had found, but the box contained six dozen of them. He had yet to find anybody else who adored them as intensely as he did.

Now he was being asked to compose himself once more in as near to his original attitude as he could manage. He tilted back his head as before, and let his left arm fall loosely across his upper body again. There was a mumble of consultation between the photographer and his assistant, and the red-clad woman approached again with something in her hand. With a murmured 'excuse me', she delicately dabbed away a tiny trace of dark chocolate from the centre of Vincent's upper lip. He rolled his eyes in deprecating apology towards the unseen photographer and, after a few seconds of silence, the camera began clicking insistently again.

It wasn't enough that the grand opening of Paradise should take the collective breath away. You had always to be looking ahead. The one thing Paradise could not do was stand still. To the combined impact of the splendour of the building itself and the thrill of its extensive first-week sale, was to be added the giddy rush of anticipating Christmas. The intention was to leave customers in a state of suspended animation while all about them went whirling. They would gasp and chuckle in a world of limitless opportunity, from which they wouldn't ever want to go home. And the one mistake you wouldn't be able to make in

Paradise was wishing your life away. There was always more life to come.

'I think we're there,' said a voice from the brightly lit void before him. The photographer was satisfied.

Various bodies came forward to help Vincent up from the set. Somebody gently prised the helmet-like silver wig from his head, while another lifted each foot in turn and eased a cushioned flip-flop on to it. A hand began dabbing at his face with a scented tissue, and Javine began to intone in a sing-song voice the rest of the morning schedule. Things were looking tight for the visit of the first press reporter, but she was sure they could condense that interview into ten minutes rather than twenty. Anything they didn't get on tape in the ten minutes would be contained in the voluminous press pack, and they could always buzz her later if anything needed clarifying. Vincent wondered about the Trade Board visit. She assured him it was mostly taken care of in advance. Their presence was simply a matter of dotting a few Ts, shaking a few hands and drinking a smidgen of champagne. The grand tour was the principal item on the day's agenda, the chance for Vincent to see in detail what the creative labours of the past year had yielded – his finest accomplishment yet, a retail vision of unbridled richness and scope. They weren't, as the publicity flyers had it, calling it Paradise for nothing.

Attended on either hand, Vincent pattered up the marble service stairs. The lifts were already working, but lifts were for people with time to dawdle and gawp, and exertion was always to be preferred to calm passivity. Onwards and upwards the flip-flops pattered, through storey upon storey, around landing after landing, until he reached the eleventh floor, his own administrative domain. At the top of the last flight, there was a broad expanse of grass-green carpet to cross, to where a rippling wall of full-length glass bounded his office complex. A member of his admin staff, seeing his approach, came forward to throw open the main door, the sheer burnished glass of which was adorned only with a small white sign, on which could be read the words: 'Knock, and you are not expecting it to be opened unto you.'

'Good shoot, VB,' said Javine.

'I'll leave that to the judgment of others,' said Vincent, sweeping through.

His own office was styled in nautical fashion. Rising from the centre of the floor, and dividing the room in two, was a triangular white sail of translucent damask, emblazoned in black with his initials. Hanging from one end of the enormous desk was a coil of rope, while inlaid in the surface of the desk, a row of instruments and dials, precise in their period engineering detail but purely ornamental, was arrayed. A shipboard telephone with a rotary dial, however, did function, and was labelled with the names and extension numbers of key personnel. An old anchor, retrieved from a breaker's yard, hung on the wall behind the desk, and along the external wall, arcing above and below the kidney-shaped window, a display of lifebelts from various old liners was hung. At the far end of the office, pride of place on the wall was occupied by a gaudily painted figurehead of a mermaid, her hair the platinum of forties starlets, her nipples scarlet dots, her shimmering silvery tail that of a heavenly mackerel.

Vincent threw down the file he was carrying. 'I'll go through these later, after the grand tour, but first, my consultation. Actually no, first – coffee.' The espresso machine in the outer office was already willingly spurting.

He stopped at the window and stared out for a few seconds. In the distance were the towers of high-rise residential blocks, budget chain hotels, multi-storey car-parks. All those buildings were bursting with people who didn't know what was about to hit them, people who would become partners in helping to shape his propulsive advance into a new path-breaking era of retail and leisure experiences. His heart thrilled with anticipation on their behalf. The old sterile boundaries were about to be demolished, the citadels stormed, the ramparts breached, by a capacious visionary generosity in which all around him shared. He was, in a real sense, everybody, and they were him.

A T-shirted male body handed him a tiny cup of espresso, and Vincent swept out, across the outer office and through another door into an almost-empty smaller room. This duskily lit space, with hessian blackout blinds at the windows, was the consultation room. It was here each morning that he would seek guidance from one of any number of divinatory practices culled with equal respect from the world's ancient belief-systems. All had endured over the aeons, and only the incurably arrogant had any right to privilege one of them over the others. They all had something to offer. A polished wood panel set into the floor was surrounded by three sofa-sized bean-bags, on to one of which Vincent serenely sank, espresso in hand. He waited.

It was Chaoyi's day. Chaoyi was a Hong Kong boy with a mop of unruly hair and a rumour of a goatee. In some other life, he was an IT student, but came on those certain days in the calendar when the style of consultation scheduled was the *I Ching*. He came in now with a tray of exciting paraphernalia, which he proceeded to lay out on the floor while Vincent sipped his coffee. There was a decanter of water and a tall glass, a black cloth parcel, and a square box decorated with a lacquer-effect design suggestive of old western *chinoiserie*. Chaoyi knelt in front of the items, his back straight as day, and appeared to be waiting for something, perhaps the most propitious moment to begin.

He was waiting, it turned out, for Vincent to finish his espresso for, as soon as he did, he half-filled the glass with water and handed it over.

'For purification? Of course,' said Vincent, and drank down the icy-cold water. 'Beautiful. Where's it from?'

Chaoyi glanced up, not having anticipated the question. 'Oh, it's a special water,' he said, 'very pure.' He unwrapped the black cloth and put the weathered-looking paperback of the *I Ching* to one side. With the cloth spread out on the wooden floor, he opened the lid of the box and shook out the fifty stalks of yarrow. The whole procedure was fascinatingly deliberative and slow, allowing you time to collect your thoughts and see penetratingly to the heart of the matter in question.

At a signal from Chaoyi, Vincent pressed his palms together, closed his eyes momentarily, and concentrated on the morning's question. There could only be one. Was everything primed with positive energy for the launch? In keeping with strict procedure, he didn't voice this question, but allowed it to strengthen, take on solid structure and weight in his mind.

Over the next fifteen minutes, Chaoyi performed the sorting of the yarrow stalks. One stalk was picked at random and laid on the cloth, then the remaining ones cast. This involved a complex manual ballet in which the stalks were picked up in bundles, which were then diminished in bunches of four until only a few were left from each bundle, these being then balanced carefully between the fingers. They were laid across the initial stalk, and Chaoyi drew a line on one of the much-marked inside back pages of the book. The process was repeated five more times until a hexagram of broken and unbroken lines had been formed.

Chaoyi consulted the book. After some flicking backwards and forwards of the pages, he stopped and read quietly to himself. Vincent understood that it was necessary for the diviner to read the oracle himself before relaying its wisdom. Chaoyi's eyes closed, and there was a prolonged hush, in which only the faint hum of traffic from hundreds of feet below could be heard.

'*Heng*,' he said at last, opening his eyes and smiling kindly at Vincent.

'*Heng?* That's good, isn't it?'

'*Heng* is Duration,' said Chaoyi. 'It means achievement. Nothing to be guilty for. Perseverence produces result. It advances the man when he has somewhere to be.'

A sensation of great warmth spread through Vincent like hot

syrup.

'Thunder is accompanied by wind,' Chaoyi continued, referring to the book again. 'The great man stands his ground, and does not change his direction. We are reminded of the saying of Laozi: "If we wish to squeeze something, we need to let it expand fully beforehand".'

That made sense, Vincent thought.

'The woman must follow the man at all times, and he must choose the right path. The male and female principles are united, their powers are balanced. All is well,' Chaoyi concluded, as indeed he always did.

He bowed his head until his nose came to rest between his knees. For a few seconds, there was a serene silence, which Vincent broke by scrambling off the bean-bag and clapping his hands.

'You are a life-line, Yingchu, you know that?'

'Chaoyi,' said Chaoyi, as he straightened up again. While he collected his belongings, Vincent swept out of the room and made a fluttery gesture with his fingers towards one of the office staff. The man took a sealed envelope out of a desk drawer, and handed it to Chaoyi as he emerged. They conferred over the date of the next consultation. The Tarot master had called in to say he couldn't make the 25th as he had just booked a last-minute holiday that week so, as long as it wasn't a problem for him, Chaoyi's next appointment could be brought forward? There wasn't, Chaoyi assured him, any problem.

On the way down in the lift, he tore open the envelope, a little self-consciously since the lift was made entirely of glass and he wondered who might see him. The amount on the cheque was correct as always, and would pay another month's rent.

As Vincent swept back into his office, Javine followed him. The reporter from the *Clarion*, Gutford's local paper, was in reception, a little early. Was this a good time?

'Why not?' Vincent replied, with an air of expansive

generosity. 'Let's do it.'

The phone jangled out.

'VB!' Vincent exclaimed into it. It was reception to tell him that the reporter from the *Clarion* was here. 'Send him up!' Vincent sang.

He asked Javine for a fresh round of espressos, and some of those heavenly Sicilian lemon cookies. Just the thought of those brought a feeling of happy munchiness over you, and they went beautifully with the coffee, the high-octane hit of which provided the adult counterpoint to the childlike indulgence of the cookies. Their other great selling-point was that, although they looked like Italian biscotti, they had none of the tooth-grinding impenetrability of true biscotti. They were cookies, basically, but like much else that found favour with Vincent, they combined the best of various elements into a rich new synthesis, and that – as he was about to tell the *Clarion* journalist – was what Paradise was all about.

Javine put her head round the door again to announce that there were no cookies left. Would Kit-Kats do? Then, just behind her in the doorway, loomed the enormous hulk of the reporter. Vincent waved Javine aside in the same gesture with which he waved the *Clarion* reporter in.

He was a very large man in his sixties, at a guess, with a huge sweating red face, across which was plastered a quantity of greying dark hair, some of which was stuffed at each side under the arms of a pair of rectangular black-rimmed glasses, the whole framed by bushy side-whiskers and a luxuriant Rasputin-like beard. He looked like a more elderly version of Bluebeard the pirate. A pair of gigantic red trousers was held up by vibrantly patterned braces, the waistband being bigger still than the man's tremendous girth, so that the strange impression was given that he was standing in something resembling a great flowerpot. He extended a meaty clammy hand.

'Hinton Richards, *Clarion*,' he puffed.

'Lovely,' said Vincent, very quickly brushing the outstretched hand with his fingers. 'I'm assuming you had no trouble finding us?'

'No end of trouble,' Hinton panted. 'For one thing, the one-way system coming off the Blackstone Road is going to be your main logistical headache. Your car-park obviously isn't open yet, but it's not easy to see how incoming traffic is going to be able to negotiate that awkward-looking right turn on to the slipway. Then, for another, my taxi-driver was grumbling about the fact that you've got to get through three – or is it four? – sets of lights as you come round the perimeter. I can't believe the car is going to be the easiest way of doing it for most people. I know you've got the park-and-ride thing, but you're hoping, I presume, that most of your customers are going to be too loaded down with goodies from here to contemplate getting them home on public transport. Anyway,' he wheezed, 'we can get on to all that as we warm to our theme. Is that coffee?' he asked Javine. 'You couldn't do me a latte, m'dear, could you? That black stuff brings me out in fierce-awful sweats, as the Irish people would say.'

With a nod towards Javine, Vincent gestured towards the seating options.

'I think if I try to recline on that,' Hinton said, casting a look of genteel fury at the bean-bag, 'I'll need a crane to get me out of it again.' He eased himself into an office-chair, settling for a demure side-saddle position between the rather narrow arms, and flailed out in the direction of his case.

Vincent retrieved the case and handed it to him. 'I'm afraid I've only got about ten.'

'Ten what?'

'Minutes. I know we said we'd make twenty available, but things have rather caught up with us this morning. I've had a shoot.'

'Turkey or pheasant?' Hinton quipped, as he fumbled about in the case for his notebook. 'Oh, well, that rather kiboshes the intention of doing the feature spread we had in mind. I doubt we'll get much done in a mere ten minutes.'

'We do have a press pack we can let you have, of course,' Vincent offered.

'Problem there being,' Hinton told him, 'that I've made a lifetime's professional habit of never reading press packs. I prefer the *ad hominem* approach. Look, let's not pootle about now. Let's get what we can down, and then the rest of it we can perhaps do over the phone. How's that latte coming along, do we think?'

Anticipating the next ten minutes were likely to be an ugly torment, Vincent ensured that the interview would consist of the first question only. Asked to outline the thinking behind Paradise, he took ten philosophical minutes to answer, revisiting his childhood delight in fairgrounds and fun palaces, and the baby wisdom he had unwittingly brought forth at six when he had asked his mother, as they waited in some long dull checkout queue, why shopping couldn't be more like going to the fairground. What mattered in life were vision and persistence and tenacity, holding on to the dream within and never letting the voice of so-called realism tear it from you. This was boiler-plate stuff, the kind of talk that usually sufficed for slow-witted journalists as shorthand biog. The truth was much more intricate and nuanced, involving a complex inner dialogue of success and failure, the latter notion continuously redefined through the prism of the former, out of which might emerge something of lasting value. Try explaining that to Bluto here, and something about pearls and swine, or seed and stony ground, suggested itself.

Throughout his speech, in any case, he noticed the man from the *Clarion* wrote nothing in his notebook, his broad perspiring face resolving itself into a misty gaze of distraction, focused somewhere a little to the left of Vincent's head.

'And the rest, as somebody nearly said,' he concluded, rising from his chair, 'will be history. With that, if you don't altogether mind, I'm going to leave you in the more than capable hands of my PA, Javine Benson.'

Hinton neither nodded nor blinked as Vincent swept out, but kept staring contemplatively ahead. Perhaps he had had a stroke.

Javine met Vincent's glance with a complicit rolling of the eyes. The tray she was about to carry in held a mug of frothy caffè latte, and a plate of two-fingered Kit-Kats.

'I think you'll find,' Vincent said in a stage whisper, 'Kit-Kat is too small a word.'

Vincent swept through the main office door and across the green expanse of carpet, shaking his arms outwards vigorously as though to cast off any lingering trace of the sudorously prosaic Mr Richards. At the opposite end to where the service stairs came up was another set of sturdy double-doors. Somebody followed him to these doors, and waited behind while Vincent paused pregnantly. He seemed to be pondering something perplexing.

'Will you do the grand tour now, VB?' asked the man behind him.

'Do you know,' Vincent replied, gathering himself, inhaling deeply, 'I believe I shall.'

He pressed his hands together over his nose as though breathing through an oxygen mask, and let the assistant unlock the doors in front of him. The last grand tour was a week ago. This one, with the whole vision so tantalisingly near completion, would be the one.

'Is this glittery stuff supposed to go all the way to the edges of the walls, or is it just running down the centre of the floor?'

The design installation team conferred over the plans.

'I'd say, down the centre, like a kind of runner.'

'There's an awful lot of it.'

'There's an awful lot of everything.'

Suddenly, without any warning, the doors at the end of the landing opened. They turned as one in time to see a man step quickly through as he flung them wide, and then just as quickly melt against the wall to make way for another to pass.

A young man clad entirely in dazzling white stepped through. His seraphic face wore an expression of placid happiness, as he slowly opened great green eyes to survey the scene before him. A small spot in the ceiling bounced a ray of silvery halogen light off the golden crown of his hair, which grew straight and soft towards an unruffled brow. His smile was the smile of Cupid at the first glimmer of his own mischief. He took a couple of tentative steps forward, and the halogen coaxed one half-second flash from the facets of a diamond in the left earlobe. A loose-fitting linen jacket flapped open over a tight white T-shirt, on which was printed in block capitals: 'If Paradise is half as nice...' The white linen pantaloons extended to just above the ankles, which were tanned and bare, crazed with a network of dark brown hairs like filaments of wire, the feet encased in white cushioned flip-flops.

Placing one foot before the other with catwalk deliberation, Vincent progressed along the landing, hardly daring to look towards the vision that opened up on his left. At the end of the landing, across an aluminium walkway suspended above a sheer drop, was a platform where the chair-lift terminated. Somebody started it up. The chair-lift had only one chair, and it was into this, a broad scarlet-painted, hooded affair that would just about have seated two, that Vincent allowed himself to be ever so gently bumped.

Falling away below in reticulating perspective, the successive storeys of Paradise opened out. There were two floors of glass-walled offices, under which the top two public floors were devoted to restaurants and bars, and below these, six floors of retail space dropped away. The levels were built around an enormous central well, the walkway walls designed in an undulating pattern that gave the bird's-eye viewer the *trompe l'oeil* impression that the walkways themselves rose and fell as they passed before the shopfronts. At the foot of the well, far far below, a fountain threw up jets of diffused water that, from this aerial vantage-point, looked no more dramatic than a lawn-sprinkler, but which, lower down, laterally emanated a fine mist of spray that danced in the cross-currents of the air-conditioning. Everywhere, at every level, lights spangled in the expanse, cobalt-blue sprays arranged on nets like spider-webs, or creamy-white dots on translucent vertical curtains. Various musics could be heard from the different levels, forming a sweet fleeting cacophony at the points where they briefly melted into one another, all muted by Olympian height. Halfway across, the chair-lift slowed and stopped, allowing its occupant to lean over the side and look down into the vast glittering chasm at the masses of overalled and hard-hatted figures.

On Fourth, somebody nudged somebody else and jerked his head upwards. The other tilted back his own head and, with a huge protective glove, pushed his welder's visor up on his forehead. Swaying far above them on a thin wire, a cherry-coloured chariot was suspended in mid-air. They grinned knowingly at each other and looked back up, the shoulders of the one shaking a little at the sight of the airborne miracle. It almost seemed, as they stared up into the kaleidoscope of lights, that the golden-haired figure in the chariot had sprouted a pair of diaphanous wings.

A single tiny printing error on the cocktail menu was all that stood between the eighth-floor High Bar and perfection. The Cachaça Cascade had become a 'Coscade', a slip that caused mixing director Coleman Tratlow some dismay. Seated at a table in the centre of the lounge, he tested the ordering system once more. Inset into the table surface was a keypad with a narrow strip of screen. You keyed the code number of your required drink into it (say, 364 for a Rotten Raspberry), pressed 'Order' and the message was relayed to the bar. While he waited, he listened critically to the music being played through concealed speakers. It was too bland, too shruggy. He made a note on a paper napkin – 'Music!'

Across the well of the eighth floor, the neon signage of Grape To See You was in full flash. A light sequence depicted sparkling wine being poured into a saucer-shaped glass, while inside the main bar, an LCD display board advertised the week's special offers in rolling wraparound text, like stock-exchange updates in a city square. 'Cranston Canyon Woodvale Malbec 2009, £5 a glass. Go large for £7.50! Fruit-drenched New World stunner!' A pair of waitresses on skateboards were practising their moves, holding glass-laden trays high above their heads, dismounting from the boards with gymnastic aplomb and flipping them up into their free hands as they did so. There was a distant insistent beat from the wine-bar, of music that sounded more vigorous than the shruggy jazz being piped into the High Bar.

Further along the walkway, an Alpine cabin was turning out steaming mugs of *glühwein* in the midst of an avalanche of polyfoam snow, while next door, arrayed along a long white-tiled counter, tall cylindrical liquidisers were juicing mangos, cucumbers, avocados, papayas, pears, blackberries and bananas, discharging crazy-coloured pulps into tall frosty glasses. Next to the juice-bar was a Bayerische Bierkeller, where monstrous steins were filled to frothing, while an oompah band did its utmost. There were vodka bars, tequila bars, single-malt whisky bars, champagne fountains, chocolate fountains and a counter selling only *tè latte*. The Gas Station would pipe pure oxygen into you, or alternatively a dose of helium. Its nitrous-oxide special was for over-18s only.

The cable-car reached its terminus on the opposite side of the cavernous space, and Vincent alighted with a little trip before it executed its U-turn and started back. Somebody hastened forward to steady him, but it was hardly necessary. Today, more than ever, he was in control. Descending through three levels, he took the service-stairs in a graceful rush, emerging amid the hectic flurry of the eighth-floor walkways.

Now he tried his luck on the escalator, where gently throbbing light panels illuminated each tread in red, yellow or green. He placed his fingers lightly on the flesh-coloured moving handrail, and a delicate velvety sensation met them. Down he sailed to the gastronomic level, where the pleasures of the tables of five continents came pouring forth, or drooped from overhanging branches above his head. A vast gastromart was the epicentre of this floor, a haven of rare and highly prized foods, where he turned in happy consternation from jars of black truffles glistening in oil to stacks of brittle bottarga, from albino caviar to dried Andean potatoes, smoked abalone to rose-red coppa, rose-petal jelly to gunpowder tea. A man in a straw hat was juggling with kumquats. Behind the breakfast counter, duck eggs were being scrambled and decanted back into the shell. The scent of hickory-smoked pecans being toasted mingled promisingly with the aroma of liquorice taffy being pulled. The pâtisserie counters were a riot of delirious colour, where frangipane tarts gleamed under apricot glazes, bon-bons were coated in sky-blue sugar, and the Cherry Bomb casings, each concealing a whole morello pickled in liqueur, were white for ginger wine, orange for mandarinette and deep blush-red for crème de cerise. A glass jar, shaped like a Greek amphoreus two-feet tall, garlanded in creamy-white mariposa lilies, was mounted on a plinth, and filled with whole baby artichokes, grilled sweet peppers, wild hyacinth bulbs and roasted shallots, afloat in Kalamata extra-virgin oil. Vincent caught up a sliver of Serrano ham and a nibble of Manchego, while he dallied over corpulent preserving-jars of goose foie gras, then gazed in pity at the piles of twitching lobsters, their claws taped together as if in penance.

At Head First, on Sixth, Dimona McGillicotty was furious. The first deliveries to arrive at her unit were not of her couture millinery creations, but frozen flan-bases. There was only a voicemail in operation on the admin line, and the person who answered when she contacted Logistics said they were 'literally snowed under' with enquiries. Considering how close they were to opening, it all looked bleak. Dimona sat on a chair in her consulting-room, looked at her anguished face in the mirror and gave way to tears. Left and right of the mirror were ebony-framed photographs of models wearing her hats, to one side a provocative cocktail hat with what looked like a scrunched-up knot of marram-grass emerging from a crimson velour crown, to the other an asymmetrical wedding piece in lilac, with downturned brim, slanted crown and an effervescence of coque feathers in vermilion. The only actual hat in the shop so far was her own blot-quilled scarlet fedora.

Next door was Only One, a couturier that specialised in producing precisely one of each item. It took exclusivity to a whole other level. None of the clothes were displayed, there were no fitting-rooms, only a predominantly white space, in which potential customers might look at DVDs of the catwalk shows, and play fridge-magnet haiku beneath a fibre-optic chandelier. Not even the paired items, such as shoes and earrings, quite matched each other. Ceiling speakers played a download of *suikinkutsu* water zither, recorded at a *chaniwa* garden in Kyoto, the gentle plash of water dripping into a basin inducing a meditative open-minded mood. A problem with the electronic till, which refused to open, was all that ruffled the serenity.

Vincent had paused on the opposite side of Sixth, where the staff at <phyzics> were undergoing a collective workout, a punitive routine of squat-jumps, which he delighted them by briefly joining. The premises incorporated treatment rooms for deep-tissue massages, facials and nail therapies. Those with the time might opt for a 75-minute You You You package, with micro-dermabrasion to encourage lymphatic drainage, a hydrotherapy bath with high-pressure aqua-jets, and the insertion of Hopi ear candles for rebalancing intra-cranial pressure. The philosophy was 'giving people their lives back'. The youngest trainee masseur was seventeen-year-old Sam Keelan, whose own life had been given back to him after a spell of institutionalisation for killing his sister when he was nine. Now he could realign impacted connective tissue, and recommend exfoliation regimes to suit a range of skin types.

Vincent's mobile chimed with the second Tchaikovsky piano concerto. It was Javine. Something had come up.

'You know what to do with things that come up?' Vincent suggested to her.

'Go on,' she faltered.

'Let them float.'

He cut the connection and floated down to Fifth.

At Get Your Rocks On, bespoke display windows had been fitted, and were being polished assiduously every couple of hours. Each pane of glass had been designed with a different whorl, stippling, frosting or convexity, so that the jewellery behind them was viewed in unexpected refraction, weirdly enlarged or tantalisingly miniaturised. The rectangular amethyst on a signet ring appeared as large as a credit card, while a lozenge of tourmaline set in a white-gold band diffused into a hundred sprinkled blue dots. Over the entrance hung an ironic strip-door, the strands of which were set with plastic spangles that clinked agreeably as Vincent swished through. He stayed just long enough to finger a silver-and-jet earring in the form of a bunch of peppercorns, and set off an alarm, before tinkling out again.

He glided past hair salons, beauty parlours, a makeup retailer called Slap. It all looked adorable but, lest anybody think that Paradise was solely about product, Vincent had ordained that at least one floor be consecrated to the idea of service, of healing, togetherness, community. There should be spaces where people could retreat from the world, from the frenzy of schedules and deadlines, and just simply be. Here dreams were realised, plans advised on, problems addressed, lives reconstructed, emotional wounds repaired.

Weddings, engagements and all other forms of partnership could be enacted, celebrated and licensed at the Hitching Post. Banks of video-screens dominated the reception-area, showing footage of marriage ceremonies from around the world. Skyrockets fizzed above the heads of an enchanted Chinese couple, a groom sheltered his bride from a pelting of sugared almonds before the door of a Florentine cathedral, Muscovites dashed their vodka-glasses to the floor. Somewhere in west Africa, the betrothed leaped over a flower-garlanded broom. A Greek bride had her gown pinned with euro-notes. Two women embraced on an English seafront at dusk, against the lights of a pier.

Vincent stepped behind the scenes, where Cheryl Rossiter was testing the light-system in the non-denominational chapel. Code 1 produced a gentle whirl of coloured spots that glided over the floor, and could be synchronised with whatever music was on the CD system. When she pressed Start, a string quartet announced itself with four strident chords, followed by a provocative pause, then a sudden plunge into romping counterpoint. The coloured spots skittered drunkenly across the floor, the whole effect, in the half-light, proving much too frenetic for the context. Cheryl stopped the CD and switched the light-system to Code 2. This created a wafting filigree of pale-green strands, intended to evoke the rustling of breeze through willow foliage. She pressed Start on the second CD deck, but instead of the sounds of soothing birdsong, the angry waffle of the string quartet re-emerged. What the crap was going on? It had taken on a mind of its own. Vincent discreetly withdrew.

At the opposite end of Fourth to the Hitching Post was where more troubled souls were received, with compassion and a breadth of therapies. The SITNOL addiction centre offered counselling and literature to people with chronic dependencies, no matter whether they be over-involved with substances, gambling or impersonal sex. There was to be no judging, no invocation of higher powers, and above all no setting of targets. As well as group therapists, there were two consultants – a shirodhara yoga practitioner and a deconstructionist literary theoretician – to provide fresh insight and surprising angles. SITNOL did not speak the language of pathology. The clue was in the acronym: Stop in the Name of Love.

Having viewed the therapeutic array on Fourth and seen that it was good, Vincent drifted down to Third, which was consecrated to fitness. At Gym Bunny, Maz Kane, personal trainer, was sitting on the bench of a pro-lat machine, breathing abdominally. Sweat coursed down his temples and cheeks, and his head was surging with exhilarated spaciness. There were people who didn't do this. The world was full of chair-bound sad sacks who would realise, either just too late or way too late, that their bodies were flabbing, drooping and clapping out even as they sat there. And even if they judged they were past help or past caring, they had kids, half-sad half-sacks who could still be redeemed, forced to look down that evil tunnel that dripped with the slime of a lifetime's pizza and turned around. Suddenly aware of Vincent lingering, Maz reached over to the adjacent bench and retrieved his towel.

'Sum up in one word what you want to achieve here,' Vincent challenged him.

'Pain,' Maz snapped back.

That was the stuff. It hurt like all hell, but that was what pain was about. A sign above the water-cooler read: IF IT AIN'T HURTING, IT AIN'T HURTING. Every pussy-assed fat-ball who'd ever come to him had begun by being afraid of pain, but by the time Maz had finished with them, they'd made friends with it. Pain was the difference. Fitness was the shining city on the hill, but pain was the place you stopped and hitched your horse. It was the place you'd never been, but where they always seemed to know you. Pain made life worth living, just because it was life. There was no other life but pain, except for that of fitness, and most travellers on the road weren't ever going to get *there* by nightfall.

Second was home to Rumble, the biggest and baddest nightspot in the county, where three dancefloors, a computerised Russian-designed lighting-system, spherical chillout zones, massage areas and cocktail robots waited to receive up to three thousand party-hounds a night, 'eight nights a week'. Its presiding genius was to be DJ Sexpest, a muscled-up vinyl-masher from south London. A multi-screen video system would show slash-movies as a backdrop to the dancing, while concealed nozzles would waft hypo-allergenic fragrances across the clubbers' heads. Anybody caught in possession of controlled substances would be banned for life.

Vincent paused at the entrance, where a life-size wax figure of a club bouncer was being set up.

He crossed towards the centre of the floor, and gazed upwards into the well of the building. Somewhere above, the sound of a nineteenth-century symphony had begun, bold and brassy, with timpani booms beneath, mingling in beautiful cacophony with a blasting power-ballad. The whole place had the aura of a theatre preparing for the last dress rehearsal. More or less everything was ready to go, but there was still the peripheral thrilling possibility of disaster to be averted while there was still time. Soon, Paradise would be overrun with real people, people wanting to spend money, or at least ready to be seduced into spending it. These people must know nothing of last-minute hitches or glitches. Out of every tiny problem arose the potential for a major triumph. From every out-and-out catastrophe came the modest beginnings of recovery. These were the wisdoms.

He looked up once more into the distant atrium roof with the pure grey sky beyond, and when he'd risen back to Eleven, he looked once more down through powerful binoculars into the gigantic wishing-well into which the place was turning right on cue. Brown and blonde heads circulated along the walkways amid the throbbing light-sequences and the plaintive contest of the musics. Here and there, figures balanced on step-ladders, or were lost in long swatches of iridescent materials, as layer on layer of decoration was applied to the shopfronts and walkways. There was an extra-special crispness to the air-conditioning that perfectly replicated the breath you drew in when you first stepped outside on a snowbound winter's morning. It was worth letting the world take your breath away, stand in your way, make you look at it anew. Adjusting and readjusting his focus, Vincent looked at it anew.

Way down on Ground, two stick-figures sat at a table outside a broad double-fronted shop window. The windows were full of what looked like postage stamps or fragments of confetti, but which must be books. One of the figures was a jet-haired woman in apple-green, the other a dark-haired informally dressed young man. Between them on the table stood two conical glasses, with something frothy and milky in them. While the man was talking, the woman nodded and made an occasional note. At one point, during what seemed to be a pause, the woman studied her notepad and the man picked up his glass and put it to his lips. It looked like a thoughtful courteous exchange. As the conversation resumed, the man leaned back in his chair in a more relaxed posture. He stretched his legs out beneath the table, one by one. He glanced up into the vastness above his head. Did Vincent imagine he caught a momentary flash, even at this vertiginous height, in the man's eye, before his attention was recalled by a further question of the woman's? She accompanied it with an ironic spread of the hands, as though performing a hackneyed piece of dramatic dialogue.

'… dumb question but, where do you see yourself in five years' time?'

'Here,' said Adam, without a thought.

Chapter 3

Inconstant

'It's always Egypt,' said Joanne, with a resigned sigh, after the briefest glance at the leaflet.

'What's wrong with Egypt?' asked Jimmy, occupied simultaneously with perusing the local paper and dolloping marmalade on a piece of toast.

'Nothing's wrong with it. It's just that it's the only ancient civilisation they assume anybody's interested in. You'd think the Babylonians or the Assyrians never existed.'

Mirabelle picked up the leaflet. 'Well, I think it'll be a nice treat for Lukey, won't it? Even Uncle Jimmy might learn something. Look, they've got Tutankhamun, it says.'

'I don't think it's the real thing somehow,' Joanne assured her, trying to adopt a tenderer tone amid the welter of general ignorance.

Luke had liked the sound of the Egyptian exhibition last night, though what remained of his enthusiasm this morning was uncertain. He carried on dipping his soldiers into a soft-boiled egg while the leaflet was passed around the table. Any sudden flicker of doubt might have killed it off, but Luke was quiescent on the subject today, perhaps feeling that doing one thing was as good as doing another, staying in quite as satisfying as going out.

'Looking forward to seeing a mummy, Luke?' Adam asked him.

Luke raised his eyes for the first time. 'Mummy?'

The museum forecourt thronged with people. There were school parties and pensioners, foreign students and families, all mysteriously having decided that today would be a good day to see the Egyptian antiquities.

'I'm surprised it's this busy on a weekday,' Jimmy declared. 'I hope you've got sharp elbows, kids.'

They managed with difficulty to jostle their way towards the entrance, around teenagers sitting cross-legged on the ground in groups, past lines of elderly people in plastic raincoats. Here and there, tour guides held up umbrellas for their groups to follow. There seemed to be three separate queues, although it wasn't clear which they were to join. Joanne pushed her way through to the entrance to read the notices, and came back to report that the left-hand queue was for people with pre-booked tickets, while the middle queue was for those who had just turned up.

'What's the queue on the right for?' asked Jimmy.

'I knew you'd ask that,' said Joanne.

As the queue on the right was the shortest queue, they joined it. Luke became mesmerised by the bobbing yellow balloons many of the other children were holding, on which was printed an image of the death mask of Tutankhamun. One little boy in a family group that came down the entrance steps was clutching the strings of three, looking delightedly up into them as he trotted along.

'We'll get you a balloon on our way out,' Adam reassured him, anticipating his next question.

Luke continued to stare at the other children's balloons, but didn't respond.

As they neared the desk some time later, it became apparent that they were standing in the press queue. A tall man in front of them showed some sort of card, and was asked who he worked for. He was given a form to fill in.

'Looks like we'll have to go to the back of the other queue,' said Jimmy.

'I'll deal with it,' Joanne said, with a sigh.

When it was their turn at the press desk, she put on a pathetic impersonation of a bewildered child, pouring out some plea the others couldn't hear, pointing at Luke intermittently with an imploring look, and clutching her chest in supplication. The next minute they were in, having been inveigled into the middle queue ahead of an indignant-looking couple, where they were sold a family ticket. It turned out that they didn't theoretically qualify as a family, as there were no parents, but at the discretion of the man from the press desk, the rule was duly bent.

Joanne unfolded the floor-plan leaflet they were given with the ticket.

'It must be time for a sit-down,' said Jimmy, nodding in the direction of the café to one side of the entrance hall.

'Should we not see a little of the exhibition first?' Joanne pleaded but, to Jimmy, any such outing ought properly to begin with refreshments, not be punctuated with them intermediately later on.

The History Hoppers café was quite as crowded as the museum entrance, but they joined the self-service queue. It didn't seem that long since breakfast, but Uncle Jimmy was obviously suffering pangs already as he put a piece of creamy gâteau on to the tray. Nobody else wanted anything to eat, but there was an extensive list of coffees, teas, juices and smoothies to choose from. Luke couldn't make up his mind. There was a hiatus of thinly contained patience behind the counter while he dithered, and then, when he asked for Coconut, Joanne had to remind him that he didn't normally like coconut things.

Jimmy shuffled the tray along a little while the others debated. There were some foot-long filled baguettes in a brightly illuminated fridge.

'What are these sandwiches?' he asked the girl.

'What do you mean, what are they?' she said.

'What's on them?'

She pointed to one the baguettes. 'That one's egg mayonnaise and cucumber?' She raised her eyebrows.

Jimmy bent a little sideways to see whether he could discern the fillings in any of the others. One of them was crammed with thick slices of some sweating green article.

'Goat cheese and avocado?' said the girl.

'Go on then.'

There were no free tables. They ended up perching on the edge of a windowsill for what seemed an eternity, the others trying not to watch Jimmy munch his way with grim determination through the baguette and then the slice of cake. Adam kept a nervous eye on Luke for the first signs of boredom, but they didn't come. He appeared beatifically composed. Indeed, it was Joanne who could barely suppress her impatience at Jimmy's ruminations.

'Why don't you go round on your own?' Adam suggested.

'I might,' Joanne replied, tight-lipped with forbearance; but just at that moment, Jimmy declared himself ready.

Starting on the top floor and working down was the correct chronological approach. One sight of the cram of people getting into the tiny lifts was enough to induce them to brave the stairs, for all Jimmy's protestations of infirmity.

The very first room they came to on the top floor was deserted. Illuminated Perspex display-cases glowed intensely in the dark air-conditioned space. Inside were arrangements of miscellaneous items recovered from tombs. Joanne explained to Luke that the objects were intended for use by the dead on their journey into the underworld. There were fragments of drinking vessels, daggers, bracelets, a box that contained the residue of some black substance for outlining the eyes, a whole comb.

'Why would they need to comb their hair?' asked Luke.

'So they would look tidy when they arrived in the next life.'

'What if they didn't comb their hair?'

'Well, if they had a comb with them, they wouldn't need to worry, would they?'

'But this comb's here.'

'Yes, sadly it is,' Joanne said.

'So the lady whose comb this is wouldn't be able to comb her hair when she got to Heaven.' Luke looked up at his sister with a look of lingering concern.

'She might have been able to borrow somebody else's.'

Luke looked back at the purloined comb. 'We could send it to her now.'

'It's probably a bit late now,' Joanne replied. 'She can probably buy a nice new one in the underworld anyway.'

'Coo, look at this,' Jimmy said, stooping to read to Adam from a display card. '"Lobed copper-headed mace, wood handle, Abydos, New Kingdom". Imagine getting cracked on the head with that.'

'Do some damage, that would,' Adam agreed.

They drifted into the next dimly lit room, where more grave goods were on display. A collection of glass bead necklaces weakly reflected the illumination in the case. There was a gold amulet in the shape of an eagle, inlaid with carnelian and turquoise. The ancient artefacts and the dead silence of the rooms after the crush on the ground floor produced in Adam the feeling of weightless detachment that always came over him in museums, as though the accumulated evidence of former lives was just sufficient to uncouple you from the present, without quite transporting you intact into the past. The cups and bowls and jewellery were startling enough in their improbable survival, buried over millennia until their sudden retrieval made them common property, but what was lacking was any evidence of their human use. You had to imagine some richly adorned princeling raising this cup to his lips, but then that seemed rather infantile, almost cartoonish.

'What did they drink?' Adam asked Joanne.

'Beer, mostly,' she replied.

'Sounds all right,' Jimmy grinned, elbowing Adam in the side. 'Mine's a pint.'

Joanne glanced round. There was no sign of Luke. He turned out still to be in the adjacent room, where she had left him, leaning with his forehead against the display-case, staring transfixed at the comb.

'Come on,' she said, taking his hand gently. 'There's lots more to see.'

On the next floor down, they came upon their first mummies. One long case contained a fully bandaged form, while next to it was a preserved body divested of its wrappings. Groups of uniformed children crowded around the unwrapped corpse, staring in mildly horrified fascination at the agonised eyeless face with its exposed brown teeth. Adults stood behind them, affecting a less gloomy but nonetheless unwavering air of inspection.

Somebody pressed a button, and an audio guide began to intone from a hidden speaker. 'During the Middle Kingdom, the practice of mummification changed from being the exclusive preserve of royalty and the nobility to upper middle-class families, although the techniques were not as elaborate as those used for the elite. In Display Case 1 in this room, we see a typical New Kingdom female burial from the twelfth-century BCE. The linen wrappings have been applied in strict geometrical patterns, but there was relatively little other adornment. Note the position of the arms, which lie by the sides, instead of being crossed over the chest in the posture reserved for kings and queens.'

'A middle-class mummy, then,' laughed Jimmy, breaking the silence that followed. One or two heads turned and looked him up and down with an air of polite disdain.

As the knot of children moved away from the unwrapped mummy, Luke glanced warily towards the case without venturing nearer. The withered limbs and flared nostrils of the body seemed indecent, the persistence of its refusal to decompose a depressing indignity.

'How did they know they would be dug up?' Luke wondered.

'They didn't, I'm afraid,' Joanne answered. 'They would have been quite cross if they'd known they'd end up here in a box, with everybody gaping at them.'

Luke considered this, his troubled frown not lightening for a second. 'They could have put a letter with them saying they didn't want to be dug up.'

'They could have done, but we need to remember that if we hadn't brought the bodies out of the tombs to study them, we wouldn't know anything about their lives.'

A display-case at the far end of the room contained another female mummy, alongside a smaller collection of bones. 'The presence of a newborn baby's skeleton,' the audio announcement was blandly saying, 'is an indication that this woman probably died in childbirth.'

Adam looked at the bones. The ambience of death and exhumation, the notion that it was the job of specialists in their field to go foraging among the long-dead, and then put their deadness on show so that others could see it for themselves, weighed on him oppressively. Luke was hypnotised. The leaflet had shown vividly coloured wall paintings, jolly hieroglyphics, beautiful faces in graphic makeup, but it was really about death.

Just before the door to the staircase was a wall-mounted case in which the light wasn't working. A life-sized face with hard black eyes stared out of the darkness.

'Who's this then when he's at home?' said Jimmy, peering at the display card. '"Linen and plaster death-mask, New Kingdom male burial, 10th century BCE. Masks such as these may well have been decorated in gold paint in imitation of royal funerary masks." Very good.'

The four of them stared at the mask. It should have been magical, other-worldly, but instead just seemed morbid and terrifying.

'Should we go now?' said Adam.

Mirabelle glanced up beadily from her high stool behind the counter where she sat knitting. A group of four bedraggled schoolboys was just coming through the shop door.

'Er…' Mirabelle called, pointing to the notice on the front of the counter.

The boys read the notice in silent unison, and looked at each other. By some process of unspoken nomination, one of them gave a shrug and made his way out again, the others uttering muffled sniggers at his departure. They fanned out around the shop, their shambling bodies foreshortened on the CCTV screen above Mirabelle's head. One of them picked up a motorbike magazine.

Dreams of some kind of retirement from the shop, selling on and shipping out, had been officially on their minds for several years. Business was slack but feasible – there was no other corner shop within half a mile's radius, the supermarkets had all relocated out of town, or else opened mini-branches that were mysteriously deficient in certain everyday items – so there was no need for them to cut their losses. It was a drab life though. Mirabelle did most of the serving, while Jimmy sat upstairs in the flat, negotiating with suppliers on the phone, keeping the books, staring at the screen of an old slow computer acquired as a management tool, but which had gradually become a problem in itself. They sometimes had holidays. Last year, they had made it to Malta to stay with old friends who had done exactly what Jimmy and Mirabelle had wanted, selling up a business and retiring somewhere sunny and cheap, where they now let out part of a rambling old farmhouse to vacationers such as Jimmy and Mirabelle. The two weeks they spent there flew by in a frazzle of trips to the local grocer, languid sightseeing and evenings around the kitchen table, eating roast dinners as though back at home, drinking litres of razor-thin red wine. Jimmy declared the trip had taken ten years off him, and attempted to prove it on return by getting his hair bleached.

The descent of Adam and family certainly threw some sort of spanner into the works. With the children not due to start at their schools until after the new year, things were going to be something of a trial. Christmas suddenly looked expensive, but Mirabelle knew that it would hardly be fair to uproot them so soon after the dislocation they had just undergone. It was all very well to talk of getting their own place once Adam had got a job, but even a two-bedroomed flat was surely beyond their means. Luke was less trouble than she had feared, at least so far. Joanne, too clever for her own good, always gave the impression that she was politely overlooking the fact that everything was beneath her, while Adam seemed as wrapped up in himself as she remembered him when he was a boy.

One of the schoolboys ambled up to the counter, and nodded at the chewing-gums. Mirabelle took a pack from the display and handed it to him. Pulling a handful of change out of his pocket, he opened it flat as though offering sugar to a donkey. Mirabelle glanced briefly at the other two boys, saw that their attention was engrossed in the magazines, and gave the boy at the counter a small conspiratorial headshake. He put his money back where it came from and winked insolently at her.

Then there was Aldo. The Aldo thing was a bit of a mess that needed clearing up, but really, where was the harm? She had a lover. So what? It wasn't as though she had gone out looking for it. Nor would she have had the opportunity. She ran a shop, mostly single-handedly, and only ever went out in the company of Jimmy. But the thing about a shop was that you got to know people, some of them anyway. You knew what they liked to eat on Saturdays, what their elderly parents were ailing from, where they were going for their holidays, what they wished they'd done in life. Sometimes they talked you, against all better judgment, into letting them run an informal credit account. Sometimes they tipped you off when environmental health inspectors were rumoured to be on the prowl. And sometimes they lingered, slouched against the counter in the late evening, laughing and chatting with a passable approximation of worldly wisdom, until you took one of their hands and turned it over, apparently to read what was tattooed on their inner forearm – something in Italian, together with a crown and some sort of prancing animal – and found their hand closing around yours.

What had started out as scandalous had become regular and satisfying, like sinking into a hot bath every other night. Aldo had a girlfriend, which evened up the disgrace, and meant that he couldn't be contacted, but Mirabelle was happy to let him take the initiative. He sent her lascivious text-messages during the day, full of unwearying sexual enthusiasm, in which he often obliquely referred to his penis in the third person. The phone would bleep while Mrs Pearson was talking about cremating her sister, and Mirabelle would surreptitiously press the OK button, allowing her eyes to flick fleetingly down while giving the bereaved her full attention. 'my best mate is telling me i shd c u again. xxx A.' 'my soldier is ready for his drill again. xxx A.' Mirabelle understood that the furtiveness was what kept it exciting, and only hoped she wouldn't ever have to deal with the consequences of its sudden exposure. A tear-streaked girl charging into the shop. Angry shouting parents. Social workers.

The boys mooched back towards the shop door.

'Thank you, come again,' Mirabelle called out sardonically.

Aldo grinned at her.

As Jimmy headed off towards the bus-stop with the kids, Adam began feeling a little brighter. The weeks of enforced idleness had taken their toll, but the new job would soon make all the difference. True, the money was fairly poor, and the hint of advancement at some future date could doubtless be discounted, but it was at least better than what he had been expecting. A job in a bookshop, and a reasonably interesting bookshop at that, Print Media. The stock was an enterprising mix of cultural theory, obscure poetry and non-mainstream history, as well as celebrity autobiographies and tragic memoirs. There was a coffee-counter of course, but no alternative spirituality section. It should be fun.

It was planned that, following the grand opening of Paradise, all the shops would have a week-long soft launch, with discounted prices to establish a base of new customers and account-holders. Print Media was offering a three-for-the-price-of-one deal for its first week, though the offer only included certain of the less-alluring cultural theorists and the more decidedly recherché historical material. A razzmatazz atmosphere had been willed into being with some post-ironic bunting and bobbling mobiles, which brushed your head as you mooched about, as though gently reminding the ditherer to get on with it.

In the main mall, there would be lucky-dip draws with opulent prizes, as well as product tastings, massages, card-reading and more. This Thursday evening, there was to be a pre-launch party on the ground floor for proprietors, staff and local media. 'Dress to express!' the invitation demanded. Adam wondered what it meant. It didn't matter what it meant. He had caught one brief rear glimpse of this Vincent guy who ran it all, holding one of the shop-owners in a tight hug as though she had just been released from a spell of wrongful imprisonment. If he was a scam-artist, as the steadily rising volume of critical opinion held, he was one of the most consummately professional. While not in the least wanting to be hugged, Adam had the impression that getting on speaking terms with Vincent, somehow, wouldn't be a bad idea.

Towards the end of the week, the days turned colder, the last of the sun yielding graciously to the harder-faced look of grey skies and low-lying cloud. The next time Jimmy suggested a trip out to Luke, he ventured as far as the side-door and looked uncertainly out, as though trying to establish by sight alone whether he liked the idea of it. He didn't, but silently shrank back among the shoes in the hallway.

Joanne had told Jimmy that Luke liked being read to, and had left some of his favourite books on the dining-table. He liked dragons and wizards of course, anything that involved fighting, but reserved his greatest glee for Alice, whom he unconditionally admired, and whose precise Victorian dialogue made him scrunch up his face in delight. When Jimmy was at the computer or on the phone to the wholesaler, Luke would scan the pictures in the books with melancholy detachment, failing to find in them the magic they glowed with when held up to him.

To Adam and Joanne's surprise, Jimmy turned out to have in him an undiscussed streak of piety. He went to church most Sunday mornings, usually alone, but occasionally accompanied by Mirabelle when Adam was willing to do a turn in the shop. Dressed in an ill-fitting suit with an untidily arranged handkerchief in his breast-pocket, he would disappear for an hour or two, returning with a little news – mostly medical – about the other parishioners. Mirabelle's attitude to his churchgoing was one of polite indifference, as Jimmy tended to seem more embarrassed about it than anybody else whenever it was mentioned. The only moments in which his self-consciousness on the subject left him were when he read the Bible, which he did sitting at the table in the evening before dinner, his mouth frozen open in an expression of earnest attention while he peered down through bifocals at the columns of text.

Sometimes, when weary of the wizards, he treated Luke to a biblical reading, revealing a solemn articulacy that the children's fantasies left untapped. Luke listened as carefully as he did to the story-books, watching Jimmy's face with fascination, evidently struck by the sudden access of conviction. If he was normally inclined to wriggling and fidgeting when being read to, contorting his body into yoga-like positions, the better to hear the familiar tales afresh, the scriptures appeared to have just the opposite effect, rooting him to the spot in a posture of keen acquiescence, as entranced by the nakedness of Noah as by the flames of Hell.

'Therefore,' Jimmy was reading, as Joanne came in to say there was no toilet-roll in the bathroom, 'since we are justified by faith, we have peace with God through our Lord Jesus Christ, through whom we have obtained access to this grace in which we stand; and we boast in our hope of sharing the glory of God.'

'Uncle Jimmy…'

'And not only that,' Jimmy continued, lifting his voice above the interruption, 'but we also boast in our sufferings, knowing that suffering produces endurance, and endurance produces character, and character produces hope, and hope does not disappoint us, because God's love has been poured into our hearts through the Holy Spirit that has been given to us.'

He closed the Bible, and gazed fondly over the tops of his glasses at Luke's bright-eyed astonishment, before turning a more prosaic look towards Joanne. 'Kitchen cupboard under the sink.'

School, Joanne felt, couldn't come soon enough. Then again, a visit from the head-teacher of the junior school at which Luke had been registered had been less than reassuring. Mrs Bigger was a tall, heavily built woman with a very soft voice and a piercing stare. She seemed to like to talk at length, but would punctuate herself with sudden questioning pauses, in which the other person was expected to make some alert response. Mirabelle hadn't taken to her manner at all, as she explained afterwards with a shudder, though she hoped at least that someone with that measure of beady-eyed self-assurance was just what was wanted to curb any fermenting anarchy. You couldn't imagine Mrs Bigger shouting, but then she wouldn't need to. Her very *sotto voce* had something about it of the crypt, and must petrify unruly infants as surely as it unsettled their elders.

The school had a strict uniform policy, which both Jimmy and Mirabelle applauded, particularly as it seemed they were eligible for a grant to help buy it. It was vividly red, the vermilion jacket and socks relieved a little by grey shorts, topped with a high-crowned red cap. As they poured off the school bus just outside the shop in the afternoons, the children looked like a haemorrhage. The girls looked cheery enough, but the uniform had the unfortunate effect of making a pale-complexioned boy look a little like a gnome. Anyway, it spoke reassuringly enough of the containment of anarchy. You couldn't run riot if you were aware you looked silly.

A notice posted at the school gates announced in minatory capitals that any child found carrying an offensive weapon, or any implement capable of being used offensively, would be summarily excluded. The provision of a special area in the playground to cater for a sudden craze for clackers last year had been withdrawn, when it had been found that some of the children were using their clackers – a pair of weighted plastic balls on strings attached to a wooden handle – to lunge at their classmates. Shifting the problem into the schoolyard had been an initial solution to incessant clacking in the corridors, which was driving teachers mad, but unsupervised clacking outdoors had only paved the way for playground battles. They had eventually been banned. The clackers were largely favoured by girls, which led to some parental disgruntlement when an equivalent ban on boys playing conkers was not introduced in the autumn term. Conkers, Mrs Bigger felt, had the richer folk history that clackers lacked, and should be preserved as a traditional pastime. Some parents strongly disagreed, and staged silent watchful protests outside the perimeter mesh during break-times. In the end, conkers too were banned. Surely, thought Jimmy, as the debate swirled into the pages of the *Clarion*, kids could be allowed some innocent enjoyment in life? But, caught between the mute surveillance of the parents and the blood-freezing murmur of Mrs Bigger, the little wretches simply didn't dare.

'Are you going to a wedding?' asked Luke, as Adam knotted his tie at the bedroom mirror.

'No, mate, I'm going to a big party.'

'You look like when you went to a wedding.'

'This is my tie for when I need to wear a tie,' Adam said, carefully loosening it back over his open top button. 'There. What do you think, Lukey?'

'Your tie's not done up,' Luke observed.

The only thing that had persuaded Luke that it wasn't worth going to Adam's party with him was that it was Bonfire Night, and a party was in the offing at home. There had been a last-minute surge of people buying fireworks in the shop, boosted by the rapacious admission charge for the municipal event, which featured acrobatic fire-sculptors from France. People were clearly intending to take their own initiatives, and Jimmy decided they should follow suit. There was a bit of garden at the side of the building that would do. Luke had only ever been to public displays, and the idea of Uncle Jimmy setting off fireworks all on his own was frightening enough to be tempting.

'Now listen,' said Adam. 'Keep well away from the fireworks won't you, and do what Uncle Jimmy says. We don't want any nasty accidents. What have you got in your mouth?'

Luke had crammed in something unwieldy and gooey that looked as though it was chewing him. His eyes widened with the effort to find a space for speaking. 'Reacle hoffee.'

The pungent smell of the toffee brought back Bonfire Nights in the fire-station yard that were as much about eating as watching fireworks go off. Potatoes baked very slowly in their mucky jackets on braziers. Plastic cups of bitty packet soup. Evil black toffee that stuck menacingly to its wrapper. The lunacy of shivering through an outdoor party at exactly the wrong time of year. At the centre of Bonfire Night was a bonfire, the only night when firemen were allowed to start a fire, instead of putting one out. There was something riveting and barbaric about seeing the effigy of Guy Fawkes start to smoulder and crumble in the flames as they sprang about him, a horror that was enhanced if you crept closer to the fire. Its searing heat was a power unlike any other, just because it was so dancingly, archaically alive. Sparks tumbled from it intermittently with each little collapse of the wood and, one year, Adam was caught by a hot glob spat out on the side of his leg, and had to be rushed indoors to have something creamy spread over the singed skin. It was a tiny little dot of agony, great for next day's boasting. The boy who got burned on Bonfire Night, just like in the leaflets, or nearly.

Inside, the explosions of the fireworks sounded even more electrifying, especially the screamers, whose frenzied whoop as they went up was a potent mix of carnival and emergency. There were little stubby fireworks whose performances extended to nothing more than modestly coughing up three small balls of colour in the same sequence as traffic signals, while others frothed forth golden and silver showers for what felt like minutes. The Catherine wheels never went round properly, and had to be coaxed into a stuttering half-revolution with a stick, while the rockets, shooting up from empty pop-bottles to burst in the sky in a handful of distant stars, put them to shame.

A cardboard box standing on the dining-table was piled with dozens of fireworks, all emptied out of their original packs.

'It's going to take you a while to get through this lot,' Adam said to Mirabelle.

'Oh don't worry, we'll be lucky to have got through half that before Jimmy loses interest.'

By the time darkness had fallen, Jimmy had had a couple of whisky-and-lemonades and it was with more than the expected reluctance that he carried the box out into the garden. There was a window on the upstairs landing that the rest of the family was to watch from, Luke kneeling on a chair, Mirabelle and Joanne to either side. The street-lamp caught the lenses of Jimmy's glasses as he grinned and gave a thumbs-up to the little group at the window. After the long process of planting a firework firmly in the ground, he applied a lit taper to it, and then turned and sauntered away. They all watched the tiny spark glow hopefully for a minute or so before vanishing.

'It's going to be a long night,' Joanne sighed.

Just as Jimmy started to approach the apparently dead firework, it burst into life, spitting golden globes in unexpected directions as it hesitantly tried to whirl. Before long, fireworks were going off in twos and threes, Jimmy hopping about amid the flares and coloured smoke as though possessed by the mood of festive vengeance. At one point, he lit two sparklers and stood, one in each hand, in front of a trio of spurting fireworks, making crazed windmill gestures with his arms. His face illuminated in the candy colours outside, Luke was properly entranced. Mirabelle stroked his head in the dark.

To judge from the press of taxis, blacked-out stretch limos and open-top buses clustered at the entrance, Adam appeared to be the only person to come to the launch party on foot. Sporadic camera-flashes greeted the disgorging of certain cars, and he found himself caught up in one of these groups, grinning randomly at the banks of photographers behind the barrier, before being ushered through a break in the rope by a towering security guard. Once inside, he took a sharp right into a cordoned-off area in which only one dishevelled-looking young man in a faintly malodorous suit was standing. They exchanged nods, and waited to see what would happen. Nothing at all happened for a few minutes until a group headed by a corpulent woman from daytime TV arrived. Whatever this area was, Adam didn't belong there. The TV presenter gave him a brief chilly smile and invited him to follow her gaze towards a photographer who was poised waiting to snap the group, into which Adam was half-intruding. He apologised and moved away. An array of professional smiles was caught on camera, and then they all dispersed as if at an order, filing out of the celebrity compound,

Adam nonchalantly behind them.

In the vast circular entrance space, a great throng was concentrated. A contortionist on a plinth whose entire body rose in a spreadeagle behind her twisted sequinned neck was unnoticed by the mass of babbling heads below her. Grass-skirted girls moved among the crowd with trays of canapés, while boys in vintage air-force uniforms and slicked-down hair offered drinks. Adam took something that looked like a Bloody Mary, but turned out to be full of horseradish, and then found a tray of mini-fishfingers being offered him by a girl who looked no more than thirteen. The fishfingers were to be dipped into some bright green substance. They were red-hot, as he now discovered. He nodded thanks as his eyes watered up, and took a gulp of the horseradishy drink. What times were these.

Insinuating himself through the thick crowds of braying cackling people, he made his way towards the lit frontage of Print Media. The windows contained a thought-provoking display of dismembered books, their scattering pages suspended cleverly in mid-air, like leaves blown up in an autumn gale. Here and there, jaggedly torn images of the authors could be seen in the confetti, smiling bravely amid the general carnage.

'Like it?' asked a voice at his shoulder. It was April Pope, his employer. 'We wanted something edgy and different, to get away from the usual reverential aura around books.'

'Yep, it's that,' said Adam.

'Not that we're encouraging disrespect for the book, only reminding the casual gawper that a book is as much a perishable commodity as a pint of milk, and therefore worthy of being nurtured and protected. We're celebrating an ancient and enduring technology.'

'By blowing it to bits, yes I see.' Adam grinned.

'Cynical too. I'm liking that,' April retorted and, with a lightning movement, turned in the direction of a passing tray, and scooped up two glasses of champagne. As she offered one to him, Adam put the fiery tomato drink back on the tray. After its cruel burn, the champagne was like cleansing soda-water.

'I don't mean to be cynical,' he said. 'This is just a brave new world for me.'

'Well, I'm just a poor girl from the sticks myself,' April said, after two hungry gulps of the fizz. 'Come to think of it, this is the sticks.'

'It's certainly a surprising place for this venture.'

'A stroke of genius, I'd say. In London, it would disappear. Yet here, it's like an alien spacecraft just landed at the arsehole end of town.'

'Who are all these people?' Adam wondered.

'Oh, the usual. Hacks, twats, local celebs. People who'd go to the opening of a cocktail parasol. I think I saw a footballer.'

'Oh? Who?'

'God, you're asking me?'

They sipped at their glasses, and took in the crowd around them.

'So, looking forward to the fray?' asked April. But before Adam could answer, a man in a jacket with a design like a crossword grid interposed himself between them, and greeted April with a series of kisses on alternate cheeks. Their words were lost in the din as they clunked glasses and yelled with laughter.

Adam was virtually the only man wearing a tie, although there was a woman dressed like Al Capone, and a battered-looking type in a singer-songwriter's hat with a striped silk tie wrapped around it. Everybody seemed engaged in exaggeratedly voluble conversation, as though they had all been waiting for a long time for this chance of seeing each other, and had to make the utmost of it. It seemed the thing to react to whatever was said to you with big theatrical facial expressions – eye-rolling exasperation, open-mouthed shock – as though you were performing for people sitting in the rear stalls. People gestured with their drinks, with breadsticks and battered langoustines plucked from the canapé trays. With an abbreviated glance back at April, who was being fully engaged by the crossword man, Adam pushed off into the press of bodies.

'Hello!' a very large man bellowed at him, pointing a small microphone into his face. 'Hinton Richards, *Clarion*. What brings you here?'

'I work at Print Media, the bookstore.'

'And what are you hoping to achieve?' Hinton shouted, looking at the volume levels on his recorder.

'To sell books, I suppose. We feel that a book should be seen as a perishable commodity, like a pint of milk, and we want to encourage people to nurture and protect their literary heritage.'

'But surely,' Hinton interjected, 'literary heritage is precisely not perishable? Isn't that the very thing that endures, by way of the great authors?'

'Well, obviously yes,' Adam replied in a slight fluster, trying to remember how the rest of April's statement had gone. 'But the book itself is something that is more, um, damageable, say, than an electronic format. If you see what I mean.'

'And what's your background? Are you from Gutford?'

'No, but I have relatives here. We're currently staying with them.'

'And are they excited by the prospect of the Paradise development opening in their own little back yard?'

'They might be more excited if they weren't likely to be going out of business,' Adam replied, realising the statement's unwisdom about halfway through.

'Oh really?' Hinton pounced. 'What line are they in?'

'It's just a small corner shop.' He had to bail out fast. 'Will you excuse me?'

'And your name?' Hinton shouted, following Adam's mouth with the microphone as he tried to walk away.

'Er, Roger. Roger Maitland.'

A man in superstar shades with lemon-and-lime-coloured frames laid a white-gloved hand on his arm. He made a stage magician's twirly gesture in Adam's face, and then directed his attention with it to the balustrade above them. He ran two fingers of the glove slowly, demonstratively, along the edge, and then held them up in front of Adam like the preaching Christ. They were black with dust. The man's eyebrows ascended theatrically above the lemon-and-lime frames. Adam gave a discreet complicit frown and blew out his cheeks.

'And on that note...' the man said, turned on his heel, and stalked off towards the exit.

Glancing round, Adam saw April's hand waving frantically at him over the heads, and dutifully returned.

'Sorry. Someone you need to meet,' she said, and cleared a space next to her for a rather majestic elderly woman to step into. 'This is your kindly benefactress, Mrs Stone.'

'Rosina Stone,' the woman said, offering a hand to Adam in a way that made him instinctively bend to kiss it.

Mrs Stone was dressed in an ankle-length black sequinned gown, with rows of multi-coloured gems around the neckline. Across her shoulders was loosely slung a gossamer-thin crimson shawl, and on her head a dramatic glossy-black picture-hat of extravagant breadth, the brim of which was set about with wispy floating tassels in shimmering emerald, some of which hung down about her face, giving her the fugitive appearance of a recklessly elegant jackaroo. Mrs Stone, as April explained while the lady herself fixed a proprietorial stare on Adam, was Print Media's chief investor. Indeed, it was fair to say that without Mrs Stone, there would be no Print Media. Adam wondered whether she had ever been connected with the publishing world?

'Oh no, dear,' she demurred. 'I'm just a silly old sausage with too much money. But I do passionately believe that a civilisation without books is like oysters without pepper. And all I see in the so-called bookshops now – if you can find one, that is – is just illiterate fiddle-de-dash. I want people to rediscover the world of letters, and I want talented people such as yourself, Mr, er...?'

'Young.'

'... Mr Young, to be able to lead them knowledgeably into the magic garden. Books are a comfort and a mainstay. I can't imagine how people live without them, but then I dare say, they think they have better things to do. Who are your favourite writers?'

Adam had barely opened his mouth to improvise an answer to this when an impertinently loud noise, like an amplified klaxon, blurted out, and produced a rapid diminuendo of the hubbub. The lights were lowered, and a brilliant spotlight was trained on the balustrade as people's heads obediently turned. Javine Benson, who appeared deceptively to be nearly nude, stepped into the light, holding a radio microphone.

'He has specifically asked me not to give him the big build-up, so I won't. And he doesn't want to interrupt proceedings by making a long speech, but I think it won't go amiss to introduce you, however briefly, to the amazing man whose brainchild this whole project is, namely Mr Wonderful himself. Ladies and gentlemen, girls and boys – the amazing Vincent Beresford.'

So this elevated figure, attired in a candy-pink suit with sky-blue tie and white shirt, who made a show of reluctantly accepting the microphone, was Vincent. His head tilted back like all the others, Adam gazed up at him. A mass outbreak of shushing rippled through the crowd. Vincent allowed the taut pause to linger, as though about to announce a competition winner, before raising the microphone to his lips.

'You know who I am,' he breathed. 'You know what this is. You know why you're here. So do it.'

A burst of lustful cheering, with a piercing squealing topnote, erupted from those clustered immediately below the balustrade. Vincent gave a low bow and handed the microphone back to Javine. Tears welling in her eyes, she could do no more than extend her arm in tribute towards Vincent, who bowed again to the crowd, gave an expansive wave to them and abruptly disappeared.

It seemed to Adam that there was something oddly familiar about the pink-suited figure, on whom he couldn't after all ever have laid eyes.

'Mister! Vincent! Beresford!' Javine screamed into the microphone, and the crowd exploded on cue again, with whoops and yells directed at the space behind the balustrade that Vincent had vacated.

'Extraordinary business,' said Mrs Stone, turning away with a grimace, her tassels levitating and sinking around her face. 'It embodies everything I can't abide these days, beginning with shouting. Why does everything have to take place at full volume?'

Adam assured her that he knew what she meant, but Mrs Stone couldn't hear amid the regathering din.

'Which firework did you like best?' wondered Joanne, sitting on the edge of Luke's bed. The evening had worn on as extensively as she had feared, Uncle Jimmy getting slowly through the entire stock of fireworks, as well as a quantity of whisky-and-lemonades carried out to him periodically by Mirabelle, with the result that, by the end of the show, the grass was littered with both spent firework cases and empty glasses. As soon as he came in, he went straight to bed, leaving Mirabelle sitting at the computer checking emails with the TV on mute. A wordless mood had descended. Joanne got Luke ready for bed.

'I like the sparkly ones,' Luke replied in an indolent tone, as though he couldn't really be bothered addressing the question. He had entered that sullen state of tiredness that wasn't worth interrupting with bedtime stories. Joanne kissed him on his forehead as he sank into his favourite position, his face half-submerged beneath the cover. She turned off the bedside lamp.

As she came back into the living-room, Mirabelle glanced jumpily over her shoulder at her. Whatever she was reading or writing at the computer clearly wasn't for prying eyes. Not wishing to be thought loitering with intent, Joanne mooched into the kitchen. Without putting the light on, she went and stood at the sink, abstractedly picked up a big glass from the draining-board, and held it under the tap for a minute. The water wouldn't run cold. When she sipped at it, it was tepid and stale. She turned round and leaned against the rim of the sink.

This wasn't going to work. It felt like a stopgap measure when they had arrived at Jimmy and Mirabelle's, and the feeling, which Joanne was sure Adam shared, wouldn't go away. They were being made welcome to disguise the fact that they basically weren't welcome.

A shaft of icy moonlight from the window behind her lit up the gurgling face of a cartoon character on the other side of the kitchen. It was printed on the side of a round tin alongside a speech-bubble that said, in furious black capitals, 'I WANT COOKIES!' Joanne didn't at all want a cookie, but found herself mechanically drawn to opening the tin anyway. There were no cookies in it. What it contained instead was a large grubby envelope, bulkily folded in two. She was about to put the lid back on, when something made her take the envelope out, as quietly as she might so as not to be heard by Mirabelle. Just inside the opening was a roughly torn scrap of paper with a few scribbled words on it. Tilting it into the moonlight, Joanne read, 'This is the last OK? It has to end now. Leave us alone please.' She peered into the envelope. It was haphazardly stuffed with twenty-pound notes.

'It's true I don't always finish a book, but I often feel I've had enough of the flavour of it anyway,' a jangly-braceleted PR woman was explaining to Adam. 'And it's finding the time, isn't it? I mean, don't you sometimes wish they'd just, like, invent something that would feed a book straight into your brain, so you'd have had the experience of reading it without the actual time it takes to go through it all?'

'I can't honestly say I've ever wished that, but I can see it would have its uses,' Adam replied, diplomatically. 'Will you excuse me a second?'

He headed off towards a door with a big red M on it, depositing his glass on a vacant tray.

In the centre of the Gents was a fountain, its fine sprays lit in shifting colours like a fibre-optic lamp. A boy in what looked like a naval officer's white jacket waited next to it with a platter of oils and unguents, and a dish for putting tips in, already festooned with a ruff of scrunched-up paper money. Adam headed into a cubicle and bolted the door behind him. On the wall above the lavatory was a framed black-and-white picture of Virginia Woolf. What was she doing here?

Adam found he didn't want to piss after all.

He opened the door again, and strode over to a wash-basin, just for the look of it. A bottle on a swing mechanism spilled some pink gloop into his palm, and he rinsed it off under red-hot water. As he did so, the door to the Gents banged open and, in the mirror, he saw Vincent Beresford sweep in.

Adam detested the sudden clutch he felt in his chest. They hadn't even met. Except that, seeing Vincent now at closer quarters, he realised they had. The Alfa Romeo.

Vincent lingered for a second by the tray. On an apparent impulse, he picked up a bottle with an outsized blue stopper, and sprayed a little of the cologne on his wrist.

'Frappé, by Gauchaud,' announced the attendant.

Vincent waved his hand about with a revolving motion in the air while he waited for the perfume to dry. He sniffed his wrist.

'Sensual woody notes, ylang-ylang, cardamom, bitter citrus,' the attendant said, discreetly glancing at his crib-notes. 'A scent for the man who builds his own contemplative space around him.'

'Aha!' said Vincent. With his nose still touching his wrist, he added, more wistfully, 'But is it me or not?'

Adam realised he had frozen at the sink to watch this scene in the mirror, a moment in which he was now guiltily caught, as Vincent met his eyes. He quickly looked away, but too late. Vincent scurried over, the sprayed wrist cantilevered in mid-air towards Adam.

'What do you think?' he demanded. 'Me?' Adam blinked at him. 'Or not me?'

With a rush of redness gathering in his face, Adam leaned forward and smelled the proffered wrist.

'Er, very nice,' he murmured, feebly.

'Me then,' said Vincent, with a conspiring smirk. The wrist swivelled into an extended hand instead. 'Vincent Beresford.'

'Yes, I know,' Adam replied with a diffident grin, clasping his hot wet hand over Vincent's. 'Pleased to meet you.'

'And...?'

'Sorry. Adam Young.' Adam rolled his eyes in self-reproach. 'Hello.'

'Are you with us?' Vincent wanted to know.

'I'm not against you,' said Adam, and instantly regretted the flippancy, as Vincent returned an unamused but not uninterested gaze. 'I work at Print Media. That is, I will be. It's a—'

'It's an independent bookshop,' Vincent confirmed. 'Very nice, as you'd put it. A man after my own heart, I'll bet. Assuming anyone is.'

'I... Yep.' This dipsy shyness was making Adam feel exposed. His throat had dried up.

Vincent stared at him a moment more, before giving Adam another unreadable smirk, and then headed to the door. '*Bonne chance!*' he called back over his shoulder.

'Yep,' Adam said again, like a daft little yepping puppy, as the door banged.

He turned back to the mirror. There was a small rouged spot on each of his cheeks, a girlish effect that made him screw his fingers into his eyes. He held his breath until the wave of self-reproach began to fade.

When he unscrewed them, the attendant handed him a towel.

'Fragrance, sir?' he asked.

Adam looked over the bottles, each seemingly trying to outdo all the others in outlandishness.

'Which one did the boss go for?' he wondered.

'Frappé, by Gauchaud. Sensual woody notes—'

'Yeah yeah.' Adam looked at the frosted blue bottle with its gigantic square top. 'Drown me in it.'

When the attendant had finished vaporising his neck and wrists, Adam took the uncapped bottle from him and stuffed it in his pocket.

'You don't mind, do you?'

'Er…' the attendant began, but Adam was already halfway to the door. He smelled of… What did he smell of? He paused at the door to think. He smelled of success, is what he smelled of.

'Success,' he said aloud, as he stepped out, and swiped up another glass of champagne.

Joanne had hardly been asleep more than a few minutes when she was woken by the sound of the side-door opening downstairs. She heard Adam's familiarly heavy tread on the stairs, his creak along the passageway, and then the light-cord being clicked in the bathroom. Turning on her other side, she slid a hand beneath the pillow, and folded it over the twenty-pound note she'd hidden there. Her heart fluttered for a moment. Tomorrow was another day, she told herself.

Chapter 4

Ambitious

What do people want?

It was a question that Jimmy and Mirabelle had occasionally asked themselves, when business slackened. Sometimes, it felt as though they were serving only the same few regulars, elderly people and stoned students whose collective infirmity prevented them from getting any further than the corner shop. It was easy enough to guess what they wanted. Bread, milk, eggs, tins of custard, cigarette-papers, vodka. But what they might be able to offer people who happily drove to the out-of-town retail parks wasn't obvious. An experiment with DVD rental hadn't worked, inasmuch as people quite often didn't bring the DVDs back. A selection of paperbacks sat on their revolving stand untouched. Unusual fruit and veg lay neglected, since nobody knew what to do with taro or romanesco. A woman had once asked Jimmy how you set about cooking a yam. Scrutinising the enormous shapeless thing, he thought that perhaps you could boil it, but the woman doubted she had a large enough pan. As to what it tasted like, Jimmy thought it was a bit like potato. It was a firm favourite with the Chinese people, or was it the West Indians?

In the end, it was better to stick to what you knew, as others in their turn likewise stuck. But Paradise promised to change all that. It was founded on the conviction that people didn't know what they wanted, only that they wanted something else, and that if you could get their attention for five minutes, you could begin to create new desires in them. It wasn't simply a matter of introducing them to novelties. The salient aspect of novelty was that it wore off, after which people would go back to their old preferences, which might at best be augmented by a single new one that would then take its place in the repertoire. What was important was to get them to think in new ways about what they might derive from the retail experience. Instead of simply selling them things, however much that was the mainstay of the enterprise, you could provoke in them an inquiring state of mind, a childlike spirit of wonder that would open their minds and hearts as well as their wallets. Instead of shopping being an agenda that had to be got through, it could instead become something more exploratory and interactive, a dialogue with the world of commercial possibility, which flowed both ways, acting to the mutual benefit of both retailer and consumer. Who knew what would happen then? All that was sure was that the sellers of goods had as much to learn as the potential buyers. Their businesses would develop and grow organically, democratically, opening up new spaces for their customers, instead of trying, as brutal capitalism did, to dictate their aspirations. For these reasons, the final publicity blitz for the grand opening of Paradise had been couched in interrogative terms, asking people to imagine what would most restore the element of adventure to shopping, and then to come along on Saturday 15th to see whether they could mould what there was to their own vision. 'Paradise wasn't Paradise,' as the posters declared, 'until Adam and Eve turned up.'

The *Clarion* did its energetic best to foment anticipation. There were sneak previews, interviews, regurgitated press releases that all assured readers the town, the county, indeed the whole south of England, was abuzz with excitement. Nobody, it seemed, could talk about anything else. Children were discovering a thrill of impatient expectation that made the approach of Christmas feel like a looming dental appointment by comparison, while their elders were discovering that, contrary to the sagging evidence of the bathroom mirror, they were just grown-up children. 'It's like waiting to go on the greatest fairground ride in the world,' a mother-of-three was quoted as saying, to the delighted hilarity of the three. She didn't know who was more excited, them or her. 'We are!' they screeched, dancing up and down to prove the point for the *Clarion* photographer.

For all these reports of uncontainable exuberance, the paper's insistence that everybody for miles around had taken leave of their senses as they awaited the opening seemed some way north of the truth. Even the choice of celebrity for the ribbon-cutting had provoked more bemusement than frenzy. The original candidate, boy-band singer Japheth Crosby, had had to be pulled, after he was quoted on the internet suggesting that terrorist attacks on Israel were God's punishment on the Jews for the Crucifixion. His replacement was a local entrepreneur who, it turned out, had signed a petition opposing the original Paradise planning application. The final choice was the eighteen-year-old Gutford Athletic left-back, Connor-Joe Mbamba, whose stuttering defensive skills hadn't yet endeared him to the Whitstock Road faithful, but who did at least have the redeeming qualification of being in a relationship with incandescent supermodel Preeta Afezuke. News of their separation, following a nightclub affray two days before the opening, didn't have to be a problem, Vincent announced. It generated more heat around the launch, and heat was a perishable luxury commodity.

But what, after all, did people want?

What emerged repeatedly from the focus groups was that people didn't know what they wanted. 'It's the Christmas-list syndrome,' Vincent had suggested to the consultant carrying out the research. 'You can hardly go through a day without thinking, "Oh, I'd love one of those," but wait until somebody asks you to make a wish-list, and your mind goes blank. All you can think about is aftershave.' Everybody nodded, as the focus group contract was cancelled. It was important, though, not to fall into the trap of thinking that, just because people were stumped when asked to list their hearts' desires, that meant you had the licence to tell them. That was the old thinking. That was the thinking that led you into opening falafel franchises at railway stations, and then watching your investment go up in smoke, as your falafel-fryers stood idle while people queued for pasties instead. Desire wasn't created from nothing. It had to be rooted organically within the customer's latent consciousness. And that submerged desire was what we were all setting out to discover. The consultant's most pressing desire, as it turned out, was to be paid the balance of her fee. Vincent made a single quick shooing motion with his fingers, a little flip that communicated assent, contempt and dismissal in one economical gesture. Henceforth, nobody was to use the words 'focus' and 'group' around him in the same sentence.

And then it was important to remember that what people wanted wasn't necessarily just commodities. More things in a world already stuffed with things could lead to a feeling of jaded surfeit, hence the anti-consumerism protests and the detox industry. What they most hungered after might well turn out to be something more intangible – a feeling, a mood, a state of mind. Could the retail experience provide that? Why not? If you created a certain environment, in which potentiality itself was the main feature, rather than the production of simple desire, did you not stand a chance of remaking the retail world? Vincent's strategy team wondered how that might work, but they needn't have, as he was about to tell them anyway.

Say you were running a juice-bar, let's call it Juice Jazz. You could decorate your frontage with huge images of tropical fruits, their sliced flesh all shiny and ripe, leading the customer into an interior that was full of the scent of mango and musk-melon, and populated with other punters drinking juice. You might want to join the party. But suppose the environment you had been invited into only hinted obliquely at a mood by creating the feel of a sun-scorched equatorial cityscape, in which, amid beeping traffic and the yells of street-vendors, you found yourself feeling a little parched. How rewarding would it then be to discover that you could actually quench your thirst as there was someone on hand to press some watermelon for you? There may also be someone to book you a holiday on Fiji, or offer you a fruit-scented massage, or even just sell you a pineapple. But the point was that the environment would have allowed you to see where your inclinations took you. Whereas, at Juice Jazz, all that was happening was that its owners were saying, 'we sell freshly pressed juices, come in if you want one'. The strategists took the point, but wondered how realistic it was to expect retailers to be able to offer a number of unrelated products and services. Besides which, the leases required tenants to state the nature of their business, and the drop-down menus didn't allow for 'whatever the customer wants'. Which, as Vincent stated with a sigh, was exactly what was wrong with drop-down menus. Pigeonholes were for pigeons. Straitjackets were for straights.

'How come,' Luke wondered, watching from his usual station on top of the bedside table, as Adam frizzed a palmful of gel into his hair, 'you've got black hair, Joanne's got white hair, and I've got brown hair?'

'It's a mystery, isn't it?' Adam replied. 'But I don't think you can call Jo's hair white. Blonde is the proper word.'

'She hates being called Jo,' Luke reminded him.

For Adam, the hardest part of this, his first day in Paradise, was that he was walking into it amid a general sense of betrayal. When he first told Jimmy and Mirabelle he had been offered a job there, he was met with affronted silence. Determined not to succumb to guilt about it, he nonetheless promptly succumbed, filling in the silence himself with weaselish disavowals. It looked an awful place but, as they knew, he had tried to find work elsewhere, many other elsewheres in fact, and come up short, and – well, needs must. They had said themselves he couldn't stay idle. The silence only deepened, until Mirabelle eventually spoke up for both of them.

'You must do as you see fit,' she said. 'You're a young man, you've still got plenty of time to make mistakes.'

'And almost as much time to learn from them,' grinned Adam, but it was of no avail. There was no word of absolution.

In the following days, one or other of them would find ways of dropping Paradise into the conversation, usually in the context of its sure and certain ruination of what remained of their business. Noting that the pricing-gun was on its last legs, Jimmy remarked heavily that there was no point in ordering another, as they probably wouldn't be pricing things up for much longer. Not until it came to putting the shop itself on the market, Mirabelle chipped in.

A feature of their antipathy to Paradise was that they both stolidly refused to utter its name. If it wasn't gesturally referred to as 'that place', it was sometimes given some withering antonym, usually by Jimmy. Adam learned one day that he was soon off to work in Hell, and on the next that it had been renamed Damnation. It was a moment of critical errancy on his pilgrim's progress, a case of wandering blindly into the darkness while blithely ignoring the cries of the condemned. It was little use insisting that it was just a job. No doubt that's what Hitler said, thought Mirabelle. 'Oh, come on...' Adam had pleaded, but the exchange was ended with a sharp bang of the living-room door. It soon turned out that the best policy was not to rise to the bait, not least because the atmosphere of frosty disapproval was beginning to be picked up by Luke, to whom the idea that Adam might have got something wrong was entirely without precedent. It came to something of a head the night before the launch party, as Adam was helping Mirabelle lay the table.

'You won't be eating with us tomorrow evening, will you?' she asked.

'No thanks, I think there's going to be food at the reception.'

'Ooh lovely, basinfuls of caviar, will it be?'

Luke's hand stopped in its tracks over his colouring-book as he caught the unmistakable sour note.

'You know, you're not making this any easier,' Adam said in an undertone.

'Oh I'm sorry, were we supposed to hang out the bunting for you? Our silly little business is about to smashed to smithereens by some ponced-up millionaire, and you're running off to join in the fun. There was us thinking that loyalty to your family who've taken you in might have counted for something, but no. Well, O damn K, mister. You scuttle off to play with your bunch of poshos. Spare a thought for us while we try to put our lives back together again, will you? Sod it!' she snapped, throwing a bunch of cutlery down on the table, and storming into the kitchen.

'Must have been a bad day,' Adam said feebly to Luke, who had looked at him for an explanation. Luke dropped his crayon and put his hands into his lap, staring with bowed head at the half-coloured tiger in front of him. Adam came round to the back of his chair and squeezed his shoulders. 'Hey,' he said, in a sustaining tone.

They could hear Mirabelle clanging saucepans disgustedly in the kitchen.

'What's smithereens?' asked Luke.

The embargoing of the topic in the days since had been a relief. And now the first morning had come, Adam hoped that passions would soon cool, once his embroilment with the enemy became a matter of regular working hours.

Joanne appeared at the boys' bedroom door.

'Off to Damnation, then?'

'Don't you start,' said Adam. 'And don't say "Damnation" in front of Luke.'

'Damnation!' Luke shouted, always happy to pick up the ball and run with it.

'We might come along later to see how you're getting on?' Joanne offered.

'You could do.' Adam leaned towards the mirror and bared his teeth for inspection. 'It'll just be me standing in a shop. Not hugely exciting. And DON'T,' he added, 'do anything to show me up, OK?' Luke gave a delighted squeal and shot his arms into the air. 'I mean it, cowboy.'

His brother jumped off the bedside table, and charged headlong out of the room, whooping with excitement.

'I think we can call that a challenge risen to,' noted Joanne.

It was with an undeniable sense of indulgence that Adam allowed himself to register both the thrill that fluttered in his belly, and his moment of due contempt at it, as he showed his staff pass to Security. On either side of the main entrance a modest crowd – not large enough to threaten a tumult, but not so small as to embarrass anyone – was being loosely hemmed in by the crush-barriers. Somewhere behind them, a couple of placards could be seen, one condemning capitalist shit, the other wondering more arcanely where the bodies were buried. A group of press photographers waited in their compound. The amorphous pink lettering of the name that rose above the entrance twinkled where it caught the odd pallid gleam of early-morning sun. Across the width of the gateway beneath, a broad pink ribbon was slung. Something stately by Beethoven was proceeding, with just a hint of reverb, from concealed speakers.

Nothing seemed to be happening for the moment, even though there were only minutes to go until the opening ceremony. One of the reporters threw an inaudible question to Adam where he stood behind the fence. There didn't appear to be any members of staff around apart from him, let alone any sign of Vincent. He was about to turn and go in, when a ripple of commotion that ascended into a sustained thin scream announced the arrival of a blacked-out limo.

Adam watched as the car swept around the bend of the approach-road, and slowed towards the main gate. The photographers turned as one. Before the car had quite come to a stop, its passenger-door flew open, and a uniformed attendant hopped out deftly, leaving the door hanging wide behind him. He stood with his hand on the handle of the rear door until the first pre-emptive burst of camera-clicking had died down again.

'Ladies and gentlemen,' he announced, in broad south London. 'Mr Connor-Joe MBAMBA!'

The door was wrenched open, and the Gutford left-back stepped out with the balletic delicacy of a starlet. He drew himself almost diffidently up to his full five-foot seven, and stood to attention for the cameras. His opaque wraparound sunglasses were positioned carefully just below the bridge of his nose, where they formed a zone of inscrutability between the runic detail of his razor-lined eyebrows, and the two pencil-thin black lines under his nose. Three diamonds were crammed in a cluster on his left earlobe. He was wearing a jet-black suit with a sprawling-wide iridescent tie and gold trainers. As the attendant began to lead him along the gauntlet of jostling people, a young woman managed to roll gymnastically over the top of the crush-barriers, timing her incursion perfectly to land at Connor-Joe's feet, screaming that she loved him. His ankles gripped fast, he began to topple, but was caught just in time by his attendant and a policeman, while security guards converged in a pack to drag the intruder off. He put his hands to his head in a pantomime of bemusement, and was then guided more securely towards the ribbon.

With what seemed like perfunctory lack of ceremony, a pair of golden scissors was produced and thrust into his hand. Obeying the bawled instructions of the photographers, he held the scissors across his chest and gave the cameras his million-dollar grin, while the shrieking of the little crowd rose to an intensity that belied its numbers. It looked as though he was probably expected to say something, but accepting that the shrieking wasn't going to subside long enough for anybody to hear it, he settled for making a V-sign, then raised a clenched fist with his head bowed for a moment, before finally cutting the ribbon.

Holding the scissors by the blades, he went to offer them to somebody in the crowd, but was quickly relieved of them by a security-man. Others closed efficiently around Connor-Joe and, leading the way, escorted him with comical briskness back to the car, as though he were being bundled out of court in custody.

And that, Adam observed, seemed to be that.

Inside, groups of young girls in ra-ra mode were milling about chatting. A couple of heads turned, accompanied by a giggle as Adam did his best to breeze past them. Outside Print Media, April was surveying the window-display and talking into her mobile. She didn't look especially happy, and as Adam approached, she appeared to look right through him.

One of the front tables was stacked with a chat-show host's autobiography. Each copy had a sticker on the cover with an endorsement quote from another chat-show host: 'Sensational stuff. Almost as good as my own autobiography!' Another table was arranged, optimistically enough, with slender volumes of contemporary poetry. *Recension* by James Frodsham. *Salamanders and Lemons* by Faith Pratt. *Savannah Gavottes,* an anthology of work by migrant workers, illustrated by—

'Yup,' snapped April, as she suddenly swept past Adam. 'Good to see you haven't given up yet. I nearly have. You'll find a cafetière in the back office. Throw whatever's in it away and make some fresh.'

'Sure,' said Adam, and turned to go.

'We've got three author appearances due this morning. Fingers crossed the bastards don't all turn up at once, but they will. You'll be in charge of calming them down after the nightmare journeys they'll inevitably have had getting all the way here from London. An hour on a train can take it out of them, especially the poets. How's that coffee doing?'

'I'm on it,' Adam replied. 'Who are the authors, by the way?'

April gave a hurried sigh of exasperation, pinched the bridge of her nose with one hand, and screwed up her eyes. 'Er, Fleur...

no, Faith Pratt, Jonah Midgley the crime writer, and... what's her damn name... Irish... Caitlin Binchy. There'll be a scrum for her and Midgley, so be ready. How's that coffee?'

Adam was on it.

Luke awoke from dribbly sleep to a room full of orange glow as the sun came through the curtains. He had heard a little high voice say Adam's name very close to his ear. He realised it must have been his own, which was a very strange feeling, as he had never heard himself talk in his sleep before. There was no sign of Adam, just a mushed-up bed in the orange glow. It was as though he'd run away and left them while they slept. A cold shaft of terror pierced Luke through.

April was now near boiling-point. She was speaking in a strangled whine on her mobile, her free hand clutching her forehead. When Adam put the mug of muddily strong coffee down on the counter, she stared angrily at it. She stuffed a handful of unopened post at Adam, with a dismissive wave at him to go away and open it somewhere. He retreated behind the counter, and sat in a swivel-chair. When he looked through the mail, he saw virtually none of it was addressed to them. Most of it was for a place called Prime Media on Second.

A young man in a puffer-jacket wandered in. April looked up sharply and cupped a hand over the mobile.

'Excuse me,' she called out. 'What are you doing here?'

'Just looking,' the man replied, nervously.

'How did you get in here?'

'The whole place has just opened,' said the man. 'Is it OK?'

April jerked a glance at the time on her phone. 'Oh my stars! Sorry, carry on. Adam!' But the voice on the phone suddenly brought her attention back to the call.

Adam stood by, awaiting instructions, as April kept up a stuttering argument, her caller and she both interrupting each other, stopping and starting simultaneously. After a minute, she gave Adam a long-suffering look, cupped her hand over the phone again, and hissed to him, 'A bottle of Rioja Reserva says you can't sell this pooch three novels in the next three minutes.'

Adam accepted the challenge with a raised thumb. 'Can I help you, mate?' he asked the man.

'Just looking,' said the man. He dithered encouragingly towards the three-for-the-price-of-one tables, turned a book through ninety degrees while he squinted at the cover, and then drifted towards the entrance and was gone. Adam straightened the book. April was still vainly trying to reason with her caller.

On the poetry table was a large black-and-white image of a woman with close-cropped hair and the intense piercing gaze of someone in a temper. The announcement said that the award-winning poet Faith Pratt would be appearing at Print Media on its launch day, reading from her latest collection and signing copies. Adam opened a copy of *Salamanders and Lemons* halfway through:

Thickening anent the day, its crusted glimmer
Thwarts all hope of loss. The bulbous lemons bind it,
While my pulse courteously dreads you, Avatar, my Enemy.
Skeins of our passion, twisted like history, mount the sheer walls
Of this palazzo until, choked on our gorgeous magnanimity,
They lie pulverised, hyperventilant, triumphant in disintegrity
On the buttresses. The soul's grout knows this season.

'Sorry about that.' April appeared at his side. 'My mother. You'll get used to it, even if I never have.'

Before too long, Adam could work the till, scan in both sales and returns, sensitively challenge a customer whose card had been declined, and tell them where they could find Food and

Drink, Military History and Object Biographies. April said she had resisted having a section for Local Interest. 'Oxy. Freaking. Moron!'

People drifted in and drifted out again. Someone asked about ordering a title, then decided it would be quicker to buy it online, and still they waited for their first sale. A small child was sent in by her mother to ask, coyly, whether they had a toilet. They didn't. Then, just as a faint gloom was settling over the two of them, a man who had been browsing at great length brought a volume of crosswords to the counter.

'Is this is in the three-for-one?' he asked.

'I'm afraid not,' Adam replied.

The man looked painfully at the cover and bit his lip, while he wrestled over the decision. He finally said he'd take it anyway. Adam scanned it, and asked him for £5.99. He took a five-pound note and a pound coin off the man, and handed him a penny, the book and a leaflet inviting him to sign up for news of future events. They were in business.

Towards midday, Jonah Midgley arrived. He was wrapped in a greatcoat and long scarf, the ends of which trailed just above the tips of a pair of filthy motorbike boots. Adam set him up at a table in the corner, behind a pile of copies of *Renegade Dawn*, the fifth book in his best-selling Dooley and Fanshawe series. The permanently squabbling couple manage once again to rise above their bitter divorce proceedings long enough to solve a mystery that opens with the discovery of a blindfolded corpse on a Ferris-wheel. Midgley did steady rather than brisk business during the half-hour that he sat there, and when his time was called with the arrival of Faith Pratt, Adam had to clear the table swiftly of *Renegade Dawn*, replace it with *Salamanders and Lemons*, and inform Midgley that, sadly, they weren't able to offer him lunch.

Faith Pratt sold one copy to a man in a three-piece suit, who told her she had been brushed by the shade of Rilke. She smiled sourly.

Recent days had been overcast for Joanne, not by Adam's consorting with the enemy, but by the sickly unease created by her discovery of the money in the envelope. The pitiful note that she found with it seemed an obvious indication of blackmail, and yet could she believe Mirabelle and Jimmy capable of such a thing? Perhaps one was involved in it, and the other not, but then the apparently open storage of the cash in the kitchen hardly suggested secrecy. The morning after she had stumbled on it, it had disappeared, but that could mean it was being belatedly hidden from her and her brothers as much as by Mirabelle from Jimmy, or vice versa. She found herself warily watching them both for any flicker of complicity or guilt, but saw none. Which of them was the more likely blackmailer? Mirabelle was full of bitter resentment, but surely not so as to make her resort to such squalor? Jimmy seemed too settled in his own placidity, in inverse proportion to Mirabelle's querulous rage, even to contemplate such a course, but then that may only be a shabby pretence of innocence, gilded over by the Bible-reading and the church-going. Or were they the expiation for the sin?

And this was before you even began to consider whom they might be blackmailing, and on what grounds. The note spoke of some final desperation, a hapless victim bled white by extortion, living in continual terror of exposure. Joanne shuddered as she thought of the threats that must have been uttered or written, and grew angry at the image of either the waspish Mirabelle or the lumbering Jimmy composing them, making them sound convincing, even ultimately preparing to act on them. How had these people come to blackmail? Peering through the landing window at the patch of garden below, where Luke was doing his best to prise a tennis-ball from Jimmy's grasp, Joanne realised she had both the moral duty and the strong desire to stop it.

She also had a twenty-pound note in her purse. She wondered whether it had been missed, whether the blackmail victim may already have had a call pointing out that the shortfall had been noticed, and threatening horrible consequences. Most likely the money had been counted before she took it, she told herself, but still, she wished she hadn't so rashly helped herself to some of it. Did that not somehow make her complicit? No, not at all. *She* wasn't the blackmailer. Except that she had indirectly profited by the sordid exploitation that was going on and, short of finding a way of furtively returning the money, it was rather late to be developing a sense of shame about it. The only thing, clearly, that would set the situation to rights was to bring a halt to it. But how?

Mirabelle now appeared on the scene below, wrapped up in an outsized black overcoat and fake-fur hat, apparently chivvying the others on to get ready to go out. With one lightning-quick movement, she snatched the ball from Jimmy's hand and stuffed it into her coat pocket. The boys' game thus stopped in its tracks, they trooped in through the side-door. Mirabelle stood for a moment, gazing down abstractedly at the scruffy grass, and then suddenly, on an apparent impulse, raised her head with a jerk towards the window. Joanne instinctively made to shrink back below the sill, but Mirabelle had already seen her. Their gazes fixed each other in some sort of uneasy stand-off. This was ridiculous, thought Joanne. She was already behaving like a police detective. Mirabelle pointed at an imaginary wristwatch. Were they due somewhere?

Luke came charging up the stairs.

'Where are we going?' Joanne asked him.

'To see Adam!' he cried.

This was an unexpected compromise after all the imprecations of the past days, but perhaps the intentions were more ghoulish curiosity than familial support. She didn't really want to go. In fact, the opportunity to prowl about the place alone seemed too good to miss, but there would be other chances, and she didn't want to arouse suspicions so soon after her discovery of the money. If Jimmy and Mirabelle had grounds to suspect she was in on it, they may be looking for evidence of the fact. She mustn't throw them any such clue. Mirabelle called her name from the bottom of the stairs.

'Coming,' she called back.

'Have fun,' said the girl who had been left in charge of the shop.

The bus was packed with people going to the launch day, the children waving balloons on sticks and wearing customised badges with their names above a bulging pink heart and the word 'Paradise'. 'Natasha loves Paradise.' 'Chloe loves Paradise.' And an entire battalion of Jacks did too. In the context of all the irrepressible gaiety, Mirabelle looked dressed for a Russian funeral. Squeezed against the window by a large woman wearing a papoose containing twin infants, she fished in her handbag for a handkerchief, fastidiously pressing it to her nose as though inhaling some sanitising specific amid the germ-infested masses. Standing in the aisle, Jimmy rested a rough red hand on Luke's head.

The entrance-gate was crammed with a seething human mass. Somewhere beyond their jostling heads, the placards of the protesters were on the point of being eclipsed. On one of them, Joanne could just make out the words, 'If you tolerate this,' and filled in the rest in her head. Jimmy warned Luke solemnly to stay within their sight and not run off. A booming voice crackled out from hidden speakers, welcoming them to the experience of their lives, and pointing out that if they looked up to the balcony at the top of the building, they would see Mr Wonderful himself, Vincent Beresford, welcoming one and all to Paradise. Arms around them shot up, pointing out to each other a stick-thin figure in pink waving from the top of the building. Phone-cameras were held up in homage.

'Ooh look, it's Willy Wonka,' Mirabelle drawled.

'Who's that?' Luke wanted to know.

'He's the man who's made all this possible,' Jimmy told him.

'And much more besides,' Mirabelle added.

They were pressed forwards with the surge. As they passed through the main doors, girls in silver Spandex body-suits were handing out floor-plans. Mirabelle disdained to take one, while Jimmy and Joanne, awkwardly unfolding the thing between them, scrutinised it for Adam's shop.

At Print Media, Adam was just explaining to yet another pair of disappointed customers that it wasn't the late Maeve Binchy who was appearing, but Caitlin, no relation.

Caitlin herself was already in position, standing behind her table with a copy of *If Love Comes Calling* in one hand, her forefinger inserted at the place where she was about to start reading. She raised a mug of cold coffee to her lips, pretended to sip, and smiled warmly at the people in the front row.

April was waving a frantic hand in Adam's direction over the heads of those standing around the fully occupied rows of chairs. He assumed she was telling him to get things under way.

Having shoved his way to the table, he tapped a teaspoon against the side of a mug for silence. The hubbub subsided a little.

'Ladies and gentlemen, I'm sure you're all as eager as I am to welcome one of our star authors today, in fact *the* star author, to judge by the numbers.' From near the till, April made a vicious throat-slashing motion at him. 'Without intending any disrespect to our other distinguished authors of earlier today. She's been hailed as "one of our most lyrical and compelling excavators of the present-day condition", an accolade I'm sure none of you need convincing of. Because you're already convinced by it, that is. She's now going to read a passage or two from her latest work, *When Love Comes Calling*—'

'*If*,' Caitlin Binchy snapped good-naturedly behind him.

'I beg your pardon, *If Love Comes Calling*. My apologies, Maeve.' Under the roar of laughter that came from the audience,

Adam instantly reddened, but his hasty correction of the name was drowned. Caitlin Binchy spread her arms in a pantomime 'I-give-up' gesture. She was used to this confusion. 'So without further ado, please give a generous Print Media welcome to Caitlin Binchy.'

An explosion of applause, accompanied by the odd whistle and whoop, rang out. Caitlin opened her book, and waited until pin-drop silence had settled before starting. She had barely got the first words out in a buttery Irish contralto – 'If every emotion has its season, and every season its spate,' – when the voice of a child at the back, hoisted into the air on adult shoulders, screamed out Adam's name.

Adam made a forbidding motion with his hand towards his brother, which Luke interpreted as a wave of greeting. 'Adam!' he screamed again, and broke into cackling laughter. Jimmy, on whose shoulders he was perched, was beaming warmly too. Adam put a finger against his lips, and Luke, catching on immediately to the rules of the game, imitated the gesture with a delighted shush like a hiss of escaping steam. 'Psssssssssh.'

'Could we have some quiet, please, out of respect for our author?' April asked from her position at the counter, which ensured that all heads turned from the endearing child towards her. 'I'm sorry, Miss Binchy, please continue.'

Caitlin began again. She read in a lilting incantatory tone at a sedate pace, which had the effect of bewitching the fans who found her prose deeply satisfying and lulling those who had never heard of her. Occasionally, a metaphor would elicit a little gasp of pleasure, which the author modestly affected not to notice. She read on, turning methodical pages, through an elaborately descriptive passage, the clotted density of its imagery precipitating like boiled cream as the voice proceeded. Adam's glance lighted on a woman in the second row, whose face had begun to take on the faintly peevish air of someone who has been kept waiting in a reception-area too long. She was blinking furiously, with compressed bloodless lips. When he looked up towards the front of the shop, the scene was dominated by the figure of Luke sitting on Uncle Jimmy's shoulders, like a more than usually diminutive jockey, stilled into barely cooperative silence, but poised in a crouching posture with his fists clenched, as though ready to join in with whatever audience eruption was in the offing. Adam lowered his head to conceal the incriminating grin that was twitching at his lips. He scrunched his buttocks together. Caitlin Binchy was panning over the lunar dereliction of Donegal, the chains of her spectacle-tabs gently quivering as she evoked the Atlantic wind. Adam didn't dare look up, knowing that the first thing he would see would be his brother's open-mouthed gape of anticipation. No power on earth would then bottle up the pee-dribbling laugh that was brewing inside him. At long last, Caitlin's voice entered its final *rallentando*.

'What dark guilt the land possesses, only the rocks know. Only the rocks and the wind. But they' – she looked up through her glasses – 'they have told me.'

There was a strained pause. Then applause and cheering rang out like bursts of artillery-fire, and Adam allowed the trapped laugh to manifest itself as an ear-to-ear grin of appreciation. He shot out his hand towards the author, like a variety-show host milking the adulation for a guest-star, mouthing as he did so her name. 'Caitlin! Binchy!' When the relieved cheering had subsided, he invited people to come up and have their copies of *If Love Comes Calling* signed, but asked them also to respect the fact that Ms Binchy wouldn't be able to personalise messages. A moo of disappointment broke through the excited chatter. Adam made a hand-rolling motion towards Luke and the family, none of whom knew what he meant by it.

Pullulating crowds swarmed throughout every level of the mall. They collected in double rows on the escalators, leaning over the sides to appreciate the bottomless depth of the space, craning their necks upwards to the sky-high atrium. The swirling, eddying din of their voices rose like congregational singing in a cathedral, overlaid with colliding cross-currents of music. Vintage soul melded into Bach, the mixture transmuting into the avian fluting of operatic sopranos, beneath whom the surging of orchestras in full flight resolved into the cheery jangling of guitar pop. Everywhere you looked, there was somebody demonstrating something, presenting something, offering free trials and tasters. Twittering toy birds flapped mechanically about people's heads for a moment, before vanishing diaphanously back into the throng. Aromas mingled like the music: frying fish and smouldering caramel, sizzling garlic, fresh-baked cornbread. Acrobats flick-flacked in belching cappuccino steam. Fairground music drowned the monastery bell on Mount Athos, which was wiped without scruple from the screen to make way for sun-seekers on Fijian beaches. Flyers accumulated underfoot like autumn leaf-litter. Everywhere, eyes bleared in the dazzle. Tears of joy glistened under the fairy-lights. Air-conditioned breath escaped in puffs of floss that floated upwards, past the woman on the podium fixed in the flamingo-like poise of Tai Chi, past the vigilant glare of the security-guards, past the disgorging lifts and the gridlock on the escalator landings, into the starry ether above.

Luke was hungry. Having briefly looked in at the bowling alley, where the queues were doubling and tripling back on themselves, the family had continued on up through the levels. Referring to the floor-plan, Jimmy said that if they persevered to the top, there was a 'wealth of mouthwatering choice' awaiting them, which half-placated Luke, but there proved to be many distractions along the way. In Bedtime, they looked at a range of king-size beds in various styles, and when Jimmy hopped on one of them and bounced a little in a seated position, declaring that there was surprisingly little give at the price, Luke was thrilled to pieces. Taking his cue, he jumped from one bed to the next, testing them delightedly for give. Mirabelle told him not to get too silly, but a place in which you could bounce on someone else's beds, and nobody stopped you, was too good a chance to pass up.

Fourth was a disappointment, for all that Joanne picked up a sheaf of leaflets at the psychodynamics centre, but when they arrived on Fifth, the avant-garde jewellery and video relays of live hair-styling proved altogether more alluring. Jimmy was stopped by a sales assistant offering him a free men's makeup advisory. By the sixth floor, fatigue and hunger were beginning to nag in equal measure, although Mirabelle found the inner resources to stop at Stomp and try on a pair of boots. They all thought the over-the-knee style suited her. It was the same story at Head First, where the cherry-red cloche made her face look spirited and younger after the massive pile of the Russian hat she had on. The assistant advised her that her own hat had an inhibiting, top-heavy effect on what was a delicate face. Removing the cloche, she replaced it with a boater in mauve garnished with a spray of polyester blackberries. Mirabelle turned her head from side to side, while Jimmy stood slack-jawed. Thanking the assistant for her advice, Mirabelle stuffed her fur hat into her bag and accepted a leaflet.

The Gastromarket on Seventh offered an unending flow of free samples with which they could take the edge off their appetites. Luke made one yucky face after another at everything he tried, from the banana and white truffle ice-cream to the sea-urchin samosas. The fermented Swedish herring being spooned out of its crumpled tin defeated everybody's sense of adventure, but Jimmy managed a chocolate termite and said it tasted of prawn.

On Eighth, they finally had to make a decision. The Swiss fondue didn't appeal, while the Western hog-roast, dripping fat on its slowly rotating spit, looked a little stodgy, thought Jimmy. Luke was asked what he wanted, and wanted the only thing he ever wanted when given a choice, an omelette with beans and chips. That looked like being a tall order until Joanne spotted a place called Good Old English Caff, which sounded promising, until it turned out that it dealt in contemporary reinterpretations of classic café fare. Everybody seemed to be having something served on a spiral cake-stand, with small brown balls and yellow discs arranged on its levels, the deconstructed elements of a cheeseburger. They all had that, apart from Luke, whose omelette arrived rolled up like a Swiss roll, filled with tomato béchamel, accompanied by one enormous dark brown chip and a portion of lemongrass-scented beans in a miniature can. It was the best omelette he had ever had, he said, and he never wanted any other kind ever again. It was a purely paradisiacal moment of contentment, until Jimmy let him have a little taste from his glass of red wine, at which the yucky face returned in its reptilian horror.

On the ground floor, things had not quite gone according to the script. After Caitlin Binchy had left, having signed copies of every one of her books, and sold most of them too, Adam became gradually aware of a peevishness in April's attitude towards him. He knew he hadn't exactly shone so far, but it was his first day after all. Maybe she was just consumed by her own preoccupations, but the snarliness did seem to be reserved for him. It was true that they had had to manage in the face of a no-show by one of the other new appointees, some girl called Brinsley, but that was hardly his fault, and in any case April seemed breezily stoical about it, declaring that she had never believed Brinsley would make it to the starting-line in the first place. But her snappishness towards Adam made him increasingly uneasy as the afternoon wore on.

Towards six o'clock, after a prolonged moment of stationary nail-biting behind the till, in which he felt her eyes following him about as he filled shelves and unpacked deliveries, she suddenly clicked her fingers. Looking up, he found himself summoned to the counter. He took his time getting up off his knees where he had been rearranging a lower shelf, and walked over. Their eyes met for several inscrutable moments.

April gave a deep sigh. 'I wonder whether this is really what we both want,' she said, finally.

'How do you mean?' Adam asked.

'I can see you getting very dissatisfied here, despite your best efforts to hide it. *Comprende*?'

'Not really, no.'

April pressed both fists to the surface of the counter in front of her, and leaned forwards on them, raising her heels from the floor. 'What I want you to do is go outside, take a walk up and down, do some serious thinking, and then come back in ten minutes, and tell me again why you want to work here.'

'But I already know—'

'Please,' April interrupted him, and pointed towards the entrance.

Reluctantly, Adam walked out.

There was an end-of-the-fair sense of deceleration about the whole place now. Most of the crowds had cleared, but for a queue beginning to form outside the cinema at the opposite end of the ground floor. The strips of sky that showed through the high windows would have been black, had it not been for the violet glow washed over them by the lights of Paradise. Adam wandered over to a fountain consisting of two walls of shivering water flowing down around either side of a kind of grotto with a bench inside. As there was nobody else about, he sat down. With his elbows on his knees and his chin in his hands, he thought hard about what April had just said.

It didn't make sense. He hadn't made any major slip-ups, apart from getting Caitlin Binchy's name and one word of her book title wrong. He had been helpful to customers with enquiries, and had even managed to sell a couple of items to uncommitted browsers. So what was the deal? Nobody gets sacked on their first day, he told himself, unless they'd cocked up in some epic way, or else, like Brinsley, hadn't actually managed to get out of bed. Possibly, as April saw it, he was only playing the part of a bookshop assistant, instead of having it imprinted in his genes. But it was a job, not a burning vocation. Maybe he had been out of work too long to have the right attitude when he was in it. Adam looked at what he was wearing. Were the trainers a bit casual?

No, he told himself, straightening up, *I'm not having this. This is absolutely not about me.*

When he walked back to the shop, he found the family hovering outside.

'Ah, the very man,' said Jimmy. 'We thought you'd gone home already.'

'Coming home soon?' asked Mirabelle.

'Yeah,' said Adam. 'There's just one other thing I've got to do. I'll be out in a minute.'

April was rearranging a row of tragic memoirs, which he had rearranged himself only a few minutes ago. She turned *Angels Guard Me While I Sleep* side-on, with *Biting the Hand That Needs Me* facing forward.

'It looked better the way it was,' said Adam behind her, making her jump a little.

She looked questioningly at him.

'I thought about what you said, and I'm fine. I'm just fine. I'm going to make a go of it, give it my best shot, and you'll see you made the right decision.'

April's face softened. She gave Adam a smile, and embraced him. Another pair of much smaller arms wound themselves around his waist from behind. Luke loved a group hug.

As they left, the first of the crowds for the evening spectacular were already gathering at the gates, waiting to be admitted to the banks of temporary seating that had been set up around a stage. They were in for fireworks, breathtaking choreography, mystery guests and a karaoke competition.

'Can you imagine anything worse?' said Joanne, reading the poster.

There seemed to be no buses, and the queue at the taxi-rank was so long, it was already getting entangled with the queues for the evening spectacular.

As they set off on foot in the direction of Flint Street, a long black car with tinted windows swept up alongside them at the traffic-signal. Adam turned towards the back window, where a slender hand, its profusion of rings glittering in the interior light of the car, waved frenetically towards them. He raised his own hand in acknowledgement, and hesitated on the pavement for a moment as his family walked on. The window glided down at a leisurely pace, and a bright white face wearing a rictus of uncomplicated joy beamed out.

'Adam!' Vincent gasped. 'Did you have fun?'

His name had never felt so extraneously applied to him, Adam felt. In the mouth of Vincent, who didn't know him after all, it sounded oddly as though it were nothing to do with him, as though there might be another Adam standing just behind him, who was being hailed with such voluble familiarity.

'Yes I did,' he replied. A few paces further on, hearing his voice, the family had turned to watch the scene play itself out. 'Definitely.'

Vincent gave him a smile all wicked complicity, and a lubricious flash of the eyes, but waited for more.

Adam tried to think. 'Mad busy,' he added. 'Thankfully.'

The eyes travelled appraisingly down his front to his shoes, and then returned with a rapid flicker to meet his.

'Then let's do it all again tomorrow!' He tapped the glass panel behind the driver, and fell back into the seat with a peal of laughter as the car lurched away.

A smile of something like affection had taken possession of Adam's face. All four of his relatives were still staring at him.

'What?' he asked.

Chapter 5

The Lovers I

There was, at this time of year, a kind of grey in the morning that wasn't at all like the hopeless grey of summer's end. At the onset of dawn, the altering light threw a lilac veil on the sky, coaxing the glowing lozenges of the street-lamps to a final bleary sizzle before they went out. The world took on an air of patience. Everything appeared to be waiting for the coming day to develop, like an old snapshot. Nothing stirred. Looking out on the scene through sleepless eyes was to accede to a bittered relief, to surrender yesterday's griefs to forgetting, your back firmly turned on today's. There was hardly a soul to be seen. All was quiet and still, as though humanity had, for a moment and without realising it, learned the ways of justice and of peace.

Then a single car made its way along the ring-road. It paused in polite isolation while traffic-signals mulled the idea of change, before it proceeded with singular care along the deserted dual carriageway. A boy with a fluorescent bag left newspapers in porches and letter-boxes. Two cats patrolled the housing estate, stopping to look about them with disdain at the surrounding human disaster, then settling to glare at each other from opposite pavements.

Patches of thin white mist hovered low, static in places, blown impressionably about in crisp drifts at others. Inhaled, it tasted as refreshing as fine summer drizzle, its diaphanous texture pretending to silken the blade-edge of November cold. It muffled what footsteps there were in the dawn streets, but gave a countervailing emphasis to the luminous grey in which the day was painted.

An unseasonably early waker heard the silence beyond the curtains evolve into the sounds of morning. A milk-float jingled past, followed at some distance by the emphatic clopping of horses being led to the racecourse. Half-drowsing, he heard the rolled-up shutters of shopfronts and mumbles of conversation as figments in a dream, until the brief scream of a night-alarm being deactivated jabbed him awake again. It was time to think of getting up. Getting up, looking out, trying to imagine yourself part of the world that was yet again reconstructing itself out there. Shivering under the shower, eating cereal, drinking two cups of piercingly strong coffee. Buttoning a shirt, disciplining malleable hair with your fingers, rummaging your pockets to check for keys, money, phone, then stepping out. Closing the door softly behind you. Pulling your jacket zip up over half your face, and hunching your shoulders as you walked off down the street. Buying a paper, and settling into what had become a regular table in the window of a corner café. Looking through the sport while you waited for a plate of fried food to be delivered to you. Checking the time periodically on your phone because you had a job to get to, but plenty of time to get to it. For now, this would do.

Things had moved on at the shop. A new recruit, Ben Avery, had been appointed to replace the missing Brinsley, and he and Adam had struck up something like a hearty friendship. Ben was sunny-natured and open-faced, in a stubbly sort of way, and had the advantage on Adam of having worked in a bookshop before, albeit one dedicated to lower-toned fare than Print Media was. What he lacked in literary proficiency, he more than made up for in glittering charm, so that, within minutes of his arrival, Adam found himself consigned to the sidelines of April's attention, where he drew the same salary as Ben, but was nonetheless elevated by him to some imagined position of marginal seniority, having been in post all of two weeks longer. Neither of Ben's twin preoccupations concerned books, which relieved them both of having to pretend to have read any. The one was his girlfriend, Corinne, upon whose erratic judgments and sudden pronouncements he doted to a degree that had helped them last through several years already, and the other, which had more the structure of a conventional love, was Gutford Athletic. He was something important in the supporters' club, it seemed, and always spent time in the players' lounge at the end of home matches, bantering briefly with the goalie over clean sheets and shots off-target, and able to inflate these brusque manly exchanges into grand narratives on the mornings after. Adam liked his unselfish manner and his assumption that the tastes of young men could only collusively coincide. For all Ben knew, he might be an anarchist or an evangelical Christian, but nothing would throw him off his stride. He saw the cheery absurdity in things unfailingly, with no penetrating wisdom, to be sure, but neither with a blockhead's clumsiness. You wondered what it would take to depress someone like Ben, but the answers – Corinne cheating on him, or the Gaffers' relegation – were ghastly enough to supply themselves. When life finally crushes even the Ben Averys, we can be sure they've pulled the shutters closed on Mount Olympus, having sickened of the entertainment below.

It was part of the constitution of a sunny-natured boy always to need something to look forward to. He approached every minor moment in the calendar, including the artificially respirated ones – Burns Night, Whit weekend, Halloween – with the gaiety once accorded by peasant communities to the major saints' days. It was a shame they'd not known each other on Bonfire Night, since Corinne's family always staged something frantic, and would have welcomed Adam with open arms. With Christmas looming, Ben could scarcely contain himself, and what he called the 'build-up' was almost as important as the thing itself. He had already had a go at inviting Adam and his whole family to Corinne's place for Christmas Day, and taken the demurral on the chin, since there was so much more to cram in before then.

Ben had established quite early that Adam hadn't got a lady-friend, and had taken it selflessly upon himself to do everything he could to help him supply the lack. There was nothing peculiar about not having someone, it just meant that Cupid hadn't got round to you yet. That didn't mean, however, that you couldn't give the little cherub a helping hand. All objection to these initiatives was in vain. For Ben, there was something a shade untidy about one of them being partnered and the other not, as it meant that they couldn't do things together in conjoined pairs. He saw enough of Adam five days a week at work for it not to be necessary to have boys' nights out together on top, other than perhaps an occasional trip to the Gaffers, a treat Adam had so far dodged. Adam didn't mind not having things to do in the evenings – there was his family after all – but Ben remained dauntless. So it was that, on a slow Saturday morning in early December, when lashing rain kept Paradise all but deserted until nearly lunchtime, Ben came back off his break to announce that he'd set something up for Sunday. A new place just off the A-road into town had opened, catering for the newest eating trend, indoor picnicking. Ben thought it sounded like a right laugh. You took your own food and utensils and a cloth and folding chairs, you were assigned a time-limited 'spot', and you bought your drinks in there. It solved the problem of how to have picnics in the winter. They even played a soundtrack of tweeting birds and droning wasps for the full effect. Al Coperto, it was called. Before Adam could say he wasn't sure he was free, he was informed that the party would consist of Ben and Corinne, himself and a girl from Something Stoopid, the gift-shop on First, who evidently had her eye on him. Essie, she was called. Corinne knew her and she was cute as party-poppers. Unbeknown to Adam, she'd apparently been in the shop, looked him up and down and liked what she'd seen. He was a shoo-in. Happy days.

It sounded like one of those situations it would be impossible to get out of, short of feigning illness on the day. There was no use trying to explain any reluctance to Ben. He wouldn't understand. Why would you ever want to get out of something when life was so full of situations it was worth trying to get into? Adam had struggled against the sense of having his days organised for him ever since he and the kids had been orphaned. The presumptuousness of this arrangement in anybody the least objectionable would have called for plain speaking, but Ben had no objectionable side. You could turn him any way you liked in the unforgiving daylight, and he was inoffensive from all angles. Adam feebly said that he felt it was less than fair that the date would be a blind one only on his side, but that, Ben explained, was the very beauty of the plan. Since Essie had already seen the goods and given the thumbs-up, he didn't have to worry. As long as he remembered to brush his teeth and cut his toenails, nothing could possibly go wrong.

'It's the perfect crime,' he said, flicking Adam's earlobes.

It certainly gave Adam something else to worry about. Neither Jimmy nor Mirabelle raised any objection to being left with the kids, although Mirabelle muttered something about him spending more and more time with what she called 'the jet set'. He even went up to the first floor to find the gift-shop but, loitering about outside, he found it copiously over-staffed with young women, any one of whom could have been Essie. And whichever she was, it wouldn't do to let her see him hanging back and peering in like this. He went off in search of a new shirt, couldn't choose between plain white and something in burnt umber with two buttons on the back of the collar, and ended up buying some socks. He went and had a haircut, despite only having had one a couple of weeks ago, and then he lingered in the fragrance section at one of the department-stores, spraying adjacent patches of his inner arms with a succession of unfamiliar scents until they all melded together in his nostrils into an impression of soapy orange juice.

Joanne noticed the renewed haircut. 'You're either going to another job interview already, or you've got a D.A.T.E.'

'What's a date?' Luke wanted to know, and the secret, if it ever was one, was out.

Everybody chipped in with advice, Mirabelle softening a little at the revelation. She told him to smell clean, talk clean and not keep going to the Gents. Jimmy thought you could never go wrong with a good suit. Adam allowed everyone to assume that he'd been bold enough to ask somebody out himself, and didn't mention anything about Ben and Corinne. Her name was Essie. He didn't know yet what it was short for. He didn't know how old she was. He didn't know where she lived. He didn't know whether she came from Gutford even.

'Are you sure this isn't a blind date?' Joanne wondered.

On the day itself, Adam came into the living-room in an ironed shirt, dark trousers and black shoes. He felt he would turn out almost certainly to be overdressed, but the time for dithering was over.

'Knock 'em dead, killer!' said Jimmy, with a chortle.

'He looks lovely, doesn't he?' Mirabelle purred.

'If a trifle formal,' Joanne put in.

'Don't be silly. Women like it when a man makes an effort.'

'Killer?' said Adam, pulling on his jacket.

He was barely halfway down the stairs when a car-horn sounded outside in a series of long impatient blares. He opened the front door to find Ben standing up in the driver's seat, his upper body twisted out of the car window, beckoning energetically.

'Where's the fire?' Adam asked.

'In your loins,' Ben shouted.

The girls were both sitting in the back. Adam climbed into the passenger-seat, and peeped through the hole in the headrest. 'Hullo,' he said.

One of the girls glanced and nodded briefly in his direction, but they were deep in conversation. Ben gave a suggestive flash of his eyes at Adam, and gunned the accelerator to produce an appreciative 'wow' from the car-engine. Then they were off.

It wasn't that Adam was impartial to relationships, nor that he lacked experience of them, for all that it had been episodic. He liked being friends with girls, especially when they didn't expect anything special from him. It was only when they did that he felt ill-at-ease with himself. There had been one or two cases of hysterical obsession over the years – three or four, in fact – where a few nights with a particular girl had been about to fade civilly into history when it turned out that she didn't want to let go. Long phonecalls, at all hours, followed, interspersed by text messages full of accusation. The politics of this were complex and intimidating. It was an inevitable consequence of a man's famous disinclination to commit, which must indeed be exasperating for his partner, but it surely couldn't only be men who didn't need to know from one moment to the next how far into the future the present was expected to stretch. What lay behind this grasping for eternity in every trick of the light? The day may well come when you yourself wanted to cling to some evanescent moment, and the other's indifference would be a retribution for all the slighted partners gone by. Well, that would be a lesson in itself, though not one that it was worth anticipating. In the meantime, you could hardly blame anyone for finding the chief alternative – being content with just having some fun – so thin and unappetising.

Ben drove assertively, taking amber lights late and using the gears rather than resorting to the brakes. He hadn't an aggressive bone in his body, as far as Adam could tell, but it was easy to see how his default setting of cheerful ebullience might be mistaken for belligerence by anyone who happened to get in his path. He chattered non-stop, shouting a little above the radio, so that Adam couldn't hear at all what the girls were saying. Their destination, which he had understood to be somewhere on the edge of town, turned out to be a good thirty-mile drive along a succession of A-roads. Little towns and villages hurtled by, the -ingtons and -ingboroughs ringing no chord of recognition for Adam, despite the fact that he must have been in these parts countless times in his childhood. Church spires rose up and hurried by. People gathered at car-boot sales in scrappy bits of field. A straggle of cyclists in matching vests clogged one stretch of the road, angrily turning to see who was being uncouth enough to sound a horn at them. Just before a roundabout junction that led to the M4, a young man with a bedraggled beard and a beanie-hat held up a cardboard sign reading 'London'.

'Good luck with that, mate!' Ben yelled, happily.

As they turned on to the next A-road, Corinne leaned forward and asked if they could stop.

'What do you wanna stop for?' Ben said. 'We're nearly at the picnic place.'

She gave a meaningful tut, and retreated. Seconds later, the satnav told them they had reached their destination. Ben slowed the car. There was what looked like a barn on the opposite side a little way ahead, with a few cars parked in front of it. Without signalling, he swung off the road and into a narrow entrance. The satnav began telling them to turn round and go back, but the sign said Al Coperto.

'Looks like a right dump,' Corinne said.

Al Coperto was indeed a converted farm building. They appeared to have no trace of the booking at reception, but it hardly mattered as there were only a few people there anyway. Ben and Adam unloaded the boxes and chairs from the hatchback, while Corinne and Essie looked on. Somebody stamped their hands with a blodgy purple triangle as they went in. A boy in a red Stetson insisted on looking through their boxes to make sure they weren't smuggling in their own drink, and then told them to go to Station 4. As they unfolded the chairs, a waitress in a jogging-suit appeared and handed Ben a bar menu. He gave it a second's glance and ordered a bottle of sparkling wine. The girls resumed their own conversation. Ben sat down, kicked off his trainers, and capably supervised Adam in unpacking the picnic cloth, plates and food.

Nobody felt like eating anything initially. As indicated on the website, the place was 'simplicity itself', in that there wasn't anything there. The floor had been marked out with white lines and numbers, but the walls were unadorned, there was no music, and nor was there any sign of a bar. Instead, the waitress reappeared from a back-room somewhere, with their bottle and four flute glasses on a tray, leaving it on the floor for them to open themselves.

Ben inexpertly did the honours, pouring all four glasses to overflowing. He raised a dripping flute, and wished everyone the best of health. Corinne reminded him he was driving.

They sat and talked, and then felt like eating something, only when they looked again at what they had brought with them, none of it seemed very appetising. Ben popped the lid from a tub of mayonnaise salad containing chunks of apple and peanuts. He dug a fork into it, chewed a mouthful of it ruminatively, before letting his face freeze into a grimace of disapproval. Essie picked up a sausage roll, took a tiny nibble and then put it back. They drank some more wine.

'What happens now?' Corinne demanded.

'Up to you,' Ben said. 'The slot's ours for two hours.'

'To do what?'

'Chill?' Ben suggested.

Whoops of delight were bubbling forth from Station 1. It probably helped if you brought your own sense of fun with you, rather than getting ensconced and waiting for the mood to take you. The place didn't really promise much in the way of diversion. They all looked about them, avoiding each other's glances. When Corinne reached for a grape, everybody's eyes flicked down to her hand and watched her pull one from the bunch. It was the nearest thing to something happening. She spat out the pip.

'It's a bit rubbish here, isn't it?' said Adam.

'It is actually total and utter bollocks,' Ben confirmed.

The girls broke out laughing.

'What we doing here then?' Adam asked.

'Yeah, mastermind,' Corinne accused Ben. 'Whose crap idea was this in the first place?'

Ben began to say that it was always good to try new things, but they had all moved already to start gathering their things together.

'Farewell, Al Omerta!' Ben shouted from the car window.

'Coperta,' said Adam.

'Whatevs.'

They drove in the rough direction of home, but there was a majority feeling that it would be good to stop somewhere again, and rescue what they could of the trip. A reflective silence crept over the party as they looked to right and left for a likely spot. Eventually, what passed for a wood appeared on the left, the girls both made an 'Ah' sound, and Ben pulled into a lay-by. It was a clump of tall pines, their sparsely layered foliage shutting out just enough of the fading grey afternoon for it to feel as though they had entered a forest. Ben stopped and gaped upwards through the yellowy-green needles, his mouth hanging open as though he were waiting for a ripe fruit to drop into it.

Adam and Essie walked on through the trees in silence for a bit, until Adam felt it only polite to ask her to tell him something about herself. This was occasion enough. Essie embarked on a generously detailed account of her family's specialist shoe business, much of which was founded on importing footwear from Poland at low cost. Their footwear industry had evidently collapsed with the end of the communist system, but had now recovered and was growing all the time. The styles often left something to be desired, but as a minimal-outlay option, they represented a good buy. Nor were they the typical shoddy rubbish you might expect from Eastern Europe. They were sturdy shoes, as people who were prepared to abandon their preconceptions and try them soon discovered. The trainers were a bit sad, admittedly, but the men's everyday business shoe had a lot going for it.

'What size are you?' Essie asked.

'Uh, I dunno,' said Adam. 'Nine?'

The shoes only came in European sizes, it seemed. Essie thought Adam would be about a 43 or 44. They both looked at his trainers, which were in fact a bit sad. He didn't wear them to the shop of course, he wore a pair of black shoes, which were fine, quite comfortable, though probably not very stylish. Essie giggled.

'We're having a shoe conversation,' she said.

'Whose fault's that?' Adam laughed. He pushed a wisp of hair out of Essie's eyes. She ran a featherlight fingertip through the hair on his forearm.

She had an astonishingly gentle kiss, from which Adam carefully took his cue. The first contact was like showers of pine-needles falling over him, so that he found himself gripping Essie's shoulders a little too forcefully. But then they both relaxed, and before too long, the note of clamorous passion had resolved itself into the overt strangeness of being so blindly intimate with someone you hardly even knew. Adam opened his eyes, as they prepared to pull apart.

'Yesssss!' came a nearby shout. Ben's face grinned out at him from behind the tree-trunk against which he was pissing. 'Re. Sult.'

Standing behind the counter, Mirabelle waited for Mrs Partridge to decide she didn't want anything after all. This was a familiar Sunday ritual. Sometimes she would ask for something she knew they hadn't got. Today, she had caught herself out by asking about tinned rice pudding, and then having to backtrack swiftly as Mirabelle strode over to the shelf where it was.

'It's all right, I didn't want it today,' she said. 'Just so as I know you've got it.'

Mirabelle resumed her post behind the counter, and waited. There was a third person in the shop, who also appeared to be waiting. It was Aldo, who had bought a pack of chewy mints and was getting through them at a steady rate.

Mrs Partridge hovered in front of him, so that he moved with a mumbled 'Sorry, lady,' but he was only standing in front of a display of babies' rattles, so Mrs Partridge had no choice, like Dick Whittington, but to turn again. She picked up a pack of dog-chews and squinted at them.

Mirabelle heaved a meaningful sigh. She and Aldo were waiting for Mrs Partridge to give up and leave, while Mrs Partridge herself appeared to be waiting for Aldo to leave. From the door behind her, Mirabelle could just make out the soporific drone of Jimmy reading something to Luke.

'Now the king had appointed the captain on whose hand he leaned to have charge of the gate; and the people trod upon him in the gate, so that he died, as the man of God had said when the king came down to him. For when the man of God had said to the king, "Two measures of barley shall be sold for a shekel, and a measure of fine meal for a shekel, about this time tomorrow in the gate of Samaria," the captain had answered the man of God, "If the Lord himself should make windows in Heaven, could such a thing be?" And he had said, "You shall see it with your own eyes, but you shall not eat of it." And so it happened to him, for the people trod upon him in the gate and he died.'

Luke pondered the text for a moment. 'Why did he die?'

'The people trod on him,' Jimmy repeated. Luke looked troubled. 'Can you imagine, Lukey, if there were windows in Heaven? The people would be able to look out and see us.'

'Why did they tread on him though?' Luke wanted to know.

'Wouldn't it be grand if we could see windows in the sky, and see everyone we loved, up in Heaven?'

Luke's lip began to wobble. What little he had heard of Heaven hadn't appealed. It sounded like a huge empty place, watched over by disturbing-looking creatures with smooth golden faces and enormous wings growing out of their backs.

'Why did they tread on the man?'

Jimmy closed the Bible. 'Where's your colouring-book?'

At last, Mrs Partridge came to the counter, holding a little jar of anchovies. 'How much are these?'

'It says on the price-sticker,' Mirabelle replied.

Mrs Partridge lifted her glasses off her nose, and peered at the sticker. 'Oof!' she exclaimed, as Mirabelle knew she would. 'Robbery!'

'They're very good ones,' said Mirabelle.

'They'd want to be, at that price. No, nothing today, thank you.' And, putting the anchovies on the counter, Mrs Partridge gathered her bags to her again, and turned towards the door. Aldo went and held it open for her, bowing courteously as she passed through. He turned the 'Open' sign round and slid the bolt.

Rain had started falling as they picked their way over the uneven ground in the pine-wood. The two couples, as they now appeared to be, walked at some distance from each other. There was an eerie quality to the acoustics as twigs snapped beneath their feet, and the boys murmured about nothing much to their girls. A trickle of wet ran down Essie's neck, and she shuddered. Adam draped his jacket about her shoulders.

Ben and Corinne stopped to examine one of the rings of reddish-brown mushrooms that had come up around the base of one or two of the trees. Ben wondered if they were the kind that would kill you if you ate them. Corinne suggested there was only one way to find out, and then had to stop Ben from picking one.

Suddenly, a piercing high squeak filled the air, like a gate opening slowly on rust-clogged hinges.

'Oh my God!' Essie gasped. 'What was that?'

They all froze and, seconds later, the squeak sounded again, this time joined by another similar sound, the two descending together into a throaty creak as they died away. Ben thought it sounded like two weird birds calling to each other, but as the cries broke out again, it began to seem as though they came from some much larger creatures. They were almost like the cries of whales, but whales whose batteries were running down. Essie didn't like it one little bit, and wanted to get back to the car.

To assure the others that there was probably nothing to worry about, Ben gave a wordless yell in the direction of the strange noises, the effect of which startled all of them, including him. It produced an abrupt scattering somewhere in the middle distance, and they just briefly caught sight of a couple of leaping grey creatures making off through the trees.

'They're deer,' said Adam. 'Cute.'

He appeared to be the only one who thought so, though. Ben strongly doubted whether deer could survive in this part of the world, and even if they could, they would surely be hibernating by now. Adam was quite sure they didn't hibernate, but Ben wasn't having it. The argument gathered a momentum that sustained it for a while, as the girls rolled their eyes at each other. It was settled when Corinne spotted a signboard a short distance away, on which visitors to the forest were exhorted not to do anything to startle the population of sika deer that lived here. Their rutting season often lasted into the winter months, during which their characteristic cries, which resembled anything from a gentle whistle to a deafening shriek, could be enjoyed. On no account was it permitted to try to feed the sika, as they were excellent foragers, and certainly not with chocolate or any meat product. Another scream tore through the forest as they read the notice.

'Doesn't sound like she's enjoying it,' Ben grimaced.

'That's probably the blokes warning each other off,' Adam said, which only started another ill-informed contretemps between them. The rain continued to fall as they bickered good-naturedly, until Corinne pointed out that, in case anyone cared, they were probably lost.

'Rubbish,' Ben said.

Joanne, drawn by a peculiar sound from below as she came out of the bathroom, was creeping very carefully down the stairs. As she delicately placed each foot, she could hear coming from the shop a more or less continuous low groan that sounded like somebody wounded and half-conscious. Up above, Jimmy was soothing Luke's muted sobs. It was a house of pain.

There were two half-merged silhouettes visible behind the screen of coloured strips that separated the darkened shop from the hallway. They appeared to be rocking slightly against the inside edge of the counter. Joanne didn't dare take another step, but stood perfectly still, her breath held, as the groan resolved itself into the satisfied purring of male sexual enjoyment. Then the sound was abruptly stifled with the unmistakable effect of a hand being clapped against a mouth, accompanied by a sharp shush.

'Wah?' the muffled male voice uttered.

'I thought I heard someone,' Mirabelle whispered.

On the rest of the journey back, Essie snuggled sleepily against Adam in the back seat, while Corinne sat in the front, staring balefully ahead at the unrolling road. Nobody spoke. The silence was placid, but told also of the frail disappointment of plans gone awry. It was a Sunday silence.

There were only a couple of weeks to go until Christmas, Adam reflected, during which it would be all hands on deck at the shop. Late opening hours promised to pay no more than the standard rate, which seemed unfair, but at least it was extra money. Constructing something that felt like a joyous family celebration at Jimmy and Mirabelle's was going to need plenty of work. Then it would be necessary to prepare Luke for starting at his new school. All in all, there hardly seemed to be time to put together something like a relationship as well. Essie's head drooped on his chest, jerking half-awake every now and then with the pitching and tossing of Ben's cornering. She was very sweet, there was no doubt of that.

When life threw something in your path that you weren't quite ready for, what was the best solution? Accept it gratefully, or regretfully pass it up in the assurance that there would always be other such chances? But would there? Always, there was this feeling of the present being a preparation for what may be to come, though it was never possible to tell whether the orchestra were still tuning up, or already midway through the crashing overture. Essie's hair smelled of lemon and lime as he kissed her sleeping head. She might make unforseeable demands on him, or her guileless smiles might light the days and months. Who was the greater risk to whom?

The car arrived at Flint Street first. Ben double-parked it, and then turned and gave a complicit wink at Adam. As gently as he could, he disengaged his arm from Essie's sleepy grasp.

'It seems I'm here,' he said. He mimed a scribble in the air, and Ben ransacked the glove-compartment for a pen. There was no paper, so Essie wrote her phone number on Adam's arm. Their mouths met with a fit degree of lingering while Ben looked on, beaming proudly at his handiwork.

'Tomorrahs, bruv,' he said, reaching over the seat-back to grip Adam's hand.

Adam stood and watched the red tail-lights recede up the street, bearing away his brand-new love. The truth was, it was probably over.

A difficult evening at home followed. For a while after the shop closed, Mirabelle seemed warm as toast and pneumatically talkative. She whisked up a giant mug of hot chocolate for Luke, despite Joanne's protestations that he wouldn't sleep if he drank it, and engaged Jimmy in conversation that ran in both directions for a while. But when Jimmy asked the kids whether they had made up their Christmas lists yet, the mood soured. Any mention of money was sure to do this these days. Adam was handing over more than half what he was earning, but it was barely enough, especially with the shop doing so badly now that it was fighting 'a losing battle against Hell'. He and Jimmy made their separate stabs at reassuring Mirabelle that it would all be fine in the end, but the emollient tone only inflamed her. It wouldn't all be fine unless something happened.

What had to happen, clearly, was another job. When Adam went into work the next morning, he picked up a copy of the weekly *Opportunities* bulletin that the Paradise admin office published. There were evening jobs aplenty in the run-up to Christmas, and in his lunch-break, Adam went up to the eighth floor, and into a café-bar called the Old Blind Possum. Avijit, the assistant manager, asked him to come back at 6.30. Adam pointed out that he was here now. What experience had he got? He said that he had worked in bars before, which was an untruth only in its resort to the plural. Had he got a UK work permit? He was a British citizen, he replied. Avijit looked him up and down, and asked him whether he would have any objection to wearing a paper hat such as the one the barman currently on duty was wearing. He wouldn't. The terms were minimum-plus-50p an hour, evenings and weekends, rising to 75p in Christmas week. Would he be prepared to work late Christmas Eve? He would. All day Boxing Day? Yep. Start tomorrow? Yep. By the time he got back on the escalator, he had two jobs.

If the measure of our desire to succeed is the amount of life we are prepared to forsake, Adam meant it. There would be no time now to do anything else at all than work or sleep. He'd try it until the new year at least, and if the regime was too brutal, he could prompt a rethink, with an honest, if self-defeating, attempt at a solution on his record. Even Mirabelle would have to credit that. And in the meantime, it was a ready-made pretext to escape the reproachful atmosphere at home.

Back on the ground floor, he walked out into the shrill December air and breathed in its brittle freshness. He wouldn't be getting much taste of this for the time being. For a split-second, a desire to get the next train out of town all but overwhelmed him. Feeling something damp and raggy in his trouser-pocket, he pulled out a bedraggled five-pound note. It was all he had.

'*Good* afternoon, honourable sir,' sang out a voice that flew by to his right.

He turned just in time to see the golden halo of Vincent Beresford disappearing into the building.

Something inside Adam whispered a suggestion.

Chapter 6

The Lovers II

To begin with, darkness was upon the face of the deep. Nothing stirred, because there was nearly nothing to stir, other than some kind of spirit, which did stir, moving upon the face of the waters. There were waters. There was an earth too, but it had no physical shape, only a kind of emptiness, other than that it had waters, upon the face of which the spirit moved. Not just moved, but blew back and forth like what would one day become autumn wind, churning itself into reckless currents that ploughed up the surface of the waters, so that they roiled in anger, but tossed nothing about because there was nothing to toss. The waves rolled and swelled, crashing back on themselves until the whole face of the waters was white with ebullition, but nobody heard or saw it because the spirit that dashed and swayed and wandered over the deep was alone, the profoundest aloneness that would ever be.

Then God – for it was his spirit – issued a command, his first intent. He summoned his will and bespoke the arrival of light. It changed the picture entirely.

Once he started making things appear, there seemed no stopping him. The light dawned, continued for some while, and relapsed into the prior darkness. That was the first day. He made a sky, and then areas of solid land amid the waters. The land was made to yield grass, herbs and trees that would ripen fruits that would contain in themselves the seeds of the next trees. Everything was plunged into a state of becoming, the several successive stages of which would mark the foundation of time, for days and seasons and years. The two shining symbols of these stages were the burning sun and the cold white moon, which he hung up in the brand-new sky to rule their domains.

The creatures followed. First the seas were set teeming, then the air was scattered thick. The land was populated with ruminants and invertebrates, reptiles and simians, their shrieking and hissing, lowing and growling, continuing without cease through the time of the sun and that of the moon, through the times of spring saps and summer effulgence, autumn ripeness and winter frost. And then he added one last touch.

'Let us make man,' he is reputed to have said to nobody, 'in our own image.' He envisaged a race of little godlings, exercising dominion over everything else, answerable only to him, having a tiny measure of his own infinite divinity breathed into them, of two kinds like the other creatures. They were set free to do almost as they wished, but there was a test, by which he hoped they would be an eternal credit to him. They failed it, disappointing him abominably, so that he was inspired to bestow pain and labour and suffering on the world into which they were now cast out. Amid shuddering storms and in a state of what looked like exposure, they fled in their little aprons and took shelter, hearing the gate bang shut behind them. Among the curses with which they were rendered wretched was the surviving memory of the state of perfection from which they had been evicted. The memory would haunt them forever.

Once they had walked in peace, conversing as they would with the Lord of all things, whom they might happen upon hovering near a lake, or rising in shimmering heat from the dry ground, or uncoiling in ribbons of mist from the edge of a bay. They were part of him, and he of them, but no more. Now they wandered apart, locked in struggle with each other, their lives soured with disappointments or blighted with atrocities. They were godlings in title rather than estate now, their dominion turned from benign tutelage to reckless tyranny.

Except that at some point, God decided to release another small part of himself directly into the murderous chaos in which his people lived. He appeared as one among them, offering himself up for murder, and was promptly chewed up and spat out again. Which happy event provoked an annual commemoration.

'What's the matter with that?' Avijit wanted to know, as Adam brought a plate of brown and green food back to the service-area.

'Table 4 ordered three turkey dinners and four veggie, but now they're saying it was the other way round.'

Avijit smirked. 'Veg conversion. They want to look veggie to their friends until they see what they've got to eat.'

It hadn't been the most unfortunate slip. That had happened when Fay, one of the waitresses, had tripped over the border of tinsel nailed around the Xmas Grotto and fallen headlong with a tray. Bright yellow soup and globs of buttery risotto splattered everywhere, much to the merriment of many of the diners. A cry of 'Encore!' went up. While staff scurried about on all fours clearing up the mess, one of the customers, a very large man in a tartan suit, drunkenly mimed the cracking of a whip over them.

Adam tried to console Fay when she returned to the service-area in tears. She was told she would be docked £20 for the wastage, but when Adam suggested to the other waiters that they could put in a fiver each to make it up, he was met with quizzical scowls.

Each day he had about fifteen minutes to get from Ground to Eighth, change into his crimson-and-yellow Old Blind Possum uniform, and start dealing with the early drinkers and nibblers. The evening shift ground on until anything between midnight and one, after which he walked home, fell into bed and got out of it again at 7.30 in the morning. He barely saw anything of the family. Either Mirabelle or Jimmy was already serving in the shop by the time he left, and whichever one wasn't was usually down in the basement stock-room. Sometimes, Luke would awaken briefly as he was creeping out of their bedroom, saying his name in a tiny voice shrunk by sleep and incomprehension. Adam would shush him gently, and creep downstairs with a pang in his heart and a piece of toast in his hand. One morning, tiptoeing about in the gloom of the living-room, he noticed that some coloured paper-chains had gone up, as well as a small tree with an oversized angel at the top.

On the 23rd, an after-hours party ('Midnight till whenever you can handle!') was to take place on Ground, courtesy of Vincent. All staff were invited, and encouraged to congratulate themselves and each other on making Paradise's first month-and-a-half such a flat-out success. Adam told Ben the evening before that he couldn't possibly do two jobs, party half the night, and come back and do two jobs again the next day. 'Unless...' Ben replied, with the kind of wink that probably implied controlled substances.

The following morning, in the consulting room, Vincent lay flat on his back, breathing deeply from the pit of his stomach. Somebody with a Polish name had just put him through 50 minutes of Thai massage, folding and unfolding his body, twisting it into graceful shapes, elegant stress postures that he held with controlled aplomb. At the end, he had sat upright in something very close to the lotus position, tingling with a corporeal sense of accomplishment, facing the masseuse, who smiled at him from a sweat-bathed face. As she left the room, Vincent sank back on the cushioned mat and contemplated the ceiling.

It had once seemed to him that it took the truly miserable to understand what happiness was, while the happy merely took it for granted. Now he understood things better. In the greatest adversity lay seeds of the greatest wisdom, and if any human attribute was closest to happiness, as cleanliness lay allegedly contiguous to godliness, it was wisdom. One should therefore not exactly court tribulation, but not fight shy of it either. It was the fighting that was wrong. One of the wisdoms of the Buddhist tradition was that, only when one stopped wishing for something, might the something materialise. So that if it didn't, you hadn't wanted it anyway. And if it did, it was an unexpected gratification, only faintly tarnished by the work that had gone into not wanting it.

Vincent's staff had put up an 'I Am' board in their office. Every morning, each employee wrote one adjective in marker pen to describe their aspirations for the day. He always stopped and read them. Today, the board was covered in words in many colours, written in bubble letters, wobbly letters and letters with smiley faces in them. Today I Am: 'EXTROVERT!', 'Ambitious', 'smoooooooth', '<u>determined</u>', 'partylicious!!', 'Self-possessed'. Vincent paused, and on a whim swiped up a marker pen from Javine's desk. In liquid green letters, he wrote across the whole width of the page, 'C A L M'. As everybody broke into applause, he turned and spread his hands. Then he disappeared into his office, where a cup of cardamom chai and a rose-petal cookie awaited him.

There was an email from a reporter at the *Clarion*, requesting a phone interview for its evening edition. Vincent pondered for a moment, then dialled the number. An obviously unprepared young woman asked him whether Paradise was the achievement of his career to date, and whether he had anything more up his sleeve for Gutford.

'I'm going to ask *you* something,' he announced. The reporter was silent. 'When you began your career as a journalist, did you imagine that all it would consist of would be inviting other people to congratulate themselves?'

'I'm not sure what you mean,' she said.

'What I mean is, there's a brand-new dream in town, honey. Don't report on it. Live it. Come and be you. It's nearly Christmas.'

'I'm Muslim.'

'A label is a libel,' Vincent said, and put the phone down.

Having watched a packed bus go past without stopping, Adam began the walk to Paradise. It was a ghost-grey drizzly morning under a sky full of threat. It was going to be a very long day, made all the wearyingly longer by the fact that he hadn't slept properly. He'd found on getting up that there was no hot water for a shower, so he'd had a strip-wash at the bathroom sink with a kettleful of boiled water. He was beyond tired, too tired even to be irritable, and was clinging against grim death to the thought that in two days' time, he would have a day off. He hadn't bought any presents.

'Hey, brains,' he said to Ben on arrival at work. 'What can I get my six-year-old brother for Christmas?'

'Save him some coke from tonight.'

'That's the one thing he really doesn't need.'

'But you do,' said Ben. 'Geez, man, you look like something out of *Zombie Apocalypse*.'

'Thanks for that.'

'Or *Zombie Bloodbath: Rage of the Undead*.'

'Warm to the theme, why don't you?' Adam said, heading for the espresso-machine.

When April floated in a few minutes later, she was carrying a large paper bag crammed with pastries. Adam stuffed down some sticky raisiny thing with a yellowish cinnamon glop in the centre, and then a muffin with red-and-green Christmas frosting. He had to take his first customer's book out of her hand between his two little fingers, the only ungummy ones he had left.

'I have now officially had enough sugar,' he announced to Ben. 'Though not yet enough caffeine. If you get my drift.'

Ben went back to the espresso-machine with his cup.

The morning press of business grew almost imperceptibly from brisk through breathless to a state of surging chaos, in which display-stands wavered visibly, books slithered to the floor, their covers progressively dog-eared through handling, and the large coffee-table picture-book of a bellicose pop sensation on tour was pawed and pored over until the sheen on every black surface in the pictures was a forensic banquet of fingerprints. People haggled over the prices, which April was content to allow, as long as no piss was taken. The chip-and-pin machine connections slowed under the weight of demand, but the only mishap of the morning occurred when Ben had to key in manually the price of a volume of Marxist aesthetic theory, and inadvertently entered £2.40 instead of £24. April shrugged off his confession, saying if he had been going to receive a Christmas bonus, she would have deducted it from that.

'Do we get a bonus?' Adam asked.

'*You* do,' she said.

The shop was sufficiently busy that both Jimmy and Mirabelle were serving, the two of them bustling and bumping into each other behind the counter, as people asked for things that had to be weighed out, retrieved from high shelves, or which required proof-of-age ID. Their hands crossed each other repeatedly in the till with the dexterous precision of piano duettists, while the electronic sounder on the door squawked incessantly as people came and went.

Upstairs, Joanne had decided to take advantage of their preoccupation by searching carefully through every cupboard and drawer in the flat. What exactly she expected to find, she wasn't sure, but she was determined to get to the bottom of something. There was a secret life going on here that remained concealed most of the time, but had emerged accidentally to view twice now, once to suggest blackmail, the second time an apparent infidelity. What more might there be? The answer seemed to be nothing, for the time being, as the tins and boxes in the kitchen turned out only to contain biscuits and bread, rather than bundles of cash. There was a safe in the living-room wall, but she knew from when it was opened that there was nothing in there but modest temporary deposits from the till. The search proved fruitless, until she arrived at the door of Jimmy and Mirabelle's bedroom.

'Stop now,' she instructed herself, her hand on the door. She could hear Luke playing some splashy-sounding game in the bathroom. He wasn't likely to interrupt her and, even if he did, wouldn't be struck with the awful significance of entering someone else's bedroom on a snooping mission. She pushed the door a little way, and stuck her head inside.

There was a twilit serenity about the room, the Venetian blinds at the window tilted to more or less closed. She could make out the white bulk of fitted wardrobes that were joined in an arch above the head end of the bed, a framed picture of some rivery landscape and a scattering of Mirabelle's shoes over the floor. A dressing-table with hinged mirror-panels was strewn with makeup and hair products, in front of which was a lopsided purple pouffe. Joanne pulled her head back from the door. She listened for a moment to Luke's splashing, and the more distant thrum of voices and activity in the shop. Both had enough of an air of continuity about them to tempt her to risk a five-minute incursion into the bedroom. She slipped in and closed the door behind her.

Making straight for the drawers of the dressing-table, she found them mostly messily stuffed with cosmetics. In the bottom one on the left was a flat white box, which turned out to contain Jimmy and Mirabelle's wedding album, the pictures of uniformly grinning groups of people in hats and suits interleaved with translucent sheets of crinkled paper. In the main nuptial portrait, Jimmy looked swarthy, triumphant, next to a Mirabelle in peach blusher and false eyelashes, her wedding veil an attenuated snood with a sprinkling of sequins. A tiny toddler in a child's military tunic in one of the group photos might have been Adam, but couldn't have been. She put the album carefully back, and turned to the wardrobes.

The left-hand one was clearly Jimmy's. It released the faintly depressing avuncular smell of old suits, hung in indecent proximity above a three-deep mound of shoes. She stood on tiptoe to peer over the shelf above, where rolled ties and a couple of flat caps were stored. On Mirabelle's side, the wardrobe was so stuffed with brightly coloured dresses and busily accessorised coats that she could have got lost among them. She pulled out a couple of drawers at the bottom, and found layers of surprising underwear, which made her roll them quickly shut again. There were drawers under the bed, which turned out to be full of towels and spare bedding, as well as more old photo albums and shoes. Clearly, nothing incriminating was going to come to light, and Joanne was just beginning to feel a little deflated, when her eyes fell upon the drawers in the fitted night-stands.

Jimmy's contained a Bible and various half-consumed packs of indigestion tablets, painkillers and sleep-aids. Mirabelle's was interestingly locked. As soon as she discovered this, Joanne was convinced that the clue to whatever was going on beneath their noses lay here. She went back to the dressing-table drawers in search of a little key, but there wasn't one. She looked inside the wardrobe again, under the pillow, in the drawers of the bed. Perhaps she could force the lock and then deny all knowledge. For God's sake, what was she thinking? She sat on the edge of the bed and mused on the conundrum. Where would you put a key that you used all the time, to hide it? Her eyes roved over the darkened room, and swept back over the carpet until her gaze came to rest at her own feet. Dropping to her knees, she extended her fingers into the narrow space below the bed-drawer. Almost at once, she found it.

Javine was growing more hot and bothered by the minute. There was some problem with the catering for the evening party. She had heard from their people that two of the celebrities were likely to be no-shows, or at least later than arranged, and now the Christmas crackers had arrived, and they were not the ones that had been ordered. In the course of explaining the series of disasters to Vincent, she had become tearfully agitated. Vincent had stepped out from behind his desk and placed healing hands on her shoulders, instructing her to breathe abdominally and gather. She gathered.

'Sorry, VB. This isn't me.'

'None of us is me, darling. Me is the mythical monster we don't believe in any more. What was the cracker issue?'

'We ordered the ones that contained luxury food items,' Javine moaned. 'What's arrived are the ones that have jewellery in them. They're thousands of pounds more expensive.'

'Then those are the ones we hand out,' said Vincent, spreading his hands and raising his shoulders at the sheer simplicity of the solution. 'We invite Positively Crackers to charge for the ones we ordered. If they charge for the ones we have, let it be. Easy.'

They went back into the admin office, where an opened box stood on Javine's desk. Vincent took out a cracker and held it towards her. She dabbed her eyes as a warm smile spread over her face and pulled the cracker. It popped sharply, and the prize, which Vincent won, fell on the floor. It was a jade bracelet. He slid it over his wrist, and yelled 'Merry Christmas!', throwing his arms above his head. Everybody took up the gesture, returning the greeting in many different pitches.

At lunchtime, Adam took a sandwich outside and stood in a huddle with the smokers, staring out into the windswept drizzle. The forecast snow had so far failed to appear, although some swore they could feel it in the air. There was enough fake snow inside Paradise to replenish the Arctic melt, but nothing compared with the feel of the real stuff crunching underfoot, or brushing your face in feathery flakes.

This was once the favourite time of year, a time that improbably united children and their seniors in a state of grateful anticipation. Its sparkles and glistenings amid lowering mornings and black afternoons melted even the hardiest indifference, and the rumblings of those who declared they hated Christmas, and couldn't wait for it all to be over, were as much a part of the seasonal cheer as carollers and paper-chains. There were always voices that mourned the commercialism of it all, claiming that it got a little worse every year, but they never described an older Christmas that sounded preferable, only one in which you were allowed a single day off work and had to be grateful to wake on Christmas morning and find a satsuma with your name on it. Now that the one-day-off Christmas had become a reality for Adam for the first time ever, festive austerity seemed all the more a gigantic oxymoron.

A voice at his right told him to cheer up, in case it never happened. It was Fay. He kissed her with a mouthful of chorizo and tomato, leaving a paprika-orange smear on her cheek. She drove her hand deep into the pocket of his jeans, and they stood in silence, watching the drizzle, Adam chewing determinedly on the tough-crusted sandwich while Fay rolled one of his testicles in her fingers. Things were fine for a second.

'They're going to let us off knock off at ten for the party,' she said.

'Going to be hard to persuade the customers to leave.'

'I expect some of them will have a go at crashing the do.'

'But only holders of the lucky golden ticket will get in,' said Adam, and they both smirked.

In the afternoon, further hordes pressed in and ascended into the glaringly lit cupola of Paradise. They brought the drizzle and the dreariness in with them, but it evaporated on the escalators, as the lights and the music and the buzzing cloud of voices deepened beneath them and opened above them. Sometimes, there was the sound of an amplified voice, barely decipherable as it interrupted the music to announce another lucky winner. Nobody threw their shopping in the air and gasped out 'I'm rich!', but rich somebody somewhere must undoubtedly suddenly be.

'Did you want to go for a pee?' Ben suggested to Adam.

'No.'

'Yeah you did.'

When he squeezed into the toilet just off the back store-room, Adam found two caterpillar-fat lines of cocaine chopped out on a DVD cover on top of the cistern. He hadn't taken anything like this in over a year. He snuffled it up through the bit of plastic straw that Ben had left. It lit up his nostrils with an argumentative peppery sting, which wasn't at all the effect he remembered. He stood for a couple of minutes until it seemed that nothing else was going to happen, and then went back into the shop. About twenty minutes later, something very gently stole into his synapses and gave him the subtlest jolt, like the regretful shake you might administer to somebody who had asked you to wake them. He winked at Ben, and carefully balanced the straw behind Ben's ear like a little pencil.

Ben snatched it away. 'Bruv! Want to get us fired?'

'Frankly, my dear,' Adam grinned, 'I don't give a damn.'

Despite the general hullabaloo, Print Media had gone strangely quiet, and he went and stood at the door. Tides of people still surged this way and that, but all in hypnotic slow-motion. Even if doom were inevitable, people weren't in a hurry to meet it. They approached it of their own volition, rather than being transported, but they were sauntering that way in all humility, inching bashfully towards the flames. Adam snorted hard. The cocaine, or whatever it largely was, had done as much as it was going to.

Vincent appeared in the admin office. Through the partition, he'd seen something like a bright-yellow concrete-mixer being wheeled with perspiring effort from the goods lift into the middle of the floor.

'*Qu'est-ce que c'est?*' he inquired.

'It's a concrete-mixer,' said Javine. 'For the grand draw tonight.'

'But of course.' The office erupted in timely laughter. 'What does the winner get?'

'A week as your PA.'

'I do remember, I really do,' Vincent deadpanned, to more giggles. 'Where will you be that week?'

'Right where I am now,' Javine replied. 'Putting the pieces back together again.'

An indrawn breath at the sudden ironic note dissolved into laughs as Vincent made a finger-clicking, here's-lookin-at-you gesture towards her. Javine could say these things.

The staff gathered round as the concrete-mixer was plugged in and switched on. Nothing happened. One of the boys dropped to one knee and, with an expert air, peered underneath the barrel of it. Vincent pressed the Emergency Stop button and it churned into life, to cheers and whistles. It wasn't as noisy as had been hoped. They watched it revolving for a minute until they discovered they couldn't turn it off, other than by pulling the cable out of the mains-socket, a *coup de grâce* that Vincent administered with a showman-like flourish.

By late afternoon, plastic beakers of Christmas punch were being passed around behind the counter, at first surreptitiously sipped, then openly swigged. April had disappeared in a temper, and hadn't come back. There had been a couple of internal calls that had descended to spitting *sotto voce*, before the phone was slammed down hard. Adam and Ben exchanged small shrugs, but kept their heads down. There was only a day-and-a-half left until the place closed for a week.

The punch was circulating from floor to floor in huge glass pitchers, at Vincent's behest. Ben had turned on just sufficient charm to persuade the girl who'd brought some into Print Media into leaving the jug. There was something bitter in it like orange curaçao, which worked cleverly to stop you wanting too much of it initially, but then as the underlying effect of the gin sank in, the bitterness politely faded. The two of them managed to keep on top of sales, giving out the right amount of change, maintaining a steady gaze when they had to tell the occasional customer that their card had been declined by the machine. In the midst of a particularly chaotic moment, as Ben embarked on a rendering of 'Unchained Melody', bolstered by encouraging whoops, a few customers accompanying him in stumbling unison, Adam disappeared behind the scenes and recklessly inhaled the remainder of the coke. His head was beginning to prickle agreeably as his nasal passages numbed.

His phone vibrated. It was a text from Fay. 'Hope yve got yr magic underpants on Superman. Looks like its gonna be madness here tonite!!! xxxxxx'. At the end was a confused smiley. The roaring of voices from the shop made it sound like a rowdy bar on Cup Final day. He sniffled sharply and, with a slop of his punch, sat down more heavily than he was expecting on a low stool. On the desk in front of him were untidy stacks of books, heaped up anyhow from boxes half-unpacked. They should all have been on the shelves by now.

'Whatever,' he heard himself slur, and broke into an idiot giggle. He reached for a book, pulling one out from halfway down a pile so that the ones above toppled to the floor at his feet. Opening it, he took another gulp of punch.

Miss Peckerton's eyes passed from one to the other of them with a keenness of vigilance. It seemed to her that, but for the havering sense of something unsaid, and perhaps unsayable, mingling in the air with a note of woodsmoke from the partly opened window, this was a finer moment of tranquillity than any she had had the fortune hitherto to share with the careless lovers. For what, while their own youthful passion flashed in the despondent tea-time twilight, could they care for her? Lettie's glance stole briefly toward the door, as though intimating that they might now be ready to be left alone, but there was further matter in Miss Peckerton's mission, and greater urgency in its telling.

'May I say one thing more?' she inquired, with a drop to suggest the compulsiveness that struggled for mastery with her natural reluctance.

'You've already, beautifully, said it, my dear,' Lettie assured her.

Adam put it back on the desk. Reading was what you did while you waited for something to happen. At best, you imagined you discovered in it an account of your own life, strung across elegant periods and the crackle of talk, and for the rest, you hoped to be entertained, awed and warmed by it. He wanted all this to be over soon, the drink, the stupidity, the over-hopeful waiting for sex. But what it might be the prelude to hadn't figured itself yet. He bent to the floor to pick up another book.

She stopped and looked again. It couldn't be. Not at this hour, not at this season, and with such a bloom of youth about him as she had scarcely ever seen. It was, though; it was Daniel, steadfast adorable Daniel, his small auburn moustache seeming to flare against the long-remembered face. Had he seen her, she wondered? Gone was the time for tremulous courtesies. They were standing no more than six yards apart, absurdly present to each other amid the bustle and rush of St James's Street, with August sun glinting on the shop-fronts and half of London gone to the country. Yet here he was, about to bring her up short, in his oh! beautifully unassuming way, for relapsing into the dither of a little nincompoop.

"Daniel!" she called, but he seemed not to hear as, with jaw firmly set, he took off in quite the other direction.

What was there to say that needed saying? Is that where he'd gone wrong before, hanging back and not speaking up when it might have counted? Much of the aggrievement in life came from an over-developed sense of its needing to imitate the structure of a story, an immature impulse towards momentousness that nothing in the actual daily round could serve. The persistent jangling question was: am I doing all I could? Of course not. But what matter? Things were either good or bad. Or something in between. Surprisingly bearable. Disappointing. But the slicing of distinctions was what gave birth to the reflecting faculty, and the unavoidable need for more. More of what, though? More than there was. He glanced down at another open page.

'Darling, you can't mean it!' Samantha cried, with only the littlest pout to spoil the overall effect of her anger.

Henry looked away from her. In all the world, there were not the words now to still the surge of despair he must inflict on her. As he was about to speak, the door flew open, and an aproned figure, not less agitated of demeanour than her mistress, tripped in.

'Beg pardon, sir', dropping him an anxious curtsey. 'There's been a smash in the village, Miss Henderson. It seems poor Albert, the farmboy, is hurt.'

For a moment, a moment that absorbed all their languid absurdity, neither Samantha nor Henry spoke. The twittering of choughs came in from the garden, borne in on the breath of hot breeze that stirred the French doors. Then the calamity, its crash muffled by the duty of their concern, was allowed its entrance.

'Good God!' exclaimed Samantha. 'Is he much injured?'

You might as well say something though. There wasn't much to recommend the alternative. Shy people didn't arouse anybody's curiosity or concern. They could be hurting horribly, or they could just be arrogantly frozen, as uninterested in the world around as the world was in them. And, other than when trying on identities in adolescence, you didn't want to be weird. *Am I weird?* wondered Adam. *Fay doesn't think so. Unless there's something weird about wanting to read while you're getting trashed.*

Kleinberg sneaked a look along the snow-grimed pavement. There was no sign of Mellie, not in either of the only two directions there were. This was a not unusual occurrence, but its regularity served only to make him wrinkle his weathered nose as though in distaste at the vulgar cold. He gave it up, and went in anyway. Inside the entrance-hall, grave-toned classical statuary receded down a classical perspective, beguiling the eye while it calmed the heart. Kleinberg walked up to the ticket-window and bought himself in. He ascended the wide, welcoming stairs to the second floor as though he belonged there, affecting the air of a curator overcoming some trifling dyspepsia as he hurried to a world-historical labour of reclassification. Kleinberg removed his hat, and the audacious winter sun poured through the atrium roof onto his shiny, liver-spotted scalp. Here, at least, he was at home.

'The Renoirs you'll not want to miss,' a voice commandingly close to his shoulder insisted. He swivelled and looked directly into the face of Mellie Curtis.

Somewhere in my crowded empty head is something I might say that will change things. Change things for someone near. I want to make someone happy, he thought. *I don't want it to be about me. I want to stop saying 'I'.*

There was that in him which declined to be stilled by the mere application of assurance. He knew that Lorna's inmost heart would ache with foreboding if he should return betimes to Dovebourne without her, on this of all nights. Will any of us, suborned by fate to a course that looks all unembarred and free of flow, find it in the least proper, for the sake of leaden conscience and its coming hour of rueful perquisition, to hesitate at the watershed while others clamorously plunge in? A day's smooth passage might be bought at the cost of an eternal night of remorse, but nothing at the present juncture persuades us to the thrift of purchasing it more cheaply.

It's just a question of forgetting who you are for five minutes, of letting someone else draw pictures on the page. The page under his gaze was one dense block of text.

Christ, the dark, the thick dark, dark enough to see your soul in, what was that word that had once come to her, come to her once when she stood by the window, did she have windows, no matter, and looking out, looking at the night that seemed the darkest night either of them had ever known, though Christ knows it was hardly without competitors, she remarked of the night that it was fearfully dark, not the slightest shyest glimmer of moonlight, not a speck, she said 'it's dark my love,' and you caught the word full in your solar plexus like a badly bowled ball, 'it's so dark it's thick, what's that word for thick, that word that always sounds made-up, yes I know, I have it – inspissated,' and she said it with an air of carelessly worn triumph

Then you could see whether you liked them. Or not. But you would have something to contemplate that wasn't just more of you. More you was a burdensome error.

'Oh Drassy, no! I'll not have it. You always say "no presents", and then you go and break your own rule.'

The speaker was Branton Pelham. The person addressed was Dracena Bemmell. They were standing in the living-room at Potsmere, where Dracena still lived with her parents and four siblings, two of whom were older than her and two younger. It was a pleasantly warm September afternoon, on a day that she and Branton had always spent together, since it was by coincidence the birthday of both of them. Branton had arrived a little later than planned, wearing an enormous padded coat and with a woollen hat pulled over his shaggy mane of dark-brown hair. He looked as though he had been expecting it to be much colder than it had turned out to be, and now he was all the more hot and bothered as Dracena had once again 'accidentally' forgotten their no-presents agreement. He hesitated to take the large gold-wrapped box from her hands.

'Go on, silly, it's nothing special,' said Dracena.

'That's hardly the point,' said Branton. 'You know it isn't fair. You make me feel such a – a – *cheapskate*. And that's a rotten thing to feel.'

Dracena laughed and kissed him quickly on the tip of his nose. 'But you're my own little cheapskate, Bran, and you can't do anything about it.'

'Hello, Branton,' said a voice from the door. Dracena's younger sister, Dorcas, entered the room, munching an apple.

'Hello, Dorcas,' said Branton. 'Look what your gilded butterfly of a sister has done again.'

'Bruv, what you doing? I'm running a solo show out here, and you're all curled up with a book.'

Ben was bright-eyed and pink.

'Yeah, I'm coming back now,' Adam replied, shaking the drunkness, along with the dreary solipsism, out of his head. 'Let me get some water.'

Ben returned to the shop just in time to see a boy of about twelve trying to stuff a hardback picture-book of great naval battles into his rucksack. The boy reddened as their gazes met. Ben jerked his head towards the exit and the boy fled, either his own or someone's Christmas suddenly solved.

Joanne looked at the tissued pictures through a film of tears. Someone had done a wonderful job on Mirabelle, who looked extravagantly young and voluptuous, her electric-blonde hair swept up into a statement of a tiara, two hanging corkscrew curls framing her face. Her lips were done in hot peach, and there was a jet-black beauty-spot dotted in just below the corner of her left eye. To her right, a young man stood, holding his arm stiffly akimbo for her to thread hers through it, his bulbously knotted tie a little off-centre to the splayed white shirt-collar. He was wearing an endearingly awful dark green suit. A slick of hair-dressing had brought up a lustrous shine on either side of his parting, and a pair of confident hazel eyes gazed manfully back at the camera. He looked like a shy man on the day of his greatest success. Joanne could – just – see Jimmy's face looking back at her.

In the next picture, a small band had gathered about the marital pair, elderly grey faces and forbidding hairdos mingling among lanky boys and demurely smiling little girls. A woman at the edge of the group held what looked like a half-day-old baby in her arms, a flap of its blue shawl hanging down unnoticed by the photographer. She had Joanne's own unamused smirk as they waited for the camera to click and whirr and click again. The baby's profiled sleeping face, pale and blank as a slice of ham, belonged to Adam.

Suddenly, there was a footstep at the bottom of the stairs. Hurriedly, Joanne closed the wedding-album and slid it into the drawer. She just had time, with trembling fingers, to lock it again and put the key back under the bed. Mirabelle bustled into the room, her head turned towards the light-switch.

'Erm,' Joanne mumbled, and was met with a shriek of panic. 'Sorry, I'm – I'm really sorry,' she stammered.

'What on earth?' Mirabelle was winded with the sudden shock.

'I don't know why I – I just needed to be in a quiet place. I'm really sorry.'

'You frightened me half to death. I was looking for Luke.'

'So was I,' Joanne improvised. 'And then I just rested for a moment.'

'I thought he was with you.'

They looked blankly at each other.

'What?'

Released from what remained of his shift when April reappeared with a couple of teenaged temps he had never seen before, Adam walked smartly away from the shop. As he left, he faintly caught Ben calling his name, but didn't look back. Pushing through the crowds towards the escalators, he shook his head like a dog coming in from rain, and then rode up and up, half-convincing himself that the fug was clearing as he left the echoing clangour of the ground floor behind. There was clangour on other floors too, but it seemed to have a less-clotted density, as though the air grew thinner with the ascent. On Fifth, arbitrarily, he got off the escalator and walked along for a bit. A row of girls sat under great old-fashioned hair-dryers like astronauts' helmets. Others were having their fingernails painted in designs from Mondrian. At Get Your Rocks On, he stopped and looked in the window.

He wondered whether Fay would like a gunmetal column ring, or a pair of shoulder-length 'ear-dangles', but the prices decided it. There was nothing in less than three figures, apart from a bootlace pendant bearing a little plaque with the word 'Fucked' on it.

Adam turned his back to the shop-window and peered up into the fathomless roof of Paradise. Beyond the glass vault, the darkening sky was already royal-blue. He took a stick of gum out of his pocket, which Ben had given him so that his jaws would have something to grind on when he was wired. It smelled like toothpaste, and he didn't want it in his mouth. He wasn't wired. Over the translucent glass balustrade of the floor above, he could see the shop-name Head First.

He didn't look at the window-display, which would doubtless be off-putting, but walked straight in and stood in the middle of the shop, looking uncertainly about him as men do when confronted with women's clothing.

'Is there something in particular?' a woman in a scarlet tunic asked him.

'Nearly. I'd like something simple, cool and cheap for a girl with a sense of humour.'

'How cheap?' the woman gently wondered.

'Dirt.'

Without a moment's hesitation, she turned and pulled a floppy woollen thing off the shelf immediately behind her. 'This is our everyday beanie. Works well with a range of outfits. Light enough for summer, warm enough for winter. Washable. A penny short of ten pounds at our pre-Christmas discount.'

'Is there any other colour than black?'

'Primrose.'

'I'll take the black,' Adam decided.

'Christmassy-wrapped?'

'I should say so.'

The wrapping of the hat took barely a moment, but a problem with the electronic till lengthened the transaction into an interlude long enough for Adam to be offered a seat. He watched women gingerly putting shapeless purple and green items on their heads, peering in the angled mirrors, and snatching them off again. The hot summery colours – throbbing cherry, smouldering cobalt, buttercup – made most of the hats look extremely childish.

All three assistants had gathered round the till to confer, occasionally pressing a button and being rewarded only with a confusing bleep. Adam inadvertently caught the eye of one of the customers in the mirror. She had pulled down over the other eye the brim of a blue raffia thing with trailing fronds at the back. He wrinkled his nose and shook his head slightly in a friendly way. 'No?' she mimed. He stuck out his lower lip in confirmation.

The puzzled bleeping at the till went on. Adam didn't mind for the time being. He was glad to take the weight off his feet. Another man of roughly his own age walked into the shop, and over to a row of bald hatless model-heads. These too were for sale. He picked up one of the heads and met its gaze frankly, as though he were about to kiss it. The woman whose eye he had caught now appeared before Adam in a bright blue pillbox hat like a hotel porter's.

'Now *that,*' he said, 'is you.'

'I thought so too,' she said.

'Though buying it might take a while.' He nodded over to the till, where the remaining two assistants were now stabbing angry fingernails at the buttons. As the discussion continued, Adam's attention drifted to the noise outside the shop. The music had momentarily paused, and an announcement was being made. As it was repeated, he caught the phrase 'Luke Young, a brave little boy who is lost'. Would anybody who knew him please come to the Lost Persons assembly-point? Adam bounded over to the till, threw a ten-pound note at the assistants, grabbed his wrapped hat and sprinted towards the escalator.

When he arrived on the floor below, he could see Luke sitting up on the edge of a counter at the assembly-point. He was staring transfixed at the policeman standing before him in a visored black helmet, who was just drawing a side-handled baton from his belt. Adam called Luke's name amid the hubbub. His brother didn't hear, but gingerly took the baton from the policeman's hand. He broke into a thrilled grin.

'Luke!' Adam shouted crossly again, as he arrived at the counter.

Luke's face lit up in merriment, and he clobbered Adam on the arm with the baton. His yell of pain provoked a burst of laughter from both Luke and the policeman.

'That's you told,' the policeman chuckled through his visor.

Adam grimaced with the agony of the blow. 'You've broken my arm, you little freak.'

'Am I to presume you know this little chap?' the policeman asked.

'Yes, he's my brother.'

'Then may I suggest, sir, that you take rather better care of him for the rest of the day? I found him standing outside in the rain.'

Luke's head flew back in mirth at hearing this account of his own naughtiness.

'Give the man his stick back,' said Adam. 'I'm not pleased with you, young man. How did you get out without anyone seeing?'

'He did what?' the policeman asked, suddenly acquiring a more serious professional interest in the case.

'We'll be OK now, thank you,' Adam assured him and, whisking Luke off the counter, he carried his brother away through the crowds before the inquiry could get any more official.

Setting Luke down on a bench with some little girls, Adam took out his phone. There were five missed calls, one from April and four from Joanne. He called his sister. There was so much din that he couldn't hear her voice on the other end, so he shouted that he would send her a text. 'Just picked up Luke safe n sound at work. WTF!!' While he stared at the phone awaiting a reply, Luke got into a face-pulling contest with the girl next to him. It had escalated to pinching when Adam intervened by pulling Luke to his feet.

'Oi,' he warned. 'That's enough monkey-business for today. You've had everybody worried out their minds disappearing like that.'

'Nobody was talking to me,' Luke whinged.

A text bleeped. They would come in a taxi to collect him, but there was a 45-minute wait. They'd text again when on their way.

'Oh great,' Adam said. 'We're stuck with each other for the

next three-quarters of an hour now.' He jabbed Luke's shoulder with a finger. 'You, mister, are a waste of Turkey Twizzlers.'

Luke returned this with a second's defiance before his face crumpled.

'OK, OK, I'm sorry.' Adam pulled him into a hug. Luke's arms remained limp for a moment, before finding their way tentatively around his brother's back. 'I'm sorry, OK?'

There was a silent clinch, and then Luke pulled away. His face was red, but he'd managed to choke the tears off at their source, perhaps conscious of making a bad impression in front of the girl.

'Should we have something to eat?' Adam offered.

Fifteen minutes later, they were sitting at a table in Choc-a-Block on Eighth. To Adam's surprise, Luke had spurned all the chocolate temptations, and was contentedly dipping vanilla tuiles in a mug of hot milk. Adam sipped his tea.

'Are you happy at Auntie Mirabelle's?' he asked.

Luke rolled his eyes to one side in a pantomime of cogitation. He nodded vigorously. 'Uncle Jimmy reads me stories, like you used to.'

'Yeah, I'm sorry I've had to work so much. It'll be different after Christmas, I'm sure.'

Luke twirled and twirled the end of a tuile in the hot milk until it grew so soggy that it broke off and fell in. He pouted ironically for Adam, and they both laughed.

'You're not a waste of space, you're a little star,' Adam said. His brother's eyes sparkled. 'Just don't run off again, OK?'

It was an hour-and-a-half before the text came through to say that the taxi was on its way, by which time Luke was lying with his head in Adam's lap, fast asleep.

A plate of loosely cooked scrambled eggs and shaved black truffle on sourdough toast was put in front of Vincent, who was on the phone. He made a heart shape in the air with one finger in the direction of the T-shirt that had brought it in.

'No,' he moaned into his mobile. 'I specifically said no more clowns. There are no clowns in Paradise.'

Outside his office, Javine was tearing about with sheaves of paper in her hand. Stopping to peer through the window at Vincent, she pointed at her watch. Vincent made an impatient whirling motion with his free hand.

'Anyway, gotta run. I've a meeting that won't take itself. Yep, fine, whatever. Byesies.'

Javine burst in. 'Sorry, VB, we've got to express this. The TV are here in half-an-hour or less, and we still have the final drop-downs to do on the MO.'

As they bustled to the meeting-room, Javine clicked her fingers at the receptionist, and gestured to Vincent's desk. The untouched plate was carried away, its contents tipped into the waste-disposal.

'Who are you?' Javine asked a boy who was playing with the lighting in the meeting-room.

'Er, Ayrden?' he stuttered. 'Technical s-s-support?'

She swept him aside as she approached the table. Everyone else was already in place, thumbing through disordered sheets of paper, conferring in mumbles. Vincent followed, customarily avoiding the executive chair at the head of the table. He kicked off his flip-flops, and sank sideways on to a beanbag with a kilim thrown over it.

'OK, boring stuff,' Javine began, 'but we have GOT to sort this out within the next half-hour, if we're to stand a cat's of hitting the ground running after Crimbo.'

The lighting turned from warm orange to a more crypt-like green.

'Why is this happening?' she snapped at Ayrden, who was just about to leave.

'Er, m-m-mood setting?'

'It's lovely,' Vincent conciliated from near the floor. 'Thank you.'

Ayrden slipped out and closed the door softly behind him. In all his eighteen months' experience, he had never had a job where he had so little minded bossy girls snapping at him. He had an A-level in physics, which the careers advisor had said might just see him through the next worldwide recession, and he was earning decent money in a place that felt like one big fairground. One day, many years off, he would be up to his beautiful neck in a frothing Jacuzzi in West Beach, California, while a movie actress, who earned more in five minutes than combined generations of his family had done since the Abdication, threw aside her last item of clothing and prepared to climb in with him. In the meantime, who cared if bossy girls sometimes ripped him about his stutter? It would turn the movie actress on.

'Drop-downs,' Javine snapped. 'Week 52. Thoughts?'

After a second's silence, Vincent spoke slowly and deliberately from his recumbent position. 'Would it help if I said that I agreed with – and/or to – everything on the agenda?'

Javine peered inquiringly over the edge of the table. For a moment, nobody moved or spoke. And then somebody at the end of the table started clapping. Hesitantly at first, then swelling to a full-blooded ovation, the applause flowed around the table. Few could actually see Vincent where he reclined, and his concluding gesture – he subsided slowly flat on his back with his hands before him clasping an imaginary prayer-book, like Eleanor of Aquitaine on the Fontevraud tomb – was missed by all except Javine, who didn't get the reference.

The meeting was over.

Safely restored to home and bed, Luke had been enjoined solemnly to promise that he would never again wander off unattended. It was extraordinary that he had managed to remember the route to Paradise after only one visit. Nonetheless, he had made his way through the drizzle, stopping at pedestrian crossings in the manner he had been taught, politely declining help from an old lady who asked him where his mum was. On arrival, he had told the security guards that he needed to see his brother, who worked at a bookshop, and was escorted to the entrance of Print Media. April had had to tell them Adam had finished for the day, and she had no idea where he would be now. A call to his mobile went unanswered.

He had woken just long enough to be taken to the taxi, and then just long enough to climb the stairs and be put to bed. Jimmy tucked the duvet under either side of his slumberous body.

To Mirabelle, the entire episode represented an obvious cry for help. Joanne was inclined to put it down to nothing graver than a small boy's indignation at being ignored, but her aunt wasn't to be placated. It surely showed that he wasn't happy where he was. He needed a proper authority-figure, which is why he was so unhealthily dependent on Adam. The discussion wound on until Luke's escapade was in danger of taking on the dimensions of a family catastrophe that would resound in their lives for years, at which point it was shrugged off.

'Still, what can you do?' Mirabelle said.

'To coin a phrase,' Jimmy put in, 'boys will be boys.'

'Yes, that helps us no end. Thank you, Dr Spock.'

Joanne turned on the lights on the tree. 'At least he didn't manage to spoil Christmas,' she suggested, in a gentler tone.

'No, we can do that ourselves,' said Mirabelle.

The waiters, Adam included, bustled between crowded tables with the jerky hurried movements of figures in silent comedy. They could barely make themselves heard above the yammering din, and customers resorted to holding up menus and pointing to their choices when ordering. One group couldn't decide how many sides of pumpkin and hazelnut purée they wanted, one of them holding up one finger, another three, another four. Other groups disputed lengthily over who should pay what proportion of their bill, so that each of the pile of cards needed to have a different amount charged on it. Occasionally, somebody queried a bill, usually the drinks tally. A prolonged investigation at one table established that they had indeed been overcharged by the cost of one coffee, while at another, it turned out that a bottle of champagne had been omitted.

'Own goal.' Adam grinned.

'WHAT?' the man shouted.

Adam couldn't be bothered re-keying the bill on his pad, and waved the issue away. 'Merry Christmas, mate.'

'WHAT?'

Fay was a far more practised coper. She dealt with disputes with ruthless efficiency, but she had noticeably fewer anyway than the others did. Avijit kept a keen eye on proceedings, occasionally clicking fingers to alert a waiter's attention to a customer's waving hand. As the clock ticked on towards throwing-out time at ten, he began to allow the staff to take slugs of drinks behind the service counter. The drink made them move even faster, whirling between tables as though driven by high-powered batteries. People wolfed their food as if they were making a determined effort to match the pace, ingesting enormous wedges of ciabatta like pythons swallowing sheep. A triumphant moment occurred when Avijit lined up all five staff in front of the counter, took the bottle of Icelandic vodka off its optic, and passed down the row of tilted heads and back again, pouring searing pure spirit into their gaping mouths. The customers hollered and cheered at the spectacle. Adam choked on the second mouthful, and ejected the vodka back down his chin and shirtfront. Fay took hers in her stride.

Eventually, at ten-to-ten, a blaring klaxon was sounded. Avijit put a bullhorn to his lips and bellowed 'Everybody out!' A groan went up. 'No fair!' they shouted, but they had all been pre-warned when seated. The announcement was also printed on the menus, and had been running continuously in an LCD banner along two walls. At every sight of somebody indignantly pointing at an unfinished bottle, Avijit repeated the bellowing instruction to get out. It took the best part of half-an-hour to clear the place, and with the dispersal of the last stragglers, he formed the staff up along the counter again, and went up and down the line with the bourbon bottle.

As everybody paused to draw breath, Adam and Fay congratulated each other on getting through it. Their faces were shining with sweat. Fay's piled-up hair was escaping its slides in stray black wisps. Patches of damp had spread from under Adam's arms all the way down his sides. He pulled his T-shirt off. Fay tweaked his nipples and a roar of encouragement came from the other boys. 'Get a room!' someone called out. He was transcendently happy, and kissed Fay as though he meant it. Retrieving his rucksack from behind the counter, he gave her the hat. She pulled it cautiously out of its paper bag and held it before her, turning it round like a valuable antique, and laughed and said she loved it. It was too hot to put it on now, but she would wear it later when they went home.

'You're my favourite person,' she told Adam, sending a responsive tingle through his genitals.

The admin-office staff had long since left their desks and gone to join the party. Only one figure remained on the eleventh floor, apart from the occasional sauntering security-guard. Vincent sat perfectly still at his desk, a coil of fading steam rising from a cup of chai. His eyes, which had been skimming lightly through the pages of a schedule printout, had paused at one of the entries. He had flicked back through several pages and stopped again. Turning from one page to the other, he appeared to have spotted some point of comparison between them. He leaned back in his chair as his eyes drifted meditatively out of focus.

If you were going to play the game – and goodness knows a

game is all it was – you may as well play it fairly. It was true the world got on better for the turning of blind eyes, but if there was a rule that everyone thought was a good rule, one that only you were allowed to disavow because you instituted it, was it not fairer to insist that its infraction be pointed out and stopped? Then the others could see that the rule meant something. They may not give it a moment's thought the rest of the time, but if the only occasion they were reminded of it was when its enforcement became necessary, then collective confidence in the rule was strengthened. The point was a painful one for Vincent to contemplate, he who had always believed as an article of faith that rules were there to be broken. But it depended on who was doing the breaking, and why.

He stood, took a small sip of the chai, and dawdled into the admin office. The whiteboard was still covered with the day's multi-coloured exclamations. After a moment's cogitation, he took the eraser and rubbed the surface back to a smeary white. With the green marker, he then wrote across it: 'We aim to please, but even more we are pleased to aim'.

He glided into the staff bathroom and stood at the mirror. The thick-lashed eyes, which always looked deceptively as though they were loaded with mascara, stared balefully back. For a moment, something ugly welled inside him. He would not, absolutely not, feel like this. He ran a small pool of cold water into his cupped hands, and then allowed it to trickle coolly over his face, as though, having arrived pale and sickly at the altar rail, he had found it curiously unattended, and had had to resort to anointing himself. Deep within, the ugly feeling discreetly continued to throb. Not all the water in the rough rude sea would wash away this stain, for it was faintly but fatally dyed with the tincture of affection.

Luke turned over in bed, momentarily half-awake, and peered in the darkness at the empty bed opposite. He mumbled Adam's name, and sank back into another sickly dream.

'You all right?' Adam bawled.

Fay nodded vigorously as she sipped something orange and filled with crushed ice. When she disengaged her lips from the straw, she mouthed some words that Adam couldn't hear. He clinked his glass against hers and gave her another wink.

The front section of the ground floor was almost entirely occupied by the party. All around were people Adam dimly recognised, though he couldn't have fitted the shop-names to the faces. Occasionally, someone paused to exchange a few words, most of which he couldn't hear in the racket of voices and the banging chart-music. He nodded and grinned, mumbled inaudible platitudes, and kept putting his arm around Fay's waist.

A dancefloor had been erected on a raised platform, with go-go dancers in cages at each side amid a whirling light-show. He wanted to want to dance, but the day and the evening, not to mention the worn-off drugs, had already drained most of his energy to a final bedrock. Fay didn't seem to want to dance, although she had taken two fat pills. The first had made her vomit a little, though the second went down with only one or two reflexive retches. Adam had declined.

He took another sip of red wine. The red wine had distinctly been a mistake. Reading the chalked-up bar menu, quite a few people had ordered what they thought was going to be something sweet and familiar, but had discovered that Squinzano was one of the best-kept secrets of Puglia, and were now therefore clutching large glasses of red wine. A couple of smashes had turned the floor crimson and sticky, the crimson fading to bruise-blue when the lights went white. Glass shards crunched underfoot until a boy in a paper bellboy's hat, whose grandparents had lived to see their country liberated from colonial oppression, arrived to sweep the remnants into a long-handled hod.

At some point while he was in the Gents, Adam missed the speeches, which were very brief. He also missed the prize draw, which apparently involved Vincent putting his hand into a turning concrete-mixer. The runners-up were a young girl from the Bayerischer Bierkeller, who was so small she couldn't be seen as she went up to collect her holiday voucher, and a monocled man with a refulgent cravat blooming from his neck. Nobody knew where he was from. The winner's ticket wasn't claimed, which seemed to add an anticlimactic note to the draw, until Vincent announced that he would personally inspect every ticket in the room until he found the Paradiser who would be working in his office in the new year. That produced a chorus of whoops and cheers, some of them a touch ironic.

'What'd I miss?' the returning Adam wondered, as the music cranked up again.

'Only the freaking draw,' Fay shouted. 'Let's see your ticket, I bet it's you.'

'I didn't buy a ticket.'

'Oh. It won't be you then. Shoulda seen Vincent though. He'd got this pink thing on his head. Hilarious.'

'He is a bit of a knobhead, isn't he?'

Fay imitated an open-mouthed shock smiley.

The party throbbed on. Indoor fireworks went off. As they craned their heads upwards, a net full of balloons in the distant atrium roof was released. More cheers went up, but the balloons took so long to float down through the floors that people gave up watching them. When they did finally arrive, they had quotations printed on them.

Fay read out the one she had caught. '"Nothing is impossble... It is often merely for an excuse that we say things are impossible." François de La Rochefoucauld, *Maxims*. So now you know.'

'Or else it's because they're actually impossible,' Adam commented. 'What a load of toss.'

A man next to him read another. '"Words... are the money of fools." Thomas Hobbes, *Leviathan*.'

'That dot dot dot bit is where they've cut out some of the quote, so it may not mean anything,' Adam advised him.

Fay caught at another, which didn't have dot-dots in it. '"I am not a man, I am dynamite." Friedrich Nietzsche, *Ecce Homo*. Oo-er.'

'They're what happened to Christmas-cracker jokes,' Adam shouted, picking one up from the floor where it was just about to be stepped on. '"No matter where you go, there you are." Confucius, *Analects*. There you go then. How profound is that?' He dug his fingers into the balloon till it popped.

'I think that's beautiful,' Fay said.

For a while, they didn't talk while the music and the chatter swirled about them. They watched the dancers on the stage, and the abstract images being projected on the video-screen behind. Trays of nibbly things came round. Fay couldn't eat after the pills, but took a miniature paper plate containing a penny-sized piece of steak and a matchstick chip, and handed it to Adam. He tipped it into his mouth, put his arm around Fay's shoulders, then let it drop to her waist as she shrugged it away. He pulled her body backwards against his, until the small of her back trapped his start of a hard-on. She shimmied against it without turning round, and a mixture of hot desire and irritation shuddered through him.

'Hey guys,' said a voice in front of Fay. It was their workmate Mike from Old Blind Possum. 'What up?'

'Yeah great,' Fay said.

They fell into a conversation that Adam could only partially hear. Mike kept putting a hand on Fay's shoulder as he shouted at her. Fay's head bobbed animatedly as she replied. Mike clenched his arms above his head in a stretch, brought them forward so that his biceps bulged, and rolled his head around from side to side. Then he thought of something else to say, and gripped Fay's shoulder again. Adam looked at the hand with its bitten fingernails and, suddenly, before he knew what he was doing, was pulling Fay away through the crowds.

'What's up?' she protested.

'Sorry, that guy does my head in.'

'He's OK.'

'He's a complete tool.'

'He's harmless.'

Adam led her, half-unwillingly, to the edge of the crush, through the unattended barrier, and off into one of the long side-aisles of the building, where nothing was happening at all. They marched grimly along into the relative darkness until Fay declined to go any further.

'Adam, this is crazy. We're supposed to stay at the party.'

'So what?' He sank on to his haunches against a shop-window full of video-games. 'It's not your fault. I've just had a tough time of it lately.'

She looked down at him where he squatted, his face in his hands. 'The party's OK, isn't it?'

'Yes, the party's OK. If only work was one big party, everything would be great.'

There was nothing she could say. Lacking for anything conciliatory, she tried a mild reproach.

'You were really rude to Mike.'

He held his hands away from his face in order to reply to her – 'I don't think he'll have been particularly hurt, believe it or not' – and then covered it again.

'That's not the point. Mike's a decent guy.'

'More decent than me anyway.'

'I didn't say that.'

Neither of them wanted to argue, but it was a difficult mode to disengage from.

'Just... Go back to the party.'

'I'm not leaving you here.'

'Go on.'

'You're acting like a big kid.'

He got to his feet again.

'Go on... I... I just need some time on my own.'

'But it's Christmas.'

'I *know*!' he snarled. 'Don't you think I know that?'

He took off down the dark walkway. She watched him go for a moment, but wasn't prepared to abandon him to solitary gloom, and followed him at a wary distance, the high heels she had changed into clacking as softly as they were able.

Adam dawdled towards the sound of trickling. The water-feature, normally turned off when Paradise closed for the night, was still running. He came to a halt in front of it, and waited until Fay had slipped discreetly into place at his side before speaking.

'Nobody ever sits in here,' he said, taking her hand.

'Maybe you're not allowed to,' she suggested.

'But there's a bench.'

The bench stood invitingly just behind the fronds of falling water.

He turned to look at her. She smoothed the front of his hair where his hands had mushed it, and asked him if he was OK. He nodded and calmed.

After a moment's pause, they went inside the water-feature, and sat on the bench.

'I'm fine, sorry,' Adam said. 'It's been a long crazy day, what with Luke and the shop and the restaurant. I'm just feeling a bit—'

As he fumbled for the word, Fay crammed her hand down inside his overly tight belt, and closed it around the gummy head of his penis. 'This is all that's the matter with you.' It wasn't, but he let her unbutton his trousers and pull it free.

Their lips had barely brushed, he had barely begun to tell her she was beautiful, she had barely begun to apply her tongue to his twanging banjo-string, when a white blur, dimly materialising before the falling tresses of water, emitted a demonstrative clearing of the throat.

'Fay,' Adam whispered, pulling her up, and cramming himself back in. They stood up as though the Lord Mayor had just arrived.

The white-clad figure moved unhurriedly to the right, until it appeared at the entrance to the grotto.

'What a beautiful scene,' Vincent declared.

'Look—' Adam began. 'This probably looks really bad.'

'It doesn't matter what it looks like,' said Vincent softly. He looked Adam steadily in the eyes. 'Would you mind giving us a minute, darling?'

It took Fay a moment to realise he meant her. She gathered up her bag, and slid past Vincent out of the grotto and a little distance along the walkway.

'I do apologise, Mr Beresford.' Adam's voice was hoarse with exhaustion, and weakened with futile guilt. 'We should go back to the party. I just needed a bit of space. To think, not to...'

Vincent gave a frosty little smile and continued to speak softly. 'There's something else.' He looked at his fingernails, almost nervously. 'What I'm concerned about, Adam, is that it would appear that, contrary to the express stipulations of your master-contract, you are currently employed in two separate capacities at Paradise. Would I be right?'

'It was only a temporary thing before Christmas. The thing is—'

'Print Media Books Ltd and Old Blind Possum plc.'

'Er, that's... yes.'

There was a pause, in which Adam and Vincent looked impassively at each other. If there was some way of negotiating this, it was escaping Adam, and yet Vincent appeared to be giving him the chance to work it out. Nothing came.

'I really can't tell you how much I regret this,' Vincent hardly dared whisper, 'but if the rules were not to be applied in one case, they would soon be contravened with impunity wherever we looked. Do you agree?'

Adam swallowed hard. 'I do, but—'

'So alas, may we ask you to leave the building now, and not please return? Arrangements will be made to inform your employers – both of them – and any remaining monies owing to you will of course be paid. I'm sorry to lose you, genuinely I am. But...' He tilted his head to one side a little teasingly, his lips forming into a rueful *moue*.

'Surely this can be sorted?' Adam suggested, in a faint unhopeful tone.

Vincent stood to one side, to indicate that the moment for leaving had arrived. For a second, their stares locked on to each other, unwavering, then Vincent smiled again and flicked his eyes demurely downwards and back.

Adam glanced down and saw that there was a strip of striped shirt trapped between his trouser-buttons. He stuffed it in.

Vincent gave a little smirk, which spread into another profoundly friendly smile. With a lightning movement that he would never in a month of rainy Sundays be able to account for, Adam's fist soared up from nowhere and smashed the smile into red streamers.

There was a scream somewhere from Fay as Vincent toppled backwards to the floor.

'You know what?' Adam growled, standing over the prone body. Fay's scream rose by an octave as he ground the heel of his shoe into the middle of Vincent's face. 'You can get fucked, you tramp.' His tongue released a gob of spit on the bleating head.

As he marched in black fury towards the fire-exit, Adam could hear the wounded cries of his former girlfriend mingle with the rising moans of his former employer. They were drowned, as he crashed through the door, by the panicked electronic screech of the fire-alarm.

It was still raining.

Chapter 7

The Wise I

It was a hard bitter day, but dazzled with defiant sun. The park was the only part of Gutford that seemed to have been untouched by the magic of Christmas, its low denuded trees and pond algae belonging to another cycle of life entirely. One or two elderly people strolled and stopped by the lake's edge, and there were mothers with all-road baby-buggies camped like covered wagons around the swings. Children squealed and chased each other, oblivious of the penetrating cold, warmed through with the absence of school and the imminence of Santa. A young woman put the brake on a pushchair with a slumped toddler in it, and looked up to see her elder child running towards a bench, where a dishevelled man in a sloppy grey coat sat with his elbows on his knees, propping a grey unshaven face between woollen gloves.

'Callum, come here please,' she called.

The little boy paused and stared for a second, his face full of tentative curiosity. Adam smiled at him, and was about to say something when Callum's mother pulled him sharply away.

'What have I told you...?'

You couldn't blame her. He must look a wreck. His face had gone first itchy, then sore, with dirty black stubble, and his hair had shrunk against his skull in an oily cringe of defeat. When he had first sat down, there was nobody about, but now the place had begun to fill up, it couldn't be too long before somebody reported him for acting suspiciously. Grown men didn't sit on park benches on their own.

When he got in the night before, he had left a note for Jimmy and Mirabelle saying that he wouldn't be going into work tomorrow as he felt he was coming down with something, so not to worry when he didn't get up. In the event, he had awoken at the usual time. Stale alcohol was slopping about his system, his head felt musty and desiccated, and an insistent nausea was sitting on his stomach, having inveigled its way into a succession of queasy dreams. The events of the previous evening played themselves through. He realised there would be a visit from the police at some stage, coupled with a probable arrest and Christmas in custody. Vincent's boundless philanthropy would have found its bounds. Adam tried to feel a kind of tattered pride at being the man to stand up to him, but the episode had only the squalid feel of a schoolday brawl about it. In Fay's eyes, he must now be a psychopath. She would tell the others at work tonight what a lucky escape she had had, and they would doubtless tell her that it would have been her turn next. These thoughts mouldered in an airless room that smelled overpoweringly of Luke, until Adam got up and threw the window open.

When he emerged in his T-shirt and joggers in the living-room, he was met by a scene from Christmases gone by. Before the tree, which had now been hung with crackers and little presents, Jimmy and Joanne were sitting at a side-table, poring intently over a game of cribbage. Luke had folded himself peaceably into the corner of an armchair with a book of illustrated Bible stories, in which two men in djellabas were pointing in fear at a wall, where a disembodied hand was writing something in transliterated Chaldee. A pot of tea was still warm, and a quantity of marmalade had, unprecedentedly, been decanted into a cut-crystal dish with a tiny spoon. Somewhere down below, the happy bleep of the till could be heard every few seconds. Otherwise, there was nothing but contented silence.

The contentment lasted only as long, though, as it took him to drift into the kitchen and put a slice of bread in the toaster. Joanne appeared in the doorway, with a look of beady inquiry.

'Not now, Jo,' Adam yawned.

'I want to know what's happening,' she said. 'No way are you off sick. You don't do sick.'

He rubbed his face with both hands, and let out an effortful breath.

'Adam?'

'Later, please. I need to think.' He doggedly refused to return Joanne's glare. There was an embattled silence until the toast popped. Then, pushing past his sister and taking his slice of dry toast with him, he went into the bathroom and locked the door behind him.

'Everything all right?' asked Jimmy. 'Adam looked a bit peaky to me.'

'Yes, a hundred or so units of alcohol will tend to do that,' Joanne replied, settling back to the cribbage.

Luke turned another page. There were grim-faced people ankle-deep in frogs in the street, shovelling them up on huge wooden paddles.

They heard much flushing of the toilet, followed by the opening and closing of doors, and then Adam's grey figure hurried past the open living-room doorway and down the stairs. Nobody spoke to him or commented on his going. It was a funny mood altogether for a Christmas Eve.

Adam slowly rose, and felt the combined heat of several pairs of adult female eyes watching to see what he would do next. He trudged back along the lakeside path to the park entrance, the shapeless grey coat protecting him from virtually none of the scything chill. He crossed the road and perched on the edge of a bollard on the pedestrian island. Traffic breezed past in both directions. Lorries with Christmas lights twinkling in their cabs, motorbike couriers, available minicabs, cars stuffed with kids. On their way to Paradise, no doubt. All on their way to Paradise.

All he could see in his mind's eye was Vincent's bloodied mouth, his upper lip sheared against his teeth. What possible defence could he mount against a charge of grievous bodily harm? He ought to be at home, explaining what had happened, instead of allowing Mirabelle to be taken by surprise when a pair of police officers arrived in the shop and asked to speak to him. She might have to close up while the family answered questions. He had deliberately left his phone behind, but when they tried calling it and it rang out in the bedroom, suspicions would only deepen. Most disturbingly of all, what might happen to Joanne and Luke, now that their legal guardian was about to be charged with unprovoked common assault?

The only possible solution sank into place before him. A direct appeal to Vincent, a prostrate apology. Why hadn't he brought the phone? He found enough change in his pockets to put into a public call-box, and rang the admin office. A softly spoken boy answered the phone, but when Adam asked to speak to Vincent, he was told that Mr Beresford wasn't able to come to the phone. Was he in the office, though? 'I'm afraid I can't answer that,' the voice said, and the line was cut. There was nothing else for it.

Aldo lounged sideways on the counter, leaning on his elbow, chewing mintily, and unwaveringly watching Mirabelle's every movement. She weighed out sweets, punched figures into the card-machine, refused to sell vodka to a pair of teenagers. When the flurry of business died down for a moment, she sauntered back to Aldo and tried to pop a sherbet lemon into his mouth. He raised a finger, removed his gum and rolled it into a ball. He handed it tenderly to Mirabelle and put the fizzy yellow sweet into his mouth without taking his eyes off her. The way his insolent full lips closed over it made Mirabelle want to scream with stifled desire. Instead she was holding a bit of spat-out gum, and choked off from saying anything by the next blurp of the door as Mrs Partridge ambled in. Mirabelle rolled her eyes as Aldo broke into a silent grin.

'Are you doing turkeys this year?' Mrs Partridge inquired.

'We had the three-in-one things, but you had to order it and it's too late now.'

Mrs Partridge wondered what they were.

'A turkey with a chicken and something else stuffed in it.'

'What else was in it?'

'I think it was a partridge.'

Aldo collapsed against the counter, his face screwed into a spasm of hilarity.

'A stuffed partridge?' said Mrs Partridge. 'I wish I'd known about those.'

'It might have been a pheasant actually.'

'Peasant is nicer,' Aldo put in. 'Stuffing an Italian peasant for Christmas is a very great tradition where I come from.'

'I find pheasant can be a little tasteless,' Mrs Partridge opined.

'That's the way we like her.' Aldo emitted a yelp as Mirabelle dug her nails into the back of his hand.

'Well...' Mrs Partridge looked about her with her customary doubt. 'I'll leave it for now. What time are you open till if I think of anything later?'

'Sixish,' Mirabelle replied.

'Heavens, is that all?'

Aldo opened the door to let Mrs Partridge out, and had just pulled Mirabelle over the counter by a fistful of cardigan towards his hauntingly kissable mouth when her husband appeared in the doorway behind her.

Jimmy shambled, oblivious, towards the refrigerated shelves and picked up a carton of orange-juice.

'Excuse me, Mrs Mirabelle, I thought you had a smudge on your cheek.' Aldo straightened the cardigan, all chivalrous humility. 'But it is not.'

Adam wrenched the bus-doors open with the emergency handle and jumped off into a sea of traffic. Horns barked and blared as he dodged between the cars to the pavement. He broke into a disorderly run, the coat flapping messily around him, as other people swerved out of his way. He was going to burst into Vincent's office if necessary and offer to work for nothing, pay him some compensation, let Vincent hit him, or whatever else might persuade him to drop the charges. But he had to do it before the police turned up at Jimmy and Mirabelle's.

As he tore round a corner, he banged straight into a child on a bicycle and knocked her flying. The girl began screaming blue murder. Adam yelled out an apology and kept running, but a policeman sitting in a parked squad car had seen the incident. He got out and began chasing after Adam, calling him to stop.

Adam ran faster for a few strides, then thought better of it. He pulled up and sank back against a wall.

'You could have killed that kid,' the policeman shouted at him in a fury.

'Sorry, I'm sorry.'

'What do you think you're doing anyway?'

'I'm trying to get to Paradise.'

The statement sat breathlessly in the silence between them. The policeman stared hard into Adam's beard, then reached for his radio.

'Red alert!' he barked.

Joanne followed the ringing tone into the boys' bedroom until she found the phone stuffed beneath Adam's pillow. Heaving a resigned sigh, she pressed the red phone symbol on her own phone, and sat down on the edge of the bed. The bedroom looked like a bomb had hit it, strewn as it was with piles of variously sized underwear, shirts, socks, mugs half-full of cold coffee, squashed plastic toys, and teddies slumped face down on the floor as though fallen in battle.

An envelope symbol was flashing in the corner of the phone screen. She clicked 'Menu', then 'Messaging'. Adam had one unread text. It was from somebody called Fay. 'WHAT was that about? Never seen that side of u b4, really scared, dont think i can c u again after that. Sort yrself out mr b4 u friten off evry1.'

There was a sudden angry shout from below, followed by a crash and three voices all clamouring together. Joanne rushed downstairs to the shop, where an outbreak of hostilities had erupted. She ran to the door and locked it.

A red-faced, panting Jimmy had both his hands round Aldo's neck, while Aldo tried to push him off with one hand in the middle of Jimmy's face. Mirabelle was trying to separate them.

'Don't be stupid, Jimmy.'

'Get off me, you crazy old duffer.'

'Jimmy!'

'What do you mean, you want to marry my wife?'

'She's more to me than she'll ever be to you.'

'Aldo!'

'I'll tan your hide, you crummy little Eye-tie.'

'Stop!' screamed Joanne. 'Stop, all of you.'

The trio staggered against the counter-edge, locked in combat stalemate, all yelling furiously.

'Jimmy, this isn't the way.'

'Get stuffed, you nasty old creep.'

'I'll teach you some blinking manners, you little sod.'

'Jimmy!'

Joanne picked up a 500-gram jar of pickled onions from a shelf, and dashed it to the floor. At the first attempt, it refused to break, but with the second, it produced the dull smash and instant stench that did the trick. The combatants stopped in their struggle and, breathless, released each other. Jimmy wheezed. Aldo bent over with his hands on his knees and made a retching sound in his throat. Mirabelle covered her face. There was a shamed panting silence.

'Adam's in trouble,' Joanne said.

Jimmy and Mirabelle looked at her. 'What kind of trouble?' Mirabelle asked.

'Big.'

Pushing and shoving through the horrendous crowds, Adam made it to the staff entrance. When his pass was swiped, however, it produced a rude electronic splodging noise and the security guard informed him that it had been revoked.

'I have to see Mr Beresford. Please. I worked here up until yesterday.'

The guard wordlessly shook his head and, with a massive padded glove, pushed Adam politely but firmly away from the barrier. He had a strong urge to sit down on the pavement and weep. He could go into the building through the main entrance with the ceaselessly flowing crowds, but he wouldn't be able to get up to the eleventh floor that way. The security guard watched him from the barrier, ready to stop him from doing whatever he was contemplating. Was it worth jumping the barrier and running? Probably not. He stepped forward to have another attempt at reasoning with the guard. The glove was raised again.

'Problems?' said a voice behind him.

It was Javine.

'Ah, yes. There seems to be a mix-up over my staff pass. I've been off sick today, but I needed to speak urgently to Mr Beresford.' Javine looked him over suspiciously. For God's sake, how much sicker could he look?

'VB hasn't been in today. He sustained a traumatic injury at last night's party, and had to go to hospital. First he said something fell on him, then he admitted he'd been assaulted.'

'God, that's – terrible,' Adam murmured.

'Yes it is,' Javine answered, 'but typically for him, whoever it was, he says he wants to draw a line under it.'

'A line?'

'I know. Ridiculous, isn't it? I tell you, there isn't enough love in the world to match what that man carries within him. Did you want me to swipe you in?'

'Er, no, that's OK. Look, give VB my best, will you? And have a good Christmas.'

'Sure. What did you want to see him about?'

'Oh, it'll keep.'

'And you are?'

Adam looked directly into her eyes. 'Maitland. Roger Maitland.'

She touched his arm. 'Wish you better, Roger.'

'Sauvignon?' Jimmy offered, waving a bottle towards him as Adam appeared in the living-room doorway.

'Don't mind if I do,' Adam responded, with his best Cheshire-cat beam.

'He can't have anything till he sorts himself out,' Joanne declared. 'He looks like he's been dug up.'

This was undeniably true, so Adam went and turned on the shower. In the echoing steamy warmth of the bathroom, he found himself singing. The net effect of the whole day, despite all the urgent hue-and-cry, was that nothing had happened, and there was evidently no prospect of anything happening. The realisation made him a little guilty, but not mournfully so. Life went on. If you sacked someone, in front of his partner too, you had to expect a little rage, and Vincent was reputed to be all in favour of self-expression after all. That he appeared to have overlooked having his face mashed in might be more tolerant than most people would have thought quite sane, but then it wasn't Adam's problem anymore. He was technically unemployed of course, but that could be worried about after Christmas, at which point he would break the news to the family. Something, like spring sunshine after the frost, would turn up.

In the living-room, the family sat and gazed at the lights on the tree, three sets of which flashed contrapuntally in uplifting primary colours. Luke announced that his favourites were blue and green, but wanted to know why there were no purple lights. The question was left to hang peacefully. Mirabelle had said she found the wine they were drinking a little sour, so Jimmy had rooted out from the back of the drinks cupboard a forgotten bottle of crème de noyau, and added a little of it to her glass. This improved it no end, she said.

Adam reappeared, his face looking baby-pink and shiny, his wet hair roughly combed this way and that, and wearing a clean yellow T-shirt. He shifted Luke along the sofa a foot or two, squeezed in between him and Joanne, and accepted a glass of the stone-cold wine. Mirabelle came over with a little glass ramekin of olives, to which everybody helped themselves with cocktail sticks, Luke's olive immediately dropping off and rolling away down the side of the sofa. Jimmy put on a CD of Glenn Miller tunes, which made everyone subliminally tap their feet, whether they liked the tunes or not, which nobody did.

Aldo Cottanera, who had been hanging about on the pavement outside since being asked to leave by Joanne, now dimly heard the Glenn Miller tunes start up. He gave a snort of derision, removed the bit of gum that he had been chewing so hard and fast his jaws felt like they were going into lockdown, and stuck it carefully over the Yale lock on the shop door, pressing it into the barrel as much as he could. Then he went home to help Mamma with the panettone. Standing lankly at the kitchen counter, he let the bullet-hard raisins run through his fingers into the mixture, while thoughts of Mirabelle ran out of his mind for good.

Jimmy took Joanne and Luke to the Midnight Mass later on, where an elderly vicar preached a sermon about justice, his eyes rolling up to the ceiling as he embarked on each orotund sentence and staying there, as though on the lookout for passing angels. The church, a vast Victorian edifice with the original pews and an ornate marble pulpit, was virtually full. People's breath billowed in front of them as they sang the hymns. Their frozen cheeks brushed each other when they were enjoined to give the kiss of peace. Ten-pound notes were crumpled into the offertory baskets, and at the end, everyone lustily sang 'Hark! The Herald Angels

Sing', their voices straining comically as the leaden melody climbed remorselessly out of everyone's range. Jimmy carried Luke home, the tousled sleeping head lolling against his uncle's shoulder.

When they got in, Mirabelle took a plate of radioactively hot mince-pies from the microwave, and handed them round. Jimmy poured everyone a tot of treacly brown madeira, proposing a toast to the year ahead, no matter what it may bring.

'God bless us, every one,' he concluded.

'Even Luke,' said Adam, and they laughed. Luke was still asleep.

'Especially Luke,' said Jimmy, and they clinked their glasses again.

Sometime during the night, Luke awoke and looked about in the grey blurry bedroom. Adam was making a plappering noise in his sleep like a horse. In the bit of street-light that strained through the brown curtains, Luke could see little glints of silver tinsel, the gold of gift-tags and weird shapes covered in shiny paper. He'd been.

Across the land, people woke to an iron morning, with the suggestion but not the evidence of snow in the air. It was the one day when you couldn't go out and buy something, though the occasional petrol-station was open, for cigarettes and dwindling supplies of milk. Council grit-bins had been installed at the sides of roads for residents to grit their roads if they so chose, but nobody chose. Joanne poked her head through the curtains. The traffic-lights on the corner changed from green back to amber and red, but there was no traffic. From the living-room came the distant jingle of 'Frosty the Snowman', and she could hear Luke already running riot with what sounded like a popgun.

Jimmy, dressed in a vividly patterned green-and-yellow dressing-gown, was mixing the first drink of the day. Mirabelle was also in pyjamas, broadly striped pink ones, with a loose-waisted shantung housecoat slung over them. Adam was in his torn track-bottoms and Donald Duck 'Oh yeah?' T-shirt. Most of the merry din was indeed being created by Luke, who was firing and reloading and firing his popgun cork as though he would never tire of it if he lived to be eighty. Jimmy rattled and rolled the ice-filled shaker, and poured out four brown creamy drinks into cocktail glasses, sticking a bit of broken chocolate Flake in each one.

'Brandy Alexanders all round,' he announced. Luke wanted to know what it was. 'Not for little boys,' warned Jimmy.

'Oh rubbish,' Mirabelle decided, 'it's Christmas.' She gave Luke a little taste of hers. The creamy, stunningly alcoholic drink made his face shake in a kind of comical epilepsy.

Adam hadn't bought any presents for the family at all, but Mirabelle appeared to have supplied the lack, marking several of the gift-tags from him, in tones that didn't exactly sound like him. 'Dearest Jo, with all my love at Christmas, from Adam xxx' wasn't going to fool Joanne. He received an England scarf from Jimmy and Mirabelle, a 'Gawrsh!' Goofy T-shirt from his sister, and something purporting to be from Luke, which had certainly seemingly been wrapped by Luke, and turned out to contain a box of after-dinner mints. Mirabelle disappeared into the kitchen and, before long, a smell of smoked bacon started wafting through the apartment.

Later in the morning, the doorbell rang, to a sharp tut from Mirabelle. Adam stiffened momentarily, as though from habitual guilt, but when Jimmy picked up the entryphone, it turned out to be Finlay and Jules Beaufort, a couple they had evidently met on holiday ten years ago, and whom they scarcely ever saw other than on Christmas Day, when they made the rounds of local acquaintances. The florid-faced, trilbied Finlay declined a drink as he was driving, but Jules gratefully accepted a glass of fizz. Her photo-sensitive lenses lightened in appreciation as she sipped. Luke took a shine to her and nuzzled his face into the fake fur of her coat-sleeve, inviting them to stay for Christmas.

'We can't, chucky,' Jules said, stroking his mop of curls. 'We've lots of other friends to see.'

'We only came for our annual drink,' Finlay shouted, and he and Jimmy guffawed. He went on to talk about how their company, an import business bringing in flowers and garden accessories from the Netherlands, was spiralling out of control. Jules had struggled manfully ('or whatever' – more guffaws) with running the office, but the time was coming when taking on someone to act as her right-hand man was going to be an essential. They had moved their HQ to the industrial estate on the bypass to the north of town. 'Best bit of business we've ever done. Business incentives, insurance, accessibility, the lot. It's all good.'

Jimmy excused himself. He had disliked this pair of braying goons the moment they'd foisted themselves on him and Mirabelle at Gatwick. The fortnight in the Caribbean had been punctuated by their insistence on sharing tables at breakfast, his long-winded business tales, her uninvited appearances at the hotel-room door just when Jimmy was about to take an afternoon nap. For some unfathomable reason, they had been stuck ever since with this hour-long visit on Christmas morning. He would soak in the bath until he heard them leave.

Tales of the press of business at HortiSol (Horticultural Solutions), and the inadequate coping of Jules in the office, continued to dominate the living-room talk, until Finlay announced that they'd better push on, or they'd be late for their next scheduled drink. Adam offered to see them out and, following a hasty exchange of formalities among the shoes in the downstairs hallway, concluding with a handshake and a slap on the back, was made office manager of HortiSol, starting January.

At some indeterminate point during the evening, the magic

began to coagulate into a sticky deposit. The main eating had been done, the drinking and lesser eating were still going on, there was a comedy spectacular on the TV with a studio audience howling as though in anguish, and Luke had had to be persuaded to give the popgun a rest and play with his other new toys. The central heating was on at festive levels, sending waves of swelter booming through the room. Jimmy opened up a huge round tin of chocolates, and handed them round until he couldn't keep stretching.

'What shall we do for Boxing Day?' he wondered.

There was a silence.

'Get some fresh air,' Mirabelle weakly suggested.

There were things that needed to be said that could wait until Boxing Day. It should be all right, Adam thought, especially now that he had another job, but Mirabelle in particular was unpredictable, one minute all smiles and twinkling earrings, the next full of waspish guile. It could go either way, but at least she ought to be pleased at his expulsion from Paradise. As if suddenly aware that she was in his thoughts, she looked abruptly to Adam. He gave her a serviceable smile and raised his glass. She turned back to the TV without a flicker.

Jimmy got up and went to the drinks table. There was some leftover Chablis that had lost its chill, but needed drinking. Adam and Mirabelle threw back the last of their madeira, and allowed themselves to be topped up, the last sweet brown drops tincturing the tepid white wine.

An uneasy feeling that wouldn't quite resolve itself settled over Adam.

The popgun popped.

When the following day came and Adam broke the news to Mirabelle, things didn't go well. In a sizzling rage, she threw them all out. It wasn't just that the family couldn't pay for its own upkeep on one paltry office salary, it was also the fact that, had it been anybody at all other than that pair of prats that he was going to work for, it might have been OK. But not the effing Beauforts, anyone but them. Was he *trying* to upset her?

'What's the deal?' Adam asked her, in genuine puzzlement.

Mirabelle flicked his pacifying hand off her arm, and flew into the bedroom with a resounding slam.

'What now?' said Joanne, appearing in the kitchen doorway. 'What have you said now, goofball?'

The day wore on and Mirabelle was not to be placated, not by Jimmy or anybody. He suggested, as tactfully as he could, that Adam might like to reconsider. Adam retired to the bedroom and considered the matter, before deciding that he couldn't reconsider. Joanne sided with him, but could no more speak reason to Mirabelle than Adam could. Jimmy suggested doing nothing until the dust had settled, but this was dust that would clearly only settle when Adam and the others had gone. It was a sad way to end Christmas, but then it had been Mirabelle herself, as she pointed out, who had said that they were perfectly capable of ruining it on their own.

'On *your* own, you mean,' said Adam bitterly, and another round of syncopated door-slamming ensued.

In the evening, Jimmy put his head round the bedroom door, where Adam was lying on the bed, letting Luke throw a teddy at him over and over.

'Phone for you.'

Adam went on to the landing. It was Finlay Beaufort. Jimmy had explained the little local difficulty that had flared up and he thought he could offer a solution.

So it was that, the day after Boxing Day, the family hurriedly gathered together its belongings, loaded them into a cheap hired van, and moved in with the Beauforts in the Bocks End district of town. Luke hadn't the faintest idea what was happening, which Joanne thought was probably best for the time being. She herself was unamused at the upheaval. What might Social Services have to say about it? The new address was at least nearer the school that Luke would soon be starting at, but considerably further from hers. Most alarming was that none of them knew anything about the Beauforts, other than that Mirabelle and Jimmy hated their guts. Just before the loaded van set off, Joanne cornered her in the shop.

'Why are you so mad at Adam? Is it something about Mr Beaufort? Or Mrs?'

'It wouldn't be right for me to say anything now,' Mirabelle replied. 'Please know that my love goes with you all. Try to forgive me.'

'Perhaps we would if we knew what you'd done.'

'I've asked you to leave.'

'Well, I imagine we won't forgive that, but we'll manage to forget it perhaps.'

Mirabelle kissed her on both cheeks. Joanne climbed into the cab of the removal van. Adam and Luke were sitting among the boxes in the back. Luke popped his gun, and the driver started the engine.

At an upstairs window, Jimmy appeared, waving forlornly at them through a gap in the net curtains. Mirabelle stared bleakly through the shop door. A boy on a bicycle skidded to a halt, tried the door, and was greeted by an angry hand pointing to the CLOSED sign and shooing him away. It looked like she was shooing them all away.

'Bocks End?' the driver asked Joanne.

Her eyes puddled for a second. 'Yes please.'

The driver emitted a low whistle. 'Someone's going up in the world.'

Mirabelle plodded back upstairs to where Jimmy was just opening the chocolate-tin. She crumpled into an armchair.

'They'll be back, don't you worry,' said Jimmy, rummaging through the rejected caramels.

'What have we done?' Mirabelle quailed.

'We?'

The removal van, its occupants entirely silent for the duration of the journey, wound its way out of town, superstitiously avoiding the A-roads, sauntering through the modern housing estates and on to the outer ring road. About half-a-mile beyond that, it suddenly swung right into a wide side-road called Chestnut Grove. A road-sign welcomed them to Bocks End, which was twinned with somewhere in Estonia, as evidenced by the blue-black-and-white flag that hung limply from a pole next to the entrance barrier. Here the driver stopped, and showed a printed manifest to a uniformed man in the booth. After careful scrutiny of both sides of the sheet, the gatekeeper made a phonecall, lowering his face into the receiver so that the peak of his cap came down over his nose. They were then favoured with a nod, and the barrier glided up.

Chestnut Grove was not so much a road as a community, it seemed, with large asymmetrical houses scattered sparsely amid the rolling acres of featureless green. Inflatable Santas and reindeer were mounted on roofs here and there. One house had a forest of illuminated Christmas trees on the stretch of unfenced lawn in front of it. Another boasted a Perspex cabinet containing a lifesize snow-figure made of real snow, its cheery pipe-chomping grin defying the thin sunshine outside. The driver paused at a curve in the road.

'Number nine,' he murmured ruminatively, glancing to left and right.

'I think this is it, isn't it?' Joanne suggested, pointing to the large wrought-iron figure 9 next to which they had pulled up.

Right on cue, the vast white front door was thrown open, and the Beauforts appeared on the verandah, Finlay in shades, Jules throwing her right arm up in a greeting that looked like a Nazi salute. The driver threw the van into reverse in order to back on to the two-lane driveway, pausing to allow Joanne to jump out first. As she walked towards the beaming smiles of welcome, an irrational feeling of dread foreboding came over her, which she did her best to quell. The effort succeeded just as long as it took for Finlay to pick her up under the arms with a triumphant cheer, and whirl her round.

It only took the van-driver and Adam about fifteen minutes to unload the few boxes into the hallway, and then what was billed as the 'Grand Tour' began. The house was a vast, evidently freshly built sprawl of a place, almost entirely composed of naked pine floors and sparsely adorned stark white walls. Room succeeded room as they were whisked about, Luke charging ahead of them. One of the lounges looked out, through a whole wall of sliding glass, on to a swimming-pool, the lawn sloping away behind it in a sunlit hillside. From there, they progressed to an elongated kitchen and dining-room complex, where gleaming islands of work-surface, above which hung pristine sets of copper saucepans, stretched down the middle, while a fully laid dining-table stood ready in the far distance, the sunlight refracting through capacious, bone-thin wine-glasses on eight-inch stems. In the main lounge, two distinct spaces had been created at either end, each with its own plasma TV and music-system, the acreage between them strewn with infinitely careful haphazardness with little cashmere rugs and deep-piled mats, arranged around a large organic form in pink Murano glass. Luke hurtled into a pouffe as he dashed about, and had to be brought sternly to heel by Joanne.

Upstairs was even more breathtaking. The number of bedrooms would comfortably have allowed the Beauforts to go into the hospitality business had they so decided. Nearly every room was white, but with colossal blotches of colour from large abstract paintings and ethnic bed-throws. Finlay and Jules's own room had a four-poster bed enshrouded by what looked like mosquito netting, as well as a TV corner and a drinks cabinet. They were all invited to choose bedrooms, and didn't resist the temptation to nominate rooms as far away from each other as possible. It was going to be quite an effort spreading their few possessions about in the virginal cavernous spaces but, as Jules put it, there would be time enough to work on that. Meanwhile, she and Fin would leave them in peace to settle in.

Joanne walked to the window in her chosen room and looked out over the estate. A delivery-van in the middle distance was unloading what looked like a catering banquet at the next house. She became briefly mesmerised by the complete silence, until Adam's voice behind her made her jump.

'We seem to have fallen on our feet then.'

'Why am I overwhelmed with an ominous feeling?' Joanne said.

'I'll leave you to work that one out.'

She heard his footsteps disappear along the endless landing. The two bags and one box of her own belongings were sitting in a huddle on the king-size bed. They would barely fill one drawer and a tenth of the wardrobe space. She slid open the louvred door of the closet and walked inside. A dangling cord turned on a soft yellowish light when she pulled it. She found herself sliding very slowly down the side wall until she came to rest on her haunches. She was crying bitterly.

In all their wanderings over the past few years, she had never felt so rootless as now. They had gone from one set of relatives to another, all of them equally proximate in blood, yet all of them equally remote. The interlude with Jimmy and Mirabelle had in the end turned out to be just that: another interlude. Another family that didn't really have much interest in them, only taking them in and working round them as though they were wartime evacuees, mildly resenting the extra outlay while appearing to have their welfare at heart. Adam seemed remorselessly insensitive to these patterns of shared obligation, accepting each one as it came and then moving on, and she could see Luke instinctively affecting his elder brother's stoicism. Who knew what effect all this discontinuity would have on him later? Certainly, other children went from school to school as the occupation of one or other parent determined, and didn't necessarily suffer, but not to have friends his own age, or to appear to miss them, surely wasn't healthy. It bred a little boy who could make just enough noise to assure himself of his own role as the youngest and wildest, but who was possibly even happier sitting transfixed while a faintly familiar relative read to him from the Bible. Meanwhile, she was conscious of filling the maternal vacancy, bringing up and helping educate her own brother as though they were living in a Victorian household, while her elder brother went out into the world of labour and left her to it. It was useless to say that it wasn't supposed to be like this. It just was. And Adam wasn't much in favour of dwelling on it, fearing that brooding over his lack of a traditional family might suggest occasions for distress to Luke, where none currently troubled him. In this he was right, but there were moments like the present when a minute of wounded solidarity would do them both – her and Adam – good. Why couldn't they incline towards each other now, like siblings sent by malign fortune into some sinister institutional house of care, clutching each other's hands in the dark as they prepared to face their first night under its roof?

Joanne pressed a lacy sleeve into her wet eyes. Half of grief was the recognition of its untransmissibility. For want of the sustenance of others, it fed itself. She could hear Adam advising her to 'get a grip', embarrassed at a girl's dismay, more embarrassed still at the dismay of his own sister, embarrassed most of all at his own discomfiture. She advised herself to get a grip, heedless as Alice of her own sound counsel. Her head dropped forward on her knees, her hair fell about her face. Let the crying cry itself through, and then take stock.

Time passed while she wept, then only wept a little, then didn't weep.

After a while, in the smeared twilight, she raised her gaze and looked again over the room. Who were these people whose house they had come to live in? How could they have grown so rich? At what point in the near or nearish future would she and her brothers stop living in Chestnut Grove and go on somewhere else, forgetting their present guardians altogether in a state of spiteful tranquillity elsewhere? A sudden urge to destroy at least one of the rooms in this preposterous house cheered her. The owners might go for weeks without noticing it, until one day, when they were all at work or school, Jules would happen along the landing in the midst of an empty afternoon, and peek through a half-open door on a scene of peaceful wreckage, the splintered closet doors, gouged mirrors and dishevelled bed just as they had been left on the day, this day perhaps, on which the occupant had vented her reasoned fury on them.

She stood up. This wasn't going to be easy. She was probably going to have to do it alone. Adam's manly sense of making do would blend with his equally manly inclination to wallow in unexpected luxury when it turned up. But, handled well, it wouldn't even need to be a long campaign. They could always, like it or not, go back to the shop, unlikely as that seemed.

Along the white landing, there was stillness and silence. Joanne walked with a sense of snowblind deliberation towards the distant staircase. She was conscious at some point in her passage of an image gliding past through an open door to her right. It was of Adam lying stretched out on an enormous bed in nothing but his shorts, his feet crossed at the ankles, his hands behind his head, his eyes perhaps closed, a shaft of the last sun falling across his densely haired chest and abdomen. At the top of the stairs, she paused.

At last, she could hear a sound. Somewhere downstairs, something like an electric blender whirred and stopped, then whirred again. Ice clattered into glasses. There was a little gentle laughter. After another silence, music began pouring through the house, booming but mellow, the bass amplification tingling subtly under her toes. An amused woman's voice assured the responding world that she got too hungry for dinner at eight.

Dinner was at seven, which confused Luke, who was used to having his tea much earlier than that. Nor was he particularly fond of roast partridge, although as Joanne pointed out, since he had never tried it before, how was he to know? Anyway, he didn't like it, but in no time at all, the caterers had whipped him up a little plate of bacon, spicy beans and a fried egg.

The evening otherwise wore the air of a grand banquet, with a white-gloved server pouring first white wine, then red, from sturdy crystal decanters. There was a twiddle of smoked trout on some scrambled egg with the Puligny-Montrachet, then velvety deep-green broccoli soup, then the partridge served with identically sculpted potato and pear cooked in goose fat, and a vivid orange purée of spaghetti squash, with which the ten-year-old Ducru-Beaucaillou was poured. Jules announced in a deprecating tone that they didn't normally eat so grandly. It was more in the way of a welcoming gesture to their new friends, but in any case they were technically still within the twelve days of Christmas, so what the hey. Following that, neither she nor Finlay spoke much during the dinner, but merely ate with set expressions of mild-mannered boredom, resting their knives and forks at the sides of their plates while they negotiated each mouthful. Occasionally, Adam and Joanne caught each other's gaze, but quickly averted it, as though in fear of succumbing to giggles. Luke caught the reverential mood, managed a couple of sips of the white wine, and then began to slump slowly in his chair.

Joanne felt increasingly uneasy. The whole scene, with its battalions of cutlery and politely soundless chewing, had an air of dented elegance. She imagined the Beauforts happily made do with improvised sandwiches and Indian deliveries most of the time. She was glad there was no conversation, for fear her thinly worn patience might have emerged in waspish evasions, but the sepulchral silence felt like mourning. To counterbalance her discontent, the food was exquisite, and a wine that tasted of molten butter, followed by one that seemed to suggest iron-clad bushels of black cherries, helped smooth her mood. Fate was neither wholly malign, nor wholly kind. To Adam, the entire outcome of the fracas in Paradise, which now seemed about six months ago, served to prove nothing at all about Fate, only that if you just went on swirling the pan, eventually you would see the flash of gold.

With Luke more or less horizontal in his seat, Joanne excused them both while she went and put him to bed. The room he had chosen was at the opposite end of the landing to hers, on a projecting corner of the house looking directly over the illuminated swimming-pool. Adam had put all his toys in neat concentric semicircles on a low table, where they stood untouched. Joanne watched him brush his teeth in the en-suite bathroom, then left him to put on his pyjamas. From the window, she saw a naked man in the next house drift up to his own window and close the curtains. She tilted the slats of the wooden blinds. When he got into the large white bed, Luke looked as tiny in it as a single shrimp on a dinner-plate. He pulled the cover up over half his face the way he liked it, and closed his eyes beatifically to receive Joanne's kiss on his forehead.

'We don't like it here, do we?' she whispered, as though there were someone standing just behind her. Luke looked nonplussed. 'I mean, it'll do for now, but we wouldn't want to stay here.'

'Why?' Luke asked, in a timorous quail.

'It's just a bit – strange. We'll see what happens next anyway. Don't worry about it.'

She turned off the light as she left, and the white glare gave way to the creamy tinge of the lights from the swimming-pool below. Luke's messy head turned against the pillow.

Downstairs, the chocolate soufflés were just coming in.

Finlay and Jules had disappeared by the time the others had got up the next morning. There was a note on the kitchen table inviting everybody to help themselves to whatever they wanted. Adam looked out over the garden for a second, decided that the swimming-pool, even in late December, looked too enticing to ignore, and went off in search of a bathroom.

Luke was unusually reticent, looking with suspicion at a bowl of cornflakes instead of crunching them hungrily down. Joanne tried to coax some explanation out of him. After much evasion, he reluctantly mumbled that he thought the house was haunted. Joanne reassured him that it couldn't possibly be, that it wasn't an old enough house, but he wasn't to be persuaded. He didn't appear to have seen or heard anything untoward. It was only that he had had a feeling that had stopped him from sleeping, and then when he did sleep, he had a bad dream. Joanne suggested that was perhaps to be expected during the first night in a new place, it would all be different tonight, suppressing the pertinent news that she had had a bad dream too.

The bad dream had played itself out in bilious slow-motion, a narrative in which the three of them were stranded in a vast featureless wheatfield, surrounded on all sides by a war-zone. They could see stretcher-bearers carrying the hideously wounded and dead from the fray towards an ambulance in the form of a double-decker bus, in front of which Finlay Beaufort, wearing a general's cap, was apparently ticking off their names on a checklist. Luke was mewling in horror. While his sister and brother tried to shield his eyes from the calamity, he kept sweeping their hands away, as though intent on witnessing it. As each stretcher was carried on to the ambulance-bus, there would be another volley of gunfire to their left or right, more screams would go up, and ragged bloodied arms would wave feebly for help through the windblown wheat. Perhaps Luke's cries, which continued to peal through Joanne's head as she awoke in a state of tremor, really had sounded from somewhere else in the house, where his own malevolent dream – something about puppets coming alive – had shaken him awake.

Later in the day, hearing the front door open and admit a babel of foreign voices, Joanne ran down to the hallway and found four women with vacuum-cleaners, mops and squeegees confronting her. Surprised in his bedroom by the entry of one of the cleaners, Adam came downstairs too with Luke, and the three of them took refuge on a large right-angled sofa while the drone of vacuuming resounded through the house. None of them found anything to say in the stillness of the lounge. Luke pointed wordlessly at their distended reflection in a convex mirror above the fireplace, in which they looked, huddled close on the sofa, like the three luckless survivors of a shipwreck, cast adrift on an open white ocean. In time, the cleaners came and vacuumed around them, never meeting their glances, occasionally murmuring something that sounded contemptuous. Glass shelves were polished, mirrors buffed and a tiny white vase of fresh snowdrops was placed on the mantelpiece.

'This is beyond weird,' Joanne declared.

'What's weird about cleaners?' retorted Adam, but when he went back up to his room, he found that nearly everything he owned had been tidily rearranged in some way, his toothbrush, razor and comb arranged in a fan position on a flannel, his discarded socks lined up in an orderly row like privates on parade, his dressing-gown hung in prudent symmetry on a coat-hanger. He half-expected to find a mint on his pillow, and the half that hadn't expected it was duly shocked to find one there.

In the kitchen, Joanne stood in front of the gently purring dishwasher, watching its digital display flash up changing temperatures and times. She wanted to kick it in and flood the kitchen.

New Year's Eve came and went. The Beauforts announced they would be having a few friends over, hoped things wouldn't get too wild. In the event, three guests turned up, a nervous young couple with rhyming names and equally rhyming scratchy bits of beard, and a large florid-faced woman. The former ran a party-organising company, while the woman was an opera-singer. They were among HortiSol's most valued customers. At an early stage in the evening, the singer was enjoined to perform, and threw her vigorous contralto into an unaccompanied aria, her upper body wafting this way and that, her gaze fixed in the distance, as though she were appearing before an audience of thousands. Luke's jaw slowly dropped at the intricately deafening sound that was emerging from her moist wobbling lips. At the end, after a pause to make sure it was the end, everybody applauded.

'Was that Beethoven?' Jules asked in a stunned tone.

'"Una Voce Poco Fa" from *The Barber of Seville*,' replied the singer, with a gracious smile. 'Rossini.'

Then she and the men left, and Finlay put on a jazz CD at incautious volume. Jules shrieked 'Party!' and jangled her braceleted arms. There was some initial awkwardness, but then everybody started dancing, Adam and Joanne non-committally half-turning this way and that, while the Beauforts rattled and shook themselves as though the years were dropping away. Catching the party mood, Luke jumped up on one of the white sofas, bouncing and cheering giddily. When they spotted anybody wandering past outside, they ran to the windows and waved like hostages trying to attract attention. Nobody waved back.

Champagne was popped at regular intervals as the music throbbed ever louder. Luke's little sip of the bubbly drew his best guttural roar from him. The others all drank it until they could face it no longer, Finlay's paunch visibly inflating under the onslaught of gas, while Joanne eventually threw most of hers up into a downstairs toilet. A tiny phone in the hallway flashed and warbled over and over, as it took unheard greetings from around the country. In a game of dare, Jules and Adam threw themselves half-undressed into the swimming-pool, and returned dripping-wet into the lounge just in time for the big TV countdown, in which a line-up of gnarled resuscitated pop legends led the country in singing 'Auld Lang Syne'. All agreed it was the best New Year's Eve they'd had in years, staggering in laughter to their respective five bedrooms at around two in the morning, the adults falling into an alcohol sleep sound enough that only Joanne heard the blood-freezing screech two hours later, of Luke waking from the tangles of the evil puppets.

Soon after, Adam began working in the HortiSol office. The job was as dull as he had expected, and involved nothing more demanding than maintaining a database, a customer mailing list and an online ordering system – all of which were variously malfunctional – and, once in a blue moon, dealing with a phonecall. All processing of the flowers themselves was dealt with by Jules, who often came charging into the shabby admin office bearing a bunch of some dripping pink things, which were sufficiently strong and sweet-smelling to bestow a pungent cloud over the whole room, so that Adam imagined that he could smell it on his clothes. Mrs Clarke, a sour-faced woman in primary-coloured makeup and a permanent red headscarf, like an embittered Claudia Cardinale, did the accounts, occasionally bowling an unfathomable query in Adam's direction, but not much minding either way whether he solved it. As far as he could tell, which wasn't far, the company didn't appear to be making money. It enjoyed a brisk trade furnishing business receptions in local hotels, and could boast a bedrock of loyal customers who bought mail-order for the sacramental moments in their lives – alternately celebrating and mourning in floral style – but the bulk was one-off orders from people who never came back, their relationships repaired or their siblings' graduations marked with a bunch or bouquet in a gesture that, once enacted, it would have been tasteless monomania to reiterate.

Taped to the wall in the office was a yellowing poster that explained the symbolic meanings of the various shades of roses, so that anybody wondering how to express their feelings on closing a business deal, being proud of their offspring, or desiring to let another person know they were more beautiful than they realised, could be directed respectively to the peach, orange or deep burgundy blooms, provided they were currently in stock. If not, as Jules advised, you couldn't go wrong with white.

People who weren't happy with the products or service were always acutely disgruntled, precisely because the flowers had been intended to mark a special moment, which was now forever ruined. Adam spent much of his time composing delicate emails, once again offering the company's condolences for a loss, or happiness at a success, while also profoundly regretting the inadequacy of the customer experience on this occasion and offering them a voucher. Sometimes he was invited to imagine how he would feel if his wedding day had been sullied by the non-appearance of the bridesmaids' nosegays. A company bidding for a contract, while not directly blaming their failure to secure it on the absence of the table decorations they had ordered, nonetheless felt that the outcome hadn't been helped by their having to fill in with sprays of dried twigs. Had Adam himself ever known bereavement? wondered one email. If so, he would surely see that anything less than a full refund would amount to the rubbing of salt into this bitterest of wounds. Attempting to reply to the woman, he found himself staring at the blank screen on to which his emollient words needed pouring, and found that they all remained obstinately choked up, like logs in a river, inside his chest. He went into the toilet and dabbed at pink eyes with a paper towel.

Finlay only seldom came into the office, and when he did, didn't say much. He would sit in his partitioned cubicle and look at a printout, smoking a furtive cigarillo with an air of resignation. From time to time, he suffered from gout, and came hopping into the office on one leg and a stick, the suggestion of Long John Silver accentuated by his wildly disarranged hair and an aroma of lunchtime drinking. Adam helped him from the car into the office, where his voluminous swinging coat swept papers to the floor as he stumbled through. Finlay described the pain as a vicious torture such as nobody should have to undergo. The quack had suggested there were certain foods he ought to avoid, but had tended not to confirm Jules's unshakable conviction that excessive alcohol was to blame. He always had it after Christmas, it was true, but if anybody was expecting him to give up drink, they may as well wait for Hell to freeze over. Adam assured him that that was the true fighting spirit. Mrs Clarke cleared her throat meaningfully.

The more printouts were stared at, the more complaints received and refunds negotiated, the more it became clear that HortiSol was not the runaway success of the Beauforts' wishful imaginations, but an unwieldy concern that had overreached itself and was in dire need of restructuring. Adam's wages were reasonably generous for the kind of job he was doing, but not really enough to maintain any sort of life, once Joanne and Luke had been allowed for. Before January was out, he found himself discreetly opening another window on the computer to scan the local employment ads. He made calls on his mobile in the toilet, and managed to arrange a couple of interviews. His leaving work early raised the thickly pencilled black eyebrows of Mrs Clarke, but she had many another axe to grind than Adam.

An interview at a social-care centre didn't go well. A man in bifocals went as critically through Adam's hastily improvised CV as though it were a piece of medieval exegesis, reading out a line here and there, weighing the words and looking quizzically up at him to invite his own commentary. He hadn't quite the secure foundation in pastoral care that the centre required, had he? Filling his chest with enough lung-power to tell a properly monstrous lie, Adam said that he had had first-hand experience of seeing the terrible damage that drug addiction could do, especially among prisoners, whom he had observed while visiting a delinquent relative who was serving time for possession of an unlicensed firearm. The interviewer blinked his incredulity. He took off his glasses and wiped them thoughtfully with his handkerchief. Which prison was that? Adam bit his lip, and let his eyes wander to a desk calendar where a young mother was cradling a newborn baby in her arms. He couldn't remember the name exactly, but it might have been Mothersville or Motherwell?

The man blinked again. 'Do you mean Barlinnie?'

'Mmmm...' Adam pretended to reflect. 'No.'

At the next interview, he was asked to produce his driving licence. The interviewer checked carefully that the face on the card matched Adam's own, and then reminded him that customers expected to be addressed with the utmost courtesy. Adam assured him that long experience of dealing with the public meant he was good at courtesy.

That weekend, he began work as a night-time car-park attendant at the Violet Star, a boutique hotel in a regeneration area in the centre of Gutford. The entrance was at the rear. Adam's job was to open the car doors to let the passengers out as they drew up, hand them to the commissionaire to take charge of their bags, and valet-park the car for them in the underground car-park. Not many people arrived after 10pm, when Adam's shift started, but those who did were usually tired enough to hand a hefty gratuity to a young man in a silver-buttoned jacket.

Some of the cars were spotless and scentless inside, though most were a fusty amalgam of stale cologne and foot-odour, the miasma of long bickering hours on motorways still pervading the interiors. Adam rolled the windows down as he drove the vehicles into the oily murk of the basement, aligning them beautifully between the white lines, sticking the numbered ticket on the inside of the windscreen. Sometimes he couldn't resist opening the glove-compartments before he got out. They often told a story, through dog-eared restaurant guides, battered CD cases, packets of condoms, half-eaten tubs of pasta salad. He would sit in the best cars for minutes, settling himself into expensive leather upholstery, closing his fist on the gearstick, turning the radio on and off. Was there any more satisfying sense of ownership than sitting in the driver's seat of a car, whether it was your car or not?

Luke sat at the back of a big gaily painted classroom next to another new boy. They looked shyly at each other as he first took his seat, saying nothing even though the teacher had formally introduced them. The other boy's name was Jordan.

They listened to the lesson as well as they could through the hubbub of other voices. It was about colours. Everything was a different colour, and the colours themselves were different colours. You could mix colours together and they made a different colour. Then they were all allowed to paint sheets of paper different colours, mixing them to see what colours they went. Jordan looked daft in his little plastic apron, but so did Luke. Some of the other boys splashed paint on each other's aprons till the teacher shouted at them to stop. The girls ignored them, and painted neatly. Luke wanted to paint neatly too, but rapidly got the inkling that only girls did that.

At break-time, he dawdled into the playground and watched the running and screaming and play-acting. A half-crumpled red ball flew back and forth over the heads. At one point, it skidded towards him, and the other boys hollered at him to kick it back, but he didn't know how to. When he turned away in embarrassment, Jordan was standing next to him.

'Do you not like football either?' Jordan said.

'Sometimes,' Luke lied.

Back in the classroom, there was a story about Robin Hood.

The teacher held up the book for them to see the pictures. Luke just caught sight of a boy in a silly green hat, before the other heads crowded in.

Lunchtime was the best bit of the day. He and Jordan sat together and ate their cheeseburgers and beans, both getting messy-faced, looking at each other complicitly as they slurped their orange noisily through stripy straws.

Only when Jules came to collect him in the car at half-past three did Luke discover that someone had put baked beans in his jacket pocket.

One fine evening, Adam was standing chewing the fat with the commissionaire, Mr Pritchard, when a red Alfa Romeo drew up. There was some kind of function going on in the Violet Star, and the earlier part of the evening, before his shift, had evidently been 'manic'. The odd car was still drifting in, though. He stood to attention and squared his shoulders as he always did when somebody drove up. There was only one person in the car. As it glided to a halt, he nipped round to the driver's door and opened it, the word 'Sir' dying on his lips as the occupant got out.

For a split-second, it looked as though Vincent might not recognise Adam, but the double-take confirmed his identity. Adam tried to meet his eyes but couldn't. Nor would Vincent quite stand sufficiently aside to let him get into the car.

'I, er – guess I – owe you a major apology,' Adam stuttered. 'Obviously.'

'Would I ever have received it had it not been for this chance encounter?' Vincent spoke softly, without a trace of resentment, even faintly rueful himself.

Adam swallowed, but couldn't negotiate the rhetorical question. Mr Pritchard was watching this mysterious encounter from the steps. The stalemate must seem incriminating.

'Shall I—?' Adam asked, nodding down towards the car.

'Come back, why don't you?' Vincent whispered. 'We can sort

something out. It surely has to be better than parking other people's cars.'

'I can't. It's good of you.'

'Were there *more* guilty secrets to be discovered?'

'No no. I just – I can't. It doesn't feel right.'

Vincent's hand moved tentatively towards Adam's lapel, and brushed away a speck. 'I don't think I understand,' he said. 'But anyway.' He tittered. 'Great hat.'

Then, in a lightning swirl towards the steps, he was gone, disappearing through the revolving door that Mr Pritchard set spinning for him.

Adam, suddenly full of muted angry embarrassment, got into the car, in the process knocking his head against the side of the roof, and sending the hat, which he had forgotten to take off, rolling across the ground.

Chapter 8

The Wise II

On a dazzling frosty morning in February, on the forecourt of Paradise, a gathering of local and national media assembled to hear a major announcement. Paradise was growing, specifically into a Victorian residential area on its eastern flank, where owner-occupiers had had no hesitation in accepting the generous purchase offers to move out. Journalists had gone about assiduously knocking on doors, hoping to find at least one elderly widow whose family had lived there since before the first Boer War, and whom wild horses wouldn't drag away, not for all the tea in China. In the event, there was no shortage of elderly widows, but they were only too happy to make way for the extension. Where the expected hopeless tenacity should have been, there was instead unfettered jubilation. Ninety-year-old Lilian Sharp was photographed in front of the main entrance, holding up her offer letter in a patched-up mitten, with a beam that said, 'What took you so long?'

Vincent Beresford joined the conference by video-link from Beijing, where some other iron was in the fire, his huge snow-white face purring almost inaudibly about dreams and opportunity. He wasn't able to take questions as the piece had been recorded, leaving his Gutford team to field the hail of queries about budgets and planning permission. Put simply, it turned out that Paradise had been a victim of its own early success. Its style was in danger of being cramped. A new multiplex cinema and twenty-lane bowling-alley would be among the prestige fixtures of the extension. But that was not all. A cyber-café on a gigantic scale would offer unrivalled connection speeds and a menu of the world's best coffees, and once you had drunk a tall cinnamon latte and checked your emails, what better way to move up through the gears than with all the fun of the fair? There were plans for a Ferris-wheel, a speedway track and more, the *pièce de résistance* a switchback with vertical drops designed by an award-winning company that had built rollercoasters around the world, from the wild west to the mysterious east, and never had a fatality.

A CGI projection of the new development was shown on the screen. As the viewpoint whirled about, the scene changed from one of dereliction to gleaming plenty, soaring buildings and fairground rides shot up and, at the end, the place flooded with people. The original section was now to be renamed Paradise Palace, while the extension was to be Paradise Park, and Gutford Borough Council had agreed to rename the approach-road, formerly Trinity Street, Paradise Way. 'Everybody's going to Paradise,' the final caption insisted. 'Are YOU?'

In the admin office, Javine tried to raise Vincent on the phone to report on the positive energy that the media call had generated, but found his message-folder was full. She tweeted instead. Moments later, a discreet bleep in Vincent's pocket was noticed only by the woman behind him in the long gliding line. Turning their heads almost furtively to their left, they moved past a refrigerated glass casket, in which an insensate figure, its pumpkin-coloured head alone visible, appeared tucked up in bed under a hammer-and-sickle blanket.

'Problems.' A voice arrived at the side of her desk.

'What problems?' Javine snapped. 'This isn't a problems day.'

It was Bellenor Hatherley, financial director. 'It is now. Can we go somewhere?'

Javine motioned to the meeting-room. They closed the door and stood immediately behind it, their heads visible to the rest of the office-staff, as though they had gone in there to settle, more or less amicably, the issue of a double-dating boyfriend.

'The auditors are pulling out,' said Bellenor.

'And...?'

'They're taking their audit report with them.'

'I beg your pardon?'

Bellenor swept the letter she was holding up in front of her face. '"It has come subsequently to our notice that the income and expenditure accounts, as presented and annotated, contain at least one and perhaps more untrue statements of material fact. In light of this eventuality, Bard McLintock's compliance coordinator has had no alternative but to suspend and temporarily withdraw its audit report, pending the satisfactory resolution of the aforesaid matter or matters."'

'So... they can be satisfactorily resolved, I'm sure,' said Javine.

'They could have been, had this letter of January 5th been actioned at the time.' Bellenor pointed to to the date. 'As it is, it contained a deadline of January 31st, which appears to have come and gone without so much as a squeak from VB. I've just taken a phonecall from Bard to say they've resigned and rescinded the audit report.'

'Why the hell didn't you action this sooner?'

'I might have done,' Bellenor replied, 'had I not just read this letter for the first time five minutes ago. It was in VB's personal file.'

'You had no *right* to go into that personal file.' Javine's voice was beginning its customary ascent through the semitones under provocation.

'I'm well aware of that,' Bellenor assured her, grimly. 'However, if I hadn't, we would have continued to know nothing about it until the financial services authorities arrived mob-handed.'

Javine thought for a second. She hated dealing with financial people talking financialese. 'What are these incorrect facts anyway?'

'Who knows?' Bellenor was gruesomely cheerful. 'I'll make a start now on seeing whether I can identify them, but it might be quicker to see whether you can persuade the organ-grinder to speak to the chief money monkey.' Javine raised an eyebrow. 'Me!'

'He's in China.'

'Yes, I know. Bitterly cold at this time of year, I believe, but beginning to look like a tempting destination for a long holiday. Unless, of course, you'd prefer a long Holloway?'

Javine waved a hand in dismissal, a tic she had unconsciously picked up from Vincent. 'This can't have any implications for us.'

'You'd think not, wouldn't you? But alas, you've signed off the accounts at every stage. As indeed have I. Still, as you almost said, there'll be some perfectly simple explanation for it all.' And with that, Bellenor snatched open the door again, and swept out through the admin office.

One of the boys, his big innocent eyes fixed on Javine, his jaws fully occupied with a sinewy wedge of pork pie, watched her lost-looking return to her desk. Very carefully, so as not to make any sound, he let the front legs of his chair resume contact with the floor, and sat up straight. He dropped the paper bag, without screwing it up, silently into his bin.

Javine tried the phone again. Then she tweeted again. 'Call if you would VB? Something's come up.'

It wasn't only Luke who had a new schoolfriend. Joanne had found herself being volubly applauded for a comment she made about *Antony and Cleopatra* in English class. Her admirer was a boy with a mass of jet-black curls spilling asymmetrically over his face. He wore a short scarf wrapped many times around his slender neck, hi-top trainers and grip-tight jeans. When she ventured another comment a little later, amid the apathetic silence of the group, the boy clicked his fingers and pointed them at her in a gun-shape.

'Do you want to say something, Marlow?' the teacher asked.

'The lady's saying it,' he replied. 'Listen up.'

They found each other at lunchtime as they were walking out

of the main building, and went and sat on a grassy bank overlooking the running-track.

'Marlow?' Joanne confirmed.

'That's me. Not Marly please, if you like your teeth,' the boy replied. 'I love what you're wearing,' he added, nodding at Joanne's sweat-top. He took a small tub of guacamole and some nachos out of his bag.

'And I love what you're eating,' Joanne said. 'Some potato salad with that?'

They shared their lunches, and Marlow kept a keen appraising eye on Joanne as they ate. Although she knew nothing about him, the attention didn't make her in the least uncomfortable. She was astonished to find herself smiling coyly at him. He shoved some of the collapsing hair back on top of his head, from where it subsided unhurriedly back down again.

'So – what you into?' Marlow said.

'Er, I'm not really in the market for a relationship,' Joanne mumbled. 'Is that what you mean?'

Marlow gave a big hearty laugh, his shoulders shaking, his elbows tensing against his sides with the hilarity of the suggestion. 'It's sweet that you would think that, honey,' he said. 'I don't mind being mistaken for straight.'

'Well, I knew that, obviously, I was just clarifying things.'

'Course you were, babe.' Marlow gave her a tweak on the cheek. 'Clarifying.'

'Probably don't tweak me on the cheek, if you like your teeth.'

'That must mean you like me. Yes!' Marlow punched the air, and pushed some of his hair up again.

'Yep. And you have beautiful hair,' said Joanne, feeling entirely excited and safe with him.

It turned out that what Marlow liked most of all about what Joanne had said in class was that she had an opinion at all. It was usually only him who spoke up, and the others all groaned and accused him of being too gay. Joanne wondered why the teachers didn't stop that sort of talk, but it was probably that they realised it wasn't about sexuality as such, it was more like saying somebody was a bit wet or soppy. The fact that they happened to be actually gay as well wasn't anything to do with it.

'That's totally unacceptable crap,' said Joanne. 'You do realise that, don't you?'

Marlow sniggered. 'Yeah, but what you gonna do?'

In the afternoon, they had to separate as Marlow went into a French class, and Joanne had Social History. But at the close of the school day, she was shown where the pigeonholes were, and discovered there was a single item in the Y box. It was a folded note on which was scribbled, 'We didn't do mobes. Here's mine.' Underneath the number was written, 'Your new best friend, Marlow Haines.'

Joanne texted him her number, and received an immediate bleep back, 'Got it', followed by a kissing smiley. She walked out under the frozen indigo sky of late afternoon, and felt ashamed of herself for recently crying in a wardrobe.

Gradually, the intermeshing patterns of their days coalesced. Adam came in at dawn from the Violet Star, slept a little, then went and did his day at the HortiSol office. About once a week, or a little less often, Finlay came into the office, sometimes yawing off the bad foot like a catamaran in a high gale, sometimes only limping a little. Jules took Luke to his school nearby each morning and collected him each afternoon. In between times, he and Jordan McLeish were inseparable. Jordan introduced Luke to his older sisters, Alicia and Carmel Obayomi, but the sisters only examined their purple fingernails and rolled their eyes. They naturally had no interest in silly little boys. 'Do one,' said one of them to Jordan. Luke didn't know whether it was Carmel or Alicia who said it, and had no idea what it was Jordan was supposed to do.

Joanne's bus-ride to her school took about three-quarters of an hour in the mornings, a little less coming back. She made other friends, and one or two boys had a go at coming on to her, but there was nobody to compare to Marlow, her association with whom was enough to deter all but the most desperate of the comers-on.

In the evenings, they all sat together for dinner, which was served three nights a week by the caterers. The awkwardness of the first evening was soon laid aside, as everybody discovered they had too many things they wanted to tell the others to keep silent. Not long after nine, Luke was put to bed, Adam went off to the Violet Star, and Joanne settled to texting Marlow, while the Beauforts, with a remote control each at their disposal, flicked chaotically between TV channels. And, because he intimated he had grown too big to be afraid of daft puppets that were only in his head, even Luke's nightmares stopped.

One evening, at Jules's suggestion, Joanne had Marlow over to dinner. He lived not far away from Chestnut Grove, and thought it amusing that Joanne and her family should have ended up among what he called the 'poshos'. She assured him there was nothing posh about the Beauforts, an estimation that he was only too happy to endorse immediately upon setting foot in the hallway, picking up a green glass mermaid ornament and making a constipated face.

Jules appeared.

'Lovely,' he told her, putting the ornament carefully back. She welcomed him with a kiss on both cheeks, calling him Marvin, and ushered them into the main lounge, where a Schumann piano CD was playing.

'Mmm, white,' Marlow purred. 'Who'd have thought?'

'Don't be sour,' Joanne whispered, as Jules hurried out to see how the caterers were getting on.

'How else will the salad get dressed?'

They sat side by side on the sofa, and listened momentarily to the music. Finlay put his head round the door, grumped a 'Hello' and disappeared again, which made Joanne and Marlow snigger. Then Luke charged in, wearing his best long trousers and braces. He stopped in his tracks at the sight of Marlow, who nodded demurely at him. There was a pointless hiatus, then all three of them burst out laughing.

'You're fun,' Marlow said, chucking Luke under the chin. Luke gave his guttural cheer, and ran away to find a toy.

Joanne took off the tentative piano music and rummaged through the CDs to find something livelier. The first bars of a sixties soul album were just ringing out when the door opened yet again. Luke came hurtling back in, ahead of Adam.

'Calm it, mister!' he said.

'This is my other brother, Adam,' said Joanne.

'Hey, Marly.' Adam put out his hand, and Marlow stood up. 'I heard you're the coolest dude at St Wilfrid's, right?'

Marlow put out his hand. His head dropped and his hair fell forward. For the first time in their short acquaintance, Joanne saw him miss a beat. He said something that came out in a voiceless whisper.

Adam crossed to the long white sideboard. 'There were meant to be some nibbles here. I'll see what's happened to them.'

As he left the room, Marlow turned to Joanne with an open-mouthed gape. 'Darling, I'm in love.'

'No you aren't,' Joanne said firmly. 'You *really* aren't. Marlow!'

He sank back on the sofa on comic wobbly knees.

'Stop it now!'

'Too late,' he whimpered, and subsided backwards, as though suddenly faint. Seeing that a game was in hand, the cheering Luke took a flying leap and landed on his hyperventilating chest. 'Agh! Guess what, Luke? I ain't ever going home.'

Conversation flowed in spurts around occasional snagging points over dinner. Jules asked Marlow what he wanted to study at university. He hadn't thought about it, but thought Joanne should do English or philosophy. Finlay poured scorn on those pointless endeavours and said that computers were where the money was. Marlow stifled a theatrical yawn. Luke had problems with his venison steak, which he had been tricked into believing would be like a burger, but so wasn't. Adam relieved him of it, while a plate of bacon and eggs was prepared. Jules asked whether everyone liked the table display, which involved winter-white gerberas and calla lilies against a spiky chive-like backing, one of HortiSol's seasonal specialities. Marlow said he could understand how some people, not him obviously, might find the smell a little sickly, especially while they were eating. Everyone looked at the staring white flowers in silence, becoming aware of their overpowering scent for the first time. Finlay said he was a hard man to please. 'Got that right,' said Marlow, colouring up vividly when Adam rewarded his remark with an appreciative smirk.

As dinner drew to a close, Luke was disinclined to go to bed. It was Friday after all. Adam spoke sternly to him, but had to leave for work. If he heard when he got back in the morning that Luke had acted up, there would be trouble. Luke turned his head aside haughtily.

In the kitchen, where Finlay and Jules had gone to tip the caterers and thank them for another successful evening, notwithstanding Luke's rebellious appetite, Finlay said to Jules, 'Do you think our friend Marly is a bit of a fondant fancy?'

'What does that mean?' Jules was always irritated by these bits of banter.

'Homo.'

'How should I know? He might just have a flamboyant manner. What does it matter anyway?'

'Flamboyant manner! He's as camp as Christmas.'

'So what?' Jules tutted. 'You should broaden your horizons. Honestly!' she added to one of the catering staff. 'This is the man who made a living out of flower-arranging.'

With Luke packed off to bed, Marlow sat and drank some

more wine with Joanne, but there was a definite tension in the atmosphere. He broke what was becoming a mildly depressing silence by saying, 'It's not like I'm going to do anything. I can see he's straight.'

'Marlow, you're fourteen,' Joanne reminded him.

'So? Am I not a man and a brother?' He fluttered his eyelids. She couldn't really disapprove of him, but she didn't want to see him hurt.

A short while later, he announced he had to go, and Joanne went out into the hallway to call a taxi. The telephone was hidden on a shelf in a little recess. She called the taxi company and waited while the phone rang. There were a couple of stamped envelopes on the shelf, propped behind the vase, waiting to go in the post. The one in front was addressed to one of HortiSol's suppliers. She absently pulled it forward to expose the address on the bulging larger envelope behind it. It was addressed to Mrs Mirabelle Blake.

Joanne's heart stopped.

A letter from Luke's school assured everyone that he had settled in very well, had made some friends, and was a very well-behaved pupil who showed 'some academic promise'. When Adam read the letter out, Luke joined in the beams of complaisant satisfaction, as though the subject of the letter were somebody else entirely.

In the weeks to come, partly to humour him and partly to placate him, Joanne gave Marlow a picture of Adam and her taken at the beach last year by Auntie Mary, in which her brother was wearing only a pair of tiger-striped swim-shorts. She didn't mind at all when Marlow carefully cut her own image out of the picture, leaving only the sun-bronzed Adam with his arm extending around some unknown back. He took to slipping the picture between the leaves of whatever book they were studying in class, so that, glancing up while her mind stumbled over a problem, she would find Marlow gazing with filmy eyes into *Factorising Quadratic Equations*. He'd got it bad. One day, doubtless, he'd have a real boyfriend, whose heart he would unintentionally shatter, but for the time being, let him have a teenage crush on her brother.

'This can only end, you realise, in the greatest unhappiness,' she teased him, as they were walking home from school one afternoon through clumps of roadside daffodils.

'As long as it's the greatest *something*.'

'Isn't there anybody at school you fancy? What about Dylan?'

'Oh, hon, it's sweet you would think of him. He only just quit believing in Father Christmas. And what makes him spring to mind after all? Are we speaking from the depths of our own unacknowledged desire?'

'No way,' Joanne said. 'Don't psychoanalyse me.'

'Ha, the raw nerve exposed. Joanne Young, you are SO in love with Dylan Sanford.'

'I am NOT.'

'The more you deny it, the more screamingly obvious it becomes. Do you want to brush his messy hair for him, sweetheart?'

'Er, messy what? Pot. Kettle.' She grabbed a handful of Marlow's tumbling hair and shook his head by it. 'Anyway, you denied it too. So that must make two of us.'

'Oh my God, we'll have to fight to the death over him.' Marlow closed a strangulating arm around her neck from behind.

'There is only one winner,' Joanne cried.

'*Absolument*.'

Locked in a mutual grip, they stumbled over the pavement and fell among the daffodils, shrieking with laughter.

A boy wheeling his bicycle past glanced contemptuously over at them. 'That's just dumb,' he said. It was Dylan Sanford.

Marlow got up and ran after him. 'Dylan, we both love you. Please tell us, who do you like the most?'

Dylan jerked the front wheel of his bike at Marlow. 'Fuck off, Haines, you gayer.'

Marlow imitated the face of a shocked smiley. 'Dylan!'

Joanne, still lying on the grass, watched the whole pantomime with deep appreciation and glee. There was some tepid spring sunshine, she could feel it on her calves, and see it painting a glisten on Marlow's coal-black fountain of hair. These were the moments she knew she would look back on with the fondest heartache when their lives had all curdled and separated like milk. It was a strange intimation, looking forward to the way you would one day look back, but she realised she had always done it. It betrayed an affinity with bleakness that she could live with for now, but that might one day become a drag-anchor, failing to connect her to what was at hand, but letting her bob about in the selfish currents.

Marlow came and stood over her, one bright orange trainer on either side of her, clashing with the daffodils. She clutched both his ankles. '*I* like you the most, not Dylan,' she said.

He sank to his haunches and lifted her upper body off the ground. And here, amid the spring flowers and the tepid sun and the drone of traffic, she had her first kiss, from a boy whose love for her would never turn carnal, neither now nor in memory, and whose luxuriant hair fell between their faces as their tongues warily introduced themselves to each other.

The glaring sun that began the day as Adam set out from Chestnut Grove one Sunday afternoon towards the end of March had turned, by the time he got off the bus in Flint Street, to bouncing hailstones. They ricocheted off the sodden boarding that covered the shop windows all the way round, and pinged in his eyes when he squinted up at the fascia, where the original red lettering, J. BLAKE, could just still be discerned beneath a layer of whitewash. This didn't look good. He went round to the side-door and pressed the bell. Nothing happened. He pulled his jacket over his head and rang again.

There was an abandoned child's tricycle in the bit of garden. He noticed the door of the tiny shed, no bigger than a ticket-cubicle, was slightly open, and decided to take shelter until the hailstorm passed. When he pushed the door, however, it immediately jarred against the leg of a wooden stool, on which a dark figure was sitting reading a book. The face turned towards him.

'Hello, Addie,' said Jimmy.

'What on earth are you doing out here?' Adam wanted to know. His uncle's hair had reverted from its blond wash to something like its natural greying sandy-brown.

'Just a little peace and quiet. I can never concentrate on the Good Book when the telly's booming out, and your Aunt Mish is in one of her moods. Come in.'

Adam did his best to squeeze into the tiny space as Jimmy drew up his knees. 'So what happened to the shop? It looks like you closed.'

'That's about the size of it,' said Jimmy. 'I can't remember a worse time than we've had in the past few months. Your aunt blames it all on you-know-where, but women get these theories. I've tried to tell her, everybody's having it bad, not just us, but she won't take it. So we decided to cut our losses and closed up last month.'

'What you gonna do now?'

'Live the life of leisure. We've a bit put by, and the accounts are in a healthier state than you'd have thought, given how little we were doing, so for the time being, we're not that bothered.'

'OK.'

There was a pause. Jimmy took one last look at the text in front of him, and reluctantly closed the Bible. 'Tea?'

'Cheers.'

'Only you'll have to step out so I can reach the kettle.'

Adam stepped back into the fading storm. 'Could we not perhaps go in? I'd like to see Auntie Mirabelle.'

'Best not,' Jimmy cautioned. 'She's been like a cat on hot bricks all day.'

'I rang the bell.'

'We've disconnected it,' said Jimmy, as the kettle began to warm noisily up.

'How's that?'

'Fear of who might come demanding money.'

'I thought you said things were OK?' Jimmy tightened his lower lip, but said nothing. 'Uncle Jimmy? What's going on?'

'Well...' Jimmy paused. 'It's perhaps not all been plain sailing, put it that way.'

'Are you in difficulties?' Adam asked.

Jimmy gave an ironic laugh. 'Who isn't?'

'Look, I can help you, I'm sure. I still feel bad about what happened. I'm not doing too badly at the Beauforts' place, and I've a night job, but I've been thinking about taking up a better-paid offer, and being able to spend more time with Jo and Luke.'

'How is everyone?' Jimmy dunked a teabag alternately between two mugs of hot water.

'Er, yeah. Jo's still Jo, and Luke, y'know. It's his world and the rest of us are just living in it.'

'I miss them.'

'They miss you too. Both of you,' Adam assured his uncle, although now he thought about it, none of them had mentioned Jimmy and Mirabelle since they had moved out. 'They'd love to see you. That is, if we're allowed to visit.'

'Ah, I see. Don't want us up at Nob Hill, is that it?' Jimmy's jaw set bitterly.

'No, not at all. It's just, I know how Auntie Mirabelle feels about them. Though I still don't know why.'

Jimmy finished the dunking and dropped the teabag into a bucket. 'Nor do I, son,' he said, whitening the tea to anaemia with a splash of milk. 'Nor do I.'

'Women eh?' Adam grinned.

'Can't live with 'em...'

'...and don't *want* to live with 'em!'

'I wouldn't go that far.' Jimmy smirked and sipped his tea.

Adam imagined that a large part of Jimmy's life was now spent sitting in this little hermitage studying the scriptures and sipping tea, like a quiescent Buddha, while some unfathomable fuming mood unravelled itself indoors. 'What time are you allowed back in?'

Jimmy looked up at his eldest nephew, and took another gulp of tea. There was an absent look in his eyes, but he smiled fondly.

While he waited at the bus-stop for what seemed like forever, Adam thought deeply. There wasn't time to think deeply, just to act. Here was one of those pivotal moments where everything depended on his being decisive instead of just accepting what there was. A pressing sense of family feeling sat more weightily on him by the minute, made up of equal parts compassion and a self-accusing sense of his own shiftless inadequacy.

He pulled out his card-wallet. Tucked at the back, he found the business card he remembered having kept. There were two landline numbers and a mobile number on it.

After a single ring, a voice answered. 'Javine Dalton.'

He said that she probably wouldn't remember him, but she had been very kind to him once shortly after he left Paradise. There had been a little unpleasantness, but he was given to understand that it was considered water under the bridge. He'd had the pleasure of a meeting recently with Mr Beresford, and Mr Beresford had been most insistent that Adam dropped in soon. He wondered how the diary was looking.

There was a long pause.

'Hello?' he said.

'Yes, I'm sorry. Who is this please?'

'It's Roger. Roger Maitland?'

'Maitland.' She tried the name out for size. 'And who did you say you were from?'

'Just freelance at the moment, but Mr Beresford – Vincent, that is – suggested that we might work on something together.'

Another silence.

'Do you mind my asking, are you anything to do with Bard McLintock?'

'Who?'

He could hear another gadget bleeping in the further pause that followed.

'Can I get VB to confirm directly with you please? What's your number?'

Adam gave her the number and thanked her. 'You might remind him that we also ran into each other, quite by chance, while having our cars parked at a reception at the Violet Star Hotel a couple of months ago.'

'The Violet Star?'

'Yes. There was a bit of a comedy scene with the boy who was parking the cars. He'll remember, I'm sure.'

'OK, Mr Maitland, I'll pass on that message, and then VB will call you if he feels it's appropriate.'

'Many thanks.'

He closed the phoneline and a queasy feeling spread through him. As he continued to stare at the screen unseeing, the bus sailed past.

On Easter Day, Jordan came over for tea, and he and Luke made a start on the Easter chocolate. Joanne warned them they would be sick if they ate too much but, despite slowly demolishing half-a-dozen eggs, neither Luke nor Jordan felt nauseous in the slightest, proving yet again that all dissuasive advice from your elders was untrustworthy, and clearly served some larger agenda. Jordan was tickled pink at discovering that Luke liked to drink tea like a grown-up. He tried a sip, wrinkled his nose, and pronounced it 'minging'. Sticking to his customary fizzy orange earned him the title of 'Babyhead' from Luke. There was no animosity though. Theirs was the rivalry of true amity, the sort of friendship that would bring a lump to your throat when, feeding your own kids Easter eggs at thirty, and warning them that over-indulgence would make them sick, you found yourself wondering whatever happened to Jordan McLeish, that kid with a heart of toffee and eyes like saucers. You wouldn't remember then that you'd once called him Babyhead.

Spring arrived in earnest just after everyone had gone back to school or work. Everything had settled into a new pattern by then. Adam no longer worked either at the Violet Star or for the Beauforts. Instead, quietly and unobtrusively, he had re-entered Paradise, if not quite by the back door, then certainly with very little ceremony.

There had been no call from Vincent, nor any meeting. Indeed, Adam had still not set eyes on him since the encounter at the hotel. Javine had called back the following day and informed him that there would be no bar to his being readmitted, which, now enlightened, she invited him to agree was the last word in magnanimity. Adam graciously concurred, and asked if there were any jobs. It transpired that an interview had already been set up, if he would just care to email his CV, for the following Friday. He wondered how much of audacity there was in it. Expelled from Eden, and having first, like humanity's parents, meekly accepted his fate, he had now hammered on the gates to be let back in. Still, it was Vincent's call.

The business was a travel agency, Dark Frontiers. Situated on Fourth, it specialised in trips to recherché destinations. Its most mainstream holidays were Arctic tours where you ate seal blubber and watched the icebergs calving. More adventurous were excursions into southeast Asian bandit country, or transhumant trekking with the nomadic peoples of the Sahel. You could be stranded on an uninhabited South Pacific island or, in due course, book a ticket to the moon. Simon, the manager who interviewed Adam and who was more or less his own age, asked him whether he had travelled much. Adam saw no point in lying. He'd been to France.

'It's a start,' said Simon.

He started on Monday. Striding in through the main entrance of Paradise, he looked about him with an air of self-possession. There was the frontage of Print Media, full of screaming posters, and there was the perfume shop and the mobile-phone shop, exactly as before. Above him in the soaring heights were the banks of escalators, rising and falling through funnels of tinny music, and right at the top, beneath the atrium roof, the cable-car line. It all looked overfamiliar, as though his few months' absence, instead of renewing the novelty and gloss of it all, had only reduced it to an everyday matt. But matt was good. It was an environment in which you could prosper and grow, instead of gasp and gaze in wonder. It wasn't a dream factory. It wasn't the Emerald City, nor even Paradise Palace. It was a shopping mall, which is what nobody ever said. Faced with the gigantic gorgeous banality of the place, he felt oddly sure of himself once more.

Adam wasn't a fan of 'Cheer up, things could be worse', not least because, in its fatuous undeniability, it ignored the plain fact that things could easily be slightly better. 'Cheer up, it might never happen' was closer to the mark, in that there was no reason that disappointment should be any less transient than happiness. But people, and not always the most fatalistically inclined, tended to believe that disappointment was how things were. A keen sense that the absolute worst was surely behind him was what mostly sustained Adam, though, and his youthful spirits, once crushed by disaster, had grown full and generous again. He had forgiven the fates, or whatever they were, for the unforgivable, and if they held their thunderbolts for good and all, he would forgive them again for not delivering him some reckless

Mary, to bathe his feet in spikenard and tearful gratitude.

In any case, he had a sister and brother to support. It was time they ceased living from other people's kindness and got along somehow in their own way. Starting now.

He strode over to the escalator, at the foot of which a man in brown overalls was just putting up a sign that read, 'This ascender is out of service. Please use alternative facilities.'

Jimmy paused outside the bedroom door, and put his ear to it. There was dead silence inside, not even the sound of sleepy breathing. It was just after two in the afternoon when he had returned from a memorial service and found an empty vodka-bottle and no sign of Mirabelle. A profound silence pervaded the whole flat. Only in his head could he hear the distant bleeping of the electronic till from somewhere below, the jarring buzzer of the shop door as it opened and closed.

'Mish.' The name came out in a hoarse whisper, followed by a clearing of the throat. 'Want anything to eat?'

Towards the end of a very quiet day at Dark Frontiers, with only a few internet enquiries to deal with, Adam looked up from his screen to find Joanne and Marlow had come in. Marlow had insisted they go and see him, to offer their support. He now made a reasonably convincing show of looking at a brochure while Joanne strolled over to the desk.

'How's it going?'

'Yeah, great,' Adam said. 'How was school?'

'Oh, y'know.'

A silence elapsed, in which neither Adam nor his sister knew quite where to look, until Marlow mooched over.

'Oh, hi,' he said, affecting surprise and pushing some of his hair up. 'Jo said you were working here.'

Simon appeared, and nodded to the visitors.

'This is my sister Joanne,' Adam informed him, 'and her best mate Marlow.' Marlow nodded at Simon, and his hair tumbled back again. 'Living proof that a guy *can* have too much hair.'

They all laughed, and early the next morning, before school, Marlow went to the barbershop and had his head shaved to blackish fuzz.

Chapter 9

Warriors of the Faith

As the spring rushed on at last, an event occurred that brought about a change in Jimmy and Mirabelle's circumstances. Jimmy's aged father died, and left behind an insubstantial estate, the chief ornament of which was an elderly person known throughout the family as Mrs Hottle.

Jimmy scarcely ever spoke of his family history. Such were its notorious convolutions that some who had heard Mrs Hottle's tale told had forgotten the salient aspects of it, but Mirabelle just about understood the pattern of affiances, desertions and reunions that Jimmy's antecedents had spun through the years, its intrications bearing witness not to the malignity of nefarious patriarchs, but to the age-long human habit of blundering through.

Jimmy's father, also Jimmy, was an unassuming man to all eyes, and yet beneath his waistcoated breast beat the heart of a hardened opportunist. He had been many things many years ago – apprenticed at a tannery on leaving school, a spell in His Majesty's Forces, gangmaster at the Tilbury docks and, latterly, a small grocer supplying esteemed orders to the discerning – and lived a succession of consequent lives with consequent ladies. The first Mrs Blake went the way of all flesh in childbirth, bequeathing the senior Mr Blake a motherless boy in whom he took no more than a proprietorial interest. The second was accounted his true life's love, readily taking on the role of stepmother and mother, in which latter part she brought up the younger Jimmy to a placid faith in the present world's benevolence, and a vigorously biblical one in the certainty of a next. At some point, however, the elder Jimmy's heart wandered in search of respite from the decencies of home. At a dockers' pub one evening, in a wartime atmosphere more reckless than convivial, he met a lady with a black eye and a battered hat, and determined on rescuing her from her tormentor. What began as altruistic tenderness transmogrified into surging passion and, before long, the affair was out. The long-suffering Mrs Blake, following an access of oceanic grief, in long course managed to accustom herself to the relation, to the degree that her husband succeeded in persuading her that they were in duty bound to rescue Esme from the baleful effects of a bad marriage, in the certain knowledge that they were doing no less than saving her life.

In early childhood, Adam had been dimly aware of the presence of a second lady in the Blake household, who sat quietly in the otherwise unutilised front parlour, and to whom he was usually briefly presented. He had once asked his mother about her, and was told, with a trace of the evasiveness with which children become acquainted, that she was a sort of companion of Mr Blake's wife. And so, in some sense, she was. She came into the living-room and drank stout ale with the Blakes at Christmas. She went on pleasant excursions to the park with Mrs Blake when the trees were white with blossom. Sometimes, the two ladies went to the theatre together to see a murder mystery, picking holes in the plot over a drink back at home, after Mr Blake had gone to bed. The one topic they both avoided, indeed, was Mr Blake, who had become a kind of mutual friend, but whose quondam relation to Esme was both a dead letter and a red herring. It was Esme who found the lifeless body of Mrs Blake one afternoon, impeding ingress to the house by dint of being slumped behind the front door, her large forgiving heart having at last given out. In the years to come, despite the rising and falling of yet a third Mrs Blake, who followed her predecessors into an eternity expected to be strongly peopled by companions with whom she had much in common, their male relict lived on with Esme, providing for her immediate needs, which were few, and accompanying her one winter morning to the funeral of her sometime husband, at which she was cursed for an evil old witch by her own successor.

Now within touching distance of her ninetieth birthday, Mrs Hottle was deemed incapable of living alone. None other of Jimmy's relatives was inclined to accept the responsibility of looking after her, as none felt at all bound by virtue of either blood or morals for her well-being. It was stoically accepted at Mr Blake's funeral that she would have to enter a place of municipal care, when Jimmy announced, with a deep uncontrolled tremor in his voice, that no such lady as his father's companion was to be entrusted to such an outcome. He and Mirabelle, the latter brooding unconsulted in the car, would take her in. So it was that, the following day, Mrs Hottle moved in at Flint Street.

She had had two-thirds of a lifetime's practice at sitting unobserved in a corner, and didn't do anything now to threaten any break. What she chiefly required was care. Staring ahead of her with melting eyes, she evidently took in nothing of her surroundings, and her translation to the house of the elder Jimmy's second son had to be explained to her in short explosive words that were thought to gain intelligibility from being bellowed. Notwithstanding, she gave no sign of having understood. Mirabelle bathed and changed her, combed her white wisps into a side-parting that marked a stylistic departure for her at eighty-nine, and turned her chair successively to face the table while they ate, and the television after. Jimmy read to her regularly from the Bible, stopping gratuitously at the end of each verse to give the sense a fighting chance of sinking in, but there was never a glimmer that Mrs Hottle knew where she was, what had happened, or why, in the twentieth year of Artaxerxes the king, Nehemiah, in the act of taking up wine and offering it to his monarch, should abruptly find himself sad.

It was proposed that at least a part of Mrs Hottle's state of isolation might be attributed to deafness, and that the deafness, rather than being a matter of a declining organism, might be accounted for by blockage in the auditory canals. Under Jimmy's supervision, Mirabelle twice a day undertook the application of olive oil to each of Mrs Hottle's ears, tilting her head first one way and then the other while the unguent was poured in, and stopping each one in turn with a finger, the better to let the oil perform its dissolvent function. The patient continued to utter never a word, but sometimes a distant smile played about the papery lips, as though, despite failing to unglue her ears' accretions, the subsequent trickle of the oil down either side of her neck had added, not scantily, to the sum of her contentment.

While the April days softened, in apology for the brusqueness of March, Paradise succumbed to Spring Fever. This was another promotional festival, intended to sweep into its ambit every last espresso machine and duvet cover in the building. People, it was decreed, were ready to spend again, putting the dreary winter months aside as they outfitted and fed themselves anew, or looked at payment plans on new automobiles. Spring Fever was to be a time of impulse buying, when the unfamiliar sun would mean the unleashing of long-suppressed desires. Businesses weren't absolutely required to join in, but a memo warned that there would be a random participation audit, during which a member of Vincent's team might turn up incognito, and enquire in the guise of a paying customer what special offers there were. Shame on those with none, and also on those whose offers, such as there were, were less than special.

Adam sat in the Beauforts' kitchen with two roughly hacked slices of toast in front of him. He found a jar of marmalade in the fridge, with a tiny residue at the bottom, liberally streaked with the week's dippings of buttery knives. He ate a mouthful of the toast, and drank back a mugful of tepid coffee at three gulps. He was already late. Luke was shouting indignantly about something somewhere, also already late for school. Things were precarious again. Adam no longer worked for Finlay but, more urgently still, he barely worked for Dark Frontiers, which had next to no customers, and was already anticipating the inevitable layoff.

On his mid-morning break, Adam strolled to the opposite end of the fourth floor, where a preponderance of unlet and vacated units had a ghost-town feel. Amid the shuttered façades, brightly posted with information about rentals, a new place had opened up. Déjeuner Sur L'Herbe, it was called, and although Adam expected somewhere selling picnic paraphernalia, or yet another deli, the shop turned out to sell not-yet-criminalised drugs. He drifted in and picked up a leaflet. 'We believe that our bodies are our own. We may put into them what we choose, whether it be the potions that led to the ancient shamanic wisdoms or the latest groovy gear from freelance laboratories. Let us take you on a journey—'

'Hi,' said a voice. 'Interested?'

The speaker was a small teenage girl with flame-coloured hair-dye.

'Yeah, maybe,' Adam replied. 'But do they work?'

'They both work and play, my friend,' said another voice behind him, and Adam turned to confront a wizened man with many missing teeth and a pirate's earring. 'At your service.'

'Hi. You're the owner, right?' asked Adam.

'I'm Fabricio,' the man said. 'From São Paulo. Welcome to your journey.' He turned and pulled a small packet of something, seemingly at random, off a revolving stand. 'These are our favourites just now, a pleasant head-rush with visual patterns, combining stimulation and calming satisfaction in one dose.'

Adam took the packet, which contained a single large off-white capsule. 'How long does it last?'

'That's up to the individual user, but the effect can be deeply energising. Let me say perhaps that your girlfriend will very much appreciate you taking it.' There was a conspiratorial wink, out of sight of the orange-haired girl.

'So it's based on erectile medication, is that what you're saying?' Adam wondered.

'But in a herbal presentation,' said Fabricio, 'nothing chemical. If you prefer a chemical version, we have that too. But these should definitely be tried.'

'I just came out for a tea-break, and I find myself discussing my sex life.'

'That's why they call it Paradise, I guess.' Fabricio leered, with another atrocious wink.

Adam felt a pressing need to wrap up the whole encounter. 'How much?'

'Five pounds only.'

Adam pulled a five-pound note out of his back pocket and offered it to Fabricio, who only showed his remaining teeth in a grin, and pointed to the orange-haired girl.

'Of course, sorry.' Just as he was turning to leave, a thought struck him. 'How's business?'

'Like I say, I don't think you or she will have any complaints.'

'No, I mean, how is the shop doing?'

They both laughed. The shop was allegedly doing 'just fine', growing all the time in fact. Fabricio was off to oversee the opening of a branch in Soho very soon.

'It's just that...'

Adam took the capsule that evening. It had no discernible effect either in his head or his shorts, although he felt a passing warm tingle in his chest for fifteen minutes or so a couple of hours after swallowing it, which was promptly quenched by the next drink. He began work as shop manager of Déjeuner Sur L'Herbe the following Monday.

At Adam's suggestion, Joanne and Marlow called in at Flint Street at the weekend, to see how Jimmy and Mirabelle were doing. After a bit of business at the door, during which Jimmy, peering through a gap of three inches, tried to dissuade them from coming in, Mirabelle appeared behind him and pulled the door wide open.

'Sweetheart, it's lovely to see you. And is this your young man?'

Once inside, they sat a little nervously in the living-room under the absently watchful gaze of Mrs Hottle, who hadn't been introduced to them or referred to in any way. They both looked awkwardly out of the window while Jimmy and Mirabelle busied themselves in the kitchen, but found it hard not to keep glancing back at the old lady, whose gaze never wavered. Finally Mirabelle bustled back in with a tray.

'Sorry, loves, I'm forgetting my manners. This is Mrs Hottle, who's living with us for the time being, till she can find something more suitable.'

'Hello, Mrs Hottle,' said Joanne, though she was scarcely surprised there was no reply. 'Does she have hearing issues?' she asked Mirabelle.

'I expect so. This isn't the ideal situation for her, as she would be the first to admit, but you know Jimmy. All heart. She suffered a bereavement recently, and hadn't really anywhere to go.' Mrs Hottle's stony eyes remained fixed on the wall opposite. She gave no indication of knowing that she was being talked about. 'I think she's interested in one of these sheltered housing places, where you're looked after but you at least have some independence.'

Joanne and Marlow looked at Mrs Hottle's immobile face, and wondered what her notional independence would look like. When they left a short while later, Joanne bent down until her eyes were level with those of the elderly lady, and said goodbye to her by name in a clear demonstrative voice. The vacant gaze registered nothing. Mrs Hottle appeared to be in an advanced state of what used to be called dementia.

Outside, Marlow shuddered. 'Ugh, I couldn't live there, with that creepy old dear sitting there watching you.'

'She's not creepy, she's just old,' Joanne insisted, and as

Marlow opened his mouth again, added in an admonitory tone, 'and if you say it's the same thing, I won't speak to you again.'

Marlow made a mouth-zipping motion and took her arm.

'Seriously, though, I've no idea who she is,' said Joanne.

'Perhaps they don't either.'

They walked to the bus-stop in reflective silence, but it seemed that Marlow had already forgotten Mrs Hottle.

'Honey, you haven't said what Adam thinks of my hair.'

Joanne looked at his haircut, which he now had shaved down to almost nothing once a week. It made him look abruptly mature, even manly, the more so as the vanished froth of hair revealed him to have dark penetrating eyes that were full of intelligence.

'I'm not entirely sure he's noticed,' she said.

At Paradise Park, one lucky ticket-holder had won the right to be the first member of the public to go on the Descent into Hell ride. Its launch had been delayed a few days by a last-minute decision to rebrand the ride, the marketing team having felt that Vincent's choice, Un Saison en Enfer, would lack the necessary traction with the public. The winner was a nurse from Gutford General, who was sent on the ride with a camera mounted in the jester-hat she had to wear, the whole jolting experience, complete with her strangulated screams, relayed on the local news that evening.

Jimmy turned Mrs Hottle's chair in the direction of the TV, and it almost seemed, as he milked her tea and Mirabelle oiled her ears, as though the fugitive suspicion of a smile began to play in the patient's eyes, if not on her determined straight line of a mouth.

'Did you ever see anything like it, Mrs Hottle?' Jimmy addressed her, as the screen blackened again at another plummet into a tunnel.

Mirabelle fancied she heard the smallest mew of a response from Mrs Hottle, but it was hard to be sure. The lips parted just sufficiently to inhale a sip of tea, the neck contracted as it was swallowed, and then all was stillness once more.

Meanwhile, at Chestnut Grove, Luke too stared transfixed at the TV, thrilled by the wild violence of the ride, but haunted by the disembodied hysterical shrieking that accompanied it. He knew that he was too small to go on the ride, too young even to say the word 'Hell', but he felt inside that one day he would measure up to it, and even if he didn't like it, he wouldn't scream. Jules remarked that you would have to pay her a lot of money to endure something like that. Joanne felt there was a last-days-of-mankind quality to it. Adam, who had come in from work halfway through, stood in the doorway until the ride had ended, then sauntered into the kitchen.

He pulled a tester-pack of two large pink capsules out of his pocket and scrutinised the instructions. They were called F3A3. You swallowed one whole, then had something to eat, then opened the other one forty minutes later, emptied out the contents and either dissolved them in a soft drink, or 'snuffed' them. He gulped down the first one. There were no caterers tonight, so he helped himself to a spoonful of last night's beetroot and calvados trifle, timed the forty minutes on his watch as he sat at the table, and then split open the other capsule. Jules came into the kitchen just as he was snorting a line of white powder off the table-top. Although she said nothing, he felt he ought to explain, but couldn't get as far as the first word before a ripping pain drilled into his nasal membrane. He screwed up his eyes as though to hold them in their sockets in case they exploded, and bent his face to the table to hide it from Jules. Somewhere in his vicinity, he heard her turn on a tap, before a colossal, agonising and copiously snotting sneeze escaped him. A bit of vomit came up into the top of his throat and, as he gurgled it down again, it set off a choking mechanism that led to a prolonged fit of coughing. While Jules put a pan of water on the stove, he teetered fumblingly to the fridge door where, with one hand clapped over his spluttering mouth, he reached with the other for a can of tonic-water. He snapped it open and poured a little into a wine-glass, then swept the remaining white powder off the table into the drink, stirring it vigorously into the fizz with his finger. Controlling his retching just long enough to get the contents of the glass down his gullet, his face crumpled up again like a boxing-glove.

Jules looked at him. 'I think I'll stick to Babycham,' she said.

Adam's mouth gasped open.

'All in a day's work,' he said.

The evening was rather dominated by Finlay's suffering a renewed attack of gout. He sat half-recumbent on the sofa with the offending foot propped on an upright chair, subsisting on a diet of painkillers, as well as the cherry juice that Jules had read would help. The pain appeared to fluctuate in a narrow spectrum between intense discomfort and screaming agony and, after a while, Finlay became convinced it was starting in the other foot too. Everybody sympathised. Adam suggested he may as well try to kill the pain with drink, and as the consensus of medical opinion seemed to be that the condition had nothing to do with alcohol, save for those few authorities who held that it was predominantly alcohol-related, Finlay was allowed a glass of wine.

As Adam went to fetch the bottle from the fridge, he felt a sudden slight imbalance, accompanied by a ringing in the ears. He paused in the kitchen to see what might happen further. Pins-and-needles rippled through his fingers for a moment, and then his sense of balance returned. By the time he was back in the lounge, pouring a glass of Chablis for Finlay, the range of effects had blown over. The F3A3 had kicked in, done its bit and cleared off. He marked it with a 2 on the report form, and put a tick in the 'No' box.

Marlow Haines lay on his front on his bed, his face crammed into a zebra-striped pillow. He ought not to have had another tear to shed by now, but still they kept pushing forth, swelling his eyeballs with salt, filling his nose. Next to him was the picture of Adam that Joanne had given him, her own image surgically excised, leaving the topless Adam of eighteen months before, soaking up sun on some pebbly British beach in glorious isolation. He was a teenager then, like Marlow in a way, only not. His smile was the smile of a man who knew nothing of Marlow, and would think nothing of him when he did know him.

Marlow's whole body screwed itself into a bundle inside again. He clutched his shaved head in both hands. He said Adam's name in a choking whisper as loud as he dared. It sounded properly desperate, brimming with soul-deep conviction, but when he repeated it aloud, he only heard his own fourteen-year-old whingy voice, and the effect was ruined. Without taking his face out of the pillow, he fumbled for the photograph and turned it face down.

At that moment, Jimmy sat with moist eyes, looking at the silent sleeping form of Mrs Hottle. She had endured much and forborne to protest, and from everything that he knew of her from his father, her model fortitude would have made her a fine mother and grandmother. And yet here she was, or here the shell of her was, in an unknown home, only partially welcome and lost to savage mindlessness. Jimmy felt a pang of love for her, whom his father had done right and then wrong by, but of what tiny portion of that tiny love its recipient might be conscious, Heaven only knew.

A health visitor attended twice a week, checking on the conditions in which Mrs Hottle was maintained. She observed her moments of eating to see that she knew how to swallow, and made forlorn attempts to communicate with her, holding up picture cards and asking her to name the animals, but Mrs Hottle only stared with a look of lofty disregard at the camel or the armadillo, uttering not a sound.

In Chestnut Grove, Jules dabbed at starting tears as the family raised Finlay's left foot too now on to the chair in front of him, his face a maze of pain, a glass falling harmlessly to the carpet from his hand. Upstairs, Luke's mouth contorted into a grimace of grief at the picture of the cackling green-faced witch who stood leering over the cowering little girl and her dog.

Nothing about tears inclined their witnesses to sympathy. This was a fact learned early. The bawling baby was allowed to test her lungs. The howling infant was left to expend her misery. Only those tears that accompanied injury were treated gently, and those were the ones that she learned to forgo as a part of growing up.

In later life, it was understood that you could be permitted tears in the picture-house or the theatre, but not in front of the television when it arrived. The expression of emotion was consecrated to large assemblies of strangers, but not the home. You could cry at a funeral – it was inappropriate not to – but not when your man roared abuse at you in rancorous drink on a Friday night. If you must wail, better run to the bathroom and do it while you treated your bleeding wound, or in the cold and dark of the unheated spare room where you sleeplessly wept while he snored in the marital bed.

The faces on the cinema screen wept in delicate silver rivulets that left their makeup unsmudged. Nor did the faces themselves crumble into pain when they cried. They remained taut and stoical, the weeping only making the eyes look deeper and softer, as though grief were a dignity and its expression an eloquence, spoken in glistening tracks on the cheeks. To be dry-faced at those moments was dumb defiance. Men in the audience sighed impatiently, and sometimes called out coarse taunts, which mixed the squalor of public heartlessness into the private moment of being moved. But the truth about weeping stared out of the dressing-table mirror. It had its own squalor, its own coarse indignity, and it never reflected what the weeper felt inside. Tears were not meant to be seen, not by others, or even by yourself. They were an accidental effluent, a release to be kept as private as the body's every other fluxion.

People came and went before Mrs Hottle, kinder people whose attentions were less oppressive. A man read aloud regularly from a book. A child with an impudent lovable face looked uncomprehendingly for several transfixed seconds before going about its normal playful business. A woman with dangling earrings hardly looked at all. Then there was a girl with a fine bloom of intelligence about her, who said things wise beyond her years. There was also this torturous soul who was holding up a picture of a carrot, and repeatedly asking the same idiot question. A relief when she retreated from the room, leaving only the girl.

'Lisa?' came a quiet girlish voice from somewhere.

Joanne jumped. Mrs Hottle was looking into her eyes for the first time. 'Do you mean me?' she whispered.

'Pray get rid of that infernal woman with her pictures, would you?' said Mrs Hottle, in a soft conspiratorial tone. 'Only don't tell her I said so.'

Now tears of unexampled joy sprang to Joanne's eyes. The health visitor bustled back into the room with a cup of tea in her hand. Mrs Hottle's own eyes snapped shut.

'We may have more luck with the fruits. They usually have high recognition value in early onset.'

'I think whatever Mrs Hottle is suffering from isn't the early onset of anything,' Joanne said. 'As you can see, she looks very tired, and I think we should give her some space, don't you?'

'Of course,' said the health visitor, grudgingly. 'I'll leave some pictures.'

Joanne saw her to the top of the stairs, and then watched her stumble through the shoes and let herself out.

Back in the living-room, Mrs Hottle was wearing a look of impish mischief.

'You are with us after all.'

'After a fashion,' said the old lady.

Joanne picked up the picture cards which had been left on an armchair. She held up an image of a lemon inquiringly.

'Armadillo,' Mrs Hottle announced, and they both disintegrated in giggles.

Déjeuner Sur L'Herbe wasn't quite the runaway success that Fabricio had claimed. During the week, Adam and the orange-haired girl, Claire, mostly had the place to themselves. They swapped accounts of their trials with some of the substances, but found that none was particularly inspiring. Towards late afternoon, there tended to be groups of browsing schoolkids, who had to be asked to leave in accordance with the over-18 policy. Business at weekends was brisker, but increasingly Adam felt a little fraudulent describing the drugs in anything but the most modest terms. At least once a week, somebody came in to complain that they had 'got nothing off' an item. These could sometimes be dispatched by asking what else they had eaten, taken or drunk at the time, and then blaming that, but one or two were tenacious enough to demand a refund, or at least the chance to try an alternative, which, Adam couldn't help feeling, was only shunting the problem a couple of days along. The longer they persisted with their objections, the more he felt tempted to ask them why they didn't just buy something illegal.

It was approaching eleven, and nobody had set foot in the place all morning, when suddenly a much-tattooed boy shambled in.

'I'm on it,' Adam told Claire.

'It's my fella actually,' she replied.

Claire and the boyfriend went into a huddle over the counter to have the muttered residue of some earlier row. Adam walked over to a wall display, and picked up a packet of dried petals. There must be a way of making the crap saleable without just parroting the lies on the packaging. Was there any way they could inveigle some actual controlled substances into them? What was he thinking?

A small figure suddenly ran into the shop. He was a Chinese boy of a little less than Luke's age, dressed in a pressed shirt with a red bow-tie and long trousers.

'Whoa!' Adam said, stepping smartly in front of him. He sank to a squat and looked into the boy's perfectly round startled face. 'Are you lost?' The boy looked back at him in frank amazement. 'What's your name then?'

There was no reply, but Adam could see in his eyes a mixture of contained trepidation and defiance.

'Haven't you got a name? It would be a very funny boy who didn't have a name.'

The boy risked the beginning of a smile. 'Guangbo,' he said in a tiny voice.

'Hello Guang. Where's your mum got to?'

'Guangbo,' the boy corrected him primly.

The name was abruptly echoed somewhere outside in a screech of panic, and Adam dashed out to find the boy's mother. They were reunited in the shop, and his mother explained that he was on his way to his school concert and didn't want to go. As she was helping Guangbo into an almost comically neat grey blazer, her glance landed on one of the packets.

'Ah, you have *lianzi,*' she said, with a broad smile, picking up a pack of hazelnut-like dried seeds. 'Good price?'

'Normally five pounds,' Adam said.

The reaction was all horror. 'Wah?'

'What do you normally pay for them?'

'Half a pound, or less.'

'That'll do,' Adam said, unaware that he had just been engaged in an exemplary piece of Chinese bargaining. He handed the woman's 50p to Claire. 'What do you use them for?'

'Very good soup, yeah.'

'Soup, really? Do you happen to know what their name is in English?'

The woman thought for some seconds, while Guangbo chafed under the restraint of her left arm.

'Lotus,' she said, proudly. 'Lotus seed.'

There was no concealing from Jimmy and Mirabelle on their return that Mrs Hottle was not a vegetable after all, but an amusing and sentient companion. She had absorbed everything and forgotten nothing that had ever happened to her. Her memories were brightly coloured, sharply delineated and full of diverting detail, and she bore no malice against anybody, not even the egregious Mr Hottle, whose conduct she rated nothing worse than 'boorish'. Had it not been for his boorishness indeed, she should never have been driven to the kindly arms of the senior Mr Blake. As to why she had chosen to remain silent for so long, she declared only that she had become accustomed not to interfering, as when her presence in the Blake household had been tolerated by first one and then another Mrs Blake, when the merest murmur of demurral from either might have been just cause for her removal. Once at Flint Street, she bided her time while she waited to see which she was – nuisance or ornament – and, finding herself neither, was overcome with the desire to become acquainted with this most intelligent of girls, the resourceful Joanne. Not that she wasn't equally enamoured of her hosts, she decorously added, though in plain point of fact, she wasn't.

This called, declared Jimmy, for a celebration. Was Mrs Hottle allowed to drink? Mrs Hottle reminded him that, since she hadn't uttered a word throughout the passing of the most recent generation, nobody had addressed himself to the question. A drink was to be risked then. The four of them duly raised little liqueur-glasses of amontillado sherry, and bade each other good health – 'and an end to silence,' said Joanne, to which sentiment

Mrs Hottle polished off her sherry more lustily than any of them.

'This is all a load of crap,' Adam declared, his temper beginning to rise incautiously. 'We're selling crap to a very small bunch of unsuspecting gullible idiots. That is, when we're not selling them Chinese cookery ingredients that you can't get in Pricebusters.'

Claire sat behind the till with her customary milk-blank expression, and shrugged. 'I think you're being a bit judgmental,' she said, 'but you're the boss.'

'I'm the boss of crap.' Adam was pacing up and down in the empty shop.

'Maybe you've not been in the right frame of mind when you tried things?' Claire suggested.

'Oh, you mean the gullible-idiot frame of mind?' He tore a packet off its display-peg. 'What have we here? R2D2? Oh no, I tell a lie, it's CSB7D. What'll this do? Send me on a rocket to the moon? Enhance my love-life? Make me party till the neighbours beg me to stop? "A life-changing energy lift combined with exotic visions provide a trip to remember." Ooh, sounds promising. I'll have some of that.' He bit open the packet and swallowed both yellow capsules inside it. 'Now then, I think we might chance mixing that with a little S5blahBTblah61Hblah, which offers "Supersonic thrill-ride with ecstatic warming energy levels". Yes please.' He swallowed the three thick round pills in that packet. 'And to top it off, perhaps a touch of whatever this is.' And he poured a sachet of white powder into his mouth like sherbet, chewing it down with grimaces of disgust. 'Urgh, that's vile. Must be good.'

Claire sat and watched with a look of profoundly unimpressed disdain. What was it with guys? 'I think you're being—'

'A little judgmental, that's right. I'm being mega-judgmental, Claire, but you know what? It's about pissing time somebody was!' And he punctuated the explosion by kicking out at a revolving stand, which crashed to the floor amid a shower of leaflets.

'I'm not picking those up,' said Claire.

Adam subsided against the counter with his face in his hands. 'I'm sorry,' he said, after breathing deeply for a few seconds. 'I'm going to get a coffee. Want one?'

'I don't do caffeine,' Claire replied.

There was a coffee-stand on an island in the middle of the fourth-floor walkway. Adam hoisted himself on to a stool and ordered a large espresso. He let go of a deep dissatisfied sigh. There must be something he could do that didn't feel like fraud, or slumming, or just getting by. If only he had any ambition to do something special, but apart from wanting to be a cosmonaut when he was seven, it had never arisen. Was it that he just lacked talent?

'Problems, bro?' asked the boy in the paper cap behind the counter.

'Just a few,' Adam answered.

'Women trouble?'

'Nope.'

'Money?'

Adam smirked.

'You can tell me to mind my own business if you like,' said the boy.

'It's OK, I don't have any of mine you could mind.'

'Then that's your problem.' The boy turned to serve another customer.

Is that my problem, wondered Adam, entertained by the boy's presumption. *I haven't any business anybody else could stick their nose into. Or stick my own, for that matter.* He threw back the hot black coffee, which jangled all over the back of his palate with metallic bitterness.

'Another,' he said to the boy in a peremptory snarl. The machine hissed again and, as it did so, the sound travelled oddly across his brain, from his right ear to his left, as though it had darted from one aperture to the other in a flash, like the Venerable Bede's sparrow.

'Like the what?' he said aloud.

'Sorry?' the boy said.

'Did I—?' His head had begun to whirl. 'Hang on a minute.' He had just enough presence of mind to hand the boy a twenty-pound note before getting off the stool, and preparing to hit the floor. When Paradise melted back into being around him, its cavernous echo reverberating round his brain, his chest rising and falling tempestuously, he was able to get back to his feet unaided. He knew the boy was watching him, but he didn't want to look at the boy's face, because it would only confirm what didn't need confirming. He was incontrovertibly out of his skull.

The realisation made him giggle like a teenager at the back of a coach, on return from a school outing on which he had learned precisely nothing. When he arrived back at Déjeuner Sur L'Herbe, the preposterous elegance of the shop's name was almost as cripplingly funny as the mute blank face of Claire, still sitting at her post behind a collapsed pile of leaflets.

'Feeling better?' she asked, a touch sourly, which turned his shuddering laughter to the shouting kind. Why did laughter go 'Ha ha ha'? Would anybody have laughed like that if they hadn't seen it written down? Adam doubled over with his arms clutched tightly round his waist.

'Must have been a good coffee,' said Claire, as deadpan as ever.

His stomach contracted painfully with hilarity. 'Give me a back-rub,' he spluttered.

'You what?'

He was in helpless tears. 'Do us all a favour, love. Work out what it is I've just taken.'

The phone rang. As Claire answered it, Adam knew that as soon as she said the name of the shop, he would choke on his own laughter, and so he did.

When the day's second customer after little Guangbo happened in a moment later, he found a girl with pumpkin-coloured hair talking calmly on the phone while a grown man lay in a convulsive heap on the floor amid a litter of leaflets, gasping and crying as though expiring.

'Well, this sure looks like the House of Fun,' said the customer, who had both the precise face and voice of the late Walter Matthau. 'Do you have a rest-room I could use?'

Adam clutched his own almost-incontinent genitals. The question was addressed to him. 'If you find one, let me know, yeah?'

'They used to sit and rattle on to each other the whole night through sometimes. I'd hear them. I suppose I should have been cross that they kept me awake, but it was too much of a good show to complain. "You said this." "Well, you said that." And I used to think none of it matters. None of it will matter this time next week, or tomorrow, or even now, you just can't see it. It's easy to be wise when you look at other people's affairs, and they get ever so tetchy if you offer advice, so of course I said nothing. And when they didn't argue, they often didn't speak at all, any more than I did. It's easy enough too to be critical of other people not talking, until you realise how much you don't talk yourself. Some people's lives are all talk, others have hardly any talk in them at all, but we shouldn't judge each other on whether we talk or not. Forced talk is prattle.'

Mrs Hottle paused and sipped her tea. Her eyes were clear and her ears were dry. Joanne, who came and listened to her in her school lunch-hours, sipped her own tea, and occasionally interjected with a question that would set Mrs Hottle off on another track. Now it was Jimmy's turn to sit silently in a corner, while Mirabelle came and went, ceaselessly working, shopping, cleaning.

'We all had a holiday once. It didn't really go with a swing. I had to ask to change rooms at the hotel, as they'd put me next to them. Well, they were still in their first flush of ardour, if you understand me. I was moved up to the next floor, but instead of hearing them next door, I only heard them from below now, her shrieking like a banshee. Nobody did it like that in those days, they weren't so deluded by all this sex on the TV. But for some reason, she was determined to be carried away on a puff of bliss. She must have read something.'

Consciousness very slowly filled the comfortable place where he had been, which now grew sticky with the admixture of daylight. He was lying on a narrow table, his upper half covered by his own jacket, surrounded by high walls of cardboard, the sides of boxes. It was perfectly silent, apart from the whistling in his ears. Somebody had taken his shoes off. There was the memory of a taste in his mouth and the hint of a headache, but nothing catastrophic. He sat up and screwed his jacket up and wiped his face with it. He was in a tiny room.

When he came back into the shop holding his trainers in one hand and the jacket in the other, Claire was sitting behind the till as always. Days could have gone by.

'Good one?' she asked, without looking up.

'How did I get there?'

'Fabricio came in. He and some American guy carried you out the back.'

'Really?'

'Yep. You've been out about four hours,' she added, anticipating the next question.

'What time is it?'

'Just coming up to five.'

The odd leaflet still lay here and there on the floor.

'I'm in a world of trouble, aren't I?' Adam sighed.

'Doubtful. Fabricio looked quite amused. Said you were a

good advert for the shop.'

Adam pondered this stupidly, but couldn't decide what to make of it. He shook himself like a dog.

'See you tomorrow then,' he said, brightly.

'You might want to put your shoes on.'

He looked quizzically at his feet for a second.

'Oh right.'

Descent into Hell had been immobilised for the best part of a week now, as the computer program that controlled it had developed what the designers called a 'glitch'. Every day that it stood idle was another dagger to Vincent's heart. He could see the ride from his office window. Dominating Paradise Park, it stood there idiotically inactive, while around it little merry-go-rounds were thronged with beaming toddlers, squawking and chuckling as their racing-cars and fire-engines revolved with functional deliberation.

'I'm almost at the end of my patience with this,' Vincent said to Javine, making a hand-rolling motion towards the window, signifying both dismissal and an appeal for progress.

'I'm on to them morning, noon and night, VB,' Javine sighed. 'It's scandalous.'

'Disappointing,' Vincent suggested. 'What's happening with the auditors?'

'We're awaiting their revised report. Bellenor is cautiously optimistic, in a suppressed-anger sort of way.'

'My least-favourite kind of anger is suppressed.'

'I know. I've suggested we meet, maybe somewhere away from the offices, once we get the report. There were mutterings that she was drafting her letter of resignation, which may or may not have been true.'

'Give her some space,' Vincent cooed. 'It's been a hectic whirl for all of us, Bellenor most of all. Once this has sedimented, we can look ahead. Which is my very favourite place to look.'

'Right,' Javine said.

A contentless silence followed, in which Vincent took one long breath through his nostrils, and let it out again very slowly and patiently.

'Where did you hear about the job?'

'Through the bulletin boards.'

'You haven't been in your present position for very long?'

'No, I'm afraid the business doesn't exactly have the right kind of model. I was expecting something more dynamic? Broadening parameters is one of my priorities, and the proprietor was more into consolidation than being ventureful. Which is not a problem for him, I hasten to add, but I thrive on challenges. If they don't come to me, I make them happen.'

'Nice. What would you say was your principal achievement at, er, Déjeuner Sur L'Herbe?'

'It would have to be expanding the range of what it offered. The proprietor was thinking very much along traditional lines, and I'm not sure he had a three-dimensional view of how the business's products might be potentialised. I proposed the combination of different materials, which had a distinctly more progressive impact than the standard product advice, which is what we were being advised to, erm, advise.'

'Forgive me, what products did the business trade in? I ought to know that.'

'Er, herbal remedies.'

'Ah, I see. Did you have to overcome a lot of customer scepticism?'

'Not really.'

'No?'

'There weren't a lot of customers. But I did lead a demonstration of some of the untapped potential in what we had, which appears to have spread by word of mouth. So that would be my main achievement, adding zeros to the bottom line.'

'I think we're all concerned to do that. So tell me what would you do differently at Deli Belly?'

'Well, the name is a major handicap, for a start.'

'Oh? What would you propose?'

'Something more communicative.'

'Such as?'

'Deli.'

There was a reflective pause. 'That I like. That I do like. We'll talk about that. Anything else?'

'Yes, there are any number of products that you could bring in that I don't see out there.'

'Such as?'

'*Lianzi*?'

'Remind me.'

'Chinese dried lotus seeds. Impossible to get elsewhere. They'll go like wildfire.'

'Really? Are you sure there's much of a demand for them?'

'Am I sure? Sorry but, you don't know many Chinese people, do you?'

Of all the memories that Mrs Hottle related during the lunch-hours Joanne spent with her, none was more surprising than that of Adam, whom she could recall as a small boy being encouraged to sing before a gathering of relatives. He stood at the kitchen table and sang some popular tune of the day, performing the actions as he must have seen the stars doing them on television. He couldn't exactly sing, Mrs Hottle recalled, but he certainly lacked nothing in boyish self-confidence. Joanne couldn't remember him as having been anything but shy, but it seemed that, prior to her own recall, he was 'quite a little trouper'. What could have happened to change him?

'I should have thought that was obvious,' said Mrs Hottle tenderly, and Joanne bit her lip.

Of Joanne herself, Mrs Hottle had no recollection, and was as sure as she could be that they had never met, or certainly not since she was a babe in arms. Joanne felt a pang of regret at not having known her as she grew up but, as Mrs Hottle reminded her, she hardly ever spoke.

'But you might have done if you had somebody you wanted to talk to? Like now.'

The old lady reached out a slender hand and placed it on top of Joanne's. 'So I might, you kind-hearted thing,' she said, 'but you're here now, and there's ever so much time to be made up.'

Mrs Hottle wondered why Joanne didn't bring her young man with her on the occasional visit, and Joanne explained that, dear as he was to her, Marlow wasn't her young man, that he wasn't that way inclined. Mrs Hottle gave a conspiratorial smile and asked if he was a 'pansy'.

'We don't say things like that anymore,' Joanne said, with downcast eyes.

'Thank goodness.' Something distantly sour, like the very first turning of the milk, hung between them for a moment. Then Mrs Hottle said, 'I *am* sorry, my dear. We knew nothing about such things where I came from.'

'Or you did probably, but they were brushed under the carpet.'

'Very true. The young are wiser than we were in so many ways, but in so many ways are determined not to be. Each generation should be free to learn from its own mistakes, it's said, but what a horrible waste of time, don't you think?'

Joanne smiled broadly. 'I do think.'

'Remind me what this month's job is?' Jules asked, as they sat down to dinner that evening.

'This month's job is Projects Manager at Deli, formerly Deli Belly,' said Adam. 'Previously just another delicatessen selling two dozen varieties of olive oil, now reaching for the stars.'

'And our credit cards too, no doubt,' Finlay put in, brusquely.

'Naturally. I would be very happy to open a charge account for you, sir, at a percentage rate I think you'll find very competitive.'

'Two words, only the second repeatable in front of minors.'

Everybody looked instinctively at Luke as they laughed.

'What's funny?' Luke wanted to know. 'Why is it funny?'

'It isn't funny,' Jules assured him.

'Everyone's laughing,' he insisted.

As the caterers served the rhubarb soup, Adam had an announcement.

It seemed that the substantial rise in salary that came with his new position made it feasible for the family to begin to stand on its own two, or rather six, feet. They would always be eternally grateful to the Beauforts for taking them in and providing for them during a sticky patch, but enough was surely enough, and as he was no longer in a position to offer any contribution to the running of HortiSol, he felt that the time had come for them to find a place of their own.

'There's no need—' Jules began, but Adam raised his hand.

He had already, it seemed, been looking into the possibility of their renting an apartment, and found that, with careful budgeting, it shouldn't be a problem. He had appointments to look at two places the following morning, Saturday, and would like Joanne and Luke to accompany him on the viewings. Both flats were available almost immediately. He was sorry that it meant yet another upheaval so soon after the last one, or last two, but this should finally be a chance for them to settle in their own place.

'Who's going to look after Luke?' Jules asked.

'I also have an appointment tomorrow to interview a registered child-minder.'

Finlay commented that Adam certainly appeared to have thought it all through, and said that, although he and Jules would undoubtedly be sorry to see them go, all good things had to come to an end. Luke wanted to know what a child-minder was.

'It's someone who minds children,' Joanne told him in a gentle tone.

'Or rather, fortunately for Luke, someone who *doesn't* mind children,' said Adam, and the entire party, including the caterers and Luke himself, broke into warm laughter, only quelled when they tasted the rhubarb soup.

Marlow wasn't sure.

'I'm not sure,' he said, as he and Joanne sat in her room later that evening.

'What is there to be unsure about? It doesn't change anything. In fact, it'll be better. You'll be able to come round more often than you do now, because we won't have to ask J and F any longer. Plus which, you won't have to eat this ridiculous food. We can slob out on instant noodles to our hearts' content.'

'With trip-choc brownies to follow?'

'*And* crappier booze.'

Marlow hugged her.

The first of the two flats was unsuitable. Joanne peered through filthy windows into a back-yard area that looked like a general dumping-ground for the rest of the building. There was a smell. It was in every room.

'Next,' said Adam.

The other flat was in a recently built block, on the second floor. Soundproofing was excellent, they were told, and there was a residents' committee that kept a sharp eye on standards of maintenance and encouraged good neighbourliness. Ordinarily, the letting agent said, with a dubious sidelong glance at Luke, the flats were not lettable to families with children, but he was sure an understanding could be arrived at.

A large white lounge opened off a kitchen gleaming with

burnished stainless-steel appliances. There was a separate toilet, a modest balcony area where a garden table stood with four chairs tilted against it, and the two bedrooms were both spacious and comfortable. The floors throughout were stripped pine, which, as Joanne whispered to Adam while they stood in the bathroom, increased the potential for racket once Luke started charging about, but Adam ruled that there would be little or no charging about. The flat was too nice to pass up, especially since the letting agent indicated that he had another viewing in half-an-hour. Was there anything else they wanted to ask?

'Is it a haunted house?' Luke wanted to know.

'No, sir, I don't believe it is,' the agent replied, with an indulgent smile.

'We'll take it,' Adam said.

They moved in the following weekend. The flat was unfurnished, although the beds were included.

'We'll have to get so much stuff,' Joanne said.

'Like what?'

'Like something to sit on.'

'Oh, we'll be fine. Besides which, there's nothing better than lots of floorspace.'

As it was, the Beauforts helped them out with some basic furniture and, by the end of the weekend, when they were all squashed up in a row on one of the squashy sofas from Chestnut Grove, watching a portable TV from Chestnut Grove, eating delivery pizza and drinking corner-shop wine, the place had already begun to feel like home.

'The Youngs are independent at last,' Adam announced, his mouth full of pepperoni.

Luke cheered hysterically.

The new minder arrived promptly at 8.30 the following morning to take Luke to school. She was a tall willowy girl called Martha, with long, excruciatingly shiny red-gold hair and an almost equally scintillant face. Adam had been surprised when meeting her to find that she was from a very well-to-do family background, and spoke with a voice of pure cut-crystal. Child-minding, she explained, was her 'absolute vocation', at least until she went up to Cambridge. When Adam opened the door to her, with Luke immediately behind him in his grey blazer and cap, Martha jumped into the hallway, throwing her arms out like a minstrel, and yelling, 'Ta-daaaaa!'

'Taaaaa!' Luke imitated.

'Oh, that's it. That's how every morning's going to start, is it?' Adam sighed.

'You betcha,' shouted Martha. 'Luke and I are going to come out fighting every morning, aren't we, buster? At least, on Monday to Friday. On weekends, you can totally slob out.'

A weekly rhythm of fighting and slobbing sounded unimaginably exciting to Luke, and the two of them went off happily prattling, their voices fading off down the stairs.

Not long after, Adam was on his way to work when he received a text alert on his phone from the Paradise job bulletins. 'Managerial position, Imporia Menswear. Highly competitive salary for right candidate. Reply YES to forward your CV.'

After a moment's reflection, he typed YES. He had been Projects Manager at Deli for a whole week now. Time to move on.

Chapter 10

Just Rulers

Sumptuary laws in Protestant northern Europe at the time of the Reformation were more conspicuously concerned with clothing than with the regulation of foods and banqueting, as they tended to be in the Catholic south. If the overfeeding of the body was undoubtedly a sin, its over-adornment was seen as more incriminating still. Gluttony might take place within the home, and in the context of private family celebrations, whereas extravagances in clothing were of necessity a matter of public display. When members of the nobility, public functionaries, even clergymen, alighted from their carriages, they aimed at being seen.

Not only the stuffs from which costly apparel was made, often imported from afar, but their brilliant colours, the richness of their decoration, and the volume of their fabric, were all indicators of status. To counter these tendencies, which risked exacerbating social tensions, not to say supporting the production of foreign textiles to the detriment of domestic industry, and falling short of the requirement of Christian modesty, sumptuary restrictions on dress were enacted during the sixteenth century, which proscribed the untoward flaunting of silks and velvets, furs and cloth of gold, and accessories in gold and silver. Elizabeth I of England issued a summary proclamation, the Statutes of Apparel, in 1574, which codified in minute detail what could and could not be worn by whom. A gentleman below the estate of Duke was not permitted to wear the fur of civet cat or lynx, nor appear shod in pantofles of velvet, although the pelts of beech-martens and North African shearling lambskin were permitted to ladies of certain ranks.

Enforcement of the sumptuary regulations was intermittent at best. They were easily flouted, and although both monarchs and

Parliament from time to time insisted that the strict letter of the law, as variously amended, should be rigorously impressed, the laws carried little or no respect among the very strata of society that were able both to afford fine clothing and negotiate the depredations of the Assize Courts.

'What are these?' asked Adam, peering into a box of what looked like open clutch-bags wrapped in layers of pink tissue.

'Pantofles, sir,' said his assistant manager, Troy Parnish.

'Troy, I've told you already you don't have to call me "sir". What are pantofles?'

'They're an overshoe, Mr Young. They're a little like American galoshes. They slip on...'

'...over the shoe,' Adam presumed. 'Are they happening this season?'

'The autumn/winter season, yes, sir.'

Adam took a pantofle out of the box, and sat down to try it on. Troy helped him fit it over his shoe, where it looked like a leather version of one of those items of protective footwear that museums insist their visitors wear to protect antique floor-coverings.

'Would you wear them?'

'If I could afford them,' Troy replied. 'Maybe.'

Imporia, on the sixth floor of Paradise, was at the cutting-edge of contemporary masculine dress. It was part of a European conglomerate, ultimately owned by a holding company in Italy, but run as an autonomous business from a London office. It retailed the work of courageous new designers interested in pushing at the limits of the way the modern man saw himself, and enjoyed a sufficiently strong profile within the couture-conscious community that it survived on magazine shoots, an online presence and word of mouth, rather than primarily on advertising. It staged a quarterly catwalk show in London and a biannual one in Paris, and had a reciprocation deal with a similar operation in New York. Troy, who had been with the store since the launch of Paradise, already knew most of Imporia's few regular customers by name. Scarcely any of them lived in Gutford, but were the kinds of people who were prepared to make a special journey from out of town to buy a scarf as much as a cashmere overcoat.

Adam held up his foot and let Troy take the silly thing off. Not everything in the store was as absurd. The navy, single-breasted, two-buttoned suit he had on right now was the most opulent outfit he had ever had the privilege to wear, impossible as it was to distinguish its undoubted stylishness from the allure of the four-figure ticket it came with. It both suited and fitted him perfectly, in a way that no other item of clothing had done before, and made him feel even more important, to himself at least, than his position itself did. Nobody would argue with the man he saw in the mirror. He looked, at least to himself, like somebody people would feel they ought to know. Adam made another minute adjustment to his tie.

Troy believed wholeheartedly in couture, and had done so since his schooldays, when a boy's interest in design might legitimately carry him into aeronautical engineering, but not into shorts. He endured the accusations of homosexuality as only a heterosexual boy could, and married his childhood sweetheart Lydia at eighteen, with his classmates' taunts still ringing in his ears. He went to design school, graduated with distinction, and took a job in a high-street chain, while he waited for an opening in one of the big houses to come up. Such an opening had so far eluded him, but at least he now worked for Imporia, where he was 'closer to the action', as he put it, than when he was selling shirts with buttoned collars to the hoi-polloi. Just after the new year, the childhood sweetheart had left him for that most stone-cold and non-negotiable of reasons – she'd had enough – and taken their two children with her. Troy was sliced in two with grief, and was still learning to cope. He had entertained hopes, when the vacancy arose, that he would be a natural choice for promotion to manager, but had seen the appointment go to an undoubtedly capable, if not wholly knowledgeable, external candidate who had apparently, until recently, been selling legal drugs, and was a couple of years younger than him. There were lessons obviously to be learned here. He just didn't feel he needed to be told how to hand a customer's purchase to them.

'Eye contact,' said Adam. 'Important. Shows we value them.' Troy nodded, avoiding eye contact with the manager. 'Yeah?'

'Yes, Mr Young.'

'Good.'

For his part, Adam had discovered one of the prerogatives of being in a senior position was that you could do everything slowly, deliberatively. You could drift about the shop, appraising the displays, checking the reflective surfaces were spotless, or even come to a halt altogether, and your every action was interpreted as tendentious. The manager is looking at the T-shirt pile. What can he mean? You could speak slowly, languidly, saying nothing in particular in the process, as though you were actually bordering on dim, but your words would have the juice loyally squeezed from them in the responses of your staff. None of the customers traduced his authority by asking him anything. They understood the structure, and always addressed Troy. When there were no customers, his perambulations of the shop appeared to take on the air of prowling. Troy stood behind the counter, aware at every given moment of where Adam was and what he was looking at, his entire body suspended in a state of hyper-intuitive tension. After some days had gone by like this, it occurred to Adam that it was best to leave Troy to get on with it. So he sat in his office at the back, made the occasional unnecessary phonecall, or scribbled some notes he wouldn't ever need to refer to, and reflected that one of the secrets of working was making stunning boredom into a state of lucrative ease.

He was aware of a change in his demeanour at home. Without intending to, he had become faintly chilly towards Joanne and oddly disciplinarian with Luke. Neither of them, it was fair to say, was unduly concerned. They had their own lives, they had each other, and if their brother had gone a bit weird, well, it was quite likely he would turn back again. He had before.

He came home one evening wearing a tight-fitting jumper in a sheer wool-silk mix. It had a shallow V, was designed to sit slightly shorter than normal to reveal a fringe of T-shirt around the bottom, and was in a shade of unapologetic mustard.

'What do you think?' he asked Joanne, who looked up momentarily from buttering a piece of toast.

'How much is it?'

Adam tutted at the perennial question. 'What's that got to do with it?'

'If it's twenty pounds, it's a little unpleasant. If it's eight hundred, it's repellent.'

'It's nearer the second than the first.'

'Well then, you can supply your own insult for it.'

'What exactly is wrong with it?' Joanne continued to ignore him, as she scraped scrambled egg on to her toast. '*What?*'

'Oh for God's sake, Adam. What's wrong with it? It looks like you woke up in a squat finding someone had stolen your jumper, and you've nicked someone else's to come home in. It doesn't fit, it's idiotically expensive, and it's the sort of colour that literally nobody in the world likes.'

Adam looked at himself in the hallway mirror through the open kitchen door.

'It's true it's not quite me. But don't always apply the standard judgments. This isn't meant to be everyday wear.'

'Or any day, by the looks of it. And don't patronise me. I don't make standard judgments about anything. In any case, it's you that's applying the standard judgments of the fashion world to it, just because it's some overpriced bit of designer tat. It's both expensive and hideous, therefore it must be good.'

Luke appeared in the living-room doorway, wondering what

the raised voices were about.

'What do you think of my jumper?' Adam asked him.

Luke looked at his brother, noticing the jumper for the first time now that attention had been drawn to it, and burst into merry chuckles.

'I think that's a 2-1 home win, don't you?' said Joanne.

'I didn't say I liked it myself, did I?'

'What the whatever are you wearing it for then?'

Now they all laughed at the jumper, and Adam pulled it off.

'That's a relief. It was cutting me to ribbons under the arms.'

Although the jumper should rightfully have been returned to the shop, Adam offered it to Marlow when he turned up later on. Marlow was speechless with gratitude and, when he put it on, was probably the only boy in Gutford whom the jumper would ever suit. Best of all, there was, for one night only, the faintest trace of Adam's underarm deodorant on it, mingled with the fainter trace still of Adam.

There being no full-time member of staff junior to Troy, only a Saturday boy who spent most of his time fidgeting behind the counter with his head in the clouds, Imporia was closed for the day that Adam took Troy with him to one of the London catwalk shows. It was already quite late to be thinking autumn/winter, Troy pointed out, which Adam pretended he knew, but thought the exercise was a useful one anyway. He was authorised to buy, and Troy was presumably qualified to know what to buy.

'The exciting thing,' said Troy, as the train pulled out of Gutford, 'is to see what continuities there are from last season, or whether everyone's going for the clean break. Are you on the lookout for anything in particular, Mr Young?'

'You already said it. Excitement is what we're looking for.' He sipped a frothy coffee that tasted of vanilla. 'And do you think, for the duration of this trip at least, you might call me by my name?'

'Mr Young isn't your name?'

They both grinned.

'Adam,' Troy said meditatively, looking out of the train window. It still seemed inappropriate.

The show was staged in a cavernous venue in the Docklands. After circulating aimlessly among other buyers, designers and journalists in a rackety reception area, patrolled by tiny servers from somewhere in the Indian Ocean, proffering trays of brutal canapés, everybody went through to the show-space. Bathed in cyclamen and midnight-blue light, it was a less-expansive room than they were expecting, one wall dominated by a set of antique wood-framed organ pipes, and with a high catwalk projecting down the centre of the floor. Those privileged to sit at the front had to crane their necks sharply upwards to see the models, which Adam imagined was making some sort of point.

Rainwear was first, as was indicated by the fine mist that was sprayed over the models as they marched to the end of the walkway, turned haughtily and marched back. Ankle-length cotton raincoats in black or dark blue didn't impress Troy ('too Nazi'), nor did the transparent cagoules with fluorescent trim ('my geography teacher used to wear something like that'). The Bermuda-shorts-and-wellingtons combination aroused a mix of gasps and chortles – 'the sort of nonsense that gives our racket a bad name,' declared Troy – but he did like the zebra-pattern umbrellas. Adam discreetly ticked them in the brochure. The ready-to-wear suits were uniformly 'unambitious' to Troy's practised eye, 'almost chainstore' in their flat hang and remorseless lack of detailing, but he brightened when the couture ranges began. A prodigiously youthful Spanish designer drew whoops of approval for his primary-coloured three-pieces, the trademark feature of which was a single long pointed tail dangling from the back of each jacket, which, as the models demonstrated, you could gather deftly under one arm as you stuck your hand in the trouser-pocket. 'Bravo,' said Troy, 'but not

Gutford.' Adam nodded wisely, discreetly scribbling out the tick he had just pre-emptively put in the brochure. An all-in-one romper suit with snow-shoes was a hit with Troy ('Now that I *do* like'), for all that it looked idiotic to Adam, but the bias-cut duffel-coats in albino white were not ('Too girly'). The military look was still in spate, producing a squadron of models in great-coats, epaulettes and combat-boots, most of the ensembles offset with ironic detailing such as sprigs of feathers or sequinned slashes to emphasise the masculine silhouette through subversion. A seasonal finale brought forth models in Christmas-tree lights and three-quarter-length cashmere coats, topped off with terrorist balaclavas that covered the face except for three irregular holes for the eyes and mouth.

'Those hoods are way cool,' said Adam, venturing his own spontaneous opinion for the first time.

'Ain't they though?' Troy concurred, and the tick Adam put in the brochure was replete with satisfaction.

After the show, they took the Docklands Light Railway back into the City, where they had dinner in a huge cacophonous brasserie. Troy tried fastidiously refusing more wine after a second glass.

'Relax!' shouted Adam. 'Unwind. You're off duty now.' Waving the empty bottle in the air produced another within a moment.

'Whatever you say, Mr Young,' Troy shouted back.

In the bar afterwards, they got chatting to two girls, who gave a reasonable impersonation of being interested in them. On hearing that they were in the menswear trade, the girls immediately assumed they were sexual partners, which misapprehension Adam and Troy fell over themselves to correct. Adam bought a bottle of champagne. As they all continued shouting at each other, the group somehow naturally resolved itself into two couples. Troy's companion, Estelle, was a makeup consultant. She had dark bobbed hair, her cheeks and eyelids done in peachy orange, and a mildly supercilious air of cool. Her friend, Shula, was more a little more outgoing, and had a mischievous smile and a way of digging Adam in the ribs at every silly joke. He began to like her.

After the champagne, they drank some white wine that was even more expensive, interspersed with shots composed of pungently bitter central-European aperients mixed with cream liqueur. Shula wanted to know what they were doing later. Adam said they had to get back to Gutford. They worked at Paradise, he was sure they'd heard of it. They had. Shula asked them whether they had to rush back. It was just they could all go back to her place. Their flatmate Carl was away. Estelle touched her arm and gave her what seemed to be an admonitory look. Adam said he wouldn't want to get them into trouble. The moment's hesitation on all four sides was quickly dismissed without having quite been resolved. The girls went off to the Ladies.

'What do you think?' Adam said to Troy as he waved for the bill. 'You up for it?'

'Sure. Who opens the store tomorrow, though?'

'We do, having got up and blown out of town at an eye-wateringly early hour.'

A flicker of doubt passed over Troy's face, but the reappearance of Estelle and Shula on the other side of the bar, their hair and makeup once more pristine, dispelled it.

'I'll be guided by your executive judgment, Adam.'

'Do you mind calling me "sir" in front of the girls?'

'Fuck off.'

When Adam's phone bleeped, it was just about light. Shula lay bundled into his side, breathing sterterously in her sleep. The alarm didn't wake her, but Adam's getting out of bed did. He trod on a condom full of cold spooge. Next to it was another, containing only the merest smear. The dangle of his balls made them ache.

'Soon enough already?' Shula mumbled.

Adam bent and kissed her cheek. 'Thanks for a great night. I'll text you.' Not that they had exchanged mobile numbers.

'Mm,' was all the response he got, so that was OK.

He pulled his clothes on, and crept furtively into the living-room. Troy was already sitting in an armchair in his overcoat.

'Mission accomplished?' he asked Adam, once they were sitting in the back of a cab heading to Paddington.

'Looked like it. How was it for you?'

'Yep. We talked and cried and talked some more. Slept a little.'

'Cried? You didn't shag her?'

'Not as such,' Troy said, with a rueful smile. 'I ended up telling her all about Liddie. By which time, neither of us wanted to go through with it.'

'Own goal there then.'

'It's as well. I'm guessing you didn't do phone numbers?'

'As it happens, no. Why?'

'The absent flatmate.'

'Callum?'

'Carl. He's her boyfriend.'

'Never! She's probably just shit-stirring.'

'Don't think so. They're engaged.'

Adam pondered this. 'No! The bedroom would have been full of his stuff.'

'Their bedroom was. You were in Estelle's bedroom.'

'Shit.' Adam giggled. 'What a bad girl. But then again... Whoo!' He punched the air.

'That is disgusting, Adam. You know that's disgusting, don't you? Tell me it's disgusting.'

'Yeah, no it is.'

'What's that shit-eating grin for then?'

At Paddington station, Adam handed two twenty-pound notes to the cab-driver and another to Troy.

'Get the coffees in, Mr Parnish, while I get us two of the finest single tickets to Gutford that money can buy.'

'What do you want?'

'What do they call the skimmed-milk version of milky coffee?'

'Skinny latte?'

'Yeah. Not that.'

Adam got home that evening to a distinctly frosty reception. Joanne, sitting at the kitchen table eating pasta, ignored his initial 'hello'. He went to the fridge, took out a bottle of elder-flower water, and swigged messily from it.

'Nice of you to call and let us know what was happening last night,' Joanne said.

Adam paused in the act of wiping his mouth. The tone was too sharp to make light of, but not so critical that a superficial lie wouldn't suffice.

'Sorry. We got caught at a reception and ended up missing the last train home. By the time I realised, it was too late to call.'

'You could have left a message.'

'You'd have been in bed by the time I got back anyway.'

'But wouldn't have got up to find you hadn't come back.'

'Do I have to report my every movement now then?'

'Yes, Adam, you do!' Joanne suddenly shouted. 'You have a responsibility to this family, whether you like it or not. Luke needs to know what's going on in his life.'

The subject of her observation appeared in the kitchen doorway, gravitating as he always did to the sound of dissent.

'It's OK,' Adam said, putting a hand on Luke's head. 'Just silly Jo blowing off about something.'

'Well you know what? Maybe silly Jo won't come back tomorrow night either. Let's all stay out. Luke can make his own tea. Or Martha could be persuaded to babysit? Isn't that what we're paying her for? To bring up our brother.'

'Jo, stop it,' Adam tried to warn her, as she stood and threw her fork into the sink. 'Jo...'

'Go to hell, Adam.'

The kitchen door slammed, and then the bedroom door slammed.

Adam sank to his haunches in front of a perplexed Luke. 'It's OK, lickle bruv. It's not you that's in trouble, it's me.'

'Why?' Luke wanted to know.

'I stayed out to play last night instead of coming straight home. Big sisters don't like that.'

'Why?'

'Well, they get worried.'

'Why?'

'In case... something bad happens,' Adam heard himself say. 'But nothing bad will happen, I promise you.' Luke looked into his eyes with a scrutinising gaze that seemed determined on finding any lie. 'Nothing bad can happen,' Adam repeated as he put his arms round his brother. 'Ever again.'

After Martha had collected Luke for school the following morning, Adam sat down at the table and wrote a note for Joanne. He apologised again for failing to let her know what was happening the other night, but asked her to confine any dispute to the two of them in future. It wasn't fair on Luke to frighten him with arguments that had nothing to do with him. He hoped she understood and would respect his wishes. He reminded her, half-ironically, that he was her legal guardian too, and then announced in a PS that he would be late back tonight as there was a stock-take at the shop. 'This is the truth,' he added at the end, and underlined it. Then he realised that that retrospectively exposed his London alibi as being untrue, so he scribbled it out heavily. The scribbling only gave the note a look of undisclosed guilt, though, so he copied it all again on a fresh piece of paper.

His phone rang.

'Hello?' said a bright female voice.

'Yeah.'

'Hello?'

'Who is this?'

'Oh hello. Mr Young, it's Martha. Luke's minder, yeah?'

'What's happened?'

'Oh no. Oh God, sorry, nothing's happened. Sorry, I didn't mean to panic you. That was totally insensitive. I'm really sorry.'

'What did you want? I'm on my way to work.'

'I was just wondering whether... Actually, no, it's OK. It's... Sorry. Talk another time.'

The call was cut. Adam allowed himself a beam of delight. Whatever it was, he'd got it going on just now.

Given that there wasn't actually much stock, or at least that the shop was designed to look that way, the stock-take proved unusually trying. It hadn't been done for far too long clearly, and although Troy had some idea of what should be where, and how much there should be of it, what there physically was on the shelves corresponded only approximately with what was in the database. Product descriptions were unhelpfully cryptic – what was 'Agave Sarape, Silver Ash', for example, or 'Kapa Malo, various'? – while the products themselves looked far less exotic than their entries suggested. Nothing was described as a shirt or a hat if some ethnic label could be appended to it, and the records of sales were full of date-gaps, as though the shop had been closed periodically through the previous year.

'What are these gaps?' Adam demanded.

'I wouldn't know,' Troy said, standing behind his chair. 'Days when nothing was sold?'

'No, because there are zero totals for those. Was the store closed at regular intervals on trading days?'

'Dunno.'

'What do you mean, "dunno"? You were working here, weren't you?'

'Yes sir, sorry.' Troy reddened. 'Could they just be system

failures in the computer?'

Adam sighed. 'Highly likely.' There was a pause. 'Go on, get on with it. We're not paying you to stand and gawp.'

'Sir.'

Troy disappeared, and Adam let his head sink on to his arms. Why wasn't this enjoyable? There was money, position, a degree of independence, but all he was doing was working in a shop that sold stuff that nobody really needed. A night of pissed sex had made him feel happy for twenty-four hours, but rather than throwing into relief the dullness of work, it had in turn been thrown into relief as a pathetic interlude.

He felt bad for having snapped at Troy. As he walked back into the shop with the aim of conciliating him, he found his assistant deep in conversation with a tall white-clad figure.

'I've been hugely impressed with what Imporia does for a while now,' Vincent was saying. 'Recognise these loafers?'

'Were they ours?' Troy asked him, in a tone that suggested he was fairly sure they weren't. Adam interposed himself. 'Mr Young, you'll know Mr Beresford obviously?'

'Hello again!' Vincent sang out. 'We must stop meeting like this.'

'VB.' Adam nodded, a trifle curtly.

'How long have you been here? What a position.'

'Er, not long.' There was a pregnant pause. 'Mr Parnish, I believe you've some stock-taking to attend to?'

Troy bustled off behind the counter.

'Keen as mustard,' Adam murmured to Vincent.

'I'll bet. I was just passing and thought you were open. I always enjoy a browse.'

'Feel free. If anything catches your eye, let me know.'

'I'll do that,' Vincent beamed.

Vincent began a non-committal mooch around the display-racks. The awkwardness of the situation was compounded for Adam by the feeling that he ought to look as though he knew what he was doing. He took a suit off the rail and looked at it, turning back the jacket to look at the label on the inside pocket. There was an Italian name on it.

Troy cleared his throat as he flicked through the printout. Adam counted some mohair jumpers. Vincent pulled the end of a scarf clear from where it was hanging, and let it trail through his fingers. An oppressive silence thickened.

Adam strode to the other side of the shop and rearranged some socks. Troy opened a flat box and rustled about in the tissue-paper. Vincent hovered in front of a mirror, and clapped a trilby on his head. The whole stalemate might go on all night, Adam thought. He straightened a pack of boxer-shorts and turned his back.

When he looked round again a minute later, Vincent was nowhere to be seen. He was about to call out to Troy to ask whether he had gone, when Vincent's voice behind his shoulder made him stiffen.

'What do you think?'

He was wearing a pair of opaque square shades. They had looked absurd on everybody who had tried them on, but came into their own somehow on Vincent's pallid features.

'Great.' Adam could see himself reflected in them. He felt himself threatening to blush.

'What horrid price are they?'

'They're yours.' Adam's eyes dropped. 'If you like them.'

'My, that's insanely generous of you,' Vincent whispered. 'You'll never inflate the profit margin *that* way.'

'Oh, you know...'

Vincent touched his lapel. 'But thank you.' Adam's mouth twitched, crushed under a pressure of embarrassment he couldn't suppress. 'I think one grand gesture deserves another.'

'Oh no, really...'

'Why don't we go to dinner?' Vincent suggested. 'I've a free evening, and I'd love to hear your plans for this place. My treat.'

'I'd love to, Mr Beresford, it's very kind of you...'

'Good.'

'...but I have to get back to my family. They're expecting me fairly soon.'

Vincent took off the shades and made a pouting face.

'I'm really sorry, I don't mean to be churlish. It's just, I've been a bit too much out this week.'

Another stalemate ensued, while Adam looked at his shoes, his face burning with discomfort. The moment continued until he raised his head and met the reproachful gaze.

Vincent gave a tiny shake of his head, with his lips compressed into a brave smile. 'Never mind.'

Then they both simultaneously said, 'Another time,' and both laughed.

Adam's eyes dropped again. He felt a cold hand briefly on his cheek, and then Vincent swept out.

For a few seconds, he couldn't move. He shuddered and screwed up his face. A feeling of smallness, as though he had been reprimanded, had somehow overtaken him. He kicked an empty box across the floor.

Troy looked up as he returned to the counter. 'Wow!' he breathed.

'What's that meaning?' Adam snapped.

'Nothing. Just... Looks like you're in the big man's favour, Mr Young.'

Adam returned him a sneer. He picked up a pair of gloves from the counter, and put them on.

'Gentleman's gauntlet. Moleskin. One pair,' Troy said, referring to the printout.

Adam raised his fists at Troy, and made a ducking motion like a boxer. They grinned.

'Troy?'

'Sir.'

'Go home.'

Chapter 11

Contemplatives

Supported on either hand, and taking tiny careful steps, Mrs Hottle could walk, but it was generally thought more commodious for her to be pushed. Where the old wheelchair had come from was lost to memory. It had been pressed into service by Mr Blake senior as Mrs Hottle's ambulant powers were thought to have begun deserting her. Mr Blake entertained the conviction that any larger testing of the remnant of Mrs Hottle's abilities, such as an outing, would be courting disaster, and so it was that she found herself severally apportioned to the old blue wheelchair, in which she was conveyed about the house, a commode, and the truckle-bed on which she slept, all of which were stationed in the front parlour.

When Mrs Hottle attended her former husband's funeral, she was presented in formal mourning in the wheelchair, being transported thus through the cemetery, despite her having walked unaided from the car into the chapel, and subsequently from the car to the cemetery gates. Those to whom the Blakes stopped and spoke while wheeling Mrs Hottle about a public place of recreation either ignored her as they exchanged remarks with her attendants, or leaned down with mouths agape, to utter something puerile at her helpless face. Mrs Hottle had accustomed herself to meeting these provocations with an answering gape of her own, sometimes accompanied by an apparently involuntary nodding of the head.

Having taken up enforced residence with Jimmy and Mirabelle, Mrs Hottle found herself still the occupant of the blue wheelchair, to which she had now grown reconciled, perhaps being more nearly qualified to occupy it. She wished it to be known, however, that she would appreciate, as occasion and climate permitted, being lifted from its embrace, and allowed to take a few careful steps while she still could.

So it was that, on a fine June day, when the sun teasingly alternated between lording it over the teeming earth below and hiding his pristine golden face behind unwashed clouds, Mrs Hottle, transported to the park by taxi in the company of Joanne and Marlow, was eased out of the familiar contrivance and on to her slippered feet on a dusty asphalt path by the lake.

'Are you all right?' Joanne asked.

'Yes, quite well, thank you,' Mrs Hottle replied. 'It's a question of getting one's balance, and then the strength to remain upright.'

'We won't let you go,' Marlow assured her, in an effort to sound helpful. He still felt a little uneasy in Mrs Hottle's company, having no elderly relatives of his own.

'No, do let me go. Eventually, at least.'

'What a lovely day, isn't it?' observed Joanne.

'A little patchy perhaps,' Mrs Hottle returned, making an approximation of glancing upwards. 'But you can't have everything. Merely being out is quite enough, though of course one hopes it doesn't rain.'

They took a few cautious but unfaltering steps by the side of the lake, and then stopped again to look at the gliding ducks. A child some distance away threw a single soppet of white bread on the water, and a turbulent frenzy of quacking ensued.

'Look at them, the fools,' Mrs Hottle scoffed. 'Every man for himself, and let the Devil take the hindmost.'

'What does that mean?' Marlow wondered.

'It means nobody cares about the ones who lose the race,' Joanne explained.

'I wasn't asking you.'

'No dissension, please,' Mrs Hottle requested. 'I had enough of dissension when it was my constant companion.'

The youngsters glared accusingly at each other across the top of Mrs Hottle's hat, and they walked on a little more. After another pause to glance over another patch of water, as crowded with gliding ducks as the previous patch, Mrs Hottle expressed a preference to sit on a bench. They turned to one close behind them, presently occupied by a young mother with two children, who immediately got up and moved away.

'Don't go on my account,' Mrs Hottle called to the departing group.

'A bit rude,' Joanne said.

'Probably just shy,' Mrs Hottle confided. 'People are, when it comes to the infirm, as though we may be carrying some contagion.'

'They could have said something,' Marlow insisted.

'They've learned probably that saying things is a dangerous business. It's what gives you away. As soon as you've said something, you've laid yourself open to attack. Best to keep your cards close to your chest, feel things inwardly, but behave to the outside world as though you'd been struck dumb by the fairies for being a beastly child.'

'Is that why you didn't say anything for so long?' Joanne shyly inquired.

'In my case, it was more because there wasn't anybody there. And when there was, they didn't say anything to me. Or nothing that made sense.'

'I don't think I'll ever shut up,' said Marlow.

'Good for you,' Mrs Hottle rejoined. 'Speak your mind at all times, and in all places. In school, in church, in the councils of the great. Especially in the councils of the great.'

'Where are they?'

'Oh, you'll know them once you get there. They have a tendency to strike you dumb.'

There was a sunny pause while they all reflected on the councils of the great. The quacking grew more peaceable as the bread-throwing stopped. A drone of unseen wasps was heard close by, then further away.

Joanne broke the silence. 'I happen to know, if you'll allow me to say so, that you will be celebrating a milestone birthday very soon, Mrs Hottle.'

'Yay! Party!' Marlow exclaimed.

'Whoever told you that?' Mrs Hottle demanded.

'Uncle Jimmy saw it in your records.'

'My records? What officious nightmare have we awoken to? My records indeed. What else do these records say about me? "Uncooperative old creature best left to her own devices. Do not resuscitate."'

'I haven't seen them of course, but Uncle Jimmy told me it was your birthday soon. It's this weekend, in fact. Now don't say you don't like birthdays.'

'I love them more than life itself,' Mrs Hottle obediently declared.

'How would you feel about having a bit of a party at home? We could invite anybody you thought of, if you like. It'll be fun.'

The suggestion was met by silence, only broken by the echo of a word: 'Invite.' Mrs Hottle seemed momentarily to have succumbed to drowsiness. Her eyelids dropped, followed by the red-hatted head.

'The sun's made her sleepy,' Joanne said to Marlow. 'Get the chair, will you?'

'Who can tell me, without looking at the sign, what this animal is?' asked Mrs Hendleton.

The gaggle of children chattered and jostled. The ones nearest the enclosure peered about, but there seemed no sign of animal life.

'Quiet, please! Anybody?'

One of the children pointed out that there wasn't any animal, but at the exact moment Mrs Hendleton turned to look for herself, a large rodent with a stupid-looking sleepy expression ambled out from behind a plant and froze. The children screamed with excitement.

'Quiet, please! You'll scare him,' Mrs Hendleton cried above the clamour. 'Does anybody know its name?'

'A rat!' shouted one girl, which set off an explosion of happy laughter.

'No, Chloe, it is NOT a rat.' A hand shot up. 'Yes, the other Chloe?'

'Is it a dormouse?' asked the other Chloe, tentatively.

'No, those are silly suggestions. It's much bigger than either of those, and it doesn't live in the UK.'

'But it's here.'

'Yes, but it wasn't born here. Or it may have been born here, but its real home is a long way away in South America.'

'Why is it here then?'

'Because this is an environmental research park, and one of the jobs of the park is to—'

The final part of Mrs Hendleton's explanation was drowned amid a renewed outbreak of laughter, occasioned by the disappearance of the animal again behind its bush. It was as though it knew what its part in the game was.

'Since nobody knows, I'm going to tell you. This was a hard one, I know. It's called an agouti. Can you say that?'

'Gooty,' yelled Jordan McLeish, setting off a chanting chain reaction.

As they moved off from the agouti's enclosure, the children who had been at the back of the pack surged to the boundary wall, but it didn't reappear.

The kangaroos' enclosure offered more to see. A shabby-looking pair flopped about on patches of dried grass, coolly ignoring each other. The shrieking of the children momentarily distracted one of them, which extended its head on its neck and examined them with timid presumption.

'Kangaroos come from southwestern Australia,' Mrs Hendleton announced, referring to the notice. 'They live in large groups known as mobs. Rather like you lot.'

Suddenly the shrieks rose to a piercing level.

'She's having a baby,' one of the Chloes squealed.

'No,' Mrs Hendleton shouted. 'She's had her baby. The baby lives in her pouch. It's called a joey.'

'Joey's a dumb name,' Jordan claimed. 'Call him Jordan.'

A tiny head peered out from the mother's belly. After staring apprehensively at the rows of human faces, it struggled half-out, its front legs coming to rest on the ground, in which position it suffered the top of its head being licked clean by its mother's tongue. Another prolonged struggle inside resulted in the rest of its body emerging, until the whole creature, looking like a giant emaciated insect, landed on the ground. It blinked against the sunlight for a second, and then, as though disgusted at the tawdriness of its surroundings, turned and lunged straight back towards the maternal pouch, misjudging its leap so that it ended in an undignified scramble on the lip, its front end buried, while its rear legs kicked about helplessly, trying to manoeuvre the rest of itself in. During the whole performance, the mother stood stock-still.

'What is the name of this animal?'

'Joey!'

'Gooty!'

'Kangaroo!'

'Well done. We got there in the end. Now,' Mrs Hendleton consulted the map, 'who would like to see the wolf?'

Screams of approval greeted this suggestion. As they straggled towards the next enclosure, two of the boys wandered away unnoticed from the pack.

The wolf didn't look like a wolf, but there it was on the sign. 'Maned Wolf.' It looked considerably more like a fox, one mounted on precariously long legs, on which it teetered about as though in stilettos.

'Native to the savannah regions of the South American

interior,' Mrs Hendleton read, her voice submerging amid the contemptuous babble. 'Who can tell me – Quiet! – Who can tell me anything about the maned wolf?'

'It stinks,' shouted a boy at the back, provoking a fresh eruption.

'Quiet!' Mrs Hendleton shouted, a livid note creeping into her voice. 'Class, I've warned you, if you don't start behaving, we'll go back to school and start on our times-tables again.' This threat prompted a round of plaintive booing.

As the pack moved on, the wolf watched them with a 'good-riddance' sort of look.

'Miss?' said one of the Chloes.

'Quiet!'

An uphill walk and a turn to the right brought them to the ostrich enclosure, which was bounded by a strip of mesh fencing. The children crowded forwards to look at the ostriches, of which there was a pair each of two species, all strutting haughtily about, like VIPs from formerly belligerent nations at a cocktail reception.

'Who can tell me what this is?'

'Ostrich!' the pack yelled in unison.

'Very good. The ostrich is the largest living bird. It's so big it can't fly.'

One of the ostriches, lured by the attention, came to the edge of the enclosure, making the children at the front shrink back a little against those behind them. Its rump feathers fluffed up, it extended its neck to its full height, and fixed the children with a piercing stare from its tiny gloating head.

'This one,' Mrs Hendleton said, in a respectfully lowered voice, 'is the red-necked ostrich, native to the semi-desert regions of north Africa.'

'Why's it called the red-neck ostrich?' wondered one of the Chloes.

'I should have thought that was obvious, Chloe, even for you.'

They looked at the ostrich, which kinked and straightened its neck again, as though aware of the object of scrutiny.

'But its neck isn't red.'

'It's redd*ish*, if you look,' Mrs Hendleton said, though she could see for herself that there wasn't a trace of red about it. 'Perhaps it turns white as it ages. We all do.'

'Eurgh, no!' shouted a boy called Sunil, with a gurgling sound, which produced another collapse into hilarity.

A peanut flew through the mesh fencing, making the ostrich just perceptibly flinch.

'Which idiot threw that?' cried Mrs Hendleton. 'We're not moving from this spot until I find out.'

An uncomfortable shuffling silence ensued, during which the allegedly red-necked ostrich continued to stare out at them, waiting even more beadily than Mrs Hendleton to discover the identity of the culprit. Eventually, a voice mumbled something.

'Was that you, Dean Brougham? Come to the front now.'

A boy with white-blond hair, wearing a T-shirt reading 'Public Enemy No 1', crept shyly to the front.

'What a stupid action that was, wasn't it?'

'Yes, miss,' the boy mumbled.

'What could have happened?' Both Mrs Hendleton and the ostrich turned their querying heads on Dean, to await a satisfactory expression of contrition. 'Well?'

'Could've frightened the hostrich, miss.'

'Spell "ostrich".'

Dean looked at the ground, profoundly discomfited at the cruel and unusual punishment. 'O... S...'

'Yes?'

'Haitch?'

Mrs Hendleton pointed, with meaningful fury, at the notice. 'Dean Brougham is on a warning. Now don't let's have any more of this babyish behaviour today.' She unfolded the map again. 'Who would like to see... the crested porcupine?'

As a few unenthusiastic hands went up, an announcement blurted from the public-address system.

'Attention, please, school groups. Attention, school groups. We have two young gentlemen in the Missing Persons area. Their names are Luke Young and Jordan McLeish.'

A spurt of cackling rose from the pack at the recognised names, as Mrs Hendleton's hands went to her face. The ostrich stared at them in lofty disbelief.

Bellenor Hathaway stood at her office window, and stared down at the car-park. She could see a people-carrier very slowly disgorging a stream of senior citizens, who were being shepherded by a young woman holding a megaphone. She had hung the 'Do Not Disturb' sign on her door, but the accounts staff could see for themselves through the partition that she was only gazing out of the window. She had seemed to have a lot on her mind in recent months, having become progressively more tight-lipped and taut-tempered. It was known that she had repeatedly requested meetings with Vincent, but these had been the subject of serial cancellations and deferrals. There were rumours of a resignation threat, but Bellenor was adept at playing the long game, keeping her powder dry against any final confrontation. It was thought that the heavily amended version of the accounts on which the auditors had eventually signed off had involved some creative bookkeeping, and possibly a little of the destructive kind too. Previously so voluble, Bellenor had gradually adopted a costive demeanour, scrutinising any piece of documentation put in front of her with a tilting back of the head, and a peering through the lower lenses of imaginary varifocals, in an attitude of the utmost suspicion. Every expense claim occasioned a query. Every incoming invoice was made to await the finest verification.

She had just emailed Vincent again, requesting a meeting later that day, and was currently weighing up her chances of receiving a reply as her eyes swept the scene below. The car-park was less than half-full. It wasn't difficult to compute, though she was increasingly disinclined to do so, the financial implications of half-full car-parks. Pensioners with next to nothing to spend. A fairground standing largely deserted in summer. Requests for reimbursement accompanied by receipts in euros. Emails and messages routinely ignored.

At school, she had learned the oboe.

'Have you ever been in love?'

'Have *you*?'

'I asked you first.'

Joanne wondered for a moment in the silence that followed whether she had overstepped a mark, but Mrs Hottle was only considering the question.

'I think if you have to dwell on the question,' she replied finally, 'the answer is probably no. You would surely have recognised it for what it was. But it comes back to what I keep saying. Being in love is another of those circumstances in which you have to keep saying things, incriminating yourself.'

'Earlier on, you told Marlow to speak his mind at all times,' Joanne reminded her.

Mrs Hottle paused, as though trying to summon any memory of having given this advice. 'Even if I did, it's a different matter for men. They're expected to give an account of themselves. The world asks them, sooner or later, what they've amounted to, by which time they've usually worn themselves out putting the self-same question to themselves. And failing of the answer.'

'Aren't women allowed to amount to anything?'

'Of course. But they're less obliged to make a public statement of it. Competition is an ugly affair, best left to men.'

'Why?'

'Because they're the ones who derive most from failure. If you lose, you're allowed to be angry. It's supposed to spur you on to do better next time, and without that constant impression of struggle, men are nothing. Women don't have to engage in these tussles because they understand that life is a tussle anyway, without seeking it out all over the place.'

'I can't agree with you,' Joanne said, in a gentle tone. 'It's as though you're saying certain things are reserved for men, and it isn't worth women's fighting for them. If they hadn't fought in the past, all the company executives would still be men. At least some are women now.'

'How lovely for them. Struggling to the top, so they can do a credible impersonation of male bullying.'

'It makes for fair play though.'

'No it doesn't. It increases the sum of human misery.' Mrs Hottle folded her hands together in front of her, as though about to pray.

'The point is, there can't be one law for men and another for women,' Joanne insisted.

'Why not?' Mrs Hottle countered. 'That is surely exactly what there should be. Otherwise, women are forever doomed to be judged by standards fit only for men.'

Joanne thought about this. She was aware of a mean streak in Mrs Hottle that made her more interesting still, but she wasn't sure she understood. 'In any case, nobody should have to live the life that you did. Being ill-treated. Insulted. Ignored.'

'No, indeed, they shouldn't. Whether they be women, men or children.'

'But that happened to you *because* you were a woman.'

'In my case, it did.'

'So that's wrong.'

'Of course it was. Who's saying it wasn't?'

There was a silence. Mrs Hottle's eyelids seemed to flicker.

'Are you tired? Would you like to sleep?' asked Joanne. But Mrs Hottle was already asleep.

'Luke and Jordan, you've shown up the whole school today with your selfish behaviour. Haven't you?'

'Yes, miss,' the two boys murmured, squirming under the collective attention of their classmates.

'What could have happened?' demanded Mrs Hendleton.

As the boys continued to look at the ground, a voice called out, 'The gooty could have eaten them'.

'Silence!' Mrs Hendleton demanded, in an eldritch scream that surprised even herself. 'I was going to suggest we go on now to visit the orang-utan, but as these two foolish boys have let us all down, I'm beginning to think we'd better not risk it.'

The orang-utan was nowhere to be seen in its outside enclosure, so the whole group, chastened into a subdued state, shuffled into the covered part. There it was, on the other side of the glass, lolling in a low tree-branch with one paw over its face suggestive of a moment's despair. As the children crowded against the window, however, it turned a kindly face towards them, appearing to smile a little beneath its shaggy auburn fringe.

'Who can tell me which continent orang-utans live in?' Mrs Hendleton asked.

'England,' someone said.

'No, it comes from Asia. It's the only one of the apes that lives only in Asia. Who's heard of Borneo?'

The orang-utan, whose name was Jezebel according to the notice, rolled off her perch in the tree, and came lolloping over to the glass. The front row of children shrank back, occasioning some jostling and pushing.

'It's all right, she can't harm you,' Mrs Hendleton assured the children, just as Jezebel began hammering with the flats of both hands on the glass. Screams went up. 'It's all right. Don't get silly.'

'Pig!' shouted one of the children, emboldened at Jezebel's evident frustration.

'Chloe, that wasn't very kind. How would you feel if you had to look at groups of cheeky children all day?'

'Miss?' another voice said. 'Jordan and Luke's gone off again.'

Marlow lay on their favourite bit of grassy bank in his lemon-yellow beach-shorts and wraparound shades. He had changed into the shorts for the lunch-break, and was claiming that he was going to go into the afternoon sessions without changing back, but Joanne didn't believe him. Surreptitiously, without anybody noticing, the day had gone from warm and bright to broiling. Now the sun sparkled in the air like fizzy lemonade.

'I used to hate the sun,' Marlow said, in an indolent drawl.

'Why?'

'I always got sunburned, and it gave me a banging headache.' He took another liquorice cake from the paper bag between them. 'Plus, I hate that everybody goes on about how great it is. Why is sunny good?'

'It's better than cold,' stated Joanne, in the unintentionally parental tone she found herself using when Marlow said something preposterous.

'Not necessarily.'

'Would you like it if it started raining now then?'

'Yeah.' He rolled on to his side to face Joanne. 'Wouldn't you? It'd be a surprise. Surprises are fun.'

'Secret policemen knocking on the door in the middle of the night is a surprise, but not fun.'

Marlow gave a snort of derision. 'Lighten up.'

Joanne concentrated on the necklace of large amber beads she was tossing about on the lap of her skirt. She didn't particularly care for Marlow's contrarian moods, not lately.

'What up?' he asked. Not receiving a reply, he supplied it for her. 'You're thinking of Mrs H, aren't you?'

Joanne had been aware for the past few days of wanting to help Mrs Hottle more, but not knowing how. A connection had grown between them, it was true, but she was acutely conscious too of falling short, being perhaps too juvenile for Mrs Hottle to find in her the refuge she surely needed. Conversations trailed away. Their hands might meet, but then the melting look in Mrs Hottle's eyes would mist up into a faint abstraction, and she was gone. Her lucidity was not in question, but was at the mercy of her almost permanent exhaustion. She slept soundly and long, and often found herself submerging into a deep drowse in the midst of prior animation, suddenly nodding and gently snoring, but having gone deeply enough that, even though she might awaken from the drowse only moments later, all connection to the previous exchange had dissolved. On occasions, Joanne held, or more precisely covered, her hand, to give the impression of some ancient bond. She knew that Mrs Hottle liked her, and she knew that, if the enormous chasm between their ages had been narrower, they might have been firm companions, as deeply interested in each other as if they had been grandmother and granddaughter, but the rift was just a little too great, and the effort at straining across it nearly all on one side.

'We'll make sure she has a ripping birthday,' Marlow said. 'All hummus and no tofu.'

Joanne smiled. 'I doubt Mrs Hottle knows what either of those things is.'

'Are.'

'Is.'

The bell rang. Marlow sighed. He sat up straight, opened his rucksack, and pulled out a crumpled white shirt.

'Y'know, honey, if you're real good, I'll let you iron my shirt.'

Joanne smirked. 'What with?'

'Love.'

Fearful of a mutiny, Mrs Hendleton had broken Education Authority rules by conducting the zoo visit single-handed, her classroom assistant having called in sick with what sounded suspiciously like a hangover. What this meant now was that she couldn't leave the class while she went off in search of its two newly missing members, so she had to lead them on an eccentric progress around the grounds, calling out the names of Luke and Jordan, and entreating the children to keep a sharp lookout for the two miscreants. Formed up into twos in a rough crocodile, the line of children snagged and straggled its way around the zoo, calling the names of the missing boys, some of them in a bored tone, others entering into the spirit of the search by pronouncing the names in dramatic urgency.

Next to the seal compound, the class found itself confronted with another school group of roughly the same age. As they passed each other, the two groups exchanged distrustful, belligerent glances. The other children were less rigorously uniformed, and the odd jeer was to be heard as Mrs Hendleton's blazered charges filed past. A moment's jostling broke out, then somebody shouted 'Stupid pigs!'

'Chloe Kittle!' Mrs Hendleton called out.

'It wasn't Chloe, miss,' someone protested.

'You're all gay,' came a voice from the other group, which provoked an uproar of indignant shouts and taunts, and even a little spitting.

'Boys and girls, stop this immediately,' the other teacher cried out, offering Mrs Hendleton a glare.

'Sorry, did you have a problem?' Mrs Hendleton queried.

'Yes I did actually. My problem is that our outing is being disrupted by an assortment of barely controlled... well, I'd better not say.'

'No, do go on,' Mrs Hendleton insisted, her tone hardening into frank hostility. 'Barely controlled what? Hooligans, perhaps?'

A thin cheer went up from her group, which was echoed more lustily by the opposing children, at the prospect of a grownups' set-to.

'I shall make representations to your head-teacher about this,' said the other teacher. 'I've never seen such a poor example set.'

'How dare you speak to a qualified teacher in that way?' Mrs Hendleton snapped.

'Mrs Hendleton is the Destroyer!' shouted one of her boys, to a resounding cheer.

'Ha!' The other teacher tossed her head triumphantly. 'From out of the mouths of babes...'

'Oh grow up.'

Suddenly, there was a new shout, followed by a fusillade of pointing fingers. 'Miss, look!'

Mrs Hendleton wheeled round to be greeted by the sight of Luke and Jordan seated, one behind the other, on the back of a half-grown elephant calf being led along the path by an elderly attendant.

'What a relief,' the other teacher murmured, with a sardonic simper. 'Their bodies won't be fished out of the canal tomorrow after all.'

Tears started into Mrs Hendleton's eyes as the elephant plodded soberly past, its small riders' arms raised above their heads like conquering heroes.

When Joanne and Marlow walked into the locker-hall, they could see a large knot of their classmates clustered around the figure of Terry Weston, who was sitting on a window-sill reading something from a notebook. Waves of jeering laughter punctuated the recital.

'I hate that goon,' Marlow said. 'Look at them all sucking up to him.'

'It's showtime all right,' Joanne noted, with barely a glance. 'Oh my God, Marlow.' She was standing before her own locker, which had been forced open, its contents jumbled about inside, exercise-books with their pages torn, textbooks split at the spines and half-dismembered. Dropping to her knees, she scrabbled frantically through the mess for a moment, before coming to a sudden halt as the blood rushed giddyingly to her face. Over to her left, the voice of Terry Weston, articulating in a parodic falsetto, became gradually distinct.

'"Don't know whether I want to continue English after this year. I'm finding it too unchallenging." I'll give you a challenge, love,' Terry added in an aside, clutching his groin to another ripple of giggles. '"And nobody else is properly interested, not even the faithful Marlow." He's not interested in you cos he's a bumstuffer, darling.' More laughter.

'He's got my diary,' Joanne said, her face flaring.

Marlow shot across to the laughing group, and was greeted by a chorus of ironic cheers.

'Hand that back, you twat,' he yelled at Terry.

'No chance.' Terry turned a few pages on, a broad malevolent grin engulfing his face. He resumed the pantomime voice. '"I'm not fond of Mr Foxton. The one-to-one sessions with him are making me feel uncomfortable." What, feeling you up, is he? "Also, without meaning to, he said something insensitive about Mum and Dad's deaths, which made me cry afterwards, despite myself." Cheer up, love, it might never happen. Oh sorry, it already has.'

Marlow, his face white with rage, his mouth twitching violently, shoved his way through the sniggering crowd. A couple of the boys tried holding him back, but he managed to push them aside as he shouldered through.

'Give me that now, you piece of trash,' he snarled at Terry. He made a flailing gesture to try to grab the diary, but Terry hoisted it in the air above his head, thrilled at the chance to humiliate someone in front of an audience.

'Beg for it, bumboy.'

Marlow made another ineffectual swipe for the diary, trying not to look into the cackling face of the tormentor, and as somebody dead-legged him from behind, found himself stumbling between Terry's legs.

'Want the girlie's book, do ya?' Terry sneered. He stuffed the diary down the front of his trousers. 'Get it then.'

Incensed beyond reason, Marlow pulled Terry off the window-sill by his belt. Terry's upper body swivelled sideways, and he cracked his head on the wall. One foot flew out in a reckless kick and caught Marlow on the side of the face. The watching group shuffled back to clear a space for the struggle. Marlow pulled the belt apart and yanked the other boy's trousers from round his waist. The diary was inside his shorts. A second's fatal hesitation before putting his hand inside allowed Terry to pull him down on to the floor. In a moment, he was on top of Marlow, his trousers round his knees. He smashed his fist into Marlow's face with a thud that raised queasy groans from the crowd. Joanne's screams tore through the corridor like the shriek of a nocturnal fox.

'Someone shut that bitch up,' Terry growled. He snatched a cola-bottle from the hand of one of the spectators, and grimly shattered it against the wall.

'Tez, no,' a voice weakly interposed, and the entire group let out one great moan, as it turned away nauseously from the sight of Marlow's face being raked with the broken bottle. After his face had been slashed, his shirt was cut to ribbons with merciless efficiency, and the bottle dragged over his chest, the grooves of blood diluted with the dropping strands of saliva escaping from his attacker's clenched teeth.

'That's enough, Tez, he's unconscious,' someone pleaded.

'Best thing for him.' Terry finally froze, his breath coming rapidly and convulsively. He let the bottle go. His hand was numb. Averting his eyes from his own handiwork, he stood up, pulled the diary out of his shorts and flung it aside. He tugged up his trousers, the reminder of which indignity suggested one more act of revenge. He undid the belt of the lifeless boy, and yanked down his trousers and shorts together. A couple of people emitted a final 'eurgh' as Marlow's genitals were exposed. He had a thick ring through the end of his penis.

'What on earth is going on here?' shouted the angry voice of Mr Foxton, from the far end of the corridor.

The crowd scattered frantically in all directions, and Joanne came running to the scene. She fell on her knees beside the grievously injured Marlow, emitting a howl of despair.

'My God.' Mr Foxton gripped her roughly by the shoulders. 'Did you see who did this?'

Rigid with sobs, Joanne could do no more than nod. The perpetrator's name rose into the back of her throat and stuck there, fouling it for all eternity.

Having declared that she didn't want to hear a peep out of anybody, Mrs Hendleton watched her class file sullenly on to the coach. The last two were Luke and Jordan, whom she had specifically detained by her side where she could see them. They were stationed on a pair of seats opposite her at the front. There was something a touch disquieting about the unnatural silence of a coachful of six-year-olds, but Mrs Hendleton wasn't about to surrender to a moment's remorse. If any of the other children happened to mention the boys' disappearance to their parents, she might be up on a disciplinary charge by the end of the week.

After some minutes, the coach became snarled in a jam at a crossroads where the traffic-signals weren't working. In the ensuing hold-up, a moment's remorse duly took possession of her. She stood up.

'Who can tell me the name of the giant birds that we saw today?' she asked the rows of morbid-looking faces. Some of the children shifted a little in their seats in acknowledgement of the fact that they knew the answer, but a Spartacist mood of solidarity had clearly settled over them, which none would betray by supplying the response. 'Begins with an O?'

The driver tutted and swore, and pulled out into the right-hand lane with a jerk that made Mrs Hendleton keel over sharply to her side. A reluctant titter went up. As she turned on her heel, the driver equally abruptly stamped on the brake, which sent her plunging forward.

'Sit down, love, will you?' he snarled in his rear-view mirror.

An ambulance tore across the junction where they were stalled, almost grazing the front bumper of the coach as it went, its siren shrieking blue murder. It went slaloming through the stationary traffic, Joanne lurching about in the back of it with every twist and turn while a paramedic held an oxygen mask over Marlow's face.

The severely panicking Mr Foxton had called the ambulance, and hadn't ceased shouting angrily at anybody he could until it arrived at the school's side-entrance. Shouting into the face of the leading paramedic, he found himself roughly pushed aside as two colleagues arrived behind him with a stretcher. One of them asked Joanne whether he was likely to have broken anything. She shook her head, but still couldn't make her voice work. What had he been cut with? She could only point to the discarded bottle, which still lay a few feet away.

With a small group of other pupils watching, the paramedics swiftly lifted Marlow's body on to the stretcher and carried him out. More children appeared at the entrance, pushing each other and craning their necks, having already heard the rumour that Terry Weston had half-killed someone.

'Cover him up,' one of the stretcher-bearers snapped at his team leader, who folded the edge of the blanket over Marlow's groin.

It was as Joanne climbed into the back of the ambulance with the paramedics that she found her voice again. Mr Foxton grabbed at the back of her skirt to pull her back.

'There's no need for you to get in the way, young lady. Go back to your class.'

'I'm going with him,' Joanne declared in a hoarse tone that wasn't her own.

'No, back to classes.'

'Piss off!' she yelled into Mr Foxton's face and, without any further consultation, the back doors of the ambulance were slammed, shutting her in. The shrill wowing of the siren started up, drowning the infuriated words of the teacher, who had now turned his compromised authority on the remaining pupils.

'Will he be all right?' Joanne asked in a broken voice, as the breathing-mask was applied to Marlow's face.

'He'll be in shock when he comes round,' said the paramedic. 'And he's going to be very sore indeed.' Joanne gave another uncontrolled choke. 'He'll need lots of TLC from his lady-love,' the man added, squeezing her shoulder. 'But yes, darling, he'll be all right. Whoever's done this to him, though, wants locking up.'

With great delicacy, his colleague sponged away much of the blood from the lacerations in Marlow's chest, peering at the wounds close up as he did.

'Make sure no bits of glass have got in.'

The other man looked up. 'Yes, Paul, I do know what I'm doing, thanks,' he replied sardonically, and set about carefully taping over the slashes with sterilised strips. Marlow's ruined chest rose and fell.

Following a dressing-down by the head-teacher, during which a sullen silence prevailed, class 2A was released. The children shuffled towards the school gates, hardly talking to each other. Many of them harboured a feeling that the sins of two of them were being visited on the rest, in a way that bore a trace of unfairness, of which Mrs Hendleton herself was uneasily aware. Still, when they grew, they would discover a similar rank unfairness popping out of every crevice of their blameless lives. Best din it into them early.

Waiting at the gates to collect Luke and Jordan, Martha was aware of a subdued air among the class.

'What up, dudes?' she asked the boys. 'Everyone looks really down.' Luke and Jordan exchanged guilty looks, but said nothing. 'Has your teacher been losing her rag over something?' They summoned a nod between them. 'Well, you know what? Pooey bum to her. We're going to have ice-cream sundaes. Let's see what she thinks of that, guys?'

Luke and Jordan brightened a little at the prospect of the sundaes, and by the time they were installed in Delfizzi's One-Long-Sundae Parlour, with tall glasses like vases in front of them, piled with scoops in many different colours, the unpleasantness of the afternoon was forgotten. Neither of the boys wanted their butterfly wafers, so Martha chomped them greedily.

'Plus,' she announced indistinctly, with a mouth full of dry wafer, 'I've got the coolest new toy to show you when we get back, yeah?'

The boys barely looked up from the ices in which they were embroiled. Neither failed to register the promise of a new toy, though each inwardly winced a little at the babyish word.

Back at the flat, Martha found a message flashing on the answering-machine. As the boys clattered about in the fridge, she played it back. It was a strained-sounding Joanne, saying something about something that had come up, she couldn't talk on the mobile for very long, but would be going on to Something Street in the evening, and would call from there. She sounded as though she had been crying. Adam could sort it when he got in.

Furnished with glasses of flat red pop, the boys now demanded to see the toy. Martha reached into the bottom of her capacious leather shoulder-bag, and pulled out a bright-yellow object with a pointed bottom. The boys looked quizzically at it.

'What does it do?' asked Jordan.

'Observe, yeah?' Martha said and, putting the top down carefully on the kitchen floor, set it spinning.

Its sides were decorated with a design of blue and green wavy lines that looked quite thin and ordinary when the top was still but, when it was set in motion, turned into a mesmeric dancing pattern like an electrical wave. The boys watched the top whirling about on the floor, emitting a very faint humming and tinkling sound, suddenly moving sideways, then drifting uncertainly back to its original spot, until its fading momentum made it wobble and lurch, and finally collapse ignominiously, like a fly overwhelmed by insecticide.

'What do you think, guys?' Martha wanted to know.

After a pause, Jordan said, 'It's *quite* good.' He looked at Luke, who remained silent. 'Does it do anything else?'

'Not really,' Martha replied and, picking up the top once more, gave it a sharp twist and set it spinning again.

After some time at the hospital, Joanne was allowed into the room where Marlow had been treated. His head and chest were swathed in bandages. For what felt like an hour, he remained unconscious, heavily sedated and breathing with slow regularity. It had proved impossible to contact either of his parents for the time being, so Joanne sat quietly next to the bed, barely taking her eyes off him.

Eventually, she was aware of a flickering of the eyelids. What she could see of his face grimaced a little, and then his eyes opened and stared blankly at the ceiling. She softly said his name.

He turned his head fractionally to the right, but could turn it no further.

'Is that you, Jo?' he said in a whisper.

'Yes, don't try to talk. You're in hospital. You've been badly cut up, but you're going to be all right.'

'My face...'

'It's OK. It'll heal. You need plenty of rest, they said. They've given you some kind of painkiller.'

A release of breath expressive of a tiny smirk escaped from Marlow's mouth. 'He's not going to look twice at me now, is he?'

'Who?'

'Your bruv. I've just been dreaming about him.'

'Oh, Marlow.' She reached out for his hand. His fingers feebly enclosed hers, and she put her other hand over the back of his. 'It's going to be OK. I'll see that Weston gets what's coming to him.'

Marlow's eyes closed again. 'Weston,' he mumbled.

'Don't think about him now. Guess what? Mr Foxton tried to stop me from getting in the ambulance with you. I told him to piss off.'

'No way,' Marlow whispered, with the smallest hint of a grin. 'Joanne Young, you bad girl.'

'Like I was going to leave you after what happened.'

There was a moment's silence.

'Jo?'

'Mm?'

'Would you like to marry me?'

Joanne's face, stiff with concern and anger for the past few hours, softened into a beam. 'I'm fourteen,' she said.

'That'll do.'

'Excuse me, mate.'

Adam glanced up from behind the counter at the man standing there, and looked around. Where was Troy?

'Somebody will be with you in a moment,' he replied, and turned back to the computer screen.

'I'm looking for Adam Young?'

'Yeah? That's me.' Adam stood up, and as he did so, an immense blinding force came crashing at him. He reeled back, as though about to pass out, and realised the man had hit him. 'What the freaking—?'

The man now grabbed him by both lapels and pulled him forwards, so that his upper body sprawled across the counter. As he sustained a second colossal blow to the face, he heard a shout from somewhere.

'Oi! What do you think you're doing, sir?' Troy shouted.

'Call Security,' Adam managed to wail, before one of the man's hands closed around his neck, and began to throttle him.

'We haven't met before, Mr Young,' the man growled, 'but we've a mutual friend.'

Adam's choking red face looked up into the face of this hysterically angry man. He could hear Troy asking somebody to put him through to Security.

'Does the name Carl Gillespie mean anything to you?' the man snarled, his spitty breath close to Adam's ear. Adam managed to shake his asphyxiating head. 'I see. Let's try another name then. Shula Marriott?'

The entire scenario clicked into place. 'Please,' Adam coughed. 'I can tell you...'

At last, the man loosened his grip a little, though without letting go of Adam's neck. 'You can tell me, can you? Go on then.'

'I don't know what you think happened, yeah? I met Shula in a bar. I didn't know she was somebody's fiancée.'

'She isn't,' the voice in his ear hissed.

'What?'

'She used to be engaged to me, but let's just say she's back on the market now.'

'Sir, Security are on their way,' Troy's voice, suddenly near, announced in a wavering tone. 'I suggest you release my manager.'

The grip was finally relaxed, and Adam slithered to his knees behind the counter. He looked up into his attacker's snarling face.

'Next time you fancy poking some other bloke's bird, might I suggest you don't leave your business card along with a couple of used condoms, you mug?'

Only moments after Carl strode out of the shop, two security guards appeared.

'Where's the fire?' one of them asked.

'Nice work, boys,' Adam said, still on his knees, his bleeding face resting on the edge of the counter. 'Another minute, and I'd have been forced to try and take him on myself.'

Troy held out a tissue. Adam took it, still kneeling absurdly behind the counter, like somebody about to give a glove-puppet show for children. He held the tissue against his red-streaked chin.

'Thank you,' he said, and looked up through blurred eyes to his assistant manager. There was a woman standing just behind him. 'Can we help you, madam?'

'What on earth is going on here?' the woman's voice imperiously demanded.

'What's going on, Troy? Oh yes, I remember now. I had sex with a girl whose fiancé, now her ex, just came in here to tell me what he thought of me. Apparently having come all the way from London.'

'And this is a regular occurrence at Imporia?'

'Do you know what, love? Why don't you—'

'Adam!' Troy quickly interposed. 'You may not have met Mrs Pelfing.'

'—get lost? I mean I'd love to kneel and chat some more, but as it happens, I've just been beaten up.'

'Mrs Pelfing,' Troy urged.

The name popped into place in Adam's battered head. 'Mrs Pelfing, I do beg your pardon. I've no idea what this must look like.'

'It looks like my store manager has been assaulted at work.'

'I do promise you nothing like this has ever happened before.'

Adam finally struggled to his feet, and offered to shake Mrs Pelfing's hand with the hand that was still holding a blood-drenched tissue.

'Perhaps not,' she demurred.

'What's the matter, darling?' Mirabelle asked, as soon as Joanne walked into the kitchen. She enfolded her niece in tender arms, making a shushing sound. Jimmy, who had let her in downstairs without apparently noticing anything was the matter, stood by helplessly and a little ashamed.

'My best friend got beaten up,' Joanne quavered at last, in a voice like someone with a heavy cold. She told the story of how Marlow had tried to rescue her diary from a cruel psychopath, and had been knocked unconscious and attacked with a broken bottle. She told of snarling at Mr Foxton, of the kindness of the paramedics, and of her desperate vigil at the bedside, which had ended only when Marlow's mother had appeared, white with worry, and after Marlow himself, barely able to see, had asked Joanne to marry him. At this last detail, she laughed a little through her tears.

Mirabelle hugged her closer. She told Joanne that, in her day, it had been decided that it was a mixed-up, shook-up world, but it was really just a sick one. Mrs Haines, who had been busy with a series of reflexology clients while the school had been trying to contact her, had shouted at Joanne for not giving the perpetrator's name to the school immediately. Marlow had tried to calm her, but his voice was too feeble, and the ensuing bitter exchange between Joanne and his mother had taken place across his bandaged body.

'Don't you worry about her,' said Mirabelle. 'She's probably just blaming herself.' She dried Joanne's face with a tea-towel and suggested that she take Mrs Hottle a cup of tea.

In the back office, Mrs Pelfing applied a fresh tissue to the dribbling wound on Adam's chin.

'This is very kind of you,' he said. 'I'm so sorry we've met under these unfortunate circumstances.'

'Unfortunate for you, poor boy. Is there no antiseptic in here?'

'I strongly doubt it.'

'Perhaps you could send the boy out for some?' Troy had appeared in the doorway.

'That's a good idea. Go and get some antiseptic, will you, boy?'

Troy raised a silent fist at Adam behind Mrs Pelfing's back. Adam grinned and split the wound again.

'Try to keep a straight face,' Mrs Pelfing insisted. 'Really, you boys. You'll do anything to avoid a quiet life, won't you?'

'Well, you know what they say.'

Mrs Pelfing stood back and took an appraising look at him. 'Remind me. What is it that boys will be? Oh, I know...'

They said the word in unison.

It was hard to guess Mrs Pelfing's age. Anywhere between thirty-five and fifty, Adam thought. Elegant in an untidy way, clothes that hung off her in random rags and tatters, hair that appeared savagely set in the middle but with bits hanging off it, makeup in ghoulish bluish-grey, long mauve fingernails, and a scent like loose change. They looked coolly at one another. She took his chin between forefinger and thumb, and tilted his head a little into the light. For a moment, it was as though she were going to kiss him. His penis glimmered, more in hope than expectation. He was covered in blood after all.

'Despite the present shambles, I'm hearing nothing but good things about you,' she said.

'From whom?'

'Whom?' It was women's job to take the piss. It redressed the balance, or something. 'Why, Vincent of course.'

'Really? I hardly know him.'

'Vincent and I go way back, to a long-forgotten amour at business school.'

'You and him?' Adam grinned, and reopened the wound. The grin became a grimace. 'I assumed he was gay.'

'I assume he is, but we weren't limited in those days by conventions.'

Adam pondered this. 'No? That's good, isn't it?'

'It's good if you take the same view. But if you're a dull straight boy who only wants girls, it'll be a monotonous handicap.'

'In what?'

'Why, getting on, of course.'

Mrs Hottle was in her usual position, her wheelchair on one side of the dining-table, facing towards the window, with its view of flat roofs and back yards. She was soundly asleep. Joanne put the cup and saucer softly on the table, and touched Mrs Hottle's shoulder. She said the old lady's name and, after a further pause, the ancient eyelids batted a little and one of the hands reached up to meet Joanne's where it rested on her shoulder.

'One of the great mysteries,' Mrs Hottle announced, as though resuming the principal topic of a homily, 'of this household is why it should be thought conducive to my well-being to turn me to face this deplorable scene.'

Joanne laughed, feeling another start of happier tears. She turned Mrs Hottle's chair away from the window to face the centre of the room, and sat opposite her. They looked at each other, each waiting for the other to say something explanatory.

'They may be the truth of the soul,' Mrs Hottle said, taking up her cup, 'but why tears?'

It came in a rush. 'My friend Marlow was attacked in school this afternoon and had to go to hospital. He was trying to defend me. His mum was furious with me, and it all reminded me how much I hate this world sometimes.'

Mrs Hottle took a sip of tea, looked with unconcealed distaste into the cup, and put it back on its saucer. She appeared to ruminate for a minute.

'Hate the world if you must,' said Mrs Hottle. 'It won't mind, but nor will it make any difference. A boy can sustain any amount of hurt for a girl he loves, and inflict any amount on one he used to. What matters more is how you feel about him.'

'Well, I love him, I think,' Joanne murmured, her eyes turned to the floor.

'You love him because he's been hurt. It's if you can love him when he hasn't done anything at all, that's what changes things. After a while, all boys stop doing things. Their lives are shaped at first by what they *can* do, and then after that, they just coast along, presuming you'll remember. It's we who have to keep doing things, coping, managing, looking after them instead of ourselves. My own mother used to believe that all men were really boys at heart, which I came to see was a lot of self-deluding nonsense. It's a thing that women say to help themselves believe they haven't married a monster.'

'Uncle Jimmy isn't a monster.'

'Uncle Jimmy never had the chance. What are you going to do, my dear? What dreams have you?'

'I don't know. Be a scholar, I suppose.'

'I should like to have done that. In my time, it would have been an indictment of a woman to want to study. She would have deserted her proper role in life, making a home and family.'

'As though you couldn't do both,' Joanne interposed.

'You can't. But the tragedy is to do neither.'

'Did you never want to have children?'

'The thought barely entered my mind,' said Mrs Hottle. 'Perhaps it should have. Children, though, make you somebody else, before you've started being yourself. They shouldn't be a vocation in themselves, any more than they should be used to mend a broken marriage. There are many other ways to be compassionate. Such as you have discovered today. What happened to your parents?'

Joanne's face flushed hot. Nobody asked her that, not even Marlow.

'They died,' she said.

'I think I'd gathered that much. In an accident?'

'No.' Mrs Hottle watched her with a look of patient sympathy. It wouldn't matter if she didn't continue, but perhaps, after all, she might risk it. 'They killed themselves.' The heavy-cold voice had returned, and with it a more ancient ache, one that time and resolution had begun to dull – those and the conspiracy of silence. In the event, the details emerged flat and inert. 'One day when Luke and I were with Auntie Mary. Adam was at school. The police went and collected him and brought him to us. He was crying. I thought he'd got into trouble. One of the policemen was going to tell us, and Adam shouted at him, saying it was his job. He took me out into the hallway, and we sat on the stairs and he told me I had to be very brave.' She came to a halt, as though there might be nothing else to the story worth telling, or that if there were, it could silently tell itself.

After a pause, Mrs Hottle asked, 'How old were you?'

'Adam was sixteen, I was ten, Luke was two,' Joanne answered promptly.

'Don't rake up these things for me.'

'You're the only person I might have wanted to tell. You might have understood.'

'Understood what, my love?'

'Why they didn't love us. They couldn't have, if they could do that. They'd thought about us just enough to make sure that neither Adam nor I came home and found them. They left a note for the woman next door, so that when she got in, she would call the police. But if they thought they were sparing us, they were mistaken. Adam said goodbye to Mum when he went to school that morning, and that afternoon, he identified their bodies.'

It was out, and sounded desperately ordinary now it was. Another silence fell. Mrs Hottle looked down at her hands, turning them palms upward, in an attitude of solemn reflection. 'Why—?'

'We don't know. They didn't leave an explanation. They hadn't been upset or arguing or anything. Nothing was wrong, but obviously everything was.'

'Obviously, yes.' Mrs Hottle sighed again, a frail sigh that ended in a tiny convulsion in her breath. 'Sometimes, in our unhappiness, we don't see that it's our view of the unhappiness that's worse than the thing itself. There are disappointments and failures and rejection and wrong turnings all the way, but acting as though each setback says something decisive about us is the behaviour of children.'

'Yes. They were cowardly really, I suppose.'

'Oh no dear, they were very brave. Not many of us could summon that amount of will-power. But that doesn't mean they weren't childish in their spite.' The words had a dry authority, efficient in its judgment, without being particularly harsh. 'But none of you gives the impression of having been damaged beyond repair.'

'We don't talk about it. It feels like it's still too soon. It's only four years ago. Luke doesn't really remember it. Sometimes he says he wants his mum, but Adam just tells him he's got us. We've had to survive, first with Auntie Mary, then here, now on our own. And we have. It's what we've done.'

'And you feel there's something callous in that. But there isn't. And it's just possible that they knew you would. They'd raised, or done half a job of raising, three healthy strong children who would pick their way through the desert and back to civilisation. Our lives are not books. They don't have logical patterns or tidy endings. But they're a process, and one that doesn't have to be mysterious.' She spoke now more slowly and deliberately, as though each sentence cost a great deal of effort. 'You have no idea why they did it, you say, but it may be that you will finally understand it one day. You may find that your mother's sense of injustice, at whatever it was, will become your own. You'll live it for her again, for a while. Then it will hurt less, because you can survive it. Just as you've survived today's...' Mrs Hottle appeared to pause as though searching for the word, but only a small gasp came.

'Are you all right?' Joanne asked.

'Of course, just a little tired.' Her eyes flickered. 'I'll wager you can make a better cup of tea than this fabulously dreadful effort.'

Joanne took the cup and saucer from her. 'Of course I can.'

Mirabelle and Jimmy had disappeared from the kitchen. Joanne took a fresh cup from the cupboard, and fancied she could just hear the murmur of bickering voices from behind a closed bedroom door, when it was drowned by the wheezing of the kettle beginning to heat up. She put a teabag in the cup. In the same cupboard that the tea was, she noticed the biscuit-tin in which she had found the money last year. It was empty this time.

When the kettle had boiled and subsided back to silence, the muffled voices reasserted themselves. It was an argument, definitely. Joanne poured hot water into the cup. Afterwards, when she tried to recall the exact order in which things had happened, she couldn't think why she had gone back into the kitchen after bringing in the tea. It might have been for the milk, but then she had thought there was a jug on the table. Did Mrs Hottle take sugar? Had she gone back for that? She couldn't remember. All she could remember was the cup of brewing tea that she put down on the table, more or less where the previous cup had been, the stifled voices continuing to insist on their separate varieties of indignation, and her return to the kitchen for something. When she came back and found Mrs Hottle asleep, she knelt on the floor before her, and rested her head in the old lady's lap, on some ridged furry fabric like candlewick, and closed her own eyes in a moment's rest. So that it was Mirabelle who came into the living-room, in high temper, to find that Mrs Hottle had slipped a little forward in her chair as her heart had stopped.

Chapter 12

Faith, Hope and Love

It was pleasant to walk the curving deserted paths of the park in early morning, the air a hubbub of bird-calls, the trees richly vigorous, their sheltering canopies shrouding and dappling the asphalt. It was agreeable to the heart to pause on the lip of the grassy bank that sloped down to the lake's edge, where some of the ducks had insinuated themselves on dry land, shaking their feathers dry and trying a few steps, surreptitiously looking to right and left as though keen to establish they were unobserved. It was sustaining to be alone on a sunlit day, away from grief and expectation and sympathy, just to walk and feel perversely blessed in the richness of a companionship just ended, of which so much more had been foregone, but which left an indelible warmth in its wake.

It was quite possible that the planned birthday celebration would have been a silly affair, discomfiting in its maniac jollity. Mrs Hottle wasn't one for celebration. It was surely better to drop the threads as they were now dropped. Her hold on them had been only of the lightest, and she hadn't been in the least given to resistance to the way things were, not even to the extent of regretting the wasted decades and the casual cruelty. They had formed a bond marked by the wisdom of mutual respect, and it was in this wisdom that Joanne intended to walk all the days of her life.

She remembered the afternoon, not long past, when the three of them had stopped here, sitting and prattling profoundly amid the strollers and the bread-throwers, the pointillist daze of the day lending the scene the tranquillity of the idyll at Asnières. And now this. Another sunny day, but just her, nurturing something heartening in an absence that might have destroyed others. Who was there, after all, to be destroyed by Mrs Hottle's death? She hadn't the taste for grief, and couldn't have found it other than disappointing in her favourite young friend, disappointing because conventional, but also so debilitating.

A young boy on a bike sped past, scattering the ducks back towards the water. An instinct to call after him to be careful came to Joanne's lips and faded there, replaced instead by a small smile.

Later, she would go to the hospital, hoping to be early enough to avoid Marlow's parents. Whether she would tell him today about Mrs Hottle would depend on his mood, but she couldn't imagine him being rendered distraught by the news. Adam hadn't been, but then he too appeared to have been attacked by somebody yesterday. But the day of violence and horror had been superseded by one that began with Luke trying, and only partially succeeding, to set a jingling top spinning on the kitchen floor, the arrival of a flushed and buoyant Martha, and now this quiet time in the park, sustainingly alone, reconciled to her various sadnesses.

She bought a mint ice-cream from a van at the park entrance. Its bright toothpaste taste belonged to an unreflective world, where nothing life-changing ever happened.

Adam had required stitches in his facial wound, and had received them at Gutford General in a room near where Marlow lay, unbeknown to him, his face also sutured back together. When he left the hospital, he had found a text message from Mrs Pelfing on his phone, inviting him to lunch the following day at an address in Chestnut Grove. As it seemed inappropriate to appear at Imporia while his face looked as though it had been involved in a boxing contest, he texted back a Yes, and contacted Troy to inform him he was Acting Manager for the day.

His taxi glided through the gated entrance to Chestnut Grove, and past the Beauforts' place, where the blinds were drawn at every window, as though there had been a death in the family. The house numbering followed some arcane sequence that even taxi-drivers hadn't disencrypted, so that some costly to-ing and fro-ing was necessary before number 50 was found. It was one of the smaller properties, its short stretch of sloping driveway occupied by two large cars, in one of which sat an unoccupied driver. For a second, as he counted out the taxi-fare, the impulse to ask the driver to turn round and leave again seemed irresistible. Instead, he found himself dolefully ringing the doorbell.

A Filipina maid answered the door. 'Mister Adam, please to come in,' she carolled, and he was ushered into a room where Vincent Beresford lay stretched out on a divan, next to which Mrs Pelfing sat on the floor, her head tilted back awkwardly against his hip.

'The man of the moment!' Vincent cooed, drowsily.

'Just in time to top us up,' Mrs Pelfing added, thrusting a lipsticked champagne-flute at Adam.

In the kitchen, Martha set the top going for the boys once more. They had nearly become proficient enough at it themselves, but still sometimes sent it careering against a table-leg. Martha now heartily regretted it. At least with the video-games at her other family's place, the kids just stationed themselves before the TV and sank into button-pressing oblivion. The spinning-top required too much in the way of tuition. For the minute or two that it whirled about the floor, though, emitting tiny whimpering sounds to itself, it held the boys spellbound. They sat on their haunches on either side of it, like Navajo elders in pow-wow, their unflickering gazes watching its tipsy progress across the floor. When it finally wobbled and fell on its side, there was always a moment of respectful silence.

'This is cool-ass,' Jordan said, not for the first time.

Luke tried to set it spinning again and sent it clattering. Jordan too had an unsuccessful go, and they turned their faces up to Martha, who had buried hers in her hands.

'Swig from the bottle,' Mrs Pelfing slurred, in a voice between suggestion and demand.

A third glass wasn't forthcoming.

'I'd rather not, if it's all the same,' Adam faltered.

'All the same as what?'

'To you.'

'Swig!' Mrs Pelfing thundered suddenly, and something told him not to disobey. He took a couple of gulps of tepid champagne.

'Now belch,' Vincent added. Adam obliged in that too. 'Gorgeous!'

Mrs Pelfing scurried across the carpet towards him on all fours. She reared up and scrabbled at Adam's trousers like a desperate dog, emitting a screeching growl as she did.

'What *are* you on?' Adam asked, with a nervous smirk. 'If I might be so bold.'

'Be bold!' Vincent cried, flinging up the hand that was holding his glass, and slopping champagne over himself.

Mrs Pelfing made a twirling motion with an amethysted hand towards a small salt-dish on the coffee-table. It was filled with a grubby-looking yellowish powder, in which a tiny spoon rested. 'Bring!' she barked.

Adam brought the dish to her, and she ladled a quantity of the drug into one of her nostrils, sneezing some of it out again straight away, and snorting the rest up in a gurgle of mucus.

'Me, me, me!' Vincent whined. Adam handed the dish to him as well. Vincent gave him his glass to hold, while he applied some of the powder to his own nose, falling back among the cushions with a grimace of agony as it went up.

'Now you,' said Mrs Pelfing, in minatory sing-song.

'I don't think so,' Adam said. 'I've only just had surgery.'

'You!' Her voice shot up and disappeared into a whispery husk in the effort at a shout.

'I'm not good at spoons.'

The amethysted hand twirled towards a side-table, where there was a length of cut straw. Of course there was. Adam sprinkled a little of the drug on the coffee-table, daubed it into a rough line with the spoon, and inhaled it into his left nostril. It stang and stank abysmally in his nose. Whatever it was, it wasn't cocaine, but he hadn't quite expected it was.

From his recumbent position on the divan, Vincent set up an ululating falsetto, in which Mrs Pelfing promptly joined, her voice lower and huskier as though threadbare from bawling. The door opened a little and the maid made a smiling appearance, unsure as to whether she was being summoned.

'Ready for lunch?' she asked cheerfully.

'Fuck you, lunch,' Mrs Pelfing rumbled, flat on her back, her face changing from hilarity to sudden confused panic and then fury in a couple of seconds.

'Not yet, OK,' the maid said.

'What's happening?' Vincent asked Adam, in the tone of a quizzical child.

'You tell me,' Adam replied. He had barely got the last word out than a thumping great weight rushed against the back of his head, knocking him to his knees. He screwed up his eyes. 'Euurrgh, fuck.' Unable to open his eyes, he could feel Mrs Pelfing's hands scrabbling at his groin again. He tried to tell her to get off, but his brain had forgotten how to speak. The words were there in his mind, and then they weren't there. What was he going to say?

A squealing started up from the divan. A squawking choir came from somewhere, picking its briskly trotting way through the finale of the Choral Symphony. Why was that? Adam unscrewed his eyes, but they screwed back up again.

Adam tried with all his might to get back on his feet. He

staggered back against something, and fell among a collection of what sounded and felt like metal objects.

'Careful, Mister Adam.'

Adam's gorge undulated as though he were going to be sick, but he wasn't.

When he opened his eyes, he was sitting on the floor. For a moment, he felt superb, then horrendous again. In a blurred frame before him were two struggling figures. He almost imagined Mrs Pelfing was holding down the maid, and trying to force something into her face, but that couldn't be. Another kind of screaming filled the air. A pair of ownerless hands began massaging Adam's shoulders from behind. His vision cleared again. The maid was screaming and fighting.

He got to his feet and stood wobbling. There was filthy powder all over the maid's face. Mrs Pelfing was growling as she tried to insert the spoon into the maid's nose. Adam pulled her back with immense force, so that the powder scattered everywhere. The maid covered her tear-soaked face as though she thought Adam was going to hit her.

'Run!' he shouted at her in a thick voice, and she ran. 'Don't come back.' He turned to the lolling head beneath him. 'You stupid bitch.'

Mrs Pelfing once more broke into her feline snarl, and scrabbled at his testicles. 'Give me.'

Vincent tottered by on all fours, apparently attempting to scoop some of the spilled powder into his hand. 'Kitty-ket,' he burbled.

'How was the lunch?' Martha wondered, as Adam appeared in the kitchen doorway.

His head was throbbing. Positively the last thing he wanted now was conversation.

'Mm, lovely,' he replied. As he walked across the kitchen, something yellow and whining, like a huge exotic insect, appeared at his feet. Instinctively, with a gasp of alarm, he kicked out at it and knocked the spinning-top flying against the wall, where it smashed.

'Adam!' a voice shouted from beneath the kitchen table, and Luke emerged, his face pale with fury.

'What's happening?'

'Oh dear,' Martha said. 'That could mark the end of the spinning-top craze.' There was relief in her voice.

The funeral took place on a sweltering day that was also the last day of term. Joanne, in favour for now having named, and secured the exclusion from school of, Marlow's attacker, was allowed to attend. There was only a small gathering at the crematorium: Jimmy and Mirabelle, Adam, Luke and herself, Mr and Mrs Blake, and an unknown woman who sat at the back and hummed peaceably to herself. It transpired that Mrs Hottle had died intestate, having nothing to leave anybody anyway, and the arrangements had been a matter of swift dispatch. The priest from Jimmy's church, Fr Dunsley, read the office while everybody fanned themselves desperately with their orders of service, and Jimmy himself read from St Paul's first letter to the Corinthians. When he was among gentle people, he was gentle. When he was among ravening people, he ravened. That way, the word was propagated. Mr Blake, to everybody's surprise and disapproval, sobbed silently throughout the obsequies, nodding vigorously when Fr Dunsley, in the caramel tones he reserved for the committal of the fondly loved, assured them that Mrs Hottle had lived a blameless life. As the service proceeded to its conclusion, and the curtains closed around the catafalque, Mr Blake released a choke of desolation. Jimmy made a motion as if to cross the chapel to him, but was sharply dissuaded by the look of daggers that Mrs Blake gave him.

At the end, as they all rose to sing 'Dear Lord and Father of Mankind', the Blakes left abruptly. They emerged into the glaring sunshine outside, climbed into their car and sped away.

The others went back to Flint Street for sandwiches and drinks. Adam loosened the immaculate black tie he had liberated from Imporia. Joanne spoke haltingly but feelingly of how much she had valued Mrs Hottle's companionship, and would always treasure her memory. When she finished, Jimmy raised his glass and murmured 'Amen'. A little later, Martha arrived to collect Luke, Joanne went to see Marlow, now discharged from hospital, and Adam returned to Paradise.

On the top of the bus, Joanne suddenly found herself crying, more bitterly than she had at any moment since Mrs Hottle's death. It was all very well to be stoical in the immediate aftermath of a bereavement, when everybody was expected to act in surprising ways. It was what you did with it when all the ceremonial was over, and you had to return to a normality that no longer included the person you loved. This was the moment the sense of loss ached at its keenest.

Marlow's face was crazy-paved with exposed stitching and mottled with odd patches of peculiar-coloured skin, livid red and necrotic white. 'I know how much you liked her,' he said. 'And hell, I did too.'

'There were so many conversations we'll never have now,' said Joanne.

'Who says you can't have them? Have them in your head. You can go on talking to her if you believe she's still out there.'

'I don't know if I do believe that. But it's a sweet thought.'

'Nothing that comes out of a face that looks like this is gonna get sweet.'

'Marlow, if only I could have done something that day.'

'You did the next best thing, hon. You nailed Weston.'

When Adam arrived at the shop, there was no sign of the Saturday boy. It seemed he had staged a work-to-rule and announced that Saturday boys didn't work on Fridays. Troy had manned the fort alone, but there hadn't been any customers anyway, so he had made a start on the sales figures. Adam pitched in with this half-heartedly, but while they were about it, a figure in dazzling pink beach-shorts and sun-hat strode in.

'Adam,' Mrs Pelfing purred, blowing a kiss at Troy. 'A word.' And she swept into the back office.

He glared at the lascivious thumbs-up that Troy gave him behind her back.

'What is it, Mrs P?'

'I wanted a word about your situation with Vincent.'

'What situation?'

'You know that he and I were once an ensemble.'

'This is really nothing to do with me.'

'Oh don't play the innocent, you little prick. You've got Vincent eating out of the palm of your hand, and God knows what other body parts too. It's no intention of mine to interrupt the course of true love, but you have to try to separate your private life from this place.'

'Can we back up a little on this? I haven't the faintest idea what you're talking about.' The sharp-tempered tone came fearlessly.

'Your relationship with Vincent. I'm not speaking from any kind of prejudice, nor the ex-partner thing, but I won't stand by and see him used and abused.'

'You've got the wrong end of several sticks. In the first place, I'm not having any sort of relationship with Vincent. I barely know him. In the second place, I'm not gay.'

'Ha!' Mrs Pelfing yelped. 'That's a good one.'

'I beg your pardon?'

'You're out and screaming, love. You've got gay coming out of your queer ears.'

Was she under the influence of something? He spoke carefully. 'I've nothing against gay at all, but you're beginning to offend me.'

'Too bloody right I am!' Mrs Pelfing's voice was suddenly a scream. 'And I'll go on offending you as long as I'm paying your wages, you little chiseller. I don't seem to be getting through to you the polite way, so I'll try it more rude. Keep away from Vincent, or I'll rip your balls off for ping-pong. Understand?'

Adam looked steadily into her flaring eyes. She was crazy. 'I can't claim I do understand, but I want you out of here now.'

There was a moment of stunned fury before she exploded. '*How dare you?*'

'Oh pull yourself together. Save it for the drug-lunches. You may be the owner, but I'm running this show, and I'm getting the distinct impression that you're bad for business. In future, if you wish to see me, you call and make an appointment. If you keep dropping in on these social calls, however charmed I ought to be, I'll find me another job. Now get out of my office.'

Mrs Pelfing's inflamed face stood its ground a few moments longer, then she backed down. She looked as though she was about to say something conciliatory, thought better of it, and turned to leave. Adam followed her to the front of the shop, a prudent but unyielding two paces behind her. As she reached the walkway outside, she turned with a sudden imploring look in her eyes.

'Adam, don't let's fall out.'

'I'm sure there's no need for that,' he replied, coldly. 'Good day.'

'You know you're always welcome for lunch.'

'Like you said, let's keep business and pleasure, or whatever it is, separate.'

'And the Vincent thing...'

'That's all.' And he turned and strode back into the shop.

Troy offered him a sympathetic shrug. 'She is basically as crazy as a bag of cats.'

'So I've learned the hard way,' Adam sighed. 'She's got some weirded-out idea that VB and I are having a thing.'

'A sex thing? Gross.'

'Tell me. She's eaten up with jealousy. It makes you wonder what he's told her.'

'Or maybe he's really got it bad. Cool.' Troy sniggered.

'Give it a rest.'

'No, think about it. You could get anywhere you wanted if you used that kind of influence. People would sell their grandads for that. I know I'd sell mine. May he rest in peace, and all that.'

'I can't think of anything in my whole lousy life I'd want enough to pretend that I was in bed with Beresford.'

'Really? Nothing at all? You're not trying hard enough, Mr Young.'

Adam covered his face with his hands in resignation. 'A funeral, a confrontation with a mad bitch, and now you putting the shits up me, all in one stinking day. What a lucky boy I am.'

Troy laughed. 'Beer usually helps.'

'You're buying.'

'You got it.'

'But.'

'But what?'

'Only if you wear one of those green flying-caps that have just come in.'

'Yeah, I'll do that,' said Troy. 'If.'

'If what?'

'You wear one of those waist-length cravats.'

Adam's scar still twinged a little when he laughed, but for the first time that day, he risked it.

As it had been a rough time for everybody lately, and it was now the start of the school holiday, the head of the household decided that a trip to the seaside was in order. He invited Martha too, to thank her for all the extra work she had been doing lately, and to avail themselves of the extra work with Luke that the trip would involve, and so that she could drive them there. A semblance of contrition had been coaxed out of Luke following the episode at the zoo, which, Adam was reminded by letter from the Principal, had brought shame on the school. As for himself, he badly needed to wash the Mrs Pelfing episode out of his system, while Joanne had been sunk in intimations of mortality for quite long enough now.

The Saturday journey to the south coast was an ordeal. Everybody else had had the same idea. It was a baking day, and large sections of the motorway were reduced to single-file traffic, which inched along or sat statically in long hot rows. Martha was a patient driver, though, and Luke had been plentifully supplied with colouring-books and sweets and bleeping toys, so they kept their tempers through the four hours it took to get there. Adam lazed back in the deeply reclined passenger-seat, sometimes snoozing a little and waking to find his T-shirt sticking to him. Joanne was reading Hume's *Dialogues Concerning Natural Religion*. The car was filled hypnotically with the comforting drone of Martha's favourite singer-songwriter. A child of about Luke's age pressed his face to the side-window of a stationary car in the adjacent lane. Luke looked at the boy with an incurious stare, until the other boy stuck his tongue out.

'This is ridiculous,' Adam sighed.

'Oh, we'll get there in the end,' Martha insisted.

'Just in time to come back.'

The boy in the car alongside had rolled down the window, and was now showing his exposed bum to Luke.

'We could always stay over, couldn't we, rather than hurry back?' suggested Joanne.

'Well, we could, if we don't mind spending the whole weekend in the clothes we're currently sweating into,' said Adam.

'Buy some more. You're earning enough to keep us in clothes now, aren't you?'

'Hey, I like your style,' Martha told Joanne in the rear-view mirror. 'Stick it to the man.'

'Or whatever.' Joanne glanced to her left. 'Oh my God.'

The boy in the adjacent car was now peeing out of the open window.

'Look at that pig,' Luke said, and they all turned to look at the appalling boy.

Adam sat up straight and rolled down his window. 'Oi!' he shouted at the adjacent driver, who stared intently ahead in a state of suspended animation. He reached out and rapped urgently on the driver's window, which was sedately lowered.

'Adam,' Joanne sighed. 'Don't get involved.'

'Do you realise your little animal is whizzing out the window?'

The man blinked at Adam with a profoundly uninterested look. 'No he isn't,' he said. And he wasn't now. 'Can I ask you to turn your music down?' the man added.

'Bugger off,' Adam said, and the two windows rolled decisively up again.

Martha laughed and turned up the soporific music.

They got there, having waited a final three-quarters of an hour in a car-park queue, and strode along the seafront in the direction of the pier. A startling wind had now got up, but everybody looked set to carry on regardless. The beaches teemed with families, pensioners, the drunk and the drug-addled. A white student in a shalwar kamiz was playing the yanaka to one whole section, his back to the indolently slopping tide. Jet-skis whined like buzz-saws, frantically chopping the undulant water in pointless circles. Small boys in long swim-shorts threw themselves from the end of the groyne, occasioning shrieks of horror from the onlookers.

The pier was teeming too, but they managed to find a tin table under a covered part of the decking, where they ordered a mixture of fish and chips, ice-creams, beer and rosé wine.

'I'll remember this day forever,' announced Martha, expansively.

'We haven't done anything yet, Martha,' Joanne said.

'Of course. The day is before us, and pregnant with possibility.'

'Steady on,' Adam chortled. 'You'll get Luke excited.'

Luke wanted to know what pregnant was.

Joanne got up from the table, leaving a half-finished plate of chips behind her and went to gaze over the pier railing. The sea surged and broke in swells in the restless wind, its surface covered in traceries of froth that formed and vanished precipitately. A dinghy violently bobbed, threatening to capsize for many minutes before it finally capsized, throwing its two occupants into the swell, while the sun still obstinately shone, glaring and sparkling in turquoise foam on the crests of water. Joanne succumbed to an entranced state amid the bustle and racketing wind, until her brother's voice piped into her ear.

'You OK?'

'Yes, I'm OK. It was a good idea to get away.'

'I think we should stay,' Adam said. 'Though we may have to tramp the streets looking for a hotel.'

'Or you will.'

'Or I will.'

Minutes later, Adam had made a mobile call and got two rooms at the Maritime Grand.

The lobby was an imposing cathedral-like space with green marble pillars, luxuriant plants climbing out of mock-Chinese jardinières, and an expansive mahogany reception-desk staffed by unsmiling name-badged women. The rooms were a twin and a double, which made for a moment of awkward decision-making. Joanne asked Martha whether she minded sharing and received the suggestion that it might be better if Luke were to go in with her. As this seemed to raise the unabashed possibility that Adam and Martha were intending to sleep together, she made the point emphatically that it ought to be one room for boys and the other for girls. Adam suggested that Martha was the person best qualified to keep Luke on a short leash, but that left Joanne and him in the same room, which was wildly inappropriate. Luke wanted to know what a short leash was. The gender-segregated arrangement was reverted to.

'We can always go musical bedding during the night,' Martha suggested.

'No we can't,' Joanne asserted. 'Why don't we just get a third room?'

'I could do you a third room on the top floor, but it only has a shower,' said the receptionist.

'No, we can't afford to go mad,' Adam decided. 'We'll make do with what we've got.' Though, since the girls couldn't possibly be expected to sleep in the same bed, that left him bunking up with Luke. 'That's OK, isn't it?' he asked Luke. Luke didn't know what bunking up involved, but instinctively felt that if it required his permission, it wasn't likely to be fun.

The rooms were unexpectedly shabby and small. There was a smell in them, a stench even, of unwashed carpet and old cigarette-smoke, the bathrooms were full of spots of rust exposed by heavily chipped paintwork, and the TV in Adam and Luke's room offered only a fizzing screen. 'What a dump,' Adam said, twiddling the tuner fruitlessly.

'Martha says she'll catch us up at the fairground,' Joanne said, when she met her brothers in the corridor.

'What's she doing?' Adam asked.

'Taking a bath.'

Martha's spirits had failed. She was lying half-submerged in chilly water, crying. This was the way it was doomed to be. The child-minder was at once part of the family, and yet not; trusted implicitly and yet waved aside when the family willed itself together again. She dabbed at her wet face with wet hands. All it was about was the obvious misjudgment of her obsession with Adam. He wasn't even that good-looking.

'Oh stop it,' she told herself, aloud. She must do the right thing. She sent a text consisting of the single word 'Sorry' to Adam, dried and dressed herself, and slipped out of the hotel. After a few minutes' further deliberation at the wheel of her car, she drove regretfully but, as she saw it, bravely back to Gutford.

Luke had discovered his favourite ride at the fair, a kiddies' merry-go-round that revolved at a pace sedate enough for toddlers. Its cars were different kinds of vehicles, and he had crammed himself inside the lower deck of a little double-decker bus. Each time the ride began slowing to a halt, he screamed out 'Again!' They had indulged him for four turns now, but it was getting tedious watching the dull plodding of the ride. Smaller children on it than Luke had the decency to look a little bored, but he was even more thrilled than he had been getting saturated on the log-flume.

'Where's Martha?' Joanne wondered.

'Yes, where is Martha?' Adam looked at his phone. 'She says sorry.'

'For what?'

'Must be having a fit of the glums. Whatever.' He slipped the phone back in his pocket. 'Who wants pizza?' he yelled, as Luke's bus came ambling by again.

'Yay!' Luke howled.

By the time the sky was streaked with poisonous orange cloud, and a distant throb of music could be heard from beach-bars below the seafront road, Adam was sitting up at the bar of the Maritime Grand with a frosty dry martini. Luke was safely tucked up in bed, while Joanne, who had greeted the news of Martha's absconding with unalloyed relief, was lounging on her bed watching TV. There was only a small straggle of guests in the bar. It wasn't the kind of town where you spent an evening sitting in a hotel drinking ten-pound cocktails. He was suddenly seized with the feeling of not wanting to go home. Home was where Martha had gone, where he was tied to a brother and sister who would need him, and need him to be successful, for a good few years yet.

Supposing, though, he was free to do whatever tonight. What would it be? He could go drinking, clubbing, find somebody irresistible, be made to feel all right. It seemed dully unambitious in its scope. Another option was sitting at this bar until he was ready to drop. Or there was going to bed with his kid brother.

'What's cool to do tonight?' he asked the barman.

The barman smirked. 'Get bitched. Make out under the stars. We lead a bohemian life down here, mate, as you'll have read in the tourist guide.'

'You're a cynical young scamp.'

'I thought you looked the same, so I wouldn't insult your intelligence.' Adam drained his glass. 'Another?'

'Did I say "when"?'

'No sirree, Bob.'

The barman scrammed the cocktail shaker through the sinkful of ice, and free-poured pale blue gin into it.

'Adam,' Adam said.

'The first man.'

'Betcha can't guess the name of the place I work.'

'The Garden of Eden?'

'No cigar.'

'Paradise then.' He dashed the dry vermouth with a tiny flick of the wrist, and didn't seem to have noticed Adam's nod. 'No way! Not that mega-mall in Gutford?'

'That's me.' The barman gave an impressed whistle that sounded almost genuine. 'And you are?'

'I am.'

'No olive.'

'Too late.' They both grinned at the complicit idiocy of one man producing intoxicants for another man. 'Joey.'

'Hey.'

They shook hands over the drink that appeared between them.

'Hey.'

An elderly man came to the end of the bar and asked Joey for a glass of ice. When presented with a half-pint glass nearly full of huge cubes, he held it up and looked ruefully at it. 'Can you spare a little more?'

'Yes sirree,' Joey said, and managed to get a single extra cube into the glass. The old man went away happy. 'This is tougher than the fight-game, I'm telling you,' he said to Adam.

'So I see.'

'So, on your own?'

'Long story. Actually, short story. My sister and lickle bruv are in bed. There was a child-minder, but she kind of blew us out this afternoon.'

'Hot stuff?'

'Kinda, but crazy.'

'Not into crazy then?'

Adam thought. 'Not really, no.' It was the first time he'd ever realised it.

'Wrong town then.'

'I guess.' They both nodded in a meaningful way, looked around the deserted bar, then looked back at each other and smirked again. 'You got anybody?'

'Yes sirree. Coming up two years now.'

'Sweet.'

'It's OK.' Adam finished another martini. 'How many more of those can you hold down?'

'About six or seven, tops.'

'I'm gonna close the bar.'

'OK.'

'And then we could go get some action?'

Leonardo di Caprio was crying as Joanne rolled her eyes,

uttered an impatient sigh and got up from the bed. She wandered to the window and looked down on the seafront, just in time to see Adam leave the hotel with some guy.

'Now there are three steps to heaven,' Joey explained. 'Step one, you find a bar that isn't full of screaming pretty-boys and big fat girls. Step two, you order a martini the way you like it, not the way some dork of a barman in a piss-elegant hotel chooses to make it for you.'

'Step three: you kiss and hold it tightly,' Adam put in, modulating into a rock-and-roll baritone.

'Well, that certainly sounds like something resembling heaven to me.'

They high-fived each other.

'We're high-fiving,' Joey pointed out.

'Eww.'

'Have a good one, boys,' a passing policewoman advised them. 'Stay safe.'

Joey replied in a Texas drawl. 'Why, thank you, ma'am, we surely will.'

Adam's phone bleeped. 'I guess you're looking for some kind of explanation,' the text began.

'It's your mum.'

'It's the crazy child-minder.' He deleted the message. 'Probably expecting to get paid for last week.'

'Stick that.'

Adam pocketed the phone. 'Did you get paid for last week?'

'In full.'

There was a club called Whirl or Swirl or something. To the untutored eye, Adam thought, it would have looked like a gay place, but everywhere here looked that way. Joey knew the DJ. The music was too jagged and abstract to dance to, but people looked satisfied. A girl in panda eye makeup came and chatted for a while. When she walked away, Joey gave Adam a quick raise of his eyebrows. Adam shook his head with a rueful air of I-would-if-I-could.

They drank a couple of martinis, then beers, then vodkas. Joey had a word with someone, following which they crammed themselves into a cubicle in the Gents and snorted two fat lines of coke each off the cistern. When they emerged, a gay boy gave them a sweet smile and said something about a traffic-jam. After about fifteen minutes, a modest delivery of numbing stimulant buzz went through their heads. Joey danced with a couple of girls, mugging and groining it to their great amusement. Adam again had the feeling of not wanting to go back. He wished Joanne were old enough to just take Luke home.

The club stayed open beyond the point where you could still hope it wasn't going to close yet. When they came out, it was still just dark, but there was the faint hint on the horizon of the navy-blue sky regressing to midnight.

'Good night,' said Adam.

'So soon?'

'No, I mean—'

'I know. You're a good guy. Good enough to put me up when I come to Gutford for the Paradise sale.'

'Sure thing.' They got to the doorway of the Maritime Grand. 'Do you live at the Maritime Grand?'

'Do I?' Joey pretended to think. 'No, I don't believe I do.'

Adam stuck out his hand. 'Listen, I'll leave my mobile number tomorrow. You're welcome to stay whenever.'

They shook hands. 'Cheers, Ads.'

'You're gonna call me Ads?'

'Looks like.'

They were still holding each other's hands. Joey had another broad grin for him. Without knowing how it happened, Adam suddenly had Joey's face in his face, and was being kissed like being chewed. It was startling and silly. He accepted it for about five seconds and pulled back.

'Whoa! I didn't see that coming.'

'I told you, we're bohemian down here. No ordeal intended.'

'It wasn't an ordeal, just...'

'Well well well.' He didn't seem at all conscious at having done anything wrong. 'First time for everything, eh?'

'I guess.'

'Don't worry about it.'

'No, it's… Thanks though.' Joey's eyebrows raised. 'You've sorted something out in my head.'

Being kissed by another man was physically a little shocking, in that it had involved more force, more texture and more intent than being kissed by a woman, but it was also somehow shallower. The moment made Adam wonder what had made Joey think he might be receptive to it, and whether it was the same thing that Vincent reportedly saw in him. It didn't seem possible to put this question to Joey, as he surely wasn't gay, or at least not in the ideological way. His was another approach entirely. Who cared what kissing might say about you? It might just feel good.

'I've not been noted for sorting people's heads out,' Joey said. 'Usually the opposite.'

Adam nodded. He felt about twelve years old. 'Anyway, you're still welcome to stay.'

They exchanged mobile numbers and final comradely smirks, before Joey disappeared along the seafront.

Back in the room, Adam found an empty bed with a note on the pillow. Joanne had written, 'Luke's in with me. Thank you for caring.'

The Gutford they returned to had taken on a sallow, pre-emptively autumnal air, as though the summer, having flirted around the coastal borders of the country, had declined to venture too far inland, where it appeared to be wasted on the inhabitants. Overcast skies and constant drizzle marked the rest of July, producing a sense of moral outrage. People doggedly went about in shorts and swimwear, their goose-pimpled skin hardening to sandpaper in the supermarket air-conditioning. In Paradise, the cool air felt particularly unreal, and confirmed people in their theory that all it was doing was circulating bacteria.

Marlow and Joanne sat in the eddies of cold outside the juice-bar on a dreary day, nursing pulpy mango smoothies, watching shoals of day-trippers drifting by. Marlow's face had settled into its scarred look; diagonal whitish creases across his cheeks, a couple of rough red lines on his forehead. He was trying to grow his hair back to disguise some of it, but the process was agonisingly slow. Returning to school would be an ordeal. For now, it was nice to be away from the smell of antiseptic and the starched breeziness of professional care. There was dutiful kindness to get you through the trauma, then the genuine sort to ease you back to normality.

'How strange.'

'What's strange?' asked Joanne, caught in the bitter effort of trying to inhale a stubborn pellet of mango through the thin straw.

'There are some people over there opening their own picnic, and no one's stopping them.'

'They need all the mugs they can get in here at the moment. Adam says business is very slow at the clothes-place.'

'That's because they sell weird crap at, like, five hundred pounds. Let's go and see him.'

'No. He doesn't like being bothered at work.'

'But if he's not busy?'

'Yeah, but there's this weird woman who owns the place, and keeps showing up unexpectedly and making life difficult for him.'

'Evil bitch,' Marlow said. 'I'll scare her off, just by showing my ugly moosh.'

'I've told you, you don't look that bad.'

'You try it.'

A posse of briskly trotting office staff came along the walkway. Amid the officious bobbing shoulders, they caught a glimpse of Vincent's electric-blond head. There was a musical hum of conversation among the group, just audible amid the tattoo of stilettos.

'The man himself,' Joanne said.

'What a wankbox.'

'What's a wankbox?'

'Duh. It's a box you wank into.'

'Oh I see. And what was in it before?'

'Tissues. Then when the tissues are all used up...'

'Thank you.' Joanne pushed away her smoothie.

In the admin office, Bellenor sat alone. She was on the final day of her notice, and had requested a meeting with Vincent to brief him before the new financial director assumed his post on Monday. Kept waiting for over an hour, she had finally had to endure the humiliation of seeing Vincent call the entire admin staff into his office before leading them all towards the lift.

At considerable risk to her own professional standing, Bellenor had been complicit in the past few months in destroying unhelpful documentation, and negotiating with an increasingly hawkish team of auditors. She had, it wasn't too presumptuous to say, saved Vincent's bacon, and wasn't sure that he understood the gravity of the potential charges she had thwarted. The price of her complicity was going to be greater control of the financial reins, but that, it was clear, Vincent had no intention of relinquishing. Her notice of resignation had been accepted crisply, and the recruitment process for a replacement set immediately in train. While she wasn't sure why she cared exactly, she had been determined to have a final riot-act showdown with Vincent, to leave with the satisfaction of making him see what a knife-edge Paradise was poised on. And yet even now, hard-faced childish denial persuaded him it was a good idea to slight her. Very well.

Bellenor rose and walked into Vincent's office. It was just a question of deciding what to smash. Should she empty the water in the flower-vase over his computer keyboard? The puerile futility of it disappointed her. Nothing that could be solved in an hour would suffice. She pulled open a drawer of the desk. It was untidily crammed with printouts, much of the information on them familiar to her, as it was her own staff who had printed them out. The next drawer down contained an open tin of apricots and a pencil. The bottom drawer was locked. A locked drawer in a building entirely dedicated to the mendacious principle of transparency was an interesting aberration. Bellenor looked around. Nothing suggested itself. She wrenched at the drawer, kicked it, and wrenched it again so hard, the desk itself moved an inch or two, exposing the unreally bright area of carpet on which its front foot had stood. The drawer remained locked fast. A quick rifling of the other drawers failed to turn up the key. Again, she looked around. Propped against the wall at the far end was a black metal rod with a flattened end like a riding-crop, a tool apparently for opening windows. There was no possibility of inserting it between the drawers, but the bottom drawer came forward about a centimetre before it engaged with the lock. She was just able to put the very tip of the window-opener into the tiny crack of space. It wouldn't lever the drawer open, but if she positioned it above where she imagined the lock might be... She took off her shoe and administered a sharp blow to the top of the rod, hoping to chisel the drawer open. Nothing happened. In frustration, she raised the rod and rammed it hard against the drawer, causing half of its front panel to splinter away. Like much else about Paradise, she grimly smirked, it was shoddy rubbish. Completing the demolition of the front of the drawer by hacking it to bits with the window-rod, she found inside a manila folder.

In the folder was another series of printouts, this time photographs that had apparently been taken on a phone and uploaded to a PC. The quality was surprisingly good, and the pages had all been neatly dated by hand. The first was a picture of the interior of a bookshop; a few customers browsing, a couple of assistants behind the counter. She studied it for any clue as to its significance, but could see none. The next was a long-shot of one of the ground-floor corridors, taken in the middle of the day, with sunlight streaming down from the distant atrium roof and a throng of people milling through. In the foreground, a man raised a carton of orange juice to his lips. What was this about? She flicked through the remaining pages, looking for anything obviously incriminating. In one of the later ones, taken inside a small shop, an apparently unconscious man was being carried with difficulty somewhere by two other men. The very last picture was dated only two days ago, and was of a pair of smartly attired gentlemen assistants standing amid the hanging jackets and trousers of a menswear shop. If the pictures represented some sort of spying operation, it was hard to see what they were evidence of. Leafing back through the bundle, she stopped at a picture of the inside of a Gents' toilet. A single man stood in profile at a urinal. With an almost perceptible click, the link fell into place.

One of the men in the clothes shop was in every picture. He was behind the counter in the bookshop. He was the unconscious figure, recognisable by the same V-neck black jumper he was wearing in the bookshop. He was the man swigging the orange juice on the crowded walkway. He was the man in the toilet. In other pictures, he was leading a small boy along by the hand. He was in the dead centre of a press of people at the launch-party, glancing above his head at something, clutching a glass of red wine. He stood outside the main entrance with a dark-haired girl who had her hand in his trouser-pocket. In the only picture not apparently taken at Paradise, he was lying sprawled on the floor of a lounge, half-propped up against a long white sofa, seemingly doped out of his mind. Bellenor didn't know who he was, but it was clear enough that he had no idea that he was the object of such persistent attention.

On the other side of the admin office, a ping and a green light announced that the lift was on its way back up again. Stuffing the printed pictures into her bag, she hurtled to the stairs and had reached the bottom of the first flight as the lift-doors opened to let out Javine.

Javine crossed into Vincent's office and picked up the floor-plan that was spread out on his desk. As she was turning to leave, she noticed the broken sections of the drawer on the carpet, together with the window-rod. She tutted. It was somehow entirely typical of Vincent to think that the easiest answer to a lost key was half-demolishing the desk. That would be something else she'd have to organise.

The autumn collections were all about reverting to a more classical look, following the extravagances of summer: long grey coats, grey cargo pants, brown boots, and the all-important woolly hats, now in zigzag patterns with smiley faces worn at the back. There was nothing to make the pulse race, thought Adam, as he looked at the designs online, but that might make them easier to shift. Shifting hadn't really been Imporia's strong point through the summer. When men did try something on, their partners often enough told them it looked ridiculous, a verdict Troy tried to overcome, but which Adam couldn't help but subtly ratify whenever he was consulted. This was not often, as he had perfected a look of rarefied disconnection that did nothing to encourage potential customers to speak to him.

He was tearing the tissue away from a consignment of crocheted scarves when Troy told him there was someone to see him. A small voice gave him a 'Hello'. He looked into a pair of limpid green eyes.

'Ellie!'

'Essie.'

'That's what I meant.' She had a little chuckle for him. 'Sorry. How's it going?'

'Yeah OK, still at the card-shop. Ain't you done good though?'

He gave a modest shrug. 'If you call running a snooty menswear shop with no customers doing good.'

'Not enough snooty men then.'

'Guess not.'

She just forgot to look away as this opening salvo concluded, which quickened his interest. She looked lovely. Her coal-black hair was wound round her head in a complicated pattern, and she had on a retro floral-print dress, like the human heroine of a fairy-tale full of coy animals.

'Not seen much of Ben then lately?' she noted.

'No. He still at the bookshop?'

'Yeah. It's just you who's been upwardly mobile.'

'How did you know to find me here?'

'I read *Paradise News*.'

'Somebody does then.' They looked at each other with vacant, but congenial, half-smiles. This could go on for half-an-hour, floating about, unless he managed an initiative. 'Time for a drink upstairs?'

'Sure.'

'Troy.'

'I'm on it,' Troy said, peering out from behind a box. As Essie turned to lead the way, he pursed his lips at Adam.

'It's a disaster-area, to be honest. I don't know what I'm going to do when the crunch comes.'

They were sitting in the cocktail-bar with vivid yellow drinks between them. Reclining in her chair, Essie was playing with a stringy bracelet that she had slipped off her wrist and was twisting into different patterns between her fingers.

'You'll get something with your CV, for sure.'

'I hope. But then, I wonder whether there might be something on the outside I could do. This place is beginning to feel like a prison.'

'People are losing their jobs outside. It's safer in here.'

'I guess.'

She took a sip of the cocktail. 'Ben says Print Media is on the slide. Mrs Stone has been in, warning she might have to pull the plug if things don't look up. How come you got on the escalator to success?'

Adam thought. How had he, after all? 'I beat up the boss.' She laughed. 'No, really. That seems to have helped. He gave me a second chance.'

'You don't look a violent man to me, Adam.'

'Nah, I'm a cuddly bear.' She gave a different kind of laugh, more reflective, not quite meeting his eyes now. 'At least I could be.' Sitting upright, she leaned seriously over the glass, and took another sip, deep red lips closing around the pristine top of the straw. His entire upper body, everywhere north of the heart, flamed up. It was like suddenly being drastically embarrassed. He faltered. 'Essie?'

'I'd like that,' she said.

They dawdled back down to the third floor, taking the stairs. After three flights, Adam crossed to her other side and took her hand. She smiled without looking at him, but returned the pressure of palm and fingers. He felt tense and hardened all over the surface, as though his outer shell were protecting him from the effect of having gone limp inside. What kind of fool had he been to let her go the first time? He dimly recalled not having felt ready. If he was ready now, it was with the intimation that there was no such thing as not ready. She had come to him both times unsought, allowing him the one mistake as a bit of male indecision, which he now had the chance to revoke.

At the entrance to Imporia, they stopped.

'Have you still got my number?' he asked.

'I do. Does that mean you haven't still got mine?'

He took out his phone and looked. No, there she was, the only

E in the list. 'Should we do something tonight then?'

'We should.'

He moistened his lips and kissed her briefly. She squeezed his hand again and hurried away. Instinctively, he wiped the other hand across his mouth as he watched her go, smearing the back with a dim trace of pink.

'*O, il est là!*' exclaimed a voice from the other side of a mirror as he came into the shop. Vincent was trying on one of the huge autumn coats. '*Qu'en penses-tu?*' He swayed across the floor like something out of Eisenstein.

This was tiresome. 'Not really you, VB.'

'*Vraiment?*'

'No, actually great, I meant. Looking again.'

'I want!'

'You'd be our first purchaser,' Troy put in, over-articulating the final word, it now having been solemnly understood that there was to be no more complimentary largesse to Vincent.

Vincent stopped again in front of the mirror, pulling the outsized coat around him like a blanket. 'You boys are going to bankrupt me at this rate. I'll take it.'

The following evening, Marlow had something like a date. A boy in another form in his year had cycled by the house a day earlier, putting a sealed letter through the door. In it, he expressed in unsentimental prose his admiration for the way Marlow had survived the vicious attack, and that he had gone up even higher in his, Myron's, estimation. There was a mobile number. Marlow read the note in a bemused state. Although he had never spoken to the other boy, he knew who he was. There was only one Myron. There was probably only one Marlow too.

He texted to thank Myron, who responded immediately, and suggested they might do something that evening. The first proposal – ten-pin bowling – wasn't Marlow's thing, but Myron was up for the cinema, and they decided to go and see *Nightmare*

Blood Orgy, a comedy horror that they were both just officially old enough to get into. When Marlow arrived at the Paradise multiplex, a layer of powder smudging his facial scars, Myron was already there and had bought the tickets.

'Looking good,' he said to Marlow.

He was an odd-looking boy, with scrubby reddish-brown hair, protuberant ears, uneven teeth, and a left eye that was turned a little inward towards his nose, giving him the air of looking fixedly at everything. Marlow smiled at him. It was too late to back out, but at least in the cinema, they didn't have to talk, and it was apparently a long film. When they took their seats, Myron, who sat up very straight so that he was a head taller than Marlow, turned to look at him and gave him an outrageously proprietorial nod, as though this was the outcome of a long and successful campaign. Marlow gulped and popped open his cola.

The film was indeed very long, but provoked alternate gurgles of disgust and screams of laughter in the audience throughout. Marlow could cope with the blood-drenched horror, but the passages where somebody was just edging nervously along a shadowy corridor creeped him out. At one such point, he slumped slowly down into his seat, hunching his shoulders, half-screwing his eyes. He was aware of Myron echoing the movement, and gave him a nervous giggly glance. An arm went boldly around his shoulders. This was beyond weird. The arm pulled Marlow towards the body it was attached to, with a gently imperious tug. He smelled piney deodorant. He leaned woodenly against Myron until, with his free arm, Myron picked up Marlow's hand and placed it on his leg. As though on cue, the audience around them exploded into repulsed shrieks. A severed head flew towards the screen, and Marlow found himself cringing into Myron's body. It was both preposterous and insanely joyful. He squeezed Myron's thigh with conviction, and had his face pulled up and subjected to a clumsy, vigorous, cola-flavoured kiss.

'You don't hang about,' Marlow told him in the foyer afterwards.

'You do.'

'I just didn't—'

'Shut up. Let's get something to eat.'

'Not here though.'

They took the lift to Eighth, where Good Old Fish 'n' Chips was still serving. Myron bought the food as he had the tickets, and they sat at a formica table and ate thickly battered pollock and floppy chips stinging with vinegar.

Myron smirked at Marlow as he ate. It was hard to see the warmth in him.

'You're not doing this for a bet, are you?' Marlow wondered.

'If I was, it's backfired.' He wiped ketchup off his lip. 'I like you, OK? Is that wrong?' Beneath the table, he trapped one of Marlow's feet between his. It wasn't wrong.

At home, Joanne was reading while Luke multi-tasked, watching a cartoon on the DVD player, colouring in his book and eating piles of bacon-flavoured snacks. They had been to the outdoor pool to see a display of synchronised swimming, only to find that it had had to be cancelled because of a terrorist threat, but he hadn't complained. The extraordinary fact about him was that he wasn't a whinger. He didn't demand things. He'd wanted Jordan to come with them, but Jordan was apparently grounded for some infraction. There was no suggestion, though, that the day was ruined, that Joanne wasn't enough, and when they arrived to find people being turned away from the pool, he made a philosophical noise and accepted it. It was a relief, but a little disturbing for the aura of crushed maturity it seemed to suggest in a boy of six. He had had a rebellious phase, but it hadn't lasted long, and while Joanne had generally failed to placate the screaming that went with it, Adam had been able to snuff it out simply by saying, in a barely raised voice, 'Enough'.

The phone shrilled out.

'Hello? Wait a moment.' Joanne carried it over to Luke. 'It's Jordan.'

'What's the matter?' Luke asked in a bright forgiving tone and, on hearing no more than the first few words of the explanation, dissolved into giggles.

On the TV screen, a bulldozer had grown limbs and an angry scowl, and was threatening a bespectacled man in a pathetic little car.

Joanne's mobile burst into song. She looked at the screen.

'Hello, darling. How's it going?' Marlow was silly with excitement, couldn't talk too long as Myron had only gone to the Gents, but it was the most extraordinary thing that had ever happened, and guess what? 'What?' she asked on cue. Myron had invited him to the synagogue. 'Are we talking about the same boy?' How many Myrons were there? He had to go now, love you bye.

Luke chuckled and dropped the phone and picked it up again and laughed again.

Everybody in the world was happy, despite all the odds. How did that happen? Was it chance or talent or what was it? Joanne saw herself on the periphery of a world of happy boys. How had she got there? She looked at her hands. For a second, the idea that she might varnish her nails came into her head, but blew quickly out again in the currents of better judgment. Perhaps better judgment was the problem. It was a luxury that boys could afford to deny themselves somehow, and they still came through the calamities. She looked at her phone. On the home screen was a picture of a quizzical-looking kitten.

When Adam arrived at the High Bar at eight to meet Essie, she wasn't yet there, but Ben and Corinne were. Ben punched him on the shoulder and upper arm, shouting his name with each violently friendly blow.

'Yeah, how's it going, Ben?'

'Only sensational, bruv. Get this one down you, then we're going to the Ski Lodge for fondues and sherbs.' Ben handed him a pint.

'Corinne, how you doing?'

'Yep,' Corinne replied, offering her cheek for Adam's kiss.

'Fondues, matey, fondues.' Ben slapped him on the back of the neck, making the pint in his hand slop. 'Woo-hoo!'

'Yeah yeah. Great to see you. I'm supposed to meeting Essie though.'

Ben roared with laughter. 'Priceless. Course you are, you kidney bean. She's here.'

And here indeed Essie was, returning from the Ladies. She was wearing a cerise peplum and white deck pants, and her hair was set in a frozen tumble across one eye. She looked unbelievable.

'The gang's all here then,' she said.

Adam smiled weakly at her, half for the unwanted crowd, half for feeling not quite worthy. 'You look amazing.'

'What about me?' Ben yelled in his ear. 'Don't I look amazing too?'

'You look amazing too, Ben. Allegedly.'

Corinne snorted, and threw down the rest of a frothy cocktail. The others were ready to go, but Ben wouldn't authorise their departure till Adam had got through the pint of brown ale he'd been bought. It was the longest couple of minutes of the evening.

At the Ski Lodge, they ate a deliquescent Vacherin Mont d'Or with boiled new potatoes, and paid an astronomical mark-up for a bottle of Swiss white wine that tasted of fresh air, before lapsing back into cocktails and beers. The conversation divided, as before, on gender lines. While the girls talked in a serious intimate way, Adam and Ben had a more fragmentary conversation about work. Ben knew his job was a 'goner', wanted to know what Adam's secret was. Again, Adam heard himself saying he just felt he'd had more than his fair share of luck, but maybe the winning streak had now hit the buffers. Imporia was struggling.

'The word on the streets, bruv, is that you've got Beresford round your little finger.'

'What? What is this shit?'

'I'm not saying nothing, I'm just saying it's like everyone sees you getting on, and you're good at what you do, but he allowed you to come back, didn't he, and ever since, it's like you're in the news-sheet every two minutes, getting promoted again. It's all I'm saying.' He'd blown himself out. 'I'll shut up now, shall I?' Adam was sunk in thought. 'Bruv?'

He was in the news-sheet every two minutes. Vincent had brought him back when he could have had him prosecuted. He was now manager of a store owned by a personal friend of Vincent's. The sense of having been guided through the past few months was simultaneously nauseating and vaguely thrilling.

He looked up. Ben was meekly sipping his drink, aware of having overstepped some invisible line. Adam gripped his shoulder.

'Ben, thanks. You've helped me make a big decision.'

Ben grinned from ear to ear. 'Ooo-wee,' he said. Then he offered the mature analysis. 'If you've got any sense, you can play this to your total advantage.'

At the evening's end, they crammed into a minicab, Ben sitting in the front with the driver, whom it turned out he knew. Adam asked Essie to forgive him, but he had an early start in the morning and an important letter to write as soon as he got in. She smiled with just the smallest trace of scepticism. They had a brief deep kiss before she got out of the taxi at her address, and he told her he would call her tomorrow evening and they would do things properly.

The taxi-door closed.

'Don't mess her about,' Corinne said, staring out of the opposite window.

'I'm not,' Adam said. 'Really I'm not.'

The flat was in darkness when he got in. There was the usual mildly angry note from Joanne on the kitchen table, together with a hand-delivered letter addressed to him. He went over to the fridge, poured a glass of white wine from an opened bottle, and read the letter by the fridge light.

Vincent began by regretting the alarmist tone of what was to follow, and wanted Adam to know that the following information was being divulged in the strictest confidence. It seemed that the fall of Imporia was now only a matter of time. Mrs Pelfing had privately confirmed as much. Understandably, he was torn between personal loyalty to an old friend and a professional desire not to see a respected contributor to Paradise be left hanging. With that in mind, he would like to offer Adam what he hoped would be a challenging and substantially rewarding position on the strategic team, as Corporate Operations Director. There was a figure written out in words that made his groin tingle. The offer was with immediate effect. He would square things with Mrs Pelfing. He only asked that Adam called to confirm his interest when he got in, no matter how late.

Adam drank the wine and tried to harness his brain into a decision-making state. It wouldn't comply. It was just a mass of firing neurons.

He called the number. Vincent seemed to know it would be him. There was no need to go into anything now. All he needed was a yes or a no. Adam left one more pause for reflection, but reflection wouldn't pour into it. It was a yes.

'Splendid,' Vincent murmured. 'We'll sort things tomorrow. Drop by my office at nine.'

'Just one other thing,' Adam put in, as the phone was about to go down.

'Yes?'

'What about Troy?'
There was a second's silence. 'I know,' Vincent said. 'Ghastly.'

Chapter 13

Angels

At the August bank holiday weekend, after a long day's cleaning and washing and shopping, Mirabelle sat down for a moment on the edge of the bed with a sudden sharp pain behind her eyes. Jimmy, sitting in the living-room studying his Bible with dimming sight that kept nearly surrendering to sleep, was jolted alert by a crash. He found his wife on her side on the floor, twitching and mumbling, a dribble of spit escaping from the corner of her mouth.

It was declared at the hospital that she had had a cerebral haemorrhage, and that it was too early to say how severely affected she might be. Jimmy returned home to fetch clothes for her, and when he returned to the hospital, was ushered into a small room to receive the condolences of a senior doctor. There was nothing they could have done. She hadn't suffered unduly, was probably scarcely aware of it. He was given something to sign. Would he like to spend a few moments with her?

He was taken to another small room by a nurse, who told him that if there was anything he needed, he shouldn't hesitate to ask. She closed the door softly behind herself.

Mirabelle lay on a bed. She didn't look well. Her face looked stone-cold, white and exaggeratedly drawn, as though she had had aggressive cosmetic surgery. Her eyes were closed and her mouth hung very slightly open. Jimmy put a hand on her hair. Her earrings were gone, her makeup erased. There was a profound silence, deeper than any silence that had ever surrounded her before. He felt he ought to say something, but she wouldn't reply. He couldn't even rely on a scornful snort if he invoked the words of Our Lord to her. He had to tell himself that this was no longer her, only an image like a photograph taken at a misleading angle, in poor light, that would never truly be a likeness.

He drew the sheet over her face and walked away.

That evening, Joanne arrived in a flutter of grief. She hugged Jimmy, sobbed and choked. She tried to say things about Auntie Mirabelle, but couldn't. Jimmy left her alone with her shock while he went to put the kettle on.

The doorbell rang again. Joanne went downstairs and found Jules Beaufort at the door.

'Oh hello, darling,' said Jules in a quavering tone, as though addressing a puppy. 'I'm so sorry for your loss.'

Joanne burst out in chokes again, and they embraced tightly amid the shoe-heaps.

Jimmy halted in the kitchen doorway on seeing Jules, and then retreated back towards the sound of the wheezing kettle. Jules followed him, and the door was rather firmly closed.

Joanne sank into a chair at the table, and bent her head while the convulsions subsided. She wiped her face on her sleeves. A low mumble of conversation that sounded incongruously businesslike and amicable came from the next room. The occasional muffled word emerged, but meant nothing out of context. She stood up, hesitated only a moment, and then pressed her ear to the door.

'I say again, it was nothing to do with me,' Jimmy was pointing out, in the reasoned tones of someone with a clear conscience.

'I'm not saying it was,' Jules assured him, evidently also repeating herself, but with clear intent to be conciliatory. 'All I'm saying is there's a lot that needs to be resolved. I know this isn't the time, but you've no idea, Jim, what Finlay and I have been through over the last ten years. She made our lives very difficult.'

As she listened, Joanne became aware of a peripheral green glow on the other side of the living-room. Still concentrating on what she could hear, she absently turned her head a little. The light from the standard-lamp was reflecting off a glass ornament on the mantelpiece. It was a half-reclining woman, whose lithe graceful body dwindled into the tail of a fish. In the hollow made by the tail's curl, a little pile of jewellery, earrings probably, twinkled in what remained of Joanne's tears.

A celebration of autumn, Gutford in the Fall, was the latest transformation of Paradise. Piles of crisp, many-coloured leaves, painstakingly sprayed with fire-retardant, were strewn about the ground-floor walkways, while cumbrous branches, denuded to order of their foliage, were suspended overhead. The fountain had been remade as a grotto, crackly with dead leaf-litter, in which costumed dryads reclined. Autumn-themed pop trickled discreetly from the speakers. A motif of wind-blown leaves decorated the boards that had gone up around the fairground to conceal its demolition.

Meetings of the management board now took place around a table in a room unadorned by light-panels or incense. There was a printed agenda, of which everybody had a copy, and which was to be completed between the times stated. Coffee was served, but not herbal elixirs, and in place of the boxes of candied fruits and Ganduja chocolates, there was a plate of digestives. Everybody had been circulated with a printout of the financial report, which they were expected to have studied and understood.

The author of the reforms took his seat at the head of the table, having appointed himself chairman of the management board without a murmur of dissent from Vincent. Seated around the table were Vincent, Javine, the new financial director Nesta Vaisey, two members of the marketing team, assistant marketing director Troy Parnish, press-relations manager Essie Collins, and Tom Fipp, the former intern who had now been appointed admin assistant.

Adam raised his eyebrows at Tom, who was bright, keen and scruffy. He had been told that a tie was now mandatory for the office and had duly bought one, but was under the impression that he only needed to wear it to meetings. Today, he hadn't even remembered that, but now blushingly unravelled it from his trouser-pocket like a magician unspooling a length of ribbon. While he wound and unwound it in his effort to remember how to tie it, Adam opened the meeting.

'OK. Many thanks, colleagues, for your time this morning. I'd like to get through the agenda as expeditiously as possible if we can. That means quickly, Tom.' A ripple of good-natured laughter went round the table as the red-faced Tom slid up the lopsided knot of his tie. 'That's still not right, but B-plus for effort,' Adam told him. 'Operations report. VB?'

Vincent, whose own tie was immaculate, sat up straight. When he began to speak, he was doing something he hadn't done in his entire professional life until the last month – reading from notes that he had prepared earlier. Adam sat back in his seat, with his hands clasped and his elbows on the arm-rests, and concentrated on a point on the table's edge while he listened carefully to what Vincent was saying. Occasionally, he interrupted to ask for a clarification, glancing around the table to make sure nobody was looking puzzled. When he made a small gesture towards the water-jug, Javine passed it to him, but as he made no move to take it from her, poured some into his glass.

The financial report was the trickiest part of the meeting. There had been some debate about how much of the irregularity unearthed by the previous financial director should be divulged. Vincent had suggested there was a lot of negative energy around it. 'Least said, soonest mended,' Adam concurred, having no idea how close Paradise had come to an investigation by the financial authorities. Nesta made it clear she had no intention of taking questions relating to events under the previous regime, and so when it came to her moment to make a report to the committee, she slapped a broad brush over the figures they had in front of them, concluding with the words, 'Steady the buffs'.

When it was Essie's turn to speak, her eyes brightened as she disclosed that there would be an eight-page pullout on the autumn season at Paradise in the *Clarion*, with a four-page digest in this Friday's edition of one of the London free-sheets. Vincent wondered in a timid voice how much that was costing. The figure was surprisingly modest, and was in any case largely being underwritten by a consortium of Paradise's leading traders. Adam pronounced the initiative excellent.

'And what have you done this week that's excellent, Mr Fipp?' he asked Tom, who gurgled coyly in response as the attention of colleagues turned to him.

'I've tidied my desk, Adam.' He giggled, his face glowing red again.

'Good lad.' Adam tidied the papers in front of him together. 'Thanks, everyone.'

Chairs scraped back as everyone rose. Javine cleared the mugs. Vincent made a twirly gesture with both hands, perhaps intended to signify that he was about to run along and get on with something. Tom shambled up to Adam, loosening the sloppy tie.

'Seriously, let me know what you want. Whenever you want, you know.'

'Are you selling me drugs, Tom?'

Tom guffawed and blushed again. 'Nah, man. I just – I need to know how to get on. Don't I?'

'Yeah. Getting on is good. Look at me. I started from nothing.'

'When was that then?'

Adam thought. 'About nine months ago.'

That evening, Adam took his brother and sister to the Gutford Playhouse to see a production of *Richard III*, for which complimentary tickets had been showered on senior Paradise personnel. Luke was under the impression that he was going to see some sort of pantomime, a misapprehension neither Adam nor Joanne felt it needful to correct beforehand. Joanne asked whether they could take Marlow, who in turn asked whether he could bring Myron, and as nobody else in the admin office appeared to be claiming the complimentary tickets, they all five went together. On sight of the tickets as they were about to go in, one of the ushers asked them to stand aside while she contacted the manager, who personally led them in and removed five people from the front row. Amid some indignation, the evictees were reseated in a block to one side, upon which two of them, discovering the inferiority of the view, stalked out.

'What was all that about?' Joanne wondered.

'Don't know.' Adam shrugged, disingenuously.

'Being top dog at Paradise clearly has its privileges,' Marlow suggested.

'I don't think it was anything to do with that,' Adam lied. 'Some kind of mixup.'

'Our tickets do say row B, though,' Joanne pointed out. 'I don't want to feel I've upset someone.'

'Don't worry.'

'Who's upset?' Luke wanted to know.

'Nobody, fella. Have you got enough chocolate?' Luke was holding what the theatre called a 'Naughty Nosebag' of chocolates and sweets. 'You have to open them very quietly once the play starts, OK?'

'Very quietly,' Luke echoed in a comical whisper.

Adam stretched his legs out and gazed absently down his front. He noticed for the first time in his life that he had begun to fill out slightly around the middle. He drew his legs smartly up again, and sat up straight. Monday he'd start an exercise regime.

'What's up?' said Joanne.

'Do you think I'm beginning to look a bit tubby?'

'Can't say I've noticed.'

'Tubby?' Marlow interposed. 'No way. I hope I look as good as you when I'm your age. Not that you shouldn't look good. But you do anyway. And definitely not tubby. Don't you think, Myron?'

Myron disdained to look at Adam's middle, but instead gave Marlow one of his withering stares. 'Shut it,' he commanded.

Marlow complied, as he had lately got used to doing, only turning silently to Joanne and rolling his eyes in a swoon of admiration. She smiled fondly back. Nobody else alive was capable of shutting Marlow up. He was enjoying the novelty as much as anyone was.

The lights went down and the curtain rose on a stage-set composed of large abstract shapes. There were some thunder-storm effects – vivid lightning flashes, deafening cracks. Luke's mouth opened wide enough to cram in two Maltesers, but didn't close again. After a minute or two of the storm, a lone figure ambled on from the back of the stage. Dressed as a medieval nobleman, with one shoulder massively hunched, Richard began his soliloquy. He was holding a large goblet, and the speech was punctuated by his taking deep gulps from it. Tottering uncer-tainly across the front of the stage, he was evidently drunk, so that when he referred to dogs barking at him, and kicked out at an imaginary mongrel, he nearly toppled over. Soon after, Clarence was led to the Tower before Richard's befuddled gape, and when Hastings subsequently entered, he did so with a flagon in his hand, from which he refilled Richard's shaking cup.

The reimagining of the play, it transpired, had Richard as an alcoholic. In every scene, he had a goblet in his hand, and sometimes a flagon in the other. He drank throughout the placating of Lady Anne, topping himself up while she hurled her imprecations at him and, at its conclusion, the line 'Shine out, fair sun, till I have bought a glass' was played to comic effect as he upended the empty cup.

'"Glass" means looking-glass,' Joanne said, in a surprisingly loud voice, as the scene changed. Luke nudged her to be quiet.

The plans for Richard's coronation marked the arrival of the interval, as he raised a pint-glass to Buckingham. 'Farewell, good cousin.' Then, with a sweep to the audience, 'Farewell, gentle friends'.

The curtain dropped to a quizzical silence. Luke thought it was over.

Adam awoke from an undisturbed snooze. 'Woot, challenging,' he said.

Joanne gave him a sceptical look. 'Not that you're in any position to judge, having slept through it. That's what comes of being fat. It makes you nod off every five minutes.'

'Adam's fat,' Luke chuckled, popping in another bite-sized Flake.

'Should we not do this?' Adam suggested. He turned to Marlow and Myron. 'What do you think, guys?'

Marlow looked at Myron. 'Whatever.' He shrugged.

There was a long queue at the entrance to Passionate Pizza on Eighth. A groan went up, but Adam winked at them. He strode to the head of the queue and clicked his fingers to attract the attention of one of the greeters. Joanne saw the shaken head and regretful expression turn to instant embarrassed joviality on Adam's production of an ID card. The girl went across to one of the larger tables and made an announcement. A group sitting there looked open-mouthed with disbelief, but she stood her ground until they all started picking up their glasses and cups, and were directed to the bar-area. Two other waiters cleared and wiped down the table, and Adam's party was waved through.

'Oh my God,' Marlow tittered. 'I so want one of those cards. It makes everything happen.'

Adam winked at him. 'When you're older, maybe I'll consider you for a job.'

'Are you going to go through life now having people thrown out wherever you go?' asked Joanne.

'I don't see you complaining.' Adam laughed.

'I'm complaining now.'

'You've still taken someone's seat readily enough.'

'Could you get some water, please?' Joanne was dry-mouthed and starting a headache. This was the last place she wanted to be. 'I just think it stinks, this preferential treatment.'

'Get over it,' Adam said. 'A bunch of plebs had to move tables. So what? They'd nearly finished anyway.'

'Exactly,' Marlow chipped in. 'Don't you think?' He gave Myron's arm an interrogative squeeze.

'I'm with her,' Myron said unexpectedly, slumping down in his seat with his shoulders hunched.

Joanne gave him a pallid smile.

'Can I have pizza?' Luke asked.

'It's pretty much all there is, matey,' said Adam. 'What's regato?'

'It's cheese,' Joanne snapped. She got up and stalked off towards the Ladies.

'Someone's in a strop.' Marlow giggled.

'Don't worry about her,' Adam told him. 'What's fontina?'

Nobody knew.

Joanne went straight to a sink and ran cold water over her wrists. She was bubbling into a fury, and knew she wasn't going to come out of it tonight. Her eyes looked narrow and tired, grey. She had grey eyes.

'All right, darling?' said a young woman in a bright orange bustier and small skirt, who had arrived at the next sink.

Joanne looked at her. 'Am I all right? I suppose I am,' she mused. 'How about you?'

'I'll be all right when I'm off my tits.' She drew some more lipstick over her existing lipstick. 'I'll be all right then.' She ground her lips together.

'Is that what you'll be doing later?'

'Yip. Hopefully not *too* much later. Depends on the fellas, if they ever shift their arses. Honestly, they accuse us of gabbing, but are they the ones?' She made a series of delicate dabbing movements at her eyelashes with a black stick. 'Are they ever the ones.'

'What's the point in depending on the fellas?' Joanne wanted to know. 'Why don't you just do what you want to do?'

'That's exactly what we ought to do.'

'So what's stopping you?'

'OK, gotta dash,' the other woman trilled. 'Nice talking, have a good one.'

Her heels made a racket on the hard floor as she hurried out. The door crashed. Joanne realised she was going to cry, but she knew too it would be an arid pointless crying. She ran some more cold water on her wrists.

Only Luke saw her come out of the toilets, and cross the crowded restaurant towards the entrance. He slurped his fizzy cherry. The taste of it and the luxuriousness of the slurping made him forget everything else.

When Joanne got down to the ground floor, she texted Adam to tell him she was going home, not to worry. Adam didn't hear the bleep, and when Marlow wondered a while later where Joanne had disappeared to, he hazarded a guess that she'd probably gone home in a huff. Everybody secretly felt it was for the best, especially Marlow, who had begun to notice that she wasn't much fun anymore. It was almost as though, he thought, she was jealous of his happiness. He snuggled against Myron's arm.

Glancing round at the hubbub, Adam couldn't help noticing the areas in which Passionate Pizza was letting down the Paradise brand. He'd come down here again before they opened for lunch tomorrow, and sit down with the manager. Nothing heavy.

By the time he carried the half-sleeping figure of Luke from the taxi to the front door of their apartment-block, it was ridiculously late. They had gone from Passionate Pizza to one of the quieter bars, where he had bought a litre-bottle of wine for the boys and started on brandy cocktails himself. A query as to whether the boys were of legal drinking age had been stilled on production of his ID card. Myron had taken the rough-textured Shiraz in his stride, but Marlow had grown progressively indiscreet, silly, and finally nauseous, only just making it to the Gents in time to throw up. Luke had fallen peacefully asleep, full of aspartame and trans-fats, as the evening had meandered on. When Marlow emerged, he said he felt better now, but didn't want any more wine. Adam ordered him some sparkling mineral water, and he was sick again.

The ID card enabled them to jump the long taxi-queue as soon as the first car appeared, which wasn't for quite a time. Myron sat next to the driver, answering the sporadic remarks addressed to him in gruff monosyllables. Luke slept in Adam's arms. Marlow sat with his head lolling and rolling on the seat-back. They stopped to drop him off first. As the taxi idled, he attempted to make a speech of gratitude for the evening, but all that emerged was a slurring gush, so he settled for trying to kiss Adam on the cheek.

'Oi, quit it,' Myron barked, craning round from the passenger-seat.

'What?' Marlow bleared.

'Acting like a fairy. Sorry,' he added, for Adam's benefit.

'See you soon,' said Adam.

When Myron was dropped off, he tapped the side-window and, as Adam rolled it down, tried to hand him a ten-pound note. Adam waved it away and told him not to be daft.

'Cheers for a top night,' Myron said.

'I hear ya,' Adam said, and they touched fists.

Luke remained half-awake through Adam's wobbling him about while he searched for his keys, but had gone off again by the time they got upstairs. A line of light glowed at the bottom of the kitchen door. He tiptoed away from it towards his and Luke's bedroom, but in the passageway, his foot caught something, and there was a crash. Luke jolted awake in the dark and started howling.

The kitchen door was wrenched open, framing Joanne in predatory silhouette. 'What is going *on*, for God's sake?'

Luke paused for breath, then let out a blood-freezing scream.

'Shh, it's OK, it's only Jo,' Adam said, bouncing Luke in his arms like a baby.

'Put him down, you idiot.'

'Can you get out of my face, please? I'm getting Luke to bed.'

'It's after midnight!' Joanne shrieked, her voice cracked and hoarse.

Adam found the light-switch. A lamp lay in pieces on the floor. Luke's face was sleep-bleared, haunted and white. When Adam set him down, his legs folded under him and he slumped against the wall.

'Look at the state of him,' Joanne shouted. 'Are you out of your mind, Adam?'

Adam stormed into the bathroom, and slammed and locked the door. He pulled open the mirrored cupboard and began searching through it for a paracetamol, but couldn't quite grip anything properly. Bottles and packets and tubes showered into the sink. He was more pissed than he'd realised. He stood swaying a little with his hands on the edge of the sink while he listened to the officious tramping to and fro in the passageway, the ceaseless indignant mutter of his sister's voice, the opening and closing of doors.

When it subsided, he came out and hesitated at the bedroom door opposite.

Joanne appeared in the kitchen doorway again. 'Don't go in there. Let him get to sleep.'

He pressed a hand over his aching eyes. Water.

Several books were spread out on the kitchen table, around a notepad full of closely printed handwriting. Adam went to the sink, ran some water and swallowed the pill.

'Bit early for homework, isn't it? School isn't till next week.' There was a grim silence. 'Or should I say a bit late?' He sniggered stupidly.

'A bit late to bring your six-year-old brother home from a drinking session, more to the point.'

'He hasn't been in a drinking session.'

'He's been *at* one. How come a small child is allowed into a bar late at night?'

Adam grinned again sloppily. 'The magic card.'

'Oh yes, of course, the card that magically transforms you into an arrogant prat.'

'Don't be boring, Jo.' He put his hand on the top of her head, without knowing what the gesture was intended to convey. Something between restraint and benediction perhaps. She tossed her head. 'What's the matter with you lately? Something you're not telling us?'

This time the silence was more desperate than resentful. Joanne sat and stared at the notebook in front of her. What had she been doing? Something to do with medieval history. What had made her want to do it now? She wished Adam wasn't there.

'Even Marlon has noticed it.'

'Who's Marlon?'

Adam blinked. What was the kid's name?

'Noticed what?'

'Your frazzly mood. Your rattiness. He wondered if you're kind of, y'know...'

'Kind of what?'

'Jealous?'

'Jealous of what?'

'Things. Just him and... his boyfriend... I don't know. Me even.'

Joanne stood and turned. Her shoulders, hunched with anger, dropped as she looked into his face. 'I will never in my life be jealous of you. Because you know what, Adam? I don't even like you. I think you're a selfish, egotistical, boring prick, and I wish I wasn't related to you. You do nothing but think of ways of congratulating yourself. You've had a series of promotions in some tacky dump only because the boss fancies you, and you're too mind-blowingly stupid to see you're being manipulated. You used to be kind and clever. You used to be like a dad to Luke. Now you give the impression of not giving a toss for him or me or anything except your own stinking vanity. You're disgusting.'

'Jo, that's enough. You don't know what you're saying.'

'I know exactly what I'm saying. It's just you don't want to hear it.'

'Enough.'

'Don't speak to me like that, you arsehole.'

'ENOUGH!' His voice rose to a roar.

'Fuck off, you ignorant ape.' She pounded him sharply in the chest, and would have done so again, but he'd grabbed her wrists. 'Get off me! Get off!'

They were struggling together now in the space between the table and the sink. Adam shouted her name, but every time he tried to command her, she only became more indignant. She couldn't free her wrists from his grip, and tried kicking his legs as hard as she might in the tussle.

'Calm down, Jo, you're hysterical.'

She jabbed a knee into his abdomen, forcing him to let out a spirity breath. Somehow, she managed to use his hold on her, combined with his evident drunkenness, to pull him over, and they clattered to the floor in a sprawl of limbs. She slapped his face and got a tuft of his hair in her fist, pulling hard on it. His face contorted, and his wet mouth hollered her name. When she let go, he tried to get up, but she picked up a book from the table and slammed it with both hands down on his face, so that his head bounced back from the floor. A last groan escaped from him, and his head fell to one side. All went still. For a second, she felt something judder beneath her knees in his chest, then stillness.

'Adam,' Joanne heard herself say, in a croaky little voice, bending over him. His eyelids were parted just sufficiently for a line of rolled-up white eyeball to be visible.

There was a creak at the door. She jerked upright and looked over the edge of the table.

Luke was standing at the kitchen doorway, wearing only a pyjama-jacket, its buttons done up wrongly. 'Where's Adam?' he moaned, eyes screwed up against the light.

Myron Stoneman turned on to his left side, finding his right side hot and numb, but his left side was hot and numb as well. His belly was jumping. His heart felt constricted. The glans end of his penis felt like a lit cigarette. He sat up in the heavy dark. The recent events of his life settled like dust around him. This was crazy-mad. It was a big bag of wrong.

Joanne touched Adam's stopped face, and whimpered his name again. She straightened the head up to look at her, and a blackish-red smear on the kitchen tile beneath revealed itself. Her gasp, and the frightened look she shot at Luke, made Luke scream like he had never screamed before.

'Luke, no!' she shouted. He was hysterical with terror.

She ran into the living-room for her phone. As she was scrabbling through her bag, there was a sudden urgent knock at the flat-door. She froze. Behind Luke's cries, she heard a muffled voice saying, 'Is everything all right?'

Finding the phone, she jabbed it three times as she went to the door. Outside was a white-bearded man in a fisherman's hat.

'It's my brother,' she choked out. 'He's had an accident.'

'May I? I'm a pathologist, I may be able to help.'

The man ventured in. Joanne realised the phone she was holding was dead. She jabbed it again.

Luke had stopped screeching long enough to listen to the

stranger, who was asking him what had happened to him.

'Not him,' Joanne yelled. 'In the kitchen. What's the matter with this?' She flung the phone at the wall in the passageway behind the pathologist's head as he moved off in search of the kitchen. A flow of unbridled grief came over her, and she buried her flooded face in her hands.

'Holy-moly!' came a voice from the kitchen. 'Have you called an ambulance?'

She was crying convulsively now, not the bitter dry weeping of earlier, but a rip-tide of remorse for everything that had gone wrong. Adam, Marlow, Mirabelle. Jules' anger. Her own empty misery. Their parents. Their selfish heartless parents. She sank into a sobbing heap on the floor.

'I need you to tell me what happened?' The pathologist was standing over her. 'What happened here, honey?' He squatted before her. 'Something bad?'

It was all bad. The shrieking siren was bad. The lights going on in windows all over the block were bad. The paramedics in their green uniforms, leaning into her face, shining a little torch into her eyes, were bad. Another journey to hospital in the company of another damaged body. The swirling ground and the crisp night air. All bad. She must have asked one of the paramedics a question because he was asking one back. 'Who's Luke?' Where was Luke? The stretcher was bad. The trolley was bad. The running nurses. The shock-machine. She sat on a seat in the corridor and cried out mucus in streamers. Somebody put a blanket round her. The shaking hands, the ringing in her ears, the echo in the corridor of her hiccuping sobs, were all bad.

'I killed my brother,' she heard someone telling a nurse, and the nurse saying, 'You haven't killed anyone, darling'. Thinking she had done something monstrous in her hatred, that was the baddest thing of all.

Meanwhile, torrential rain had begun to fall, accompanied by gales that blew up out of nowhere, raging through the dark in inscrutable limitless fury. Myron got out of his sleepless bed and looked between the curtains. Great sheets of rain, lit yellow by the street-lights, were driven this way and that in the high winds, spitting disgust in his face at the window. Black recycle-boxes were shunted along the pavement in the gusts. Next door's cat glowered under a bush. Who could sleep amid this much bristling rage?

He opened the window a little, and sat down on the end of the bed to listen to it. His skin prickled with the intensity of it. It came up in pimples under the scarves of cold air. He felt it in his feet and his hands and all over his scalp, a great invigorating wash of cold to awaken himself to himself. He felt it in the edges of his protruding ears and in his genitals. He felt it behind his eyes.

At around seven, he awoke in a shiver. The rainstorm had gone. He was lying sideways on the end of the bed. His whole naked body was cold, and there was a sharp acidic feeling in his sinuses. On the nightstand, his phone was emitting a pulsing white light. It was a text from Marlow, wondering whether he'd seen the weather last night, accompanied by an entirely black picture. Myron composed a reply that began 'Sorry, I don't think I can do this anymore', and then deleted it. Maybe the best thing was to say nothing.

He climbed back into bed. A delicious and sickening feeling was in full possession of him. It was an intimation of a kind of masculinity he had never felt before, something gruesome and powerful. He smooshed his face into the pillow, but it didn't go, not even when he heard other people getting up and going downstairs. Only when he got up again to find a pair of discarded shorts to wipe himself off with did the feeling finally begin to retreat.

He looked at Marlow's black rain-picture again. Now it made him laugh. He looked at his phone-picture of Marlow, then texted him. 'Sorry I been arsey lately. C U lunchtime? M. x'

A group of visitors had assembled in the waiting-room before the nurse came to tell them they could see Adam now, but not to over-tax him with questions as he was still a little groggy. Jimmy had arrived – unexpectedly, as it was Mirabelle's funeral that afternoon. Marlow and Myron were there, both dressed with comical formality. They too were going to the funeral, and so was Essie, who looked as though she was dressed for a red-carpet premiere in pulsing violet. Joanne, holding Luke by the hand, led the whole band into Adam's room.

'Whoa, what a mob,' he said, in a weak high voice that none of them recognised. He was sitting propped against a barrage of pillows with a swathe of bandaging around his head, and a heart-monitor clipped over one of his fingers. He smiled faintly and nodded, but appeared to think better of moving his head too much.

They gathered on either side of the bed. There were only two chairs, one of which was taken by each of the girls, with Luke balanced on Joanne's knees. Essie took Adam's left hand.

Having arranged themselves in this vigilant grouping, they found that none of them knew what to say. Joanne asked Adam how he was feeling, and he said he was feeling much better. The headache had gone, and he was beginning to think straight again. Essie joked that that would be a first, and everyone smirked. Adam regretted that he was in no fit state to come to Auntie Mirabelle's funeral, and Jimmy whispered that he understood. He should concentrate on getting better.

Essie continued to press Adam's hand and lean forward at the bedside, training her luminous black eyes on him. Joanne's sense of remorse for what she had done to Adam came over her in such titanic waves that she couldn't look at him, only bite her lip and concentrate hard on not letting her eyes fill up. Luke fidgeted a little, and looked at anybody but Adam, finding himself particularly fascinated by Essie, whom he had never met. Jimmy stood behind Joanne's chair, steadying himself on its back and breathing a little roughly. He had other things on his mind. Myron and Marlow stood side by side like toy soldiers, the outside edges of their hands just touching. Adam looked down at his hands, stroked Essie's hand with his thumb, and wished somebody would say something.

The silence went on a while longer until Luke swivelled round on Joanne's lap and asked what they were all waiting for. A peal of relieved laughter went round, which made Luke want to know what was funny. Adam said he had to admit he'd been to better parties than this one, and the laughter murmured on a little before subsiding back into silence. Then Marlow remembered he'd brought Adam a banana.

When the party dispersed a while later, Joanne touched Adam's hand with the desire to express something like regret. Adam asked her how she was. She wasn't sure, but she looked forward to him coming home, within the next day or two, seemingly. Adam warned Luke he'd better be behaving, and Joanne said he'd been fine. She looked at Adam, who was looking at Luke, who was looking at her.

In the waiting-room outside, Jimmy took charge of Luke, taking him off to get ready for Mirabelle's funeral. Myron and Marlow got into a situation with a vending-machine that wouldn't dispense its chocolate. Essie lingered.

'I know you're going to the funeral later, but if you have time to talk?'

'What about?' Joanne asked, a little suspiciously.

'What's been going on. Things aren't great with you, are they?'

'Has Adam said something? I'm fine, really.' She could hear the tired croak in her own voice.

'No you aren't,' Essie insisted gently, and she drew Joanne into an embrace, letting the suddenly wet face collapse on her neck.

The funeral that afternoon was a tearless affair. Jimmy stood implacably at the graveside in a skewed black tie, having delivered a short methodical eulogy in the church. Myron put on a yarmulke before entering, and had a withering glare for Marlow when told he looked cute in it. The thin wind fluttered their loose clothing as they stood in the cemetery, trying its knife-edges against knuckles and ears, while the vicar intoned the obsequy. Joanne found her head subsiding against Essie's shoulder. Luke stood a little apart, his shoulders militantly hunched inside his small overcoat, a look of grim regret etched on his face.

They each gathered a little clod of brown earth from the holy shovel, and formed a queue to toss it in the grave. Off to their left, behind a stand of beech-trees, the cemetery workers waited respectfully to fill in the hole. After a final prayer, they were referred to their orders of service again, and the vicar led the way quaveringly in the final hymn – 'The day thou gavest, Lord, is ended' – the others taking up the measured tread of the melody in a variety of pitches. 'The darkness falls at thy behest'. Myron scanned through the lyrics of the five verses for any reference to Jesus and, finding none, joined in with the discomfitingly familiar tune.

As they walked away, Essie, still with her arm about Joanne, said that the service had been beautiful and made her wish she had known Mirabelle. Nobody spoke for a moment, until Jimmy proposed that what they all needed was a drink. They were invited back to Flint Street, where there would be champagne and whatever else anybody wanted. Mirabelle would have wanted it that way. The residual tautness in everybody's chests that the burial hadn't quite managed to dissolve was relieved when, in the taxi back, Luke said that he wanted a banana-fudge milkshake with chocolate sprinkles.

In the event, Jimmy poured a mouthful of champagne into an eggcup for him. Everybody stood in a rough circle in the lounge, toasted Mirabelle's memory, clinked glasses and, at the unexpected bidding of Jimmy, sang 'Auld Lang Syne'.

'What a weird day,' Myron said outside in the garden, where Marlow had followed him while he had a cigarette. 'Hospitals, funerals, champagne. What next?'

'Do you really have to ask?' Marlow threaded his arm through Myron's.

Myron exhaled a long plume of smoke, his face bitterly serious in the cold. 'Do you ever think about anything else?'

'Do you think it's unappropriate?'

'*In*appropriate.'

The blare of a car-horn made them both look towards the road for a moment. A cat leaped on top of the garden wall, bristling with indignation, another of its lives discarded.

'You've still got your cap on.'

'So I have.' Myron took another hungry drag on his cigarette.

'Look at me.'

'Why, what you gonna do?' His slightly skewed eyes fixed Marlow's own.

Marlow buried his face in the fleecy checked shirt. 'I love you so much I could scream,' he declared in a muffled voice.

'I can't tell what you're saying,' Myron said, the note of irritability resonating in his chest. But Marlow could hear the smile too.

Jimmy came back into the living-room with some crisps he'd poured into an oven dish. Joanne was unsurprised to find they were stale. Luke wolfed them down at least.

'I first met your Auntie Mirabelle at a meeting at the town hall,' Jimmy said, settling himself into an armchair while the others stood around. 'There was some big argument going on about whether to build a car-park that would have blocked off one of the bus-routes. Everybody was fired up, all talking at once. The chairman kept calling for order and asking whether anybody had anything sensible to say. Then this lovely young lady stood up, raven-black hair, figure trim as you like, and she asked how this decision had been kept from the people until it was so late. Well, the man from the council didn't know what to say. You could tell he had something to hide. This lady kept pressing him for an answer, until everybody in the room was cheering her.'

'So she was a real crusader,' Essie commented, as Jimmy drifted into the memory.

'Eh?'

'Mrs Blake.'

'Oh, that wasn't her, love,' Jimmy said. 'No, she was some firebrand from the Communist Party. No, I met Mirabelle in the room where we had coffee after. We agreed that the meeting had gone well, and that it was the dark-haired lady who'd swung it. From that moment on, it was as though an invisible magnet was pulling us together.' Jimmy's eyes clouded again. He took another gulp of his champagne, and broke into a burst of coughing.

'Are you all right?' Joanne asked, taking the shaking glass from him. 'Some went down the wrong way?'

The coughing went on for a while. Neither of the girls quite knew what to say. Luke had drained his eggcup and was looking a little red in the face himself.

'Sorry, love. I had a frog in my throat,' Jimmy choked out, and set off coughing again.

The boys reappeared in the living-room doorway.

'We're going to go back now, if that's OK,' Marlow said.

Joanne said something in reply that he couldn't hear because of Jimmy's coughing.

'Uncle Jimmy,' Joanne said in a tone of sudden concern. 'Are you all right?'

Jimmy tried to nod, but his face had gone white and he was suddenly holding both arms in a huddle across his chest. He gasped in pain.

'Shit!' Myron shouted. 'Call an ambulance.' Everybody looked at him. 'Where's the bloody phone?'

Marlow called on his phone.

Vincent stood at his office window, gazing down on the thin trickles of people entering and leaving by the main entrance, eleven floors below. He had come to feel oddly detached from everything. Once the unmoved mover of his world, he now held the status of a mere epiphenomenon. It wasn't as though anybody else had manoeuvred him out. He had authored every change, had willed things to happen, and yet the unforeseen effect had been to marginalise himself, as though he were the ageing capo of some family business, now reluctantly but graciously stepping aside for the next generation.

He had just taken a phonecall from Essie, to say that, having attended Adam's aunt's funeral, she had now got caught up in a further situation, an emergency of some sort that had left her minding Adam's six-year-old brother, while everybody else dashed off somewhere. Vincent couldn't remember what it was that was supposed to be happening this afternoon. With Adam in hospital anyway, everything was in a state of suspension. Through the glass partition, he could see Javine simultaneously talking on the phone, eating a sandwich and typing on her keyboard. She presumably had things in hand. The driving force, the power to initiate, had flowed away from him. The energy was now around Adam. And wasn't that what he had envisaged? It was, but not in such a way that he himself had become largely ornamental, another body at the table during strategy meetings, someone whose views were politely heard and then, nearly as politely, disregarded. Things flowed on more efficiently now, it was true. There was less space for lateral thinking, for sudden satoris. On the other hand, things got done. Is this what organisations cried out for after all? People liked the sound of radical innovation, but they didn't want to live it. They complained of routine, but they liked its certainties. They wanted to feel grounded, not endlessly afloat.

But then, whose damn business was this?

He buzzed Tom for some coffee, and saw the boy get up from his desk and go into a dither of indecision about how to make it happen. He realised suddenly that the new dispensation had reduced him, Vincent, to the status of a Tom Fipp, hesitating between options he didn't understand, required to make a call in a world that would be indifferent to his predicament only until he got it wrong.

Some time later, Tom came in with a Styrofoam cup of cappuccino, which he had probably gone down to Eighth to buy on expenses. Meanwhile, Vincent had come to a decision. It was rather in the nature of another wrenching key-change, but would undoubtedly serve the purpose. In his best tradition, he decided to let the office junior be the first to know of it.

Tom stared back, unprompted by anything in what Vincent had said that a reply was expected.

'Well, what do you think?'

'Yeah, great,' Tom stammered. 'He'll be made up with that, for sure.'

'Thomas, I'm asking your advice. Should I do this?'

Tom began to shake inside. This wasn't in his job description. It was obviously a test, to see whether he had initiative. 'Er, I think you should do what you think is right.'

Vincent laughed, but there was an ironic edge to his usual merry twitter. 'Oh, Tom,' he said, as though he were going to pronounce a judgment, but then didn't say anything else.

Whatever the test was, Tom felt he had failed it. 'But if you're asking me, go for it.' He grinned weakly, but it was already too late.

He waited to be dismissed, but Vincent only continued to eye him without apparently seeing him. When he took a sip of the coffee, he gave a thoughtful grimace. See, even the coffee was wrong. Tom knew he was a goner.

As Jimmy was admitted to hospital, Adam was being discharged. A taxi delivered him home to an empty flat. Texting Joanne produced no response. Eventually, he got through to Marlow, who told him in a tremulous voice that Jimmy had been rushed to hospital with a heart attack. The world was careering out of control. Adam put the phone down and was about to go and get changed when he noticed two messages flashing on the answering-machine. The first was from somebody insisting he make an urgent call to a premium-rate number to discuss refinancing his debt obligations. The second was Vincent wondering whether he'd had time to consider his offer.

There was a small bundle of post on the table, mostly rubbish, but including an item that appeared to have been delivered by courier. Adam opened it. It was a letter from Vincent. After a preamble about the distinctive and authoritative way he had so far discharged his duties as operations director, he was urged to see that the time had surely come to put his relationship with the Paradise project, the greatest days of which were still ahead of it, on a more permanent footing. In short, he was invited, at no financial risk to himself, to become a partner.

Adam sat down at the table. Marlow's banana, now very dark brown, was in the bowl. It felt mushy but, on peeling, turned out to be perfectly unblemished, soft and ripe. While he ate it, he looked at the letter. There seemed behind it all Vincent's insecure impulsiveness. The proposal had presumably been nowhere near a legal advisor. There were no two ways about it. You didn't start off as a shop assistant, and end as partner in a business with a turnover in the millions, in less than a year. It spoke all too resonantly of personal obsession, a final piece of enormous benevolence that would require something in the way of return. What kind of obligation might he be under? Then again, he would be the partner. The last vestige of hierarchical relationship between them would have gone. He could say no.

Among the other post was an A4 envelope with his name and address printed in childish block capitals. Inside was a set of badly photocopied images of various interiors at Paradise, together with a letter from one B. Hathaway, headed 'URGENT – DO NOT IGNORE'.

For the first time since he was a child, Adam found himself singing in the shower, a disco hit from years ago with a complicated hook that slid out of tune towards the end, so that he had to keep starting again. Life was absurd, but it was the best kind of absurd. It promised to be interesting for years to come, even when jointly presiding at the helm of a titanically unstable business promised to give him sleepless nights. He wasn't a lucky man. There was tragedy and uncertainty in his family's story, but now it had changed. It wasn't luck, though. He'd arrived at this juncture, he sincerely believed, through his own native talent. Even when he was down, people wanted to be like him. They wanted to be near him and make his life agreeable. It would be wrong to deny it, or try to forestall it. Somehow, he thought, as he stuck a fat piece of soap between his buttocks, he had become a success. His head fell back, throbbed a second at the spot where his sister had concussed him, and a spray of tepid water ran over his teeth. This time, he got the tune right.

As he dialled the taxi number to go back to the hospital, it occurred to him that next week he would buy himself a car.

'I'm not sure about this one, VB,' said Javine, winding a skein of her hair around a pencil.

'Why not?'

'What experience does he have?'

'What experience do any of us have, when we start out? There's so much CV-ism in the business. What have you done? Prove you can do it.'

'It's just that those things are usually helpful indicators of suitability.'

'And then again, they may not be. Look at that dreadful woman who was doing the money. Bella?'

'Bellenor. She was at least qualified.'

'Yes, and she spent her entire time here acting as a screw-anchor. We don't want screw-anchors, we want hang-gliders.'

'Pardon?'

'People who soar, take to the skies.'

'And you think Adam Young is that person?'

'He's perfect. Young, keen, has an air of authority, and yet he's grounded.'

'Not the best attribute in a hang-glider.'

'Oh stop it.'

Javine stared towards the window. A small aircraft crossed the patch of sky framed by it, towing a banner that read, 'PARADISE IS A PLACE ON EARTH'.

'Who authorised that banner?'

'Authorised, schmauthorised. Think big.'

Javine looked back to the photo-booth snapshot of Adam attached to the document. She saw an impassive well-proportioned face, comfortable with itself, mildly distrustful of others, with a fugitive hint of sadness behind the deep green eyes.

'You do know...?'

'Know what?'

'He has a girlfriend.'

'Indeed. Who knows? We might be paying for a wedding this time next year.'

Javine pressed her fingers into her eyes.

There were several Mr Blakes being treated at Gutford General, it turned out, and Adam was initially directed to the bedside of a young man who had been in a motorcycle accident. After another spell at reception, the correct Mr Young was located, and Adam arrived at his intensive-care room just as Joanne was returning to it.

'Everything OK?'

'No, everything is not OK,' Joanne sighed.

'Where's Luke?'

'He's one of the things that isn't OK. About ten minutes ago, he announced that he'd pooed something funny. Turns out it was a worm.'

'Eurgh, gross.'

'You didn't have to look at it.'

'What did it look like?'

'It looked like a worm. It was about an inch long and brown. Oh, and it had nostrils. Roundworm, the nurse thinks.'

'So he's being treated. They ought to name a wing of this place after the Young family. Good place to discover it though.'

'Yes, it's just perfect. Thank goodness Uncle Jimmy had that heart attack, otherwise we might have had to go to the doctor's.'

'Heart attack? Is he OK?'

'No, he's not OK, he's had a heart attack.'

'Jo—'

'What are you even doing here, Adam?' She turned away from him abruptly, and opened the door of Jimmy's room. 'Uncle Jimmy, Adam's here to see you. Don't overstress him. The nurse says he needs complete rest.'

'Where are you going? Don't go.'

'I've been here forever. I'm sure you'll think of something to say.' She went off down the corridor, her shoes squeaking indignantly on the floor.

Jimmy was attached to a number of machines, including one with a screen on which a wiggly line gently pulsed. His head looked unnaturally white and decayed. With his glasses missing, his eyes looked small and sightless. His hands lay before him on the sheet. Adam wasn't sure whether he had registered that there was anyone else in the room.

'Uncle Jimmy?'

'Hello, Adam.' His voice was a feeble croak of exhaustion.

'What we going to do with you?'

'Measure me up for a box, son, by the looks of it.'

'Don't talk like that. You're in the best place you could be. You're being looked after, and we're all on your side. You had a scare.'

'I had a heart attack, lad. You weren't there.'

Adam drew a chair up to the side of the bed. 'I'm here now.' Jimmy continued to stare ahead of him with dead eyes. 'You're going to be OK.'

The assurance was met only by a further tightening of the compressed lips. In the silence, only the purring of the monitors and the distant sound of trolley wheels could be heard. Adam was sick of hospitals.

'What does the doctor say?'

'I should take it easy,' Jimmy replied.

'Well, that sounds right. It's been a hard time for all of us lately, but especially for you.' Adam looked at his hands, which had roped themselves together for safety or supplication. 'Guess what?' he said in a loud over-eager tone, which he had to hush for the announcement that followed. 'The guy who runs Paradise has only asked me to be a partner.' He gave a nervous laugh. 'I can hardly believe it.' Raising his eyes to Jimmy's blank ailing face, he found no response, and had to fish for one by asking softly, 'What do you think of that?'

There was a long silence, a silence of little electronic peeps and slow breathing. He had manoeuvred himself clumsily into a cul-de-sac. There was nothing for it but to wait out the long gestation of a reply.

At long last, Jimmy's pallid face turned on its enormous pillow. The eyes looked somewhere in Adam's direction. It was hard to see his uncle in them at all. Not just Jimmy, but everybody, had been changed, himself perhaps least of all.

'Will you take it?' Jimmy murmured.

'Yes, of course.'

'Well then, what does it matter what I think?'

Adam swallowed. 'You probably find it hard to understand.'

'Yes.'

'But it's a stroke of luck, Uncle Jimmy. The most massive luck this family has ever had. If I hadn't have come here, with Joanne and Luke, to live with you and Auntie Mirabelle last year, none of this would have happened. We'd still have been struggling along, living on benefits, trying to make both ends meet. Now the whole world can open up for us. And you too. I'm not going to forget you, you realise? Your kindness to us.'

'You've already forgotten it,' Jimmy declared severely, painfully raising himself up a little against the pillow. 'Perhaps you forgot it the minute you stopped helping us and threw in your lot with that bloodsucker.'

The tremulous words and the angry myopic face were nothing that Adam could recognise of Jimmy. He didn't want to be led up an avenue of recrimination. Reaching into his pocket, he pulled out a crackly packet. 'I brought you some caramel shortbreads.'

'You knew what that monstrosity was going to do to us. You can see what it's done all around the town. Empty shops, shutters going up, families living on the breadline, and you've joined in the destruction, closing your eyes to the consequences while your family suffered.'

'Uncle Jim, please.'

'It's everything that's wrong with the world. Greedy, selfish, stupid, and proud of it. And now you've joined it. Your aunt was disgusted with you, and I'm beginning to wonder whether she was right.'

Adam's forbearance cracked. 'So you're disgusted with me. Well done. Obviously, the heroic thing to do would have been to carry on struggling on a fiver a week, trying to look after my family, whose protection is my legal obligation.' The face on the pillow turned away. 'Legal obligation, Jimmy!' He was shouting and his voice and mouth were trembling, but a moment later, he had them back under control. 'I've done no more than what any man would do in my position. I've taken the opportunities I was offered, and I've done my best. Life is about taking chances, not stagnating where you are out of some misplaced sense of loyalty.'

'Is that where we've been going wrong then? Stagnating? Is that why we've ended up with nothing? So that the likes of you can step over our bodies on your way to the top?'

'Don't be melodramatic.'

'Our life's efforts are in ruins, you stupid little shit. What are we supposed to do, celebrate your luck?'

'How dare you talk to me like that? You did us a favour that you didn't need to. Right now, I wish you hadn't. But that is all. We don't owe you for it forever more.'

'I didn't say you did. But you could have left us to get along in the way that suited us, instead of driving us into the ground.'

'I haven't driven anybody into the ground.'

'The nasty piece of work you're sucking up to has.'

'That's not my fault!'

'You've gone along with it every step of the way, so from where I'm sitting, it *is* your fault. You couldn't wait to get ahead, and hang everybody who got in your way. Even your own family.'

Adam was breathing hard. There was a singing in his ears and he could feel his cheeks burning. He wanted to walk away from this squalid locking of horns, but he needed to make peace first.

'Listen. I know this has been hard for you. Not just for you, for lots of people. But you can't expect the world to stand still. I know you feel cast aside, forgotten about, but some good has to come out of this. Like I said, I'm not going to let you go without. I'll help you find another place, get away from that flat and the empty shop. It's bound to have painful memories, but you can put those behind you and concentrate on the good things.'

'Adam, you don't know what the good things are. You've been tricked like everyone else into thinking it's all about some kind of shopping utopia. Loads of choice, where the choices are all the same thing. Sign up, join in, and you'll be showered with rewards. Nobody believes that crap. All people want is just to be able to buy what they need, at a price they can afford, without having to talk to robots or be part of some gigantic funfair. There isn't any fun. Look at people's faces as they're trudging round. It's all misery.'

'But they were miserable when there wasn't any choice. Poor and miserable.'

Jimmy gave a sneery little laugh. 'That's all it's about for you, isn't it? Getting rich will make you happy. You take from the pockets of people who can't afford it, and then offer it back to them when you've destroyed them. And we're supposed to be thankful for your generosity.'

'There's no need to see it as us and them. Why can't you accept that people can just take what they want from it and leave the rest?'

'Because there isn't anything else. It can only survive on destruction. It's taken the means of their living out of the hands of people who were just getting by, and handed it all to some fat rich pig that doesn't care about them.'

'What's made you so hateful, Uncle Jimmy? I know you've had a big health scare, on top of everything else, but you're going to be OK.'

'You mean despite losing my livelihood and then my wife at the hands of a vampire who you've become best mates with?'

Adam sighed. The caramel shortbreads were looking gooey in the packet he was still holding in both hands. He hated Jimmy's rage, but it was beyond him to know how to appease it.

'OK, how about this? I'll tell Beresford that I'm declining his offer. I'll stay where I am.' There was no word of response. 'Unless you'd like me to resign from my current position too?

How far back down shall I go? Back to working in the bookshop?'

There was another smirk, and the sightless eyes wandered back towards him again. 'That gives it all away, there, in one little word.'

'What does?'

'"Down," you said. "How far back down?" To you, honest people trying to earn a living are lower than you.'

Adam covered his eyes. 'I didn't mean that. You know I didn't.'

'Our words give us away though, so often. Your word was "down". Down to the level of the family that you despise.'

'I tell you what, I didn't despise them when I walked in here fifteen minutes ago.'

'But now you do? Because you've heard the truth and you don't like it?'

'I don't like it any more than you do. I don't like what's happened to you, and it hurts me if you think I'm part of the cause of it. But the world is moving on, Jim.'

'You're not hurting, you're stone-cold. Is that the price it comes at, success?'

For the first time since whenever, Adam felt a burn behind his eyeballs. 'Please don't,' he heard himself say. 'What you're saying is not the truth.'

Jimmy caught the tattered tone, and peered harder to see the face he couldn't seem to see. 'Not tears? Leave the crying to the little people.'

Adam blinked hard. 'You bastard,' he whispered.

'Are you talking to me, Adam? Or yourself? Or your father? What about him?'

'Stop it!' He was on his feet, his face red. 'You're in some weird place that I can't understand, but I'm not taking this. You're not the only person who's had it bad since Paradise opened, but nobody, I'll bet, is feeling so gloriously self-pitying as you are. You don't like me anymore, I accept it.'

'I don't like what you've become,' Jimmy interjected.

'OK, that's fine. At least you've told me now. I'm going to do you one big favour, though, before I go. No, two actually.'

'I need to rest,' Jimmy murmured.

'Number one. I will not breathe a word of this poison to Luke and Joanne. If they still want to come and see you, I won't stop them. Unless of course you don't like them either.'

'Don't twist my words, son.'

'And listen.' Adam leaned down and rested his fists on the edge of the bed. 'This is the way it has to be. Things change, you have to cope. I had to cope with the worst thing that's ever happened to me. Joanne had to cope. Luke was a tiny kid. Even he had to cope. Coping is what we do. Small businesses go to the wall when big businesses move in. You can spend the rest of your life moping about it, or you can see it as an opportunity. There's a crisis, there's a way out. You look at the problem, you find the solution. When did you stop being able to do that? I offered to help you. You've flung it back in my face. That's your privilege. But nothing, nothing at all, about the way the world is will change because of that. You're not making a stand, you're cutting your own throat. So you live in your little bubble of moral purity while the rest of us make the best of things. If you feel better doing that, I won't deprive you of the self-righteousness. But remember this. Nobody respects you for it. Nobody. You're just a bitter old fool who hates his own family almost as much as he hates himself.'

Jimmy looked away with the same smirk as before. 'I thought there was going to be a second favour?'

'That was it,' said Adam.

Chapter 14

The Empyrean

No one would have believed, in the first years of the twenty-first century, that this world was being disregarded, lethargically and obliviously, by intelligences greater than ordinary people's and yet as mortal as their own; that as people busied themselves about their various concerns, they were being overlooked and ignored, perhaps almost as carelessly as a man with a microscope might barely notice the transient creatures that swarm and multiply in a drop of water. They swarmed and multiplied across the car-park, tiny and frantic as infusoria to the watching eye from way above, erratic in their progress but all bound surely in the same direction, united in common thoughtless purpose. The watching heart could yearn with compassion for them in a moment, and as easily turn away, unable to distinguish individual features among the mass, where individual features mattered not. Looking over the river plains where the first cities arose, the earliest eye might have discerned in the splendour of endeavour all the future glory of human achievement – a tower rising as high as the heavens, a single man in a craft leaving the earth's atmosphere behind in an ecstasy of weightless fright – and already have ceased to notice the careworn faces, the bowed backs, the tide of tears that paid for it. With the events and occasions of history would appear beliefs and assertions, contentions and dreams, that sought to recall the scrutinising eye to the suffering stream but, where they satisfied the mind, they proved elusive to the heart's grasp, and where the heart had hold of them, the mind let them dissolve to silt. By the period just before our own day, the scene had once more resolved into an image of amorphous toil, and there was no more discerning the singular fate than there had been in Eridu and Uruk.

As it was French month, a man in a beret sat just inside the main entrance of Paradise, toasting what were billed as 'crompettes' over a gas-fuelled fire. Children were bemused to see something being cooked on the end of a long fork over naked flame. As each crompette was declared done, it was pulled off the fork by an assistant in a tricolor neckerchief, who slathered it with saltless butter and handed it, wrapped in a paper napkin, to the next taker. They were too hot to hold or eat, and half the fun consisted in jiggling them between buttery fingers until they had cooled sufficiently to chance the first nibble. Gone in a trice, they didn't, as was expected, make you want another, the less so as a second one had to be bought, and pleasure bestowed in the sweetness of gratiation quickly bitters in pecuniary gall.

A new sale was in full swing. In acknowledgement of the earlier autumn sale, this one was entitled the Mid-Autumn Sale, a chance to take stock before the festive season. It was declared to be a good time for cleaning the house, sorting things out, recycling. Sorting yourself out was as important as sorting the house. Since you knew how inevitable it was that you would pile on the pounds over Christmas, it was worth losing a little now to make space for the extra later. Diet products, exercise equipment and gym memberships were all being vigorously discounted, but it should not be forgotten that, within all the careful self-husbandry, there was yet room for the occasional reward, so chocolates, luxury travelware and weekend breaks were also on offer.

Crowds filled Paradise from top to bottom, dawdling, looking, dropping pound coins into the slot of the speak-your-weight machine, squealing in merriment at the insolence of its android voice disclosing your measurement. '*Fifty-three-point-nine kilograms.*' Tarot-readers foretold happy disasters and disappointing triumphs, palm-readers the exact opposite. A phrenologist sat at a table on Fourth, measuring skulls with a caliper. At the Loving Room, a sex therapist guided couples through the pitfalls and potentialities of what she called their 'erotic arrangements'. People were encouraged to see that a sex life wasn't a competition. You didn't become a better or worse person in proportion to the numbers of partners you had, but if one partner in a relationship was convinced the arrangement was monogamous, while the other preferred an open approach, then 'Houston, you have a problem'. The way through this problem was talking, rather than silent seething, although one of the problems was often that the partner wasn't there to talk about it, being engaged elsewhere in deepening the problem. Where a couple was mutually committed to monogamy, it was important they didn't fall into unconscious gender roles. It couldn't always be one partner's job to take out the rubbish, and the other's to flip through the TV channels. Nor could it always be one partner's habit to point out such disparities, and the other's to nod guiltily and continue dabbing at the remote. What we all want is a satisfying sex-life. Without it, we grow as bored and blameless as giant pandas.

Bored and blameless, the operations director sat at his desk viewing an internal document outlining takings as a coefficient of throughput. It seemed that the former rose in parallel with the latter, but not proportionately. If twice as many people came to Paradise on Saturday as on Wednesday, they nonetheless didn't spend twice as much. They spent about forty per cent as much again. Looked at another way, there was a hard core of people who didn't spend anything, and more of those people came at weekends, when more people had more free time. In midweek, there was clearly a greater likelihood that shoppers were there for a purpose, whereas because the weekend was defined as leisure time, browsers were represented in greater numbers. Responses to questionnaires established that, among those who self-identified as browsers, seventy-eight per cent said they would be open to the possibility of making a purchase if something caught their fancy. Of those seventy-eight per cent, thirty-four per cent said they would consider buying a big-ticket item, such as a digital TV or a Pacific island. And yet takings did not rise by anything like seventy-eight per cent. So either nothing caught their fancy, or more likely, as the operations director's admin assistant suggested, 'they're basically lying'. Nobody is going to admit to a stranger with a clipboard that they can't afford to buy anything.

Ideas for growing revenue were tossed around at meetings of the traders. The OD felt that endless deep discounting was a one-way street, with which most of the traders heartily concurred, though all of them were doing it. Someone proposed a Paradise loyalty club.

'Go on,' Adam said.

'Well, you create a loyalty scheme like the supermarkets, where every purchase earns points for the punter, and every now and then, they get a set of vouchers, or the chance to enter something to win something. Create a flashy card, send them a monthly magazine, the usual bollocks.'

There was some traction behind the proposal, but others thought it would just create another expensive overhead for participating businesses. They needed something simpler.

'What would be irresistible?' Adam said. 'Regular prize draws?'

'That's patronising crap,' a woman interjected. 'Everybody's wise to that nowadays. "Give us your email address and you could win a blowjob." People need something guaranteed, not "A chance to win! It could be you!".'

'It doesn't have to be a giveaway. Just something that adds value,' another voice called from the back.

'Something that adds value and a sense of belonging to something exclusive,' said another.

The meeting broke up inconclusively. Adam went back to his desk and stared at the jotter on which he had scribbled down, 'Value. Exclusivity. Belonging'. Eventually, it came to him.

Vincent OKed it, which was to say, he held up his hands with the palms facing Adam, as though to indicate that it was nothing to do with him, it was all in his, Adam's, hands.

There was a little adverse comment in the *Clarion*, which swelled to a chorus of derision in the national press, with accompanying vitriolic online chat-threads in which subscribers poured hysterical anger on the proposal. An opinion piece in one of the broadsheets, entitled 'Come friendly bombs...', received thousands of supporting comments. Adam's legal team drafted a threat of litigation, but he decided not to send it and, sure enough, the indignant clamour was drowned after about a week, when a bishop in Sussex called for more immigration.

Paradise introduced an admission charge. The idea was beautiful in its simplicity. It lent weight to the idea that a trip to Paradise was a special treat and created a horizon of expectation in the customer's mind. Why, after all, would you pay for admission to something that you didn't then take full advantage of? Where individual shops ran their own special offers, the vouchers or prizes were for so many free admissions. Some shops issued free admissions every time the customer clocked up a certain spend, so that the next time she came to spend, it didn't cost her anything. At the same time, the admission charge conveyed the sense of belonging to a members' club. They had opted in. For the businesses themselves, the scheme worked because they weren't sacrificing anything on their own margins. They were simply letting people come to shop again. For Paradise as a whole, every paid admission could be seen as a bonus, with the complimentary admissions doing no more than reflecting the *status quo ante*. Nobody was losing. It was a little cheaper to get in during the week than it was on Sundays, which were a little cheaper than it was on Saturdays. There was even a wholly gratis period between 8 and 9am on Sunday mornings, which produced the biggest crowds Paradise had ever seen on Sundays, crowds that spent nearly in proportion to their numbers, precisely because they didn't want to have to come back again when there was an admission charge.

Soon after the introduction of the admission charge, the operations director was voted a six-figure bonus by the board of management, on Vincent's initiative. The OD offered to split 10% of the bonus among the other members of the board, Vincent excepted, and was chaired out of the room at the meeting's close by Troy and Tom.

'You'll really like this,' Joanne told Luke and Jordan, as they waited side by side at their table in One-Long-Sundae. They had ordered a Pharaoh's Delight, which looked in the menu picture like a gigantic pink pyramid of strawberry ice-cream and red jelly, piped with pink-dyed cream. Three spoons had been provided.

'Where's Adam?' Luke wanted to know.

'He's at work.'

'Why? He's always at work.'

'He's working very hard to look after us all.'

'My sisters go to work,' Jordan put in. 'Work is rubbish. You have to be there all the time.'

'Some people say they like going to work,' Joanne told them. 'The thing is to find something you enjoy. What do you like?'

'I like One-Long-Sundae.'

'Me too!' shouted Luke.

'Well, maybe you can both work here.'

'I can work here on Monday,' Luke suggested.

'You're going to be free on Mondays, are you?' Joanne smiled. 'What about school?'

The boys gave a groan of simultaneous disgust.

'School stinks,' Jordan said.

'Yeah, school stinks,' Luke agreed, adding for emphasis, 'it stinks like stinky poo.'

'Nevertheless,' said Joanne, which was a word she always felt needed no elaboration.

The Pharaoh's Delight arrived. A shapeless mountain, a long way off pyramidal, it was composed of messy layers of variously coloured jellies and green ice-cream with a cherry on top.

'It probably tastes nicer than it looks,' Joanne said, observing the fallen faces opposite.

Jordan dug a spoon into the green ice-cream. 'Eurgh,' he gargled.

Luke scooped a little on to his own spoon, and immediately mimicked Jordan's reaction.

'What flavour is it?' Joanne said, picking up her spoon.

'Poo!' Luke shouted.

'Luke, don't be stupid.' But when she tried the ice-cream herself and made a face, the boys took it as a green light for hysterical laughter. 'What flavour *is* it?'

They all tried another spoonful, the boys managing to cram it into their giggling mouths, but not swallow it in their hilarity, while Joanne continued to ruminate.

'It's not mint. Or pistachio. Excuse me?' A waitress was gliding past. 'What flavour is this green ice-cream?'

'Er, cucumber?' the waitress guessed.

'Cucumber?'

'Would you like me to find out?'

'Perhaps not. It might turn out to be something even worse.'

The boys, always appreciating a bit of backchat to waiting staff, exploded again.

'Well, they're enjoying themselves anyway,' the waitress added, before hurrying away.

'Cucumber,' Joanne announced, laying her spoon on the table with deliberation. 'You know what? Cucumber ice-cream is poo.'

The boys clung to each other as they bellowed.

Adam had not accepted Vincent's offer. That his decision not to do so had not resulted in any reconciliation with Jimmy couldn't be helped. He hadn't, in any case, declined the offer for Jimmy's sake. Nonetheless, the decision felt right. He knew that, in not having seized a chance, he had also dodged a period of anxiety. Not every stroke of luck was an uncompounded blessing. It was sometimes necessary to walk away from the scene of a triumph, as long as the ground for doing so wasn't cowardice but a deeper intuition that you might not have seen the palace of achievement from all angles. Its façade might shine with the lustrous accretions of plunder, while at the back, they were hurling out the tried-and-found-wanting with the cabbage-stalks. They had enough. They lived in a nice place. His brother and sister were being properly schooled. Despite the recent ructions, they were each in one piece and more or less loved each other. If Jimmy's disapproval stained the outer margins of the picture, the picture would just have to be reframed.

Jimmy survived, the cardiac episode being diagnosed finally as less serious than had at first appeared, and made his way back to Flint Street, armed with advice to take plenty of rest and avoid stress. Everywhere he looked, his home offered reminders of the departed Mirabelle, but this was only proper. To have removed them in the interest of lightening the burden would only have augmented it. Framed photographs of anniversaries and Christmases gone by populated the surfaces in living-room and bedroom, and for the first time in his life, the unsmiling Jimmy saw what the point had been of smiling for the camera. If it felt like extorted joviality at the time, it looked like happy assurance when one of you had gone. All about him were Mirabelles laughing and radiantly beaming, like messengers from the other side sent to solace the survivor with the news that the show wasn't over. Was she waiting for him? Was there impatience in the afterlife, or did they know all along when the time would be, and that, inasmuch as it wasn't now, they could go back to the unimagined things that had been prepared for them?

By contrast, the notion that he had been in some sense created sat uneasily with Adam. He didn't find it hard to deal with the idea that his destiny was his own to write. But some believed, along with Jimmy, that destiny was created for you, not as a matter of irresistible fate perhaps, but as a path already laid through the garden that you might choose to follow. What worked against his believing this was Adam's sense of his own compassion. It wasn't conceivable that one sinner's destiny could be success and self-esteem, sitting at the top table with the mighty and high until you mistook yourself for one of the elect, while another sat in a factory making badges. If there was equality, why did it have to manifest itself in so many exceptions, under the rank totalitarian logic that their existence proved the rule? And yet, having made the decision he had about Vincent's offer, an intimation of entire rightness had come upon him and hadn't gone away. No shriek of brakes had accompanied it, and no recrimination, within or without. To Jimmy, the grace of God shone out from moments of correct decision. For Adam, they were the moments when you were most fully true to yourself. Neither of them quite saw that the two views of the matter were wholly compatible, any more than did those who insisted on the strikingly ordinary truth that everything in life happened for a reason.

Vincent watched Adam at work, and Adam was conscious of being watched. There was no air of surveillance about it, nor even much of vigilance, only an implied fascination, as though – and he was quite sure of this – Adam's refusal of the offer had only added to his moral stature in Vincent's eyes. Through it all, Vincent sat in his little office, screened off now in precisely the way he never thought he would be, in a place apart from the machinery of executive control. He saw Javine put a piece of paper in front of Adam, waiting while he disengaged his attention from his screen and looked at the document. He saw a brief laugh, a comment, an answering laugh from Javine. Then they turned their heads sharply towards Tom, who had evidently just chipped in, his idiot grin spreading into a bigger laugh as Adam said something back to him. It worked. This was how people got things done, not through bursts of wild creativity, or of spontaneity under duress, but by calmly dealing with what needed to be dealt with. You worked, you relaxed, you worked again. It wasn't brain surgery. Or then again, it was. That was what was impressive about it.

'Oh look, there's a place there,' said Jules, as they crawled along the seafront in her worn-out estate car, looking for somewhere to park.

A nagging wind had whipped in off the sea, intermittently blowing drizzle at the windscreen. It didn't look the day for an outing, but she had been most insistent, and Jimmy wasn't yet well-versed in Mirabelle's old faculty for saying no. It was a long drive too, nearly three hours, and he didn't feel comfortable with Jules, despite their years of association. Conversation was patchy until Jules realised that Jimmy wasn't likely to be forthcoming, and she took on the chattering role at which she was so proficient. She talked of Finlay's troubled encounters with doctors, the renovations they were having done at the house, of a fantastic meal they had had in one of the new restaurants in Paradise – Phase or Phrase or something – and she talked eventually, delicately, of Mirabelle, and of his own need not to sit and brood, but occupy himself.

To Jimmy, this was a torment. He'd never liked Mardon Hollacombe. Fairgrounds and crabsticks weren't his sort of thing, although it looked as though they'd spruced the place up a bit. A big Victorian hotel at a junction, where he and Mirabelle had once been guests at a wedding, had changed its name to Ocean Dreams. The lights changed and they plodded on, attended by discreet little beeps from the car behind, until Jules spotted a parking-space.

The Golden Sands café hadn't been spruced. They sat at a

weathered formica table in the window, gazing out on the raindrops, some of them dancing in the air, others splashing the glass.

'Don't let me intrude, obviously, Jim, but what are your plans?'

'What, for today?' Jimmy asked.

'No, for the foreseeable future, I mean.'

He shrugged. This was infuriating but, for now, he was stuck with her, and must bear the kindnesses with a goodish grace.

'I'll just have to make my way really. It's taken some getting used to, but I'll get there, God willing.'

Jules looked into his eyes with a mix of scrutiny and pity. 'I'm going to make you a proposal.'

'No, really...'

'No.' She raised a ring-laden hand. 'Hear me out. Why don't you consider moving in with us? We've got oceans of room. We wouldn't intrude. You'd be left to your own devices when you wanted. But when you needed a friendly face, you'd have at least one of them, and sometimes two. It would be a change of scenery.'

Jimmy couldn't think of a polite way of declining.

'I can see you're struggling with the idea,' Jules said, 'so I'm going to leave you to think about it. Also, there's no problem about giving the arrangement a trial run if that would help. All I'm thinking is, what if you had another health scare, when you're on your own and can't get help? Where would you be?'

'What does Finlay have to say about all this?'

'He's right behind me.' So it was her plan. How much had he had to be talked into it?

'Well, thank you, it's certainly a kind offer. And one I shall mull over, if I may, and get back to you,' Jimmy replied, a little stiffly.

'No hurry. No pressures.' And her crimson-nailed hand descended softly on his and stayed there, leaving a deeply strange sensation where it rested. There was no eye contact. Jules looked at their hands, and Jimmy looked out to sea, where massed banks of grey cloud were just beginning to come adrift at the seams, letting whiter patches show through.

'Would you like to try them on?' the girl in Sock Monster asked Myron.

'Why would I do that?'

'To see whether they feel right. It's something we offer that other sock-retailers don't.'

Myron and Marlow exchanged glances.

'Does that mean other people have tried these ones on?' Myron asked.

'Oh no, we wouldn't sell a pair that had been tried on. Except to the person who'd tried them on, of course.'

'Don't you end up with loads of socks you can't sell?'

'Not really,' the assistant said. 'Not many people want to try them.'

'I think you should try them on,' Marlow insisted.

'What for? They're just black socks. How complicated can it be?'

'Like the lady says, you don't know how they feel.'

Against his better judgment, and with a reddening face, Myron sat down and undid his trainer laces. 'This is beyond daft.'

The assistant said she would come back when he was ready, but hardly had she drifted away than a trio of girls stopped to watch.

'They feel nice and soft,' Marlow said.

'Shut up and give me a sock.'

Marlow carefully took a pair out of the pack and separated them. Myron's bare foot was hovering in the air as though he were trying to avoid putting it in a wet patch.

'Why are you holding your foot like that?' Marlow started to laugh, which set the girls off too.

Myron snatched the sock from his hand, and bent over to pull it on. He stood up and, not sure how he was intended to assess it, took a few lopsided paces along the floor. One of the girls wolf-whistled him, and they burst into yells of laughter.

'Are they to your satisfaction, sir?' Marlow giggled.

'Actually,' Myron frowned, 'it feels a bit weird, thinking about it.'

Marlow was nearly helpless. 'Weird how?'

'I dunno,' Myron said, 'just kind of – prickly.' Standing on the one trainered foot, he flexed the foot with the sock on it. 'I'm not sure.'

'You might get used to it.'

Myron, oblivious to the scene around him, looked down at the foot he was waving about. 'I haven't got it on inside out, have I?' He held his foot up for Marlow to examine. 'Is it on right?'

Marlow was in paroxysms, and couldn't help at all. Myron sat down and lifted his foot on to the other leg to peer closely at the sole of the sock.

'Success?' The assistant had reappeared.

Myron looked up at her. 'Not really. They feel a bit funny. I think I'll leave it for now.'

'See?' Marlow said, as they walked away. 'If you hadn't tried them on, you might have bought a pack of funny-feeling socks. That would have been a waste.'

'Not really, cos I could have used them to stuff in your mouth.'

'Oh, honey!' Marlow put his arm through Myron's, and had it instantly shaken away again. He didn't like public affection. 'I love shopping with you. Something weird always happens.'

Not long after Adam informed Vincent of his decision to decline the partnership, Essie announced she was going to step down from the board of management. Instead, she was going to rent an exhibition space on Second, and showcase the work of local artists. Adam wondered how many local artists there were, which only proved how out-of-touch he was.

'This is what happens when you sit at a desk on the top floor,' she said. 'You become as detached from reality as a politician.'

Adam offered to help her with sorting out the lease and setting the place up. It was called Paradigm Shift, and opened in late October with an exhibition of photos taken on mobile phones. There were shots of people in parks, sun-struck shots of people on beaches, empty skyscapes, seascapes, sections of buildings, images of childbirth and funerals, teary eyeballs and rotten fruit. The show was called *Timeline* and received a short enthusiastic notice in the *Clarion* from Hinton Richards, who called it 'an amateur snapshot of the state of contemporary Britain'.

Most days, the place was empty, but one morning a group of sixth-form photography students happened in. One of the schoolgirls opened a large sketchpad and began drawing one of the images, of a church steeple at dawn. Essie brought her a little stool. Adam came in at lunchtime, ate his sandwich leaning on the front counter, and found himself shushed by Essie when he tried to speak. She didn't want anything to interrupt the girl's meticulous concentration. He ate his sandwich with quiet gusto. The girl continued to copy the picture, oblivious of the respectfully maintained silence going on around her. When she was satisfied with her drawing, she got up and carried the stool back to the counter.

'Would you like to take the picture?' Essie offered.

'Really?' the girl replied.

At a nudge from Essie, Adam, his mouth still full of ham and mustard, carefully detached the photograph from the wall and handed it to her.

'What's your name, sweetheart?' he asked.

'Freja,' she said, and was gone.

'I've had plenty of really positive feedback,' Essie said.

'Yeah?' Adam replied, scrutinising his next sandwich as he chewed his way through the first mouthful of it. 'Great.'

'All apart from you, of course,' Essie sighed. 'You haven't said anything.' She twirled her pencil.

Adam's glance was distracted for a moment as two young women with identical long blonde hair walked in. They moved from picture to picture, their initial giggles subsiding into bored politeness. He stared at them as he chewed, with unwavering gaze, until they drifted out again. 'Yeah, right,' he said, turning back to Essie.

She blinked at him. 'What's right?'

'What you said.'

'Yes it was,' she sighed.

The conventional view that happiness is boring because, as Rousseau's Julie has it, the imagination has nothing more to do, prolongs the misconception that happiness is a state – not only a state of mind, but something like a nation-state with securely patrolled borders. But it seemed there was a constitutive happiness that had to undergird all relationships, otherwise they would fall to ruin. Adam neither believed, nor was especially interested, in that idea. Happiness wasn't a town. It wasn't somewhere you visited for a holiday, and then decided to move to. The important thing was to live without delusion.

In the late night, in the bedside light's soft gleam, Essie got up to go to the kitchen for water. She was heading out of the room naked when he reminded her that Joanne might still be up. She picked up a sweater of his to put on, and that was how he liked to see her. Something that fitted trimly on him looked big and sloppy on her, like she was wearing an adult's clothes. He settled comfortably in bed, his legs flung wide, hearing a little clumsy clattering in the kitchen. When she reappeared, he was ready again, stretching up his arm to welcome her back to bed, pulling her close, spreading his hands over her back. They embraced until everything about his body felt bigger than it was, bigger than hers, and his desire was even stronger. When she lowered herself on to him, he held his breath in acutest pleasure. When he opened his eyes again, she was pulling off the sweater.

Just do happy, don't talk about it.

'One of the infuriating things,' Finlay confided to Jimmy, 'is that people think it's funny. It reminds them of Laurel and Hardy.'

They looked at the offending foot, which was encased in an enormous slipper, resting on a cushioned stool.

'That takes the pip, doesn't it? The ladies think they have a monopoly on suffering,' Jimmy mused.

'Puh!' Finlay took a thirsty draught of unmixed rum. 'What they mean is that you never bloody stop hearing about it. It's left to us to suffer in silence.'

'Ah yes,' Jimmy concurred, taking a cautious sip of his rum, which wasn't a drink he was partial to, 'true enough.'

The Chestnut Grove experiment hadn't appealed to Jimmy. He didn't feel that he liked the Beauforts well enough to move in with them. Joanne, though, had tried to get him to see that it was at least worth trying, and that, even if he only stayed a week or so, it would surely make a change. They were generous people, and you certainly ate well, even adventurously.

The change-of-scenery argument cut no ice with Jimmy. He found it faintly insulting, as though Flint Street had somehow become ritually unclean since Mirabelle's death. He wasn't ashamed of his solitude, nor did he succumb to morbid thoughts or weeping. There was no disputing the point, though, that perhaps a little human contact might bolster him. There would be more to talk about perhaps, more to explain. So it was that he found himself one Sunday packing a small holdall, and being whisked up by Jules in the sports car and translated to Chestnut Grove, where nobody knew their neighbours, the pretend streets were patrolled only by luxury cars and delivery-vans, and the silence had an undeniably different quality to the silence of Flint Street.

For the first couple of days, Jimmy sat alone in the living-room, reading newspapers and magazines, occasionally being brought a cup of weirdly scented tea by Jules. It became apparent that he was being deliberately left to himself, and it was only over dinner on the third evening, that Jimmy proposed they might like to do something the next day. Finlay demurred, blaming the incapacitating foot, and so Jimmy and Jules went on an outing to the aquarium.

They drifted about the dim deserted galleries, peering into little tanks where, as often as not, the advertised creature was nowhere to be seen. Where was the African dwarf frog? Their two heads bobbed about, trying to spot it in its glass enclosure, until Jules said that it was obviously so 'dwarf' it was invisible to the naked eye, and they broke into warm relieving laughter. There was no sign either of the spectacled caiman in the dank water of one of the larger enclosures. Jules asked a man in wellingtons, who strode past carrying a bucket of dying fish. He put up a hand to deflect the question, as though it were a recognised flashpoint of controversy, about which he had been advised to say nothing.

'Makes you wonder how many things go AWOL before they give you your money back,' Jimmy said.

'Oh look, though,' said Jules, pointing to a tank full of tiny iridescent fish flashing about the gloomy water in bustling circles. 'Neon tetra.'

They stooped a little to look in. There was something mesmerising about the movement of the fish in their wafting single-minded shoal, the spaces between them geometrically perfect, their wild circulation a hypnotic dance they appeared to be enjoying for its own ecstatic sake.

'"Native to clearwater streams in eastern Peru and western Brazil",' Jimmy read. 'You'd think it'd be too cold for them here.'

'They can control the water temperature, though.'

'I doubt that'd fool them,' Jimmy said. 'What do they eat?'

'Tiny aquatic crustacea, apparently,' Jules replied, referring to the notice. '"Neon tetra can spawn every two to three weeks." Goodness.'

'They don't look like they ever hold still long enough,' Jimmy chuckled.

He tapped on the glass, but the tetra continued swooping around the tank, oblivious to the huge alien faces gawking in.

'Please don't tap the glass,' said the wellingtoned man, passing behind them with another squirming bucket.

Jules gave Jimmy a nudge.

'All right, Hitler,' he said in a stage whisper, and they gave way to childish giggles, before continuing arm-in-arm towards the Sumatran tiger-barbs.

'How was the aquarium?' Finlay enquired.

'Oh, you know,' Jimmy replied, grimacing a little as another corrosive siplet of rum slid down his throat. 'Once you've seen one, you've seen them all.'

'Never went in for fish much myself.'

'No. An acquired taste.'

'I don't mind one on my plate, of course, with a wedge of lemon.'

They chuckled.

'Now you're talking,' Jimmy said. He held up his glass. 'Is there something else I could try?'

No sooner had Jules freshened Finlay's glass, mixed Jimmy a gin-and-tonic, to which he was scarcely any more partial than rum, and discreetly withdrawn, than Finlay put the question.

'Well, James, what's to stop you coming in with us?'

Jimmy swirled the ice-laden glass and wondered. 'I'm not sure it's right at the moment.'

'Considering other options, are you?'

'I'm considering the option of carrying on as before.'

'Pah!' Finlay spat. 'You don't want to do that. Where's the

point in that? More of the same.'

'I don't know.'

'It's a terrible thing when the woman goes first. It's not the natural order. Knocks you back. But at least if you've people around you, looking out for you, there's a chance of getting back to some kind of life. Besides, who else have you got?'

'Nobody really.'

'What about that nephew of yours? He's doing well for himself, isn't he?'

'Sore point,' said Jimmy, swirling the glass again.

'How so?'

Jimmy wasn't sure how much of this he cared to explain. 'Let's just say he turned out to be a viper in the bosom.'

'A what?'

'A prat, basically.' He took another gulp of the perfumed frothing drink. 'Let me mull it over anyway.'

'You said that a couple of weeks ago. How much more mulling is there to do?'

'What's in it for you?'

'The usual. Company. A little help.'

'A bloody waiter, you mean,' Jimmy said, nodding towards the raised invalid foot.

'That too.' Finlay tittered.

Jimmy swirled his glass again. It was the liquid equivalent of toying with your food. 'Is there anything else to drink?'

It was in the nature of acquisition that it took many forms, but they were a paltry few compared with the number and variety of things that may be acquired. Moreover, there were many different ways of defining the impulse to acquire, from simple whim to dire necessity. What was much less scrutinised, however, was the emotional charge that acquisition carried. One moment an item was on display. You were standing and looking at it, wondering whether you wanted it. And the next moment, by some mystical process of transfer only partially accounted for by purchase, it was yours. It became part of your life, part of who you were, sometimes only for the length of time it took to eat it, sometimes forever as it stood on a shelf or hung at the back of a wardrobe.

At a certain point, Mrs Pelfing's relation to acquisition had undergone a transformation. Enriched by settlement of divorce from a husband whose unreasonable behaviour had reduced her to brittle spite, but whose unwillingness to contest the detail of her suit in court had ensured a swift and lucrative dehiscence, she had first celebrated the measure of her liberty in a spree of spectacular acquisition. She had bought jewellery, clothes, furniture, had travelled extensively at a merely fractional depletion of her resources, and had found in those activities the momentary satisfactions that her married years had denied her utterly. Somewhere, Mr Pelfing simmered, and the thought of his dereliction couldn't help but add further lustre to the emerald necklaces, and extra sublimity to the ocean sunsets she snapped from the observation decks of cruise-ships. She acquired, above all, new friends, an entire new social set whose brilliance matched her own, the more so as some of them were divorcees like herself, the previously injured, now merely calloused, and from whom no secrets were hidden. They shuddered with horror, and then with hilarity, at the memories of their abandoned blimps and boobies, but rejoiced in the freedom that had come upon them now that 'he' was gone for good and all. They drank to that.

At another certain point, Mrs Pelfing came to realise that there was another way of acquiring beautiful things. It was possible – why not – just to take them. Taking them was what she had been doing since the settlement, hovering about among lustrous objects, pointing to one, trying it, liking it, buying it. And then, quite unexpectedly, the last element was subtracted from the equation. Nobody seemed to notice if you didn't pay.

The staff didn't notice, because they all assumed that the ubiquitous cameras would notice. Shoppers didn't notice the cameras. They were as benignly extraneous as light-fittings, their dark globes offset with winking red eyes, into which nobody looked. Meeting the camera's gaze, Mrs Pelfing intuited, would be a sure signal to whoever was watching the monitor that you might be contemplating a crime, and because nobody looked up at the cameras, nobody looked suspect. Not even the panoptical vision of the cameras, though, could penetrate solid objects, and all you needed was ensure that the item you were taking was eclipsed by a larger item, or by part of your body, and it was yours. At first, she took small packets of screws, needles, boxes of staples, tubes of mascara, items of obvious insignificance. It wasn't as though she started by purloining a diamond ring. She started by purloining paper-clips. Single items soon became two or three, and eventually a trip to the shops – hardly now a shopping trip – would result in a bag rattling with dozens of liberated items, now hers as though by some process of osmosis, rather than money conventionally changing hands. Was there a thrill to this activity? she reflected. There was, but it wasn't the tarnished allure of having got away with something. It was more to do with her not behaving as she was expected to, and therefore not being suspected. Mrs Pelfing, the ornament of a rigorously exclusive ladies' club, of many a private dinner-party and many a captain's table, was a shoplifter.

Whether one called it stealing or thieving hardly mattered. Mrs Pelfing didn't view herself in that light. She was an unorthodox taker perhaps – put it that way – but she considered her little vice in the manner of a peccadillo only. Theft could be vicious in a certain sort, but viciousness wasn't in her nature, as anybody who knew her could vouch. True, they didn't know that she took things in shops, and likely wouldn't approve if they did, but it couldn't dim their view of her whole character, because she did many other things that were wholly virtuous. And what did the shops mind? The paper-clips they could hardly miss, and while it was true that her acquisitiveness had gone on to grander aspiration, so that her wardrobes were restocked, her table accoutred in fresh napery, her own body more richly bedizened, it wasn't as though everybody were doing it. This she told herself in the anxious evenings, when something like a sickly remorse might begin to lap at her, only to be repulsed by a fresh assertion of her essential goodness and a fresh examination of the damask napkins.

The advent of Paradise had been to Mrs Pelfing a trove of opportunity. Its walkways and escalators were usually crowded enough to permit of quick escapes, during which her heart still beat as rapidly as it had when she had begun her career of taking. And now here she was again, having paid her way in, embarking on another productive sweep from floor to shining floor. On Ground, she had acquired a couple of best-selling novels, on Third a pair of wristbands, a set of paisley pillow-cases and a bathroom plunger. Fifth was where it grew more interesting still. Small cosmetics were child's play, bottles of tinting lotion in the hairdresser's a little more challenging (you had to sit in the waiting-area and leave just before somebody asked if you had an appointment). Jewellery, the holiest of grails, required an elaborate pantomime of trying on, until the serendipitous moment arrived when the assistant, distracted by fetching out another cushioned tray, didn't notice you very slightly but deftly rearranging the rings on another that was already out, to cover the evidence of your having taken a sapphire cluster. On Seventh, Mrs Pelfing always declined the free tasters that were being handed out – she scorned the condescension of licitly receiving something for nothing – and headed straight for the display-stands. Here was no need for subtlety. If you took the topmost tin from a pyramid of truffled foie gras, an assistant appeared a moment later and replaced it. At an earlier stage, Mrs Pelfing would always pick up a basket at the

Gastromarket, the better to decoy the store detective by putting in one or two items and paying for them. She had come to view that tactic, however, as naïve, almost an apology, at any rate a poor way of saying, 'Don't look at me'. The basketless browser was far less likely to be suspected, precisely because she looked at once too discerning and too uncommitted. She would as readily drift out untempted as pick up a packet of oolong tea. It was more important still to engage the staff rather than avoid them. She had heard folk-tales of takers who had solicited two shop assistants to help them carry some heavy electrical item to their car, and while she doubted she would ever tempt fate to that degree, she was nonetheless adroitly practised in asking staff to describe the taste of Criollo chocolate to her, dexterously turning over a bar of it between gloved fingers as she let a second fall into her bag. This morning, she had acquired a jar of caper pesto, a side of smoked blue trout, a can of spiced pistachios, a bottle of Taggiasca olives in rosemary oil, another of chipotle popcorn, a packet of casareccia al zafferano pasta, a quarter-bottle of blood-orange vodka and a carambola. She was feeling almost sated, and ready to part with money on the next floor up for a well-earned coffee, but just as she was leaving the Gastromarket, her eye chanced on a basket of baby artichokes on one end of a counter. She selected a particularly beautiful one, and let it drop into the opening of one of the two bags.

'Excuse me,' a voice immediately behind her said.

She turned. 'I beg your pardon?'

The voice belonged to an unexpectedly familiar, smartly suited young man. 'I believe you just put an artichoke into your bag.'

'I'm sorry, do you work here?'

'Not in this shop, madam, but I am employed by Paradise.'

'Then perhaps you don't realise that these artichokes are free samples.'

'I don't think so. Would you mind coming with me to the

customer-service counter?'

Mrs Pelfing allowed her gaze to drop swiftly to the interior surface of her bag, where she could see the little artichoke resting on top of a tin. She snatched it out.

'Oh really, have the wretched thing back if you must.' She put the artichoke back in the basket and, turning to go, made one of the shoplifter's classic mistakes, unconsciously tightening her grip on the handles of the bags.

Adam stood in front of her. 'I'm sorry, Mrs Pelfing, I really am going to have to ask you to come to the security office.'

'You!' Mrs Pelfing had barely stuttered out when, at a hand-signal from Adam, two uniformed security officers came hurrying along the walkway to the Gastromarket entrance.

'Control,' said one of the security men into his radio. 'Suspected lifter on Seventh. OK, lady,' he added, gripping Mrs Pelfing's upper arm, 'let's roll.'

'This is wholly unacceptable,' she spat at Adam, as she was led to the staff lift. 'I hope you realise what a very grave mistake you are making, young man.'

'We can sort this out in private, I'm sure,' Adam assured her in his kindest voice.

'What the blazes has this got to do with you anyway?'

'I'm operations director of Paradise plc.'

'Operations director,' Mrs Pelfing sneered. 'I'd like to see Vincent immediately.'

'Now we both know that's not going to happen,' Adam replied, with a gentle smile.

As they descended in the lift to the ground floor, Mrs Pelfing jabbed angrily at the keypad of her mobile phone. The security men exchanged amused glances.

'VB?' Mrs Pelfing shrilled into the phone. 'VB darling, it's Laura. Sorry to bother you. I seem to be caught up in some horrible little business with your security Gestapo.'

'May I?' Adam took the phone from her.

'Laura, sweetheart, what on earth do you mean?' Vincent was saying. 'Where are you?'

'How now!' Joanne screamed. 'Is he dead?'

'His death's upon him,' Myron replied, 'but not dead. Look out the other side of your monument; his guards have brought him thither.'

Two boys carried Marlow's limp and nearly lifeless body forward and set it down precariously.

'O sun!' Joanne wailed. 'Burn the great sphere thou movest in.' As she looked down at Marlow, he gave her an unhelpful wink. 'Darkling stand the unvarying shore of the world.'

'Peace,' Marlow moaned, coming in too soon, before Joanne had had chance to shriek his name three times. He followed the word with a throaty death-rattle.

The class erupted in shouts of laughter.

'Quiet, please,' bawled Mrs Grellop at the top of her voice. 'We are in the presence of tragedy.'

'Got that right, miss,' one boy yelled out, and they erupted again, including Myron.

'Not Caesar's valour hath o'erthrown Antony,' Marlow cried in a high squeaky voice, 'but Antony's hath triumph'd on itself.'

The laughter was now accompanied by the coordinated banging of desktops.

Myron gave Marlow's prone body a shove with his foot. 'You knob-end,' he smirked.

'So it should be,' Joanne shouted, 'that none but Antony should conquer Antony.' But she was laughing too now, despite herself.

'But woe 'tis so,' cried Mrs Grellop. 'And woe to anyone trying to drill some culture into a bevy of snot-nosed heathens like this.'

The bell rang, and the hilarity dissolved into the mass scraping of chairs as the entire class rose and made a rush for the door.

'Act Five next week,' Mrs Grellop hollered, unheard, above the din.

Myron stepped over Marlow's body to go to his own desk, but Marlow grabbed his ankle and tumbled him over. 'Diomedes, I love thee,' he squeaked, and got a trainer in his face for his pains.

'Mark Antony is not in love with Cleopatra's flaming servant.'

'He has hidden depths.' Marlow giggled.

'Who's up for ice-cream and cocktails at mine?' Joanne asked, swirling out of her improvised robe.

'Yes!' they yelled as one, still flat on their backs.

'Pomegranate vodka!' Marlow cheered.

'Score!' Myron responded.

'Pomegranate what?' asked Mrs Grellop, from the back of the suddenly deserted classroom.

'Pomegranate squash,' Joanne insisted, none too convincingly, giving Marlow a kick.

Mrs Grellop tutted. 'To what shall I compare this generation?' she intoned. 'They are like children sitting in the marketplace.'

She stood over the prone bodies of the boys, and raised her eyebrows.

'Philip Larkin?' Myron hazarded.

'Go and get drunk,' Mrs Grellop sighed.

Adam, freshly frazzled from a late-night row with Vincent over the decision not to press charges against Laura Pelfing, slipped out of Paradise by a rear entrance. He felt a little pleased that, in a conversation that had turned on several crucial decisions, he had established where his own moral boundaries lay. Vincent listened to him these days, where once he would have blustered and flannelled. That said, though, he was also aware that Vincent's shapeless vision of how to run an enterprise, which was largely responsible as Adam saw it for the floundering financial performance, and which was all too evident in Vincent's determination to see an unrepentant criminal pardoned for her actions, would see them all go down bubbling and spluttering, were it to be allowed to continue unchecked. It was an exhausting business trying to persuade Vincent of the demarcation lines, and his preferred strategy of beating a tactical retreat when he sensed that his obduracy was antagonising you, without having surrendered any real territory, was exasperating. Adam might be inexperienced, but he knew he was better equipped to decide things than was Vincent, whose tactical awareness consisted in nothing more than improvising through any dilemma in the hope that a solution would present itself. Whether it was the right solution didn't concern him unduly. He slept the sleep of the proverbially innocent, but it was an innocence in both senses of the notion: he was at once unsullied by experience and preternaturally naïve.

Ever since his first day in Paradise, Adam had nurtured a thrilled feeling that there was unprecedented opportunity here. He was playing a navigational role, and a more and more important one, in a vast dynamic machine. Machines could break down and blow up. Machines could eat you alive. But you could also experience the energising sensation of being in control of them, so that it was not just the inherent power of the thing that was intoxicating, but the fact that you could make it obey you. For now, he had no idea which way this would go, but he knew that there was something about the whole monstrous enterprise that made it worth tenaciously clinging on for dear life.

The moon was full and silver. It shone through the feathery rain to light up the whole empire of human folly, through which a man, who felt like the first man, had to pick his way. He walked along the deserted midweek pavements looking for transport and, finding none, grew progressively wetter and more ebullient as he went. Past the boarded shopfronts, past plate-glass windows pasted white on the inside, past dimly lit bars in which machines flashed out angry demands for attention while single patrons sat oblivious in their drink, past furious red-faced traffic-signals, glowing cashpoints, illuminated advertisements in bus-shelters that urged him to take his family on the steam-train, to the coast, to Paradise. He walked the senseless streets in strengthening rain until he felt invincible. Invincible in his skin and his decisions, invincible to his own residues of self-doubt. A vacant taxi crept past him, and stopped at his nod. He uttered his address through the window, and as the car swept unhindered through the empty roads and the downpour, he abruptly recalled the rainy taxi-ride of the night they had arrived, when another long journey had ended at another temporary staging-post in uncertain territory. He was not now the man he was then. He was someone else.

Putting his key in the door, he could hear the distant thrum of music. It was louder in the hallway, and there was a line of bright light under the door to their apartment. When he let himself in, it was to a barrage of hysterical shrieks and thumping techno.

In the living-room, Joanne, swathed in a huge red duvet and with a cake-tin on her head, was sitting on the back of the settee. Standing before her was Myron in his undershorts, his body crudely smeared in zigzagged red makeup, while Marlow, also down to his underwear, was sprawled on the floor, his arms wrapped around Myron's ankles. All three were trying to choke out bits of speech in between their convulsions. 'Diomedes, I love thee. Do with me as thou wilt!' 'Stay thy hand, my noble servant. This cur is not worth kicking.' 'I know it well, my queen. The slave will not take heed, save to his own lusts.' 'Oh come on, thou know'st thou wants to.' There were half-finished glasses of some bright pink drink everywhere. Adam strode over to the music-system and killed the volume.

'It's midnight, people!' he shouted above the giggles.

'But soft, it is the angry god Adamus, wet of jacket and ugly of countenance.'

Adam took a little sip from one of the glasses. The drink was at once acidic and rancidly sweet.

'Enough to drink,' he told them. 'And keep the noise down. You'll wake Luke.'

'What is this Luke, of whom we have had knowledge?'

There was a light on in the kitchen too, and when Adam stepped in, he was surprised to find his brother sitting at the table. Luke gave him the briefest glance, before turning his attention back to the colouring-book he was filling in, its crinkled pages thick with crayon. To one side, there was a glass of milk, which he had evidently been replenishing from a litre carton. His face wore the tireless expression of someone in a library late at night, bent on mental labour.

'Why are you still up?' Adam asked him.

'Joanne's noisy friends woke me up,' Luke said. 'I've got lots of colouring to do.' He carried on sweeping a green crayon back and forth across the page, making an expanse of countryside appear out of the dull white paper.

Adam sat down next to him, and wrapped an arm around his small shoulders. 'You can do your colouring in the morning. It's bedtime now. I'll tell them to shut up. They can go to bed too, come to think of it.'

'I don't mind,' said Luke, picking up a yellow crayon without taking his undimmed eyes off the page. 'I've been to sleep already.'

'But not for long enough.' Adam scruffed his messy tangled hair. 'How much milk have you had?'

'It's all right, there's some left for you.' Luke pushed his glass across the table to Adam. 'See.'

'Thank you.' It came out in a whisper. He lifted the glass to his lips and found they were trembling. It wasn't milk or colouring or fun or even lots of sleep his brother needed most of all. It was a mother and father.

He put the glass down and covered his face with his free hand, pulling Luke towards him with the other. Luke didn't resist, but dropped his crayon and waited in a grown-up way for this grown-up moment to see itself out. Adam's grip on his chest tightened. After a while, Luke half-turned in Adam's grasp and looked up at his brother. Very cautiously, he reached up and caught a drop from the trail on Adam's face, examining it on his own fingertip as though satisfying himself that it was real. Both his arms tunnelled under Adam's zipped-up jacket, and he rested his face in the rain. He heard only a low kind of gasp from Adam, and in the minute that followed, while his brother's head was full of memories of evil news that broke the world to pieces, he slid into the thick embrace of sleep.

It was all wrong, Adam knew. There was no saying why one thing happened rather than another, but sometimes the way things fell out was right, and at others it was quite wrong. When the right was stronger than the wrong, there was hope. When the wrong was older than the right, it was all wrong, even the right that was barely more than two hours old. Everything had happened at such an unquestioned pace that it served to suppress the memory of the ancient wrong, but here it was again, expanding inside, digging sharply into his ribs. They were free but it wasn't right. He had brought up a family in which youngsters, silly with drink, saw no dignity in anything, in which even his sober sister had surrendered her wisdom to the luxury of foolishness, and in which his infant brother, schooled by contrast in self-restraint at seven, had learned to distract himself on a sleepless night. The world was upside-down, and wanted righting.

He bent his head over his brother's, hearing the softening thump of the music from next door, which had now taken on a plaintive tone of its own. His head was light and passive, a cork bobbing in water, what was left of his conscious mind only a function of the oddly steady breathing of his chest. There was a big wide sunlit classroom, a teacher droning, a huge pristine poster of the periodic table taped to the wall, its numbered boxes arrayed in sober pastel. He was aware of his breathing having almost synchronised with Luke's. Into the classroom came a small kind-looking woman, who conferred with the teacher. Then the teacher was pointing him out, and he clung grimly to the sides of his chair, the veins on his hands distending, as if to sit there and be burned alive now would be better than whatever was coming next. He trembled from head to foot as he walked the corridors behind this woman, his head reeling with the panic of an infant at thunder. He was ushered into the head-teacher's office, where two uniformed police officers were waiting, a man and a woman, holding their hats under their arms. His hand tightened on Luke's skinny arm, raising a little sleepy murmur of protest. He had fallen on his knees in front of the officers, his upper body jerking rhythmically as though an electric current were passing through it, the kindly woman clutching his shoulders. The policeman squatted before him and told him he knew how difficult this must be, but there was something he would need to do, and it was better to get it over with now. They drove him to the hospital where, amid a roiling mist of tears and snot, he was made to look at first one body, then the other. It was raining hard, and the splits in the soles of his trainers had soaked his feet as he walked across the car-park. He signed first one piece of paper, then another, and was left in the company of a psychiatric nurse, who gave him a plastic cup of thin brown soup. He held the cup untouched throughout the interview until, as he moved to take a booklet he was offered, his hand suffered a spasm and the soup went over him. The day had started nice and ordinary. It had ended with his reduction to a shivering child, different kinds of wetness plastering his face and trousers and feet.

After some time, Adam carried Luke's leaden body to the bedroom. His head slid sideways on the swirly pillow as he kissed it, and he pulled the cover up to his ear in the favoured manner.

In the living-room, the show was subsiding. Joanne took the

cake-tin off her head. Myron hopped about as he pulled his jeans back on.

'Plenty of water now, kids, or you'll suffer in the morning.'

'I'm suffering now,' Marlow moaned from the floor.

Joanne shot Adam an apologetic look.

'It's OK, but you should have thought of Luke,' he told her.

'Did we wake him?'

He smiled at her. 'He's fast asleep.'

Adam pulled out the sofa-bed for the boys.

'Do your parents know where you are?' he asked them.

'Yeah,' they both said, a little ashamed at the way a particularly adult kind of irresponsibility had turned so puerile in the presence of an adult.

They fumbled ineffectually with the bedding while Joanne went to brush her teeth.

'We're really sorry, Adam,' Marlow said.

Their two faces, poking out from under the blanket, looked as palely remorseful as the severed heads of the nobility during the Terror.

'It's OK, I'm not angry,' he said. 'Just concerned you don't go too wild too soon.'

Neither of them quite fancied giving him that assurance.

'That's my job,' he added with a wink, as he flicked off the light and left them to embrace each other coldly in the dark.

At Vanity Hall, the servants all walked backwards when they withdrew from your presence, to demonstrate their obliviousness to any other purpose than you. There were baubles and bonbons and garlands wherever you looked. It was where Mrs Pelfing had imagined she would one day live, and was now, divorced from its precincts by the long acres of ordinary boredom, quite content only to look upon. Vincent didn't dwell there either, but the avenues were not blocked to him, and as long as he was content to entertain himself dawdling in the grounds, she too could learn such forbearance, only occasionally surrendering to the impulse to pelt stones at the orangery windows.

'You've too many *things*, Laura,' Vincent slurred, as he picked a stolen carriage-clock off the mantelshelf.

'Why shouldn't I have things? People only ever say that to people who could have everything if they chose.'

'Exactly.' Vincent assumed a tone of gravity. 'You know, I can't defend you again, when you have one of these spills.' It was why he was here.

'I promise to be good.'

'Promise instead to get help.'

Mrs Pelfing tutted. 'Help!'

'We have some very good places in Paradise, on Fourth. Nobody need know, and you'd be doing yourself a favour.'

He picked up a silver egg-coddler.

'Isn't that beautiful? I had to have it.'

'But you could have paid for it, my dear.'

'How did that ghastly man know I was there? Are you training vile people to spy on me, you turncoat?'

'He just happened to be there, and he's not vile, he's superb. And you'd better get used to the idea, because he's going to be part of it all in the deepest sense.'

'Whatever do you mean?'

'He's my partner as of tonight.'

'No!' Mrs Pelfing would have turned pale if she knew how to.

'It's true. I had a little difficulty persuading him at first, but he's brooded and stewed over it for a few weeks, and now, *voilà*. More or less exactly as I anticipated.'

'But what does he know about running such a huge concern?'

'Right now, nothing. By next year, whatever he'll have learned from me.'

'But I don't get it. Why him?'

Vincent considered. 'Sometimes you have a feeling.'

'Oh dear,' Mrs Pelfing sighed, knowingly.

'And you've probably made exactly the same misconceived assumption as him.'

'Explain, you tiresome thing,' she drawled, on her way to the decanter.

'Mr Young is perfectly convinced that I have designs on him. I, who have no need. By this means, he has been at first repelled from, and then drawn inexorably towards, the centre of things. Expecting to have to resist unreasonable demands, he has succumbed to demands that are considerably less unreasonable.'

'But why wouldn't he succumb to such a splendid offer?'

'He feels he is selling his soul, which makes a man at first reluctant, and then happy to go along, because he tells himself that, at least now, he knows what he's doing.'

Mrs Pelfing poured another brandy, and thought about it. 'I still don't get it,' she said. 'He doesn't want to be a partner, you don't want him to be *that* sort of partner, so why are you both doing it?'

'Because we are each arriving at our heart's desire by the classic means of refuting it. He has squared it with his conscience and is on his guard, so he feels master of his destiny. He has persuaded himself that he has made his own decision. I have swallowed a momentary passion for him and promoted him into the inner sanctum, to show that I'm precisely *not* going to let it stand in the way of a good man's advancement. In the great days of the movies, they used to have the casting-couch. It theoretically brought shame on all concerned, but that didn't mean the stars who rose dishevelled from it were at all tarnished. In some senses, they were better for it, because they'd got the most demeaning parts of their careers over with. What's happened here is that a sort of metaphorical casting-couch has been negotiated. He will forever believe that he only got the job because he was attractive to me, but will congratulate himself on having sidestepped that without the need for an awkward scene.

And for my own part, I've appointed an extravagantly talented man.'

Mrs Pelfing sipped and pondered. 'But how could you be sure he knew you liked him?'

'And remain within the bounds of decency? A good question. I prepared a crude but effective dossier of evidence. It was going to be left around carelessly one evening for him to find after I'd left. But before I could deploy it, somebody rifled my desk and took it.'

'Him?'

'Oh no, he wouldn't stoop to that. I've no idea who did take it, but whoever it was did me the enormous favour of showing it to him.'

'How do you know?'

'Given the fact that they took it, who else would they show it to?'

Mrs Pelfing picked up a cigarette between a pair of chopsticks and lit it. 'Unless of course, whoever it was was also madly in love with him, and kept them to herself?'

'Unlikely,' Vincent replied. 'I haven't come across a single other person who thinks he's anything but decently dull.'

'Which makes it all the more of an enigma why you think he's such a pip. Really, sweet, the whole thing is goo-goo bananas to me.'

'That's the way I like it.'

'Still, at least there's one good thing to come out of it.'

Vincent raised his eyebrows.

'He's going to be too busy to snoop on little old me from now on.'

He offered her a smirk. 'I wouldn't be entirely sure of that, Mrs Pelfing. Like the cherubim and seraphim, my boy never sleeps.'

The sight of Jimmy and Finlay pretending to smooch together

was at once hilarious and dimly distasteful, but in another sense entirely heartening. Jimmy, after much dither and doubt, had settled at Chestnut Grove, and moved in the remainder of his things. He had a room at one end of the house, where he was bothered by nobody, and once he had firmly established that he did not want outside caterers to decide what he ate, all the early friction was dissolved. Finlay, for his part, got on with Jimmy as never before, and was now on allopurinol, which had wonderfully restored his mobility. Jules had never been happier, and had taken to referring to the pair of them as 'the two men in my life', a fancy that everybody soon stopped noticing apart from the neighbours, who took it to be an official *ménage à trois*, which didn't in the least upset the Beauforts since they didn't know the neighbours. Not long after Jimmy's installation, they threw a welcome party.

On the Saturday following the pomegranate vodkas, Adam took Joanne, Luke, Jordan and the boys to Chestnut Grove for what was described as a 'harvest home'. He would have taken Essie too, but for her having broken off with him that morning, citing boredom. The clinically brief phone conversation left Adam with an ache that persisted through the day. It ached when he thought of her wanting him and now choosing to pass. He still hadn't breathed a word about his latest promotion to anybody. That must come later. There had been tears enough already this week, in the present and in memory, seemingly all of them his. A dry-eyed evening of recreation suddenly looked good.

There was a handful of other guests. Adam was reintroduced to Mrs Clarke, the normally headscarfed accountant from HortiSol, now barely recognisable in a silk shift and diamante ear-drops. A couple from what were referred to as 'our Vietnam days', Mr and Mrs Dinh, smiled politely, could almost have been brother and sister but for their obvious conjugal imbrication, and spoke only to Jules. Adam had been invited to bring colleagues with him, and had brought Ben and Corinne, as well as Troy, who didn't yet know he was about to be abruptly elevated to operations director. And there was somebody called Zack, a large burly man with elaborately bushy facial hair, who had the air of an ageing heavy-metal singer, was head-to-foot in leather and, during intervals between CDs, bashed out ham-fisted renditions of rock-and-roll tunes on the piano.

'Help yourself to drinks!' Jules squealed at intervals, as scarcely able to contain herself as if the party were her own tenth birthday.

Marlow and Myron had arrived wearing similar black shirts, which had earlier in the evening been a source of contention between them, but had now been resolved by Myron peeling down to a white vest. When Marlow waited to see what drink Myron would take, and then chose exactly the same beer, Myron snatched the bottle out of his hand.

'Don't copy everything I do,' he snarled.

'I'm not,' Marlow protested.

'You don't even like beer.'

'I thought I'd try it again.'

'Have a Cherry Kaboom, that's more your speed.' Myron handed him a fizzy red drink.

'Meaning?' Marlow was stung by the implication, though there hadn't necessarily been one. '*Meaning?* Ron, don't blank me.'

'DON'T freakin' call me Ron.' Myron was livid. 'How many more times?'

'Is this your time of the month?'

'What's that meant to mean?'

'I don't know, don't you have to do something Jewish at the full moon?'

Myron blew out a mouthful of beer-froth. 'Do you even know how dumb that is?'

Marlow bit his lip, and sucked on the Kaboom. If he could enrage Myron like this his whole life, he would have all he wanted.

'Too bad about Essie,' Joanne told Adam.

'Yeah, well. She'll be back,' he grinned, knowing it was rubbish.

'She was kind to me when I was very low. I'll always remember that.'

'Things got weird back there, didn't they? It was all a muddle. I never thought I'd find myself standing in the same building as Uncle Jimmy again though. He looks as though he's recovered enough strength to punch me.'

'What did you say to him?'

'I think I told him he was pathetic.'

'Adam.' She rolled her eyes. 'What would we have done without them?'

'I dunno. Starved?'

'That's right. Well, as you're here and he's here, you can apologise.'

'Later. This is Ben and Caroline. Ben and I worked together when I started at Paradise.'

'Yes, I know, it wasn't that long ago,' Joanne replied, giving a conspiratorial roll of the eyes to Corinne.

'It's Corinne,' Corinne said, clinking Joanne's apple soda.

'It's like he's been asleep a thousand years.' Ben chuckled.

'I'll just go and hide behind a plant,' said Adam.

'Thanks so much for coming. We've been very worried about you,' Jules told him.

'Worried? Why?'

'You don't call. You seem to have lost track of things. Jimmy...'

'Oh, I know what Uncle Jimmy felt. We had a frank exchange of views when he was in hospital.'

'I think he'd like to bury the hatchet.'

They turned and watched Jimmy and Finlay jiving mechanically to the rock-and-rolling piano. Zack was grinning greasily, pulling on a bottle of beer during the one-handed passages.

'It's up to him, not me, though,' said Adam.

Jules smiled and sighed. Male pride was both delicate and so stubborn, admirable and utterly pointless.

'How do you know Mr and Mrs Beaufort?' Mrs Clarke asked Joanne.

'I'm Adam's sister.'

'Poor you.'

Joanne smiled at the Dinhs, who smiled sweetly back from their perch on the edge of a settee. They had no idea where they were. She glanced at Troy, who was helping himself to another bourbon, twirling a straw in the glass. He strolled over to a tall stool by the fireplace and hoisted himself up, placing one polished Chelsea boot on one of the rungs, adjusted the knees of his trousers with exquisite care, touched the knot of his loose tie, and took a gulp from his glass, which he held between his thumb and first two fingers. He then noticed her watching him, and gave her a courteous, faintly gratified grin. She wished she was just a little older.

Luke was wearing long trousers, clearly feeling a little self-conscious in them, striding around stiffly and continually checking the backs of the legs to see if they looked as funny as they felt. Jordan hadn't helped by roaring with laughter at the sight of them.

'What's the matter?' Luke had asked, as they squeezed up together on the back seat of the taxi.

'You look a right goop in them,' Jordan said.

'No I don't,' Luke declared, and the matter was closed for the time being.

Jules put on a CD of chart-hits, and Jordan danced in the middle of the hearthrug as though performing in a video, his agile liquid movements compelling everyone's attention.

Finlay, having upended the remains of a half-bottle of gin to his lips, tried a spot of limbo-dancing to show off his restored agility, but fell backwards on a coffee-table, scattering a pile of magazines.

'Careful, you klutz!' Jules shouted, and shook her head in disbelief at Joanne.

'There's no hope for the youngsters really, is there,' Joanne said, 'when this is the example they're set?'

'Not really,' Jules replied.

She smiled at Joanne with more than a trace of meaning. It seemed as good a moment as any.

'Jules, tell me if I'm interfering, but something's been concerning me for ages. I found out that Auntie Mirabelle was...' How to put it?

'Was what?'

'Extorting money from you and Finlay. I'm not asking what it was about, but I want you to know I'm glad it's over.'

Jules bit her lip. She sucked a strawful of gin-and-orange.

'It doesn't really matter, but I'd rather you didn't imagine it was anything worse than it was.'

Joanne waited.

'We all met on holiday ten years ago. It was the Caribbean, it was hot, we were all full of the spirit of adventure. Something happened between your Uncle Jimmy and me, only a silly holiday fling, but I suppose it carried on a while after we got back, and she found out. They were really struggling at the time, and it wasn't hard to feel sorry for them in that dingy little shop. She sent me a pathetic letter, suggesting I might like to compensate her for the trauma they'd been put through. She said they came to the brink of splitting up, but she forgave Jimmy. Now she wanted reparations.'

'Or else what?'

'Or she would tell Finlay.'

'He didn't know?'

'No, not at first. I sent her some cash – a very modest amount – but I felt so awful about it that I soon confessed the whole thing. He barely batted an eyelid. It was over, and he felt sorry for them too.'

'But the money... You kept on sending it, right up to this year.'

'As I say, we sympathised with their plight, especially when they had you three to look after, and with Paradise opening. It was only going to end one way. I'm only sorry she had to believe she was our enemy. We had them round every now and then. She would sometimes help herself to things from around the house – toilet-roll holders, little knick-knacks, you know – and we let her have them. I hope it helped.'

Joanne let it sink in while she looked vacantly at the cavorting adults. 'Do you think Uncle Jimmy was in on it?'

'Oh no,' Jules said, in some alarm. 'You must never tell him.' She'd after all done that herself. 'When all's said and done, I think he'll be happy here. And I don't want anything to upset that.'

As the revelation dawned, Joanne turned slowly to Jules, who was watching Jimmy's clowning with a smile of the warmest indulgence. 'You know that Mirabelle herself had a fling last year?'

'Perfect,' Jules whispered.

'Did I tell you we're tying the knot?'

'Ben! Of course not, I haven't seen you forever,' Adam said, grasping his free hand in congratulation.

'She's making an honest man of me.'

'That'll be the day.'

'Adam...'

He jumped in. 'No way, mate.'

'You don't know what I'm going to ask you.'

'You're going to ask me to be your best man.'

Ben blinked. 'Well yeah, but...'

'No, please. I'd be hopeless at that. All the speeches and stuff.'

'You only have to make one. I'll write it for you. But listen. The theme is – wait for it – *Star Wars*.'

'No! Ben, really no.'

'It'll be a scream.'

'What does Corinne say?'

Ben looked across the room at her. She was sitting on the edge of a sofa, listening patiently to Mrs Clarke.

'She's coming round to it.' He chortled.

A canteloupe melon flew through the air and landed with a thump at Mrs Dinh's feet. She drew back in momentary alarm, and then remembered her smile.

'Chung ta nen de lai som,' she hissed to her husband.

'Nonsense, it's too early,' said Mr Dinh. 'The party is just starting.'

Mrs Dinh glared at him. *'Tai sao cac ban luon luon nen gai?'* she spat.

'I am not without a spine, you are mistaken. Please only speak English.'

Mrs Dinh waved a hand in a flurry of dismissal. *'Tai sao toi da cuoi ban?'*

'You married me because our parents wished it.'

'Puh.'

'Please only speak English among English people.' Mr Dinh gave a pained smile to Jordan as he flew past, and flashed a glare at his wife.

Beneath her disgusted gaze, he reached forward to the table and helped himself to a handful of spiced peanuts.

Mrs Dinh turned aside as he ate them. *'Ban dang nhu mot dua tre.'*

'I think it is you who are behaving like a child,' he told her, crunching the nuts contentedly.

'Everybody happy?' hollered Finlay, dancing past the Dinhs with a bottle in each hand.

Mrs Dinh managed a wintry smile. *'Vang.* Ah... yes we are, please.'

Marlow and Myron had found the bottom of the staircase. They were now both drinking Cherry Kabooms. A long-suffering look of disappointment had settled on Myron's face. It was a look that Marlow could live with, as long as he was reassured from time to time that it wasn't terminal. He sat two stairs below, between Myron's feet, clutching one of his knees with a lazy arm.

'I always seem to get on your tits,' Marlow began.

'No you don't,' Myron sighed. 'You're just a bit full-on at times. You don't always have to be so gay.'

'Er, hello. This just in.'

'I know, but don't make a thing of it all the time.'

'You're ashamed, are you?'

'Of course I'm not ashamed. But it's just, not everything in the freakin' world is gay.' Marlow was silent, so he ploughed on. 'I'm just saying. It's not like I'm embarrassed. Everyone knows. My folks know. Your people know. Get over it now.'

'Yeah, cos it's like your Dad's really cool with us, isn't he? We can't even go round to yours.'

'Of course he's not cool with it, he's my Dad. Dads want their sons to have a girlfriend, then a wifey, then kids. I can't bring home a ditzy gay-boy, can I? How's that going to look?'

Marlow's string, tensed to quivering for weeks, now snapped. 'Fuck off then,' he snarled in starting tears, but when he tried to get up and storm off, Myron pinned him between his knees. A struggle developed, but Myron's arms gripped him round his neck too. 'Get off me, you twat. Get off!'

'Listen!' Myron's voice was close enough to his ear to catch him a thwack on the side of the head. 'Marlow! Listen!'

The arms and legs refused to relinquish their grasp. It was the strongest embrace he had ever been in, but for all the wrong reasons. He gave up the struggle and let the brutal scene play itself out.

'Look at me.'

Marlow refused. Myron took his jaw in one hand and swivelled his face round. His furious asymmetrical eyes fixed Marlow like crossed lasers.

'Look at me.'

Marlow lifted his eyes. Myron was mad as fire, and quite as determined to take possession of everything. 'I love you, you daft boy. Don't you get that yet? I'm not embarrassed, I'm not ashamed and I'm not going to let go. You're mine. Understand?' He smudged the stupid tears away. 'Give me a kiss. Come on, kiss your man.'

It seemed only right.

'Are you ever going to stop ordering me about?' Marlow asked, the fury and misery strongly dissolved in warm joy.

'Sure I am.' Myron's voice had gone comically soft and tender. 'The first fifty years I give the orders. Then it'll swing the other way one day when I'm least expecting. You'll see.'

Marlow grinned and put his bottle to Myron's lips. His Adam's apple rose and fell while he sucked on it. The red ran down his chin and on to Marlow's shirt until they both smelled of benzaldehyde.

'Are you going to marry me then?' Marlow asked.

Myron caught the note of challenge. 'Wow,' he whispered. He pressed his lips into the back of Marlow's neck. 'Ask me again when we're old enough.'

'I'm guessing you've got some news for us,' Joanne said.

'What makes you say that?'

'Oh just a hunch. The endless phonecalls in hushed tones in the kitchen. The general air of smug overachievement.'

'I'm not smug.' Adam was insistent. 'This is what's gone wrong with us, Jo. You've got this messed-up idea of all that's happened in the last year, and it isn't me. You know me better than anyone else alive now, and you know it isn't.'

She held his gaze. He meant it.

'OK, I hear you.'

'But yes, as a matter of fact, I have.'

'You changed your mind about the partnership.'

'Don't hate me. I can back out any time I choose if it doesn't suit. That means, suit all of us, not just me. And I understand

Vincent much, much better than he thinks I do.'

'I don't hate you. I'm pleased. Well done. I trust you to make it into something that's about you, not just him.'

'That's exactly what I plan to do.'

'All you have to do now is square it with Uncle Jimmy. Only please don't offer him a seat on the board or something.'

'One step at a time.'

'Has he spoken to you yet?'

'Kinda. I said hello, he said hello.'

'That's great. You can start again.'

'Too true.'

Joanne hugged him. It was the first time she had touched him since she smashed his head on the floor. He stroked her hair for a moment, then kissed her hand.

'Now then people,' Finlay bellowed as he lumbered past them, noticeably beginning to limp a little. 'Save the smooching for later.'

They looked at each other.

'That is beyond gross,' Adam said.

'Talking of smooching,' Joanne deadpanned, 'I think I'm finding myself physically drawn to Zack.'

Adam doubled over.

'I'm serious. There's an animal lustre there.'

Zack was just lowering himself shakily on to the piano stool again.

'Luke would run rings round him.'

'At first, maybe.'

Zack yelled out something about shaking and rattling, pointing a hairy finger at the ceiling. Some of the adults joined in, Jules leading some hand-clapping that quickly disintegrated. Nobody noticed the Dinhs sidling out to the hallway, where they discovered the coat-rack had come off the wall, leaving Mrs Dinh to tunnel furiously through the mound of clothing to find theirs.

'Toi noi chung toi khong bao gio nen da den!' she screamed.

'Please do not be illogical,' said Mr Dinh calmly. 'If we do not come to things, how will we know if we like them or not?'

'You can come to my birthday party if you like.'

Luke looked suspicious. 'When?'

'Soon,' Jordan said, not yet wishing to give away too much. 'It'll be much wilder than this.'

'OK.'

'But you have to get me a present, yeah?'

'What present?'

'Something cool.' He considered. 'A train set.'

Luke thought about it for a moment. 'OK.'

'Deal?'

'Deal.'

They slapped hands.

'A real train set?' Luke asked.

'May I have a moment's silence please?' Jules shouted over the hubbub. 'My husband would like to say a few words.'

Finlay, his face drenched in sweat, tried to get up from the sofa, yowled in pain and collapsed back.

'What is it?'

'This buggering foot again.'

A peal of good-natured laughter rang out, and Zack began hammering the piano into submission again.

Jimmy, as red-faced though not as agonised as Finlay, swayed off in the direction of the kitchen. He crashed through the toilet door, and stood gently oscillating while a prolonged gush released itself. This whole thing wasn't at all what the doctors had prescribed, and yet he felt liberated from a world of care; weightless and strangely youthful again. He made two attempts at flushing, to which the cistern responded only with half-hearted gurgles, before turning and giving up.

'Crap, isn't it? You need to hold it down,' Adam advised him.

Jimmy shrugged, so he slipped in and flushed the toilet for him.

'Expert in everything these days, it seems,' Jimmy said, a trace of sternness just hardening the edge of his drunk voice.

'Flushing toilets is my limit. After that, I just make it up.'

'Good for you, son.' Jimmy studied him through glasses that had slipped most of the way down his nose. 'Good for you.'

There was a silence in which they looked frankly at each other.

'You know, I'm glad you've found a refuge here. They're good people.'

'They have what are known as their moments,' said Jimmy, in a tone that suggested he was reluctant to concede any point.

'Don't we all?'

Who owed whom the apology? It was hard to say. Jimmy picked up a salt-cellar from the table, and cracked first.

'Adam, I'm sorry about what happened. I regret saying what I did.'

'No, I regret what I said. More, in fact. I didn't want to cause you any hurt, and I didn't stop to think I might be.'

'No, you were right. Time marches on. I had no right to stand in your way, but I did hear what a principled thing you did.'

'Oh?'

'Joanne told me you'd turned down Mr Big's offer.'

'She did?'

'Good for you, son. Your aunt would have been proud of you, I'm proud of you, and – well, you know.'

'You can say it.' Jimmy scrutinised the salt-cellar. 'Please say it, Uncle Jimmy.'

Jimmy chewed the inside of his cheek as he worked up to a great effort.

'Your mum and dad would have been proud of you too, Adam.' He looked into his nephew's shining eyes. 'Yes they would.'

They shambled round the table towards each other, and constructed an awkward embrace which got less awkward the longer they held it. A feeling of purgation began at the bottom of

Adam's lungs and spread strenuously upwards, pushing an accumulated weight of sediment slowly ahead of it as it rose.

'They would indeed,' Jimmy said hoarsely.

In the doorway, Luke waited decorously for another of these unfathomable grown-up scenes to elapse before daring to cut in. He needed somebody, it didn't matter who, to buy a train-set.

The antique office-fittings were being ripped out as Vincent emerged from the lift on Monday morning. Adam had stipulated he wanted an office to himself with normal office things in it. There was really only one candidate for such a space on the admin floor, and Vincent had made the obvious sacrifice. He could mingle with the rest of the staff, the way it ought to be. Adam hadn't been particularly interested in the point, but was more concerned that his office should have shelves. The whole thing was going to be, for Vincent, an exciting journey into conventionality.

Nobody was to address Adam as anything other than Adam, a stipulation that had arisen as soon as Javine had called him 'AY'. Meetings were to be held daily at 8.30am, and were limited to himself and Vincent, the finance director, the operations director and Javine, other staff being invited as required. Outside catering was to be cut to lunchtime sandwich orders, unless an especially important client was being entertained, in which case any of the restaurants on Eighth were to be invited to tender for the one-off contract. It was agreed that the admission fee would as soon as possible, before Christmas at any rate, be rescinded. A deal was negotiated with the principal gym on Sixth for discount rates for the admin staff. Gym membership wasn't compulsory, but Adam would like to know of anybody's reasons for not joining. His first discovery in executive authority was that nobody dared assume anything you said was ironic. Tom began going to the gym three times a week. Javine enrolled in the expectant-mother classes, prompting a chorus of generous congratulation.

'Gym?' Vincent whispered pallidly.

'It'll do you more good than the *I Ching* ever could,' Adam declared, sounding sufficiently stern that Vincent hardly dared correct the pronunciation.

The conventionalising weighed heavily on Vincent's soul, Adam could see. It was going to be necessary to allow him his little moments of conceptual frivolity. He hadn't had a sensible idea in years, and in between getting people's backs up and stymieing the normal administrative procedures, his purely ornamental appearances throughout the building were of decreasing significance. Only Adam took him entirely seriously, realising that his value to the business was symbolic. It was the sort of role you couldn't pay a salary for, but all such enterprises needed a character. The idea that somebody, however much of an obvious dingbat, had invented the whole thing, putting an enormous gaudy tinkling clanking something where previously there was nothing, was not to be underestimated. It was like a gigantic work of art, glorious in its pointlessly existing for its own sake alone. It was the sort of thing God must have had in mind when he sat in the infinite void of his own power and decided one day to make something happen, pausing only to make the day itself on which it could happen. To begin with, it was beautiful. Then it was a mess, then a tragedy. Now what was needed was to redeem it.

The cable-car was to be torn out. It had only been used a couple of times, and it only linked the admin offices with the storage and electrical areas at the opposite end of the eleventh floor. Its removal would necessitate closing the entire building for a weekend. Couldn't they just leave it there, Vincent wondered. Adam wasn't in favour of non-functional installations, and pronounced its death sentence. It was only necessary to allow Vincent one more go on it, on an afternoon when Paradise was in full cry. And it was difficult not to accede to the demand that, to emphasise their new partnership, they should go on it together.

On a teeming Saturday, when the walkways were cross-hatched with lines of people snarling and snagging, drifting this way and that in search of temptation and whatever else they hoped to find in Paradise, Adam and Vincent stepped out of the office and on to the little platform where the carriage was waiting. The staff, Javine and Tom to the fore, stood in a little huddle at the door to see them off, wishing 'Bon voyage' and 'God speed' as apposition suggested.

'I feel I ought to be wearing a flying helmet,' Adam said.

'Then you shall,' Vincent quavered.

'Don't be ridiculous.'

Vincent stepped into the cable-car first, shunting along the red seat to make room for his partner. Adam felt a curious lurch of nerves in his abdomen as he set foot into the swaying car. He wasn't good at heights.

'Can anybody fly this thing?' he said.

'We can!' shouted Vincent. 'Away!'

'Don't make it judder.'

'It's perfectly safe,' Vincent laughed. 'Why, Adam, you're not afraid, are you?'

The cable-car jerked roughly out of its station, and Adam's heart jumped into his throat. After a few rickety yards, it emerged above the resplendent depths of Paradise. He looked down once into its bottomless kaleidoscope and closed his eyes. Vincent laid a protective hand on his arm.

'Be brave,' he breathed. 'I'm here.'

Below them, the swarming multitudes began to crane upwards and point. Many of them were doubtless laughing. Others retained a sense of awe at the spectacle of two men dangling in the wide echoing space above them, bobbling along with the world beneath their feet for no reason other than the wonderful hubris of it.

A mingled swirl of music reached Adam's ears. The car jolted and swayed, its instability aggravated by Vincent's rocking about in the seat to point at things.

'Sit still,' Adam hissed.

The hand squeezed his knee in teasing affection. He was crammed claustrophically close and suspended acrophobically high. Nothing about this was pleasant. He should never have agreed to it and, just as he thought so, with the cable-car at the midpoint of its journey, it came to a sudden halt, at exactly the point it had halted when Vincent had ridden it alone, before the gates of Paradise were opened.

'Oops,' Vincent giggled. 'Don't worry. They'll rescue us.'

'This is horrible,' Adam managed to choke out.

'Don't worry,' Vincent repeated. 'Just enjoy the view.'

Between his feet, Adam could see rows of upturned merry faces, their eyes trained on the two of them, but especially, he fancied, on him. They could sense his fear, the vertiginous panic that had overtaken him and that rattled through his frail frame with every jounce of the carriage. He couldn't decide which was worse, to look down or to look ahead. Or not to look at all, but close his eyes tight and wait to be rescued. And how did you rescue two people who were hanging in midair with nothing to cling to? And why should you? It was their own stupid fault after all.

'We won't be here forever,' said Vincent, in a soft purr very close to his ear.

Was it reassurance or regret? Adam's head was whirling and he couldn't tell. He couldn't tell.

His heart beat fast.

'You have to conquer your fear.'

'That's right. Never give in to it.'

He had almost edged back from the platform, but the whole school and the rows of parents were watching, and every other boy had jumped. Jumped into the cold clear air in rhythmic sequence and now only he was left. Their bodies had fanned out in the water below, and they looked up. They called out his name to encourage him. It would only be a moment more before the encouragement turned to jeers, the jeers of boys that would ring in his head for a lifetime. So he jumped in too.

Ready with towels to cloak his shocked skin, affecting not to notice the shivers of fear that drove out the shivers of cold as he came to them at the poolside, they embraced him, slapped his dripping back and told him that fear had to be conquered, and he had conquered it. He doubted it, but everyone pretended it so.

'I don't know,' he stammered, cold but comfortable in the thick towel.

'Oh but we saw you.'

'My brave darling.' He received the kiss heroically. She pressed her cheek against his. 'He's always had the strongest heart.'

It was his heart that had been tested first. Just as he was about to emerge to the light of evening, it had stuttered or stopped, something unhelpful, when faced with entry to the great world. A flurry of concern, gabbling voices amid the monitors, and then he was drawn forth by means of an outsized pair of pincers, which gripped his reluctant stubborn head and made him be. Coated with uterine slime and coughing his first breath, he was cut free and wrapped and handed on, undamaged after all. An authoritative kindly voice told his mother what sex he was.

At Roundfire we publish great stories. We lean towards the spiritual and thought-provoking. But whether it's literary or popular, a gentle tale or a pulsating thriller, the connecting theme in all Roundfire fiction titles is that once you pick them up you won't want to put them down.